Advanced Praise for *Framed and Burning*

"Lisa Brunette continues to develop vibrant characters in a stunning story that will keep you reading well past your bedtime!"

- On My Kindle

"*Framed and Burning* is the second book in the Dreamslippers series. It's easy to follow and hard to put down, making readers who may not have read the first book race back to give it a try!"

- InD'tale Magazine

Praise for *Cat in the Flock, Book One in the Dreamslippers Series*

"The launch of an intriguing female detective series... A mystery with an unusual twist and quirky settings; an enjoyable surprise for fans of the genre."

— Kirkus Reviews

"Clearly author Lisa Brunette has a genuine flair for deftly crafting a superbly entertaining mystery/suspense thriller. *Cat in the Flock* is a terrific read…"

— Helen Dumont, Midwest Book Review

"Brunette's portrayals of Cat and Granny Grace are nothing short of genius."

— On My Kindle

"A fascinating plot populated with interesting and engaging characters."

— The Wishing Shelf Awards

"Already hooked, this reader intends further sojourns in Cat's dreamslipping world. Highly recommended."

— Frances Carden, Readers Lane

"Filled with twists and turns, humor, a little romance, and suspense, this refreshing take on the world of private investigating will appeal to readers of many different genres."

— Janna Shay, *inD'tale Magazine*

"A fascinating tale of mystery, romance, and what one woman's dreams are made of. Brunette will keep you awake far into the night."

— Mary Daheim, bestselling author of the Bed-and-Breakfast and Emma Lord/Alpine mysteries

"Gripping, sexy and profound, *Cat in the Flock* is an excellent first novel. Lisa Brunette is an author to enjoy now and watch for the future."

— Jon Talton, author of the David Mapstone Mysteries, the Cincinnati Casebooks and the thriller *Deadline Man*

"A drinkable, page-turning thriller that poses questions about faith, family, sexuality, and secrecy in an authentically rendered Seattle landscape."

— Corrina Wycoff, author of *O Street*

"Lisa Brunette's *Cat in the Flock* is the satisfying launch to a new detective series featuring Cathedral Grace McCormick, your average Jill with a twist—she slips into other people's dreams. Putting these psychically received clues together with her daytime gumshoe misadventures makes for a clever and entertaining murder mystery."

— Rev. Eric O'del, Amazing Grace Spiritual Center

Included at the end of this edition of *Framed and Burning*:

Book club discussion questions.

The prologue and first chapter of Dreamslippers
Series Book Three. This excerpt has been set for this
edition only and may not reflect the final content of
the forthcoming editions.

Framed and Burning
by Lisa Brunette

Copyright © 2015 by Lisa Brunette

Cover Design: Monika Younger, www.youngerbookdesign.com
Author Photograph: Allyson Photography
Early Draft Copyediting: Christine M. Roman, Ph.D.
Developmental Editing: Elisa Mader
Line Editing: Jim Thomsen

ISBN 13: 978-0-9862377-5-1

Published in the United States of America

Published by Sky Harbor Press, Sky Harbor LLC

P.O. Box 642
Chehalis, WA 98532

skyharborllc@gmail.com

Direct inquiries to the above address

Author Web Site: www.catintheflock.com

Framed and Burning

Book Two in the Dreamslippers Series

by Lisa Brunette

Nancy —
Thanks so much
for your support
of my work!
Happy Birthday!
Lisa Brunette

For Tino, and his son

Prologue

Brickell Lofts, Miami
December 5, 2013
10:37 p.m.

Donnie Hines was passed out, drunk, in a corner of his studio when the flames made their way to the painting he'd just finished.

It was a true work of art, and he knew it. Not just good, but great. He knew it even as the whiskey made his tongue thick in his mouth and his eyelids droop. A diabetic, he knew he had no business drinking that much. When he could no longer hold a paintbrush, he sat back in a metal folding chair and realized that he had finally done it. He'd captured, perfectly, the fractal shapes he'd been chasing his whole life.

Ever since his father took him to the Cleveland Science Center when he was ten, he'd seen them in his imagination. That day a scientist showed the crowd how fractals could be found everywhere: in mountains and rivers and on seashells. The never-ending patterns that repeated themselves in an ongoing feedback loop were the most beautiful things Donnie had ever seen. For the past thirty years, he'd been trying to capture them on canvas.

And in the end, all he needed for inspiration was a bowl of broccoli.

Not just any ordinary broccoli, either. This was special. "Romanesco broccoli," the woman at the market stall called it. Lime green, with florets spiraling into fractal shapes. He bought a bag of it, had it sitting in a bowl on an old Formica table. Mick, whose studio Donnie shared, kept threatening to cook it up for lunch. But he agreed it was special. "Froccoli," Mick called it.

Donnie had worked feverishly that night as a way to tamp down the loss he felt after the worst conversation of his life. Working always helped, always freed him from feelings he couldn't sort through. But in the end, his masterpiece at last finished, the drinking won out. A bottle of whiskey, three-quarters empty, sat on the floor by the cot where he slept.

Donnie hadn't even signed the painting.

But it didn't matter. The fire that raged through the studio that night, devouring his masterpiece, knew no names and took no prisoners. The paint was still wet when it went up in a shimmer of orange, igniting the wooden two-by-four easel behind it.

Mick's paintings caught fire next. An angry slash of black on a field of red curled easily into charred shreds. A thick decoupage of mixed media first melted, its bits of metal and rock sliding down before the canvas disappeared in flames. One painting after another—some finished, some not—went up in flames.

The fire leapt to a stack of framed paintings leaning against the wall like oversized dominoes, first eating their stretched cloth and then attacking their hardier wooden frames. Bottles of turpentine, paint thinner, and oil paint fed the flames, as did the men's bottles of whiskey, wine, and gin, all of them exploding, their glass shattering.

Donnie did not stir.

Perhaps he was already dead.

Or maybe he dreamed in his sleep as the fire raged, smoke pouring in behind the curtain surrounding his cot, enveloping his passed-out form and invading his lungs. Those who knew him would expect him to dream of the fractals that were his singular obsession, how they would keep repeating into infinity, so small his eye wouldn't be able to see them.

First his skin fried. The flames licked across the surface of his body, the top layer quickly peeling off. Then the fire attacked the thicker layer underneath, causing it to shrink and split. As it split, Donnie's own body fat leaked out, feeding the fire as another kind of fuel.

Maybe in his dream, he was eating the broccoli. Maybe since the florets were made of the energy of fractals, they kept repeating inside him. He could feel them spiraling through his gut. Soon he could only watch as they emerged from his belly, bursting out of the core of his body, rippling in space, turning him inside out. He was a vibrating, swirling entity of math and matter. His body dissolved.

But as Donnie died, maybe he still existed in a larger way, his spirit flowing as part of the energy that is everything in the universe at once, the largest supernova and the smallest quark and everything in between.

Maybe Donnie's true masterpiece was this: He *became* a fractal, never ending.

Chapter 1

Holding a sweaty gin and tonic in one hand, the napkin under the glass damp, Grace watched her granddaughter out of the corner of her eye.

Cat had lost too much weight. The young woman's cocktail dress seemed to hang on her. Her face lacked color, her spunk gone. It had been more than a year since Lee Stone, Cat's childhood sweetheart, died. Grace thought the trip to Miami for Art Basel would knock her out of the Seattle doldrums. But surrounded by vibrant art and tropical sights, sounds, and smells, Cat remained sullen, uncommunicative.

It was all Grace could do to get Cat to attend the party tonight. Her granddaughter had wanted to stay in the hotel, reading statutes and case law.

"You're worried about her, I can see," said a voice at Grace's elbow.

She turned to find Ernesto Ruíz, an old Miami flame of hers she'd bumped into a few days ago. He'd been hovering around her ever since, trying to get her alone for a bit of the nostalgic, trade-wind-fueled romance they once enjoyed. At seventy-eight, Grace commanded as much attention from men as she had in her twenties. Even more, in fact. She was self-possessed, and she understood that this quality radiated from her, drawing men like Ernesto to her despite the wrinkles, the gray hair, the natural aging of her physique. A smart man like Ernesto knew he would find Grace a much more satisfying partner than any of the young, inexperienced, waifish artists in line for the bar.

Ernesto cut a dashing figure, his hair perfectly trimmed, his fresh face giving off a musky aftershave scent. His impeccable suit appeared tailor-made. His shoes reflected the light of the crystal chandeliers as if they were a source of illumination themselves. Grace had to hand it to Miami men. No matter how hot the weather, they turned out as if every event were red-carpet.

But she knew she was too distracted to take full advantage of Ernesto's charms this time. Grace allowed his arm to nestle her waist, drawing her toward a nearby alcove. But Grace's gaze returned over his shoulder to Cat, who was slumped against a balcony railing opposite them, a plump Miami full moon hanging overhead.

"It is simple." Ernesto's speech was correct but inflected with Cuban rhythm. "She still thinks the shooting was her fault. That's what we do. Blame ourselves for that which we cannot control."

The truth in Ernesto's statement singed her. And Ernesto didn't even know the half of it. He had no idea that Grace and her granddaughter were both dreamslippers, and that a good deal of Cat's depression had to do with her gift. Dreamslipping was, in Grace's estimation, a rare gift, something to cultivate and hone. But Cat regarded it as a curse and blamed it—and herself—for Lee's death.

Ernesto took her hand. "But she is young, my Grace." He lifted her hand to his lips. "She will survive this. It will pass. In time."

"You're right." Grace shifted her gaze at last from Cat to Ernesto. "But it's been a year. She needs to move on. And you know it's never been my style to wait around for time to take care of things."

Ernesto laughed, revealing unnaturally white teeth. The band, which had been on a break, picked up again. "Care to dance?"

She accepted his hand with a nod. The two slow-danced across the room, Ernesto a gentle but firm lead.

A commotion at the entrance to the ballroom stopped them. A group of uniformed police appeared, a woman officer and two wingmen. "We're looking for an artist," she said, and the crowd chuckled at that.

"Almost everyone in this room is an artist," someone called out. "This is Art Basel. One of the biggest art shows in the world."

"The one we're looking for is Mick Travers."

Grace felt alarm at the sound of her brother's name. Where was Mick, anyway? She scanned the room but didn't see him anywhere.

Someone in the crowd near the door motioned toward Grace, and the police approached her. Grace caught Cat's eye, and her granddaughter drifted over.

The officer asked Grace, "You know where we can find Mick Travers? There's been a fire at his studio."

The gin and tonic in Grace's hand slipped to the floor, where it shattered, shards of glass prickling her exposed toes and ankles.

"He-he's supposed to be here," she muttered, reaching out to Cat. She felt uncharacteristically wobbly in her heels, and it wasn't just from the glass underfoot. "I'm his sister."

"What happened?" Cat directed her question to the police officer. And then, as if it had just dawned on her: "Was anyone hurt?"

The look on the officer's face caused Grace to fall further into Cat's arms. "Oh, God…"

"We need to talk to Mick Travers. If you two are his family, please tell us where to find him."

Cat pulled out her cell phone, and Grace watched as she tried to call Mick. He did not answer.

The officer turned to her crew. "Ask around, find out if anyone's seen him here tonight."

The wingmen broke formation. The officer stayed with Grace and Cat, introducing herself as Sergeant Alvarez. She asked them who they were and what they were doing at the party.

"The two of you are from out of town then." She said this not as a question but as if noting its suspicious nature.

"That's correct, Sergeant Alvarez. We're visiting from Seattle."

Alvarez shook her head. "Such a long way to come for an art show." Grace bristled at the way she said it, as if the distance in itself suggested guilt.

Fifteen minutes later one of the officers returned with Mick, whose eyes were watery. He swayed, obviously unable to stand straight. "We found him in the lounge downstairs, drinking. By the looks of him, he's had more than a few."

"Wh-what happened? This guy says there was a fire." Mick rubbed his chin. And then, as if it had just dawned on him: "Donnie."

"We need to speak to you in private." Alvarez's hands dropped to her belt, which supported a sidearm and nightstick.

She led the way, with Mick following. "Is Donnie all right?"

Alvarez took Mick by the elbow and steered him into a side room. Grace followed, and when Alvarez held up a hand as if to keep Grace out, she set her voice hard. "I'm Mick's older sister. I should stay with him."

Mick looked surprised. "Oh, I'm okay by myself."

Grace shot her brother a reprimanding look, and he shifted gears. "Uh, yeah, Pris should be there. She's a PI. She gets this police stuff."

Grace ignored Mick's use of her birth name and spotted Cat. She slung an arm around her granddaughter. "This is my partner. And she's Mick's great-niece."

"A family of PIs," said Alvarez. "That's all we need." Her voice softened. "This is a shock, I realize. So I suppose you can be present. But please, don't interrupt. We need to talk to Mr. Travers now."

Then Alvarez's gaze settled on Ernesto Ruíz, who politely hung back. "Don't tell me you're somebody's third cousin twice removed. And that you're a PI as well."

Ernesto chuckled. "No, no. Just a friend ... who's perfectly content to wait out here."

The officer nodded for her staff to close the doors to the room.

"Now then, Mr. Travers," Alvarez said, motioning for Mick to sit. She introduced herself and her deputies, Speck and Santiago. Santiago sat near them and began to take notes.

"I know this is hard," Alvarez continued, "but I need to ask: How long have you been here?"

"You mean at the hotel?" he asked.

Alvarez sighed, and Grace detected a weariness in her bearing that suggested the sergeant was at the end of a long shift. "Yes. In the lounge downstairs."

"I don't know. What time is it now?"

Alvarez checked her cell phone. "It's nearly two in the morning."

"A couple hours, I guess..."

"I know this is a lot to take in. But you're going to have to be more specific with us here, Travers."

Grace's feeling of alarm worsened. Come to think of it, where *had* Mick been? He was supposed to meet them at the hotel, but he'd called and told them to go ahead, that he would be at the party later. And then he never showed up.

"Why? You think I torched my own studio?"

"When was the last time you were there?"

"Not since this morning."

Grace broke in, "He was busy entertaining us for most of the day. Cat's never been to Miami before..." She glanced at her brother for assistance.

"Say, why don't you tell us what this is about," said Mick. "Where's Donnie?"

Alvarez sighed again, this time with genuine feeling, not weariness. "I'm very sorry to inform you of this, Mr. Travers, but Don Hines is dead."

"No," Mick said, running a hand through his hair. "He can't be. He didn't want to go to the party. He hates parties. He wanted to paint. His own stuff, not mine. He said he was onto something big..."

Mick covered his face with his hands.

Grace wobbled a bit on her heels and went to embrace her brother, as much to steady herself as to comfort him. Mick's body felt tense, as if rejecting the news in a physical way. Grace hadn't known Donnie well, but she found him to be a charming character, always ready with a smile. And she was a great admirer of his art. *What a loss for the world*, she thought. And Mick was so fond of him, too.

Over Mick's shoulder, Grace tried to catch Cat's eye across the room, but her granddaughter looked away. Cat didn't know her great-uncle very well, so even if she hadn't already been lost in a cloud of her own grief, it was understandable that she didn't seem drawn to comfort him. Grace felt the heaviness of their double losses, and her own inability to ease their pain.

Mick's grief seemed to take more of the edge off Alvarez's questioning. She waited a few beats for him to regain his composure, and when she spoke again, her tone had softened further.

"I'm sorry to ask this, Mr. Travers, but I'm going to need a full account of your timeline for the evening."

"Where is Donnie?" Mick stood. "I want to see him."

Grace touched her brother's arm. "Mick, wait," she said. "The fire marshal, forensics—they're probably still on the scene." She glanced at Alvarez, who nodded. Grace lowered her voice. "And he might be unrecognizable."

Mick sat down again. "Jesus."

Alvarez touched Mick's hand. "Take it easy tonight, Mr. Travers. We'll deal with the details in the morning."

She nodded a good-bye to Grace, who did the same.

Cat fetched a cup of coffee for Mick, who took it in both hands as if it were the only thing he had left in the world.

"She's right, Mick," Grace said. "Let's head back to the hotel. I don't think you should go home tonight. You can stay in my room. I have an extra bed."

Mick gulped the coffee and set it down. He wiped his eyes. "I don't know how I could sleep."

There was nothing Grace could say to that, so she squeezed her brother's shoulder instead. She and Cat watched him finish his coffee. When he was done, he let the cup clatter onto the tabletop. "I've got to get out of here."

The three went back into the ballroom. Grace saw Speck and Santiago talking to people. She overheard Alvarez on her phone with a member of the forensics team, which was most likely crawling over the wreck that was her brother's art studio.

They left the scene behind, Grace leading them through the corridors of the convention complex to the hotel adjoining it, where she and Cat had rooms. The hotel had seemed so impersonal at first—Grace would have preferred rooms in a boutique hotel or a bed-and-breakfast, were it not for the convenience. But now it seemed like a refuge.

Grace let them into her room. She slipped off her heels and sat on the bed, wondering vaguely where Ernesto had gone, realizing she hadn't said good-bye to him. Cat slumped into a chair by the window, the lights of South Beach garish behind her. Mick went straight for Grace's laptop, which was sitting on a desk.

"What are you doing, Mickey?"

"I've got to get his parents' phone number. I need to call them."

"That can wait till tomorrow."

"I don't want them to find out from the news." Mick pecked away at the keyboard.

7

Grace put her hand on his shoulder again. "It's two in the morning," she said softly. "You don't want to wake them, tell them like that."

Mick slowed down, his face crumpling again. "Here's their phone number and address."

"That's great," she said. "We can give it to Alvarez in the morning."

Grace motioned to Cat to hand her a pad of hotel stationery and a pen. Then Grace copied down the information.

"I'm not going to sleep," Mick announced. "How can I?"

They were quiet a minute, and then Grace said, "All right then. Let's talk about your timeline for the evening, before you forget the details." She slid the pad of paper and pen in front of him.

Mick crossed his arms over his chest. "What am I supposed to write?"

"Write down where you were every hour today, and who you were with."

He stared at the paper. "No."

Cat finally spoke up. "But Uncle Mick, the police are going to make you do this anyway. It's better to be cooperative."

Mick glared at Cat. "Did they teach you that in cop school?"

"It was a bachelor's program in criminal justice," Cat said. "And yes."

Grace winced a bit at Cat's defensive tone. If Grace weren't glad to see her granddaughter finally exhibiting something other than passivity, she would have lightly reprimanded her. Instead, she turned to her brother.

"Cat's right, Mickey. You need to be as specific as possible."

"Not right now." He put the pen down and stood up. "I want to see Donnie."

"That's not a good idea," Cat protested. "You've been drinking."

"Nonsense. I've had coffee." He stood and made for the door.

Grace had no choice but to follow her brother. She grabbed the pad of paper with the contact information and ran after him. Cat followed.

By the time they got to the parking lot, they'd managed to talk him out of driving. He wasn't in shape for it, and besides, Grace regarded his small brown Fiat convertible as a death trap. It was a '78 and on its third clutch, which Mick had a tendency to ride hard. He'd acquired it in a trade for several of his paintings.

Grace knew the authorities wouldn't be keen to let any of them into the crime scene until investigators were done, which might not be till the next day. By the way Alvarez and her crew were acting, they must already suspect arson.

But she couldn't keep Mick away, and she owed it to him to find out whatever she could.

So Cat drove the rental car, with Mick riding shotgun and Grace in back. As they turned onto Coral Way, Grace smelled the smoke. Where Mick's corner studio had been was a mass of charred beams and broken glass. Water left over from the firehoses pooled and dripped. Tendrils of smoke drifted up out of the sodden, burned mess. A palm tree that had filled the two-story bank of studio windows was nothing but a burned stump, its pot cracked and leaking water and soot.

As the three of them gaped at the wreckage, a woman in a pink peignoir clapped over to them in silver mules. Her unnaturally red hair was in curlers, a gauzy yellow scarf tied around them. Grace had met Rose de la Crem the night before; she was one of the artists with studio space in the same building as Mick. Her prominent brow ridge and masculine feet revealed the gender of her birth. But other than that, the transformation to woman was a convincing one.

"Mick!" she exclaimed. "Oh, Mick." She wrapped her arms around him.

The four of them gazed at the burned structure, one whole exterior wall now gone, the studio's remnants exposed to the full moon's judgment.

"I'm the one who called nine-one-one," explained Rose. "I smelled the smoke. Oh, God, Mick. Donnie. I can't believe it. At first the cops thought he was you—but I told them you were at the party. They found Donnie's ID bracelet on him."

Grace remembered that Donnie was diabetic. He wore a Medic Alert bracelet, which would have made his identification easy, no matter the condition of the body.

Sergeant Alvarez was on the scene, chatting with the fire marshal. Grace sidled toward them and stood within earshot. She heard the word "accelerant" several times. She waited for a break in their conversation and then moved in to talk with Alvarez when the fire marshal returned to the burnt studio.

"Do you suspect arson?"

"That's police business." Alvarez began to walk away.

Grace raised her voice to Alvarez's departing back. "If you do, it won't be a secret for long."

The sergeant turned. "If we determine this was arson, your brother is a suspect. He arrived at the hotel after this fire was set. And he has no other alibi so far."

9

Grace set her voice to calm. "I believe my brother was the intended victim. If it weren't for our visit, he would have been working in his studio tonight. The only reason he went to the hotel is because I insisted." Then Grace motioned toward her granddaughter, who was talking with Mick and Rose de la Crem. "I thought the party would cheer up Cat. She's been depressed."

"That's very interesting." Alvarez did not seem swayed.

A stretcher was wheeled into view, toward an ambulance. It held a body bag.

Mick went to it. "Can I see him?"

Alvarez blocked him. "I'm sorry, but it's better if you visit him in the morgue."

Wanting to leave with a gesture of cooperation, Grace drew the paper with the contact information for the Hineses out of her pocket and handed it to Alvarez.

"Here's how to get in touch with Don Hines's parents. Let Mick call them first, though. Please. Give him some time."

Alvarez nodded and took the paper.

Cat stepped in then, speaking to Alvarez in an authoritative voice, the likes of which Grace hadn't heard much since Lee's death. Her granddaughter had been distant and cerebral ever since, and she'd shied away from any case that seemed the least bit exciting. They had yet to take a murder case, and it had been more than a year.

"We'd like to see the evidence reports," Cat demanded. "We'll need to see the lab and autopsy reports, too. We're happy to comply with any further questioning you have for us."

Alvarez surveyed the trio. "Don't any of you leave town."

Chapter 2

For the past year, and especially the past six months, Cat had consistently wished Granny Grace would leave her alone about Lee. Ever since he died, her grandmother had been trying to make sure Cat "healed properly," which meant constant invitations to grief workshops and meditation events. Once Cat found a brochure on her bed for a four-day course on "healing with color therapy," which would begin with a questionnaire meant to identify her "one true color" and end with an exercise that promised to "integrate her color's vibrational harmony with the universal rainbow."

The old Cat would have confronted her grandmother with such a ridiculous brochure, and the two would probably have joked about it. The new Cat tossed it in the trash without a word.

She didn't need poking and prodding around the wall of sadness lodged in her chest. What she needed was work and time, and to get clear on her new life as a committed single person. For Cat had no intention of ever getting entangled again. As a dreamslipper, how could she? The people around her would only get hurt. Even friendships were off limits; her friendship with Wendy, made possible by Cat's undercover work in the Plantation Church, had ended in pain and betrayal. No, it was her duty to focus on her purpose—her work—and leave relationships to normal people.

She kept this to herself, though. Everyone had so many expectations of her grief, as if she were supposed to follow a script. Even her Granny Grace was guilty, with her pressure on Cat to heal *correctly*.

Being in Miami had helped lift the persistent heaviness off her chest, even if she hadn't shown it. Cat figured this was partly due to an infusion of vitamin D from the sunshine.

In drab Seattle, people tended to paint their houses in equally drab colors. But in Miami, a riot of tropical flowers and ostentatious birds, people drenched their homes in tangerine, aqua and pink. It made her wish her grandmother lived here, near Great-Uncle Mick, instead of in the Northwest. Why did the two siblings live on extreme opposite ends of the country, anyway?

The fire in his studio had pulled her out of a fog, though, that was for sure. She'd liked Donnie right off. He was intrigued by her name, and when she said it was short for "Cathedral," he launched into a rambling account of the cathedrals he'd visited in Europe.

"By far, the most amazing cathedral in the entire world is the Sagrada Familia," he'd pronounced. He retrieved his phone and showed her a slideshow of images. "Look, here we are creating monuments to

God, and Gaudí instead found God down here on Earth, in nature. The columns are like trees!"

That was the first thing she'd thought of in the hotel room when Sergeant Alvarez said Donnie was dead. He was so gleeful about that church in Barcelona. He made her promise to visit it sometime, saying, "Cross my heart and hope to die."

She wished he hadn't made her say that. It was such a silly, girlish thing, and now…

She had to put on her PI hat to stop from thinking about what a schmuck God was to take people like Donnie and Lee. She focused on the puzzle of that night: Who set the fire? Did the arsonist mean to kill Donnie, or was that an accident? Then there was the worst question ever, the one she could not vocalize to her grandmother: *Could it have been Mick?*

Cat didn't know Mick very well. He'd visited her family in St. Louis only twice, and they were short visits. She remembered the watercolor set he gave her. And how, frowning at her drawing of him, he told her not to try to paint people the way they really looked.

"Paint the way they feel instead." He had a bushy beard back then, and she saw him as a kind of magical creature in his paint-splattered clothes. But Cat had never been able to figure out how to paint people the way they feel. She still didn't know what Mick meant by that.

The night of the fire, Granny Grace took Mick back to her hotel room. She hadn't wanted to leave him alone. But it was clear neither of them got any sleep. "He went back to whiskey and then tried to sober up again with hits of coffee before our trip to the morgue," her grandmother had told her.

Cat did not accompany the two of them to the morgue the next morning, but she understood that Mick needed to see Donnie to believe that he was gone. When Mick returned, he asked to be left alone to call Donnie's parents.

Afterward, he promptly got drunk again and stayed that way. Cat counted five bottles of Bushmill's in two days. And he still hadn't written down a solid timeline for the evening or done anything to strengthen his alibi.

With his studio torched, the three of them had moved into a rental house, one in Coral Gables owned by Granny Grace's friend Ernesto. Mick's beach house was off limits since Granny Grace suspected Mick was the target of the fire, and that the killer would hit it next once he found out Mick hadn't died in the studio fire. It was too small for the three of them anyway.

This put three dreamslippers together under one roof, which was a challenge.

"Mick's in no condition to control his dreamslipping right now," said Granny Grace their first night in the rental. They were in the kitchen cleaning up after a thrown-together meal of plantains and Cuban rice and beans. Cat knew her grandmother was warning about what she might find if she slipped into her great-uncle's dream, or vice versa.

"And frankly, my dear," her grandmother continued with an emphatic swipe of a rag across the countertop, "neither are you."

"Thanks, Gran, for your confidence in me."

"Oh, I didn't mean it as a criticism. Just an observation. But no one is expecting you to have it under control. Nor Mick, for that matter. I know he cared a great deal about Donnie, and there's almost nothing more upsetting than knowing someone wants you dead."

"Well, unless you know of a tinfoil hat or something that keeps us from dreamslipping, Granny, I don't know what we're supposed to do."

Her grandmother laughed. "Remember the rules."

Cat nodded. In her apprenticeship with her grandmother, they'd established ground rules that governed their dreamslipping ability, giving it dimension but also keeping it in check. The first rule is not to *try* to dreamslip in your loved one's dreams. This one was pretty challenging, as Granny Grace claimed to be able to keep herself from slipping into people's dreams most of the time, but the more she loved them or the closer she felt to them, the harder it was for her to keep from picking up their dreams as if they were her own. Cat had not mastered this ability, and Granny Grace herself had trouble staying out of Cat's dreams. Cat wondered if this was because it was easier to slip into another dreamslipper's dream or if it was because of their emotional connection.

Thinking about rule numero uno made Cat realize how little she knew about Granny Grace's relationship with her brother, especially where their dreamslipping was concerned.

"Gran?" she asked, "can you keep yourself from slipping into Mick's dreams?"

Recognition seemed to flicker across her grandmother's face. She smiled.

"Oh, such lovely dreams that man has, when they're his own. I remember one from our childhood to this day. He must have been three or four at the time, as I'd just entered puberty, and my dreamslipping had recently started. We'd been given our own rooms by then, after having to share one for forever, or so it seemed to me at the time. But my room was still next to his, not that it mattered. I was regularly picking up my parents' dreams, and they slept downstairs.

"Anyway," she continued, "the dream was so lovely, so fanciful. The circus was in town, and little Mickey dreamed he was riding on the back of an elephant, which flew! I think he thought of it as Dumbo. We flew up above the clouds, looking down on our farm town, and a pretty accurate aerial depiction, I must say, especially considering his age. He got the Catholic church steeple right, and the dairy plant on the edge of town. I remember the feel of the elephant's back under my hands, its hair bristly and its skin dry... I think they let Mick touch the elephant at the circus, so he got that detail right, too. We flew through the clouds, doing loop-de-loops! There were giant hot-air balloons going by us, and then things got really strange, as a World War II flying ace zoomed by, and then a pirate ship.

"The captain spotted us in his spyglass, and then his crew began to shoot at us with cannonballs! So Mick swerved to avoid being hit, and they missed us every time. Then a dinosaur so big it could reach into the sky tried to swipe at us, but again, Mick swerved to avoid him.

"The elephant set us down softly back on earth when we were ready, and then it presented us both with giant lollipops held out in its trunk, the old-fashioned candy that looks like a swirled ribbon shaped into a disk. Back then those were a rare treat. Oh, the dream was grand and beautiful, the kind of dream you think children should have."

"But how about now, Gran?"

Mick walked in without a word to either of them and began rifling through the cupboards, looking for more liquor.

"Maybe you should ask Great-Uncle Mick if I've picked up any of his dreams," Granny Grace proposed, her voice a bit stern.

He startled. "What's this? Oh, the dream thing. Humph. No sister sightings in many a year, thank God." He found the bottle he was looking for and practically cuddled it to his chest, as if it were an old friend.

"Well, we're all under one roof now," Granny Grace cautioned. "So who knows what will happen."

That first night, what happened was this: Two of the three dreamslippers got very little sleep.

Cat didn't necessarily agree with Granny Grace's rules, especially in this instance. Even though Mick refused to write down a timeline for the evening, Cat made a mental note of the whole evening, and she could not account for Mick's whereabouts after they met him at seven p.m. for dinner at the Blue Pineapple.

"Nobody eats dinner in Miami before eight," Mick had complained. But he gave in, and they'd had the early dinner. The next

14

time they saw him was at the hotel when the police came just before two a.m. That left nearly the whole evening unaccounted for.

Cat tossed and turned before finally giving in to the temptation to open herself up to any dreams her uncle might be having. It was a skill she'd honed over the past year, thanks to her grandmother's mentoring. Using their ability this way, they'd been able to catch two embezzlers and a woman cheating on her husband.

As she drifted to sleep, she entered her uncle's mind space by imagining one of his paintings, the big, abstract one that sort of resembled a seashell. She pictured him creating it in sweeping, broad strokes....

There were no pirates, dinosaurs, or flying elephants in this one, but it did strike her right away as most likely Mick's.

She was in his art studio, before the fire. Donnie was there, painting, and Rose de la Crem clopped in on her heels and tossed a cup of coffee at the painting, mixing it in with the paint Donnie had applied to the canvas.

"See?" she said, a hand on one hip. "Isn't that better?"

Cat heard herself say, "Yes, it is better" in Mick's voice.

Rose broke down crying and threw the cup to the floor. It shattered, the pieces flying. "Why can't I do this with my own work?"

Donnie hugged Rose till she calmed down while Cat-as-Mick knelt to pick up the pieces. The mug was one of Rose's thrift-store finds. "Florida Quacker" was printed in bold pink on an image of a duck wearing a trucker cap that was more redneck than ironic. The duck was sitting in a beach chair, sipping a cocktail. Cat could tell this through the broken pieces, putting them back together as if they formed a puzzle.

"C'mon," Donnie coaxed Rose. "Let's go take a look at what you're working on."

He motioned for Mick to follow, and the three walked down the hallway to Rose's studio. But when Rose opened the door, a swirl of black smoke blew out, swallowing them up. Cat couldn't breathe. She coughed, choking on the smoke as she saw Rose drop to the floor, overcome by the fumes. Cat could feel herself about to go down next. But then the dream changed.

They were in Mick's studio. She caught a glimpse of Donnie, asleep on a cot behind a curtain, a bottle of Bushmill's open on the floor next to him. Cat rode along in her uncle's consciousness as Mick picked up pots of paint thinner and turpentine and began dumping them out around the room. He opened the curtain and poured the liquid onto Donnie, who woke in time to see Mick and yell out. But Mick lit a match and threw it onto him, everything going up in a burst of flame. Donnie screamed and screamed until he couldn't scream anymore....

And then Mick woke up, and Cat was forced out of the dream.

She sat up, sweaty, her heart pounding. She heard Mick stumble to the bathroom, coughing and clearing his throat. Did he know she'd slipped into his dream? He hadn't seemed to show it within the dream. She lay in bed for a long time, considering her uncle's possible guilt and how she could tell this to Granny Grace.

But then Cat fell into her own recurring nightmare, one that had plagued her for the past year, a dream within a dream.

She is sleeping in bed with Lee and begins to dream. The killer, Anita, slips into Cat's head. Anita was not a dreamslipper in real life, but in Cat's dream-within-the dream, she has the ability. She fuses with Cat's consciousness so that Cat can feel Anita in her head; she can hear Anita's thoughts.

Cut out the rot to make the wood strong. In Jesus's name. You will be the Church's salvation.

Quickly, Anita overpowers Cat so that Cat becomes Anita. She gets up and looks in the mirror, and it's Anita's face staring back at her. The dream always ends the same way: Cat-as-Anita opens Lee's dresser drawer, pulls out a gun, and shoots him there in the bed.

Only this time, as Cat/Anita turns around with the gun, she finds there's someone else there, sitting in a side chair, drinking whiskey.

"Whatcha doin' there, my mild-mannered grand-niece?" Mick says, motioning with his drink at the gun in her hands.

Cat hears herself as Anita answering him. "I'm going to shoot that man," she says, pointing the gun at Lee, sleeping in the bed.

"That'd be a waste of time," Mick says, taking a drink. "Seeing as how he's already dead."

Cat turns to the bed with a start and sees Lee as he looked that terrible day on Granny Grace's front porch, after Anita shot him, with part of his head blown away and blood spilling out around him like a halo.

"No!" she cries, and suddenly she's Cat again. Anita is gone, and Cat crouches down to stop the blood.

Cat awakened from the dream in a panic, and it took her a few moments to realize where she was. Then she heard the sound of her uncle, shuffling to the kitchen for another drink.

So he had the ability to appear and talk to her in her dreams, as Granny Grace did.

The next day, Cat tried to broach the subject of Mick's possible guilt to her grandmother, but she couldn't find the words. "I think your brother might be an arsonist or murderer" didn't exactly roll off the tongue.

Mick came out of his room only to piss or get more alcohol, helping himself to Ernesto's ample stash. Cat was sure Alvarez and her posse would identify the hole in his alibi soon, if they hadn't already. But they were probably waiting for the forensics reports. They'd want more evidence on Mick before interrogating him further. Granny Grace went to the precinct station but got no more information.

When Granny Grace was out, Cat called her mother to let her know what was happening. Mercy was upset, and as always, worried about Cat's safety. She was relieved to hear they weren't staying at Mick's beach house. Cat took the opportunity to ask her mother about her family history.

"What do you know about your uncle, Mom? Why do Granny Grace and Mick live on opposite coasts?"

"Oh, those two had some kind of falling-out in the Eighties." Her mother clicked her tongue in judgment. "Tedious, if you ask me."

"Do you know what it was about?"

"No idea. They used to be extremely close, and then... It probably has to do with you-know-what."

Cat's mother didn't like to talk about the dreamslipping thing. Up until Cat proved she could do it by relating the content of her mother's dreams exactly, she had denied its existence. It apparently skipped a generation.

As she said good-bye to her mother, Cat wondered if there wasn't a personal reason Granny Grace had set up those rules.

The next night, things were a bit better for Cat. Mick had had so much to drink his dreams were washy and disjointed, and that made it easy for Cat to pop out of them when she inadvertently slipped into them. And he didn't slip into hers.

And now after a couple of days, Mick was sprawled out on the lanai, which he was using as a sort of makeshift studio, a giant easel on two-by-fours set up in the middle. But not much painting was getting done, Cat noted. She took him some coffee and a sandwich, setting the plate on a side table next to where he was reclining on a vintage Sixties-era sofa. Ernesto was a collector of Mid-Century Modern furniture.

"Uncle Mick," she said sharply, "you've got to eat."

"Right." He opened his eyes halfway. "Eat." He slumped back down on the sofa.

Cat snapped her fingers in front of his face. "Uncle Mick!"

It startled him into opening one eye. "Whaaat?"

"It's lunchtime, a couple of days after your studio was torched. You've been wallowing in drink long enough. It's time to get up."

He lifted himself up into a sitting position with great effort, placing his bare feet on the floor. He was wearing the same pajamas he'd put on two days ago. She could smell his sourness.

She gestured to the food on the side table. "Eat."

He set the plate in his lap and then lifted the coffee to his lips.

"This isn't Cuban," he said. "And it's pretty weak, besides."

Cat resisted the urge to smack him.

He put the cup down and took up the sandwich, grinning after the first bite. "Say, this is tasty, Cat. Thanks."

She smiled back. His bipolar nature caught her off guard.

He polished it off handily. "Got another?"

She stepped into the kitchen, made another sandwich, and returned. He was up and standing in front of a blank canvas on his easel, stabbing into the surface with charcoal. Cat watched as he worked.

Slowly the image took shape, and she gasped: It was Donnie's burnt body.

"When I look at the canvas, that's what I see."

He put the charcoal down, went to his bedroom, and came back dressed. "I'm heading out for some real coffee."

Before she could offer to tag along, the door slammed, and he was gone.

Cat went back to work, shrugging off her great uncle's loss-infused rudeness. She was researching every square inch of his storied art career to see if she could turn up anyone who hated him enough to torch his studio. There were plenty of jealous types, including a couple of suspicious ones from his grad-school days, but were they envious enough to try to kill him, especially after all these years? She'd have to find out.

After an hour or two, Mick hadn't returned, but Granny Grace swept in. "Still at the computer?" she asked, disapprovingly. "You know, Cat, in my day, we never used computers. We had to do our investigating on foot."

"On foot? I thought you went around on horseback."

"All right, Smarty Pants, we've got more interviewing to do. Here, I've marked a few we haven't met." She tossed Cat the Art Basel artists' directory. "Today's the last day of the show, so let's vamoose before these *artistes* leave town."

Cat groaned. So far, talking to artists had turned up nothing other than a few choice anecdotes for future cocktail-party fodder. She and Granny Grace had tackled a few the day before, wanting to do something other than sit and wait for Alvarez's team. Cat had her fill after meeting with the performance artist whose entire shtick involved making music with an electric razor as his instrument.

Cat scoped the directory, finding the entry Granny Grace starred in a purple pen. "South Beach?" Cat questioned, her voice edged with sarcasm. "This requires travel. In a car. Across the causeway."

"Better wear sunscreen," Granny Grace advised.

What should have been a twenty-minute drive took them twice as long due to traffic, and they were nearly wiped out by a guy doing ninety and swerving from lane to lane while watching TV on a screen built into his driver's-side visor. Even a short drive in Miami meant risking your life.

But soon they were in the loft space belonging to the first artist on the list, Kazuo Noshihara. He'd rented the space for the show. It offered a commanding view of the beach from floor-to-ceiling windows. His work was scattered around, and he and his assistants were busy crating it for the return trip to Japan.

From what Cat could tell, his work amounted to nothing more than white canvases with pieces of lint stuck to them. But Granny Grace gasped as if impressed when she saw them.

"Brilliant," her grandmother pronounced, and there came Noshihara, in his crisp white jeans and equally crisp white shirt, to greet her. Cat drifted away from them as they lapsed into a conversation about the artistic influence of Yoko Ono, whom Granny Grace said she'd once met in person, as had Noshihara. Cat wondered briefly if every artist in Miami had once met Yoko Ono.

Walking the length of the paintings awaiting their crates, Cat kept expecting to see something more than simple white canvases with a single piece of lint stuck into the middle of each, but that's all there was to see.

As she returned to her grandmother and Noshihara, Cat watched as Granny Grace reached into the pocket of her linen trousers, grabbed what lint was there, and offered it to the artist.

He accepted the gift with tears in his eyes. "You have a deep understanding of Minimalism, of the detritus of living, in a small way," he said. "My English fails me. But I think you know."

"I think I do," said Granny Grace, nodding.

"I will title my next piece 'The Gift of Grace,' for you." The artist bowed.

Cat had to hand it to her grandmother. She really knew how to connect with people. But as for shedding insight on the case, Noshihara had not much more to offer than, well, pocket lint. He knew Mick only by reputation and had a solid alibi for the night of the fire, which had been verified already by Miami PD, which had been by for a chat.

Cat felt the time was wasted, but she also knew from her criminal-justice classes that most of detective legwork wasn't glamorous or even relevant. In the white elevator of Noshihara's building, Granny Grace turned to Cat. "You know, you should really take more of an interest in our potential suspects."

"Do you know how much his lint sells for?" Cat spat back. "Fifty thousand dollars! For the fuzz some hipster scraped out of his pockets, Gran! It's ridiculous. The whole art world is a joke."

Her grandmother raised an eyebrow at her. Sizing Cat up and down, she asked, "Let me see your lint."

"What?"

"Let's see it. Whatever you've got in your pocket. I want to know."

The elevator chimed, and they stepped out into the white-and-turquoise building vestibule, To Cat, it felt like walking into an iPod. Granny Grace steered her over to a white leather bench perched on aluminum legs.

"There," she said, pointing to the bench surface. "Take it out and set it there."

"We have two more people to interview on South Beach," Cat protested.

"Humor me."

"Fine." Cat reached into the right pocket of her slacks, not expecting to find much, as they were warm-weather slacks and not appropriate for Seattle most of the year. She'd hardly worn them before this trip.

She turned out her pocket, and a scraggly array of fibers fell into her hand. She set them on the bench.

Granny Grace knelt to look at them closely, taking her smartphone and flipping to a light-bulb app, which illuminated the pocket lint. "Let's see..." Amidst gray fibers from Cat's pants, there was what looked like the corner of a dollar bill. Cat had to admit it was visually sort of interesting, but not earth-shattering or surprising in any way.

"A bit of money. Big deal."

Also caught up in the gray pants fibers was a crumb from the pastry they'd had that morning at the Cuban bakery on Calle Ocho. "Yeah, that's a cool detail," Cat conceded. "But art worth tens of thousands? Hardly."

"The detritus of everyday life," Granny Grace pronounced. "It tells the story of what we do with our hands, and what we value enough to keep with us."

"Sure," Cat said, smiling. "So apparently I value food and money. Can we go now?"

"What's in your other pocket?"

"Really? We're doing this?"

"Yes," her grandmother said, motioning to the bench.

Cat emptied the contents of her other pocket.

Granny Grace bent forward like a forensics examiner. "Oh, look at this," she said. "It's paper..." She unrolled a piece of paper fiber that had obviously been through the wash. Faded but still readable were the words *Dave's Drive-In* and a logo of a frosty soda mug with a happy smiling face superimposed on the white mug froth.

Cat took it from Granny Grace's hands. Seeing it instantly brought her back to the day that Lee had shown up in Missouri, worried about her, foolishly playing the white knight come to rescue her. She had no choice but to take him with her on a trip to Johnson's Shut-Ins, where she found a clue, etched into the rocks there, that was relevant to her case. They'd stopped at Dave's Drive-In for lunch on the way, and the two of them had scrunched up the papers around their straws and then siphoned soda onto them, watching them grow like worms. She'd felt like a kid again, laughing with Lee.

Her eyes began to water.

"What is it, Cat? Is it something from your trip back to St. Louis?"

"Yes. I went there with Lee."

Cat felt her grandmother's arms around her as the tears came. "Oh, my poor dear. You just got socked with the power of art."

Cat recovered, and, laying a hand on her grandmother's shoulder, she said, "Gran. I need to ask you something. I hate to ask it, but I have to." She cleared her throat. "Should we consider Uncle Mick a suspect?"

"Certainly not!"

"He doesn't have an alibi...."

"Yes, I know." Her grandmother looked away. "He's hiding something about that night. But he didn't set that fire. He lost most of his art, not to mention his best friend, in that fire. So get that out of your head."

"It's just…" Cat hesitated, swallowing hard.

"What, Cat? Say it."

"I, um, dreamslipped with him."

"On purpose?"

"Yes."

Granny Grace silently regarded Cat.

"I couldn't help it … I wanted to know… And I found something. He dreamed—"

"—Whatever he dreamed, it doesn't matter."

"But what if you're in denial because he's your brother? He dreamed that he set his studio on fire and killed Donnie."

Her grandmother sat there for a long time, not saying anything. Then she picked up the remnant of the straw wrapper, which Cat had set in her own lap. "Like you keep dreaming that you shot Lee. That's not the same as this, is it? Hard evidence. Always remember that, dreamslipper."

Cat let the words sink in. Her grandmother was right. But then Cat realized something. "Hey, you've slipped into my Lee nightmares! What about the rules?"

"As you illustrated, Cat, rules are meant to be broken." And with that, Granny Grace hoisted herself to her feet. "C'mon. We've got more artists to interview."

Chapter 3

I
t was the worst conversation Mick Travers had ever had in his life.

Telling Donnie's parents that their precious son was gone, their precious boy, no matter that he was a forty-three-year-old man who hadn't yet made it as an artist—to them he would always be their precious boy sitting on the living room floor drawing like a boy genius—that was the worst conversation he'd ever had. It wasn't even so much a conversation as a verbal bloodletting. Poor Mary Ellen Hines and Donald Hines, Sr., sitting in their suburban kitchen in suburban Ohio, getting this information over the phone.

Mick had let Donald Sr. cry in that silent, wracking way a man not given to shedding a tear finally does when something happens that is so painful, even he can't hold it back. "No," was the first thing the man said. Just "no."

Mick waited while Donald told Mary Ellen.

"We should come down," Donald finally said through choked sobs. "We should ... see him."

Mick thought of Donnie's unrecognizable body. No parent should have to see that. He also knew they couldn't afford several trips to Miami or funeral costs. Mick had heard from Donnie that his parents struggled financially after the airline company Donald had worked for all his life defaulted on his pension. The two survived solely on their small savings and Social Security. Donnie hoped to make it big as an artist so he could help them. They'd never been able to visit their son in Miami, not that they were the traveling type anyway. Unlike their free-spirited son, the two had barely ever left Ohio in their own lifetimes. Donnie had driven up to see them whenever he could, usually making the trip in a record two days in his aged Datsun.

"You don't have to do that," Mick told the man. "Really. It's better ... if you remember him the way he was."

Seized with a galvanizing sense of guilt, Mick said, "Please, let me handle the wake. We'll have it here. You can come down then. It won't be long. Just a week or two."

The two agreed, and Mick left them to their black hole of grief.

There was nothing for it, nothing at all, not even five bottles of Bushmill's. When he came out of his stupor, he was still angry enough to carp at his well-meaning grandniece. He left the house just so he didn't end up saying something he'd regret.

Donnie hadn't deserved to go out like that.

It should have been me, Mick thought, about fifty times an hour.

He drove to a Cuban bakery in a strip mall where he knew he could get some decent coffee. He would have preferred a walk or a bike ride, and maybe one of those would have cleared his head, but nobody really did that in Miami. Both activities were in fact dangerous; the head of the city's transportation department had recently been mowed down by an SUV while biking to work. That was Miami for you.

He sat in a booth and ordered a cortadito, though he preferred the taste of the colada. But coladas were meant to be shared. He, Donnie, Rose, and some of the other residents of the Brickell Lofts often took communal coffee breaks that way. One of them would go out and get a colada in a big Styrofoam cup and pour the syrupy coffee into tiny plastic thimbles, one shot each. It was the perfect afternoon pick-me-up. They'd stand around in Mick's studio shooting the shit, Rose complaining about her boyfriend (in Mick's opinion he seemed to only come around when he needed something from Rose), and the three of them criticizing what they'd read in *Art in Our Time* that month.

Donnie was Mick's studio assistant. His first. Donnie could handle the large canvases Mick painted, the twenty-by-twenty-foot behemoths his patrons and collectors loved to put in their big Miami manses. Mick could no longer stretch and manage them on his own. Everyone told Mick to work with the local colleges to get an intern to do it for free, but Mick didn't believe in slave labor.

Donnie reminded Mick of himself twenty years prior: an artist with amazing work ethic and experience who hadn't ever hit it big. So Mick hired him and paid him, even gave him health insurance through the Miami Artists' Guild. And when Donnie's escalating rent had forced him out of his apartment, and Mick found out Donnie had no savings whatsoever for "retirement," whatever that was to an artist, or anyone anymore for that matter, Mick let Donnie move into Mick's own tremendous studio space.

Mick's cortadito arrived, but then he added a guava pastry. Cat's sandwich had already burned up in his stomach, which hadn't been fueled in forty-eight hours. The waitress was Cuban and either knew no English or refused to use it. So Mick was forced to tap into his Cuban-styled Spanish, still accented by his Midwestern roots despite his long stint in Miami. "Pour fahvor, dee gamey una pasteleez con hwava."

While he waited, he swirled the sugary coffee in his cup and contemplated the target of his anger, and that was whatever piece of excrement coated in five layers of vomit and snot had come into his studio and set fire to his works-in-progress, killing his friend in the process. His sister was right; clearly the intended target had been Mick himself. Outside of Rose and some of the other live-work tenants, nobody knew Donnie had been sleeping in Mick's studio. But before he'd let Donnie have it, Mick often slept there, when he worked late at night and didn't want to drive back to his beach house in South Dade.

Mick had already been killed a million times by other artists' jealousy. This had begun to happen even before he'd had any success.

As early as junior high, it had set him apart. In the small town where he and Priscilla, aka "Amazing Grace," grew up, it had already started. In his junior high class, no less, which was made up of Mick and eleven other kids. They didn't have locks on their lockers, which were stacked against one wall of their homeroom. In art class, Mick painted Johnny Cash performing on *The Ed Sullivan Show*. His teacher, who was a Cash fan and encouraged Mick's talent besides, held it up for the whole class to see. Later, when Mick went into his unlocked locker to take the picture home to show his parents, it was no longer there. Someone had stolen it.

In graduate school, his talent quickly became known, and one of his professors declared, "We have a real artist in our midst." But that professor's rival was a man who'd recently been granted tenure without the level of artistic success the others in the department enjoyed. He had made it his personal mission to destroy Mick not only as an artist but as a human being. Chester Canon, or "Chester the Molester," as Mick liked to call him, screamed and threw things at Mick during crits, described him as a "no-talent hack" to anyone within hearing, and ridiculed his work with insatiable glee. Canon enlisted into his campaign several of Mick's fellows, students who couldn't find the perspective in a painting if it were diagramed into the canvas like a paint-by-numbers kit.

Canon got his comeuppance, though, when he refused to enter Mick's painting in a national contest of MFA art students' work. Several of the professors wanted to enter Mick's *Pink Splash*. To create *Pink Splash*, Mick had taken an old advertisement for facial bleaching cream, decoupaged it onto a canvas, set the canvas on the floor, climbed to the top of a very tall ladder, and then dripped pink paint over it. Canon's vote was trumped by the other faculty, and *Pink Splash* was submitted against his wishes. In competition with the work of hundreds of students throughout the country, it won.

"A riveting commentary on the nature of racial complexion," said the judges. That had taken the wind out of Canon's sails, for sure, since Mick's talent had been vindicated by an independent panel of judges whose opinion he had to accept, even if he vehemently disagreed.

Mick ran down the list of hating grad students in his head, wondering if any of them still bore a grudge. It was possible. A year after grad school, *Art in Our Time* published a Letter to the Editor that bad-mouthed the work of one of Mick's professors, making it sound as if the letter had been written by Mick. It was signed *Mick in Miami*, which is where he'd fled after graduate school. He was the only "Mick" in the Miami art world. Coupled with the letter's references to the professor's work and the classes Mick took, it was easy to assume that Mick had written the letter. That professor had been one of Mick's staunchest allies, and it pained Mick to think the professor believed he'd written it. Mick tried to get the magazine to print a retraction, but it refused. And the professor refused to take Mick's calls.

The worst part was, Mick *had* criticized some aspects of that professor's work, over beers with the other students, in confidence, but never to the professor's face. Whoever wrote the letter cribbed some of Mick's details from those conversations. So the letter had an air of authenticity to it, and Mick knew whoever betrayed him had been close enough to be involved in the regular round of criticism most art students doled out against their professors, especially when drinking.

The pastry was a delicious concoction of orange guava jelly between layers of buttery, flaky crust. Mick wolfed it down and gulped his coffee. Then he took his flip sketchbook out of his back pocket and began to jot down some names. It was something Priscilla and Cat had been asking for since the night of the fire. It was a humiliating task, compiling a list of people who might want him dead for no other reason than jealousy over his knack for putting lines and colors together on canvas. And he was alarmed to find that it was a rather long list, one that had grown through the years.

When he was finished, he sat there staring at the ring of milky brown coffee left in the bottom of his cup. He could give this list to the police, but they would still think of him as a suspect unless he coughed up his alibi.

But he feared his alibi would make him look guiltier.

He flipped the cover closed on his sketchbook and decided to talk to the one person who could verify he hadn't set the fire that night: A goth chick named Jenny Baines.

Chapter 4

Grace was sitting in the cottage in Ernesto's living room listening to her granddaughter complain about Mick when the man himself burst into the house. He tossed a crumpled sheet of notebook paper at Grace, said, "Here's your damn list," and announced that he was leaving again.

Grace smoothed out the paper. He'd done a good job, at least, with names, dates, and details. In the silence after he slammed the door, Grace read the list aloud to Cat.

"Let's split up this time," Grace said. "These first two are here in South Florida, but after that, it looks like we're going to the Big Apple." She gave Cat the task of interviewing one of Mick's former professors up in Fort Lauderdale and took it upon herself to interview the number-one hater on Mick's list.

This happened to be a woman.

With whom her brother had once slept. There it was in Mick's chicken-scratch handwriting: CANDACE SHREVEPORT, EX-LOVER. Grace remembered meeting Candace, but only briefly. Back then—more than thirty years ago—she'd been a young beachcomber with stars in her eyes about Mick. When Grace called to set up the appointment, the woman sounded surprised, then suspicious.

"It would be great to talk to someone who's practically an expert on Mick Travers," Grace said. There was no response, so she added, "And his art." The woman agreed to meet.

Candace lived on Sanibel Island, on the Gulf side of the Florida peninsula, but Grace was keen for the drive. It took her across the Everglades along Alligator Alley, a straight shot she'd traveled many times during her visits to see Mick. The name was not a misnomer, as Grace spotted several alligators without leaving her air-conditioned car. She gave herself the luxury of a stop at Shark Valley, which was a misnomer, since there were obviously no sharks slogging through the swampy glades. But a long, paved path led to a hummock, an area of solid ground where a few slash pines bravely fought for their existence.

The alligators lining the pavement seemed fat and happy, lazing in the sun without much care for how close she and the other tourists approached. The gators yawned, wide-jawed, and looked away. She was mercifully glad when she reached a shaded kiosk at the end of the paved trail. A clever crow lifted a silver-sheathed energy bar out of her backpack, making off with the treat before she realized it.

Without the energy bar, she was famished by the time she arrived in Sanibel. A restaurant on the edge of the shell-lined beach called to her, but she was to meet Candace Shreveport at her beach bungalow. Perhaps she could entice the woman into an early dinner.

The bungalow was a delight from the outside, reminiscent of the gingerbread Victorians of Key West, and painted in pale pink with aqua trim.

"What a lovely home," Grace remarked when Candace greeted her. The woman was holding a black-and-white cat balanced on her ample middle when she came to answer the door. Her hair had gone gray some time ago but was dyed black; Grace could see it was time for a root touch-up.

"Well, Mick would hate it," Candace said, gesturing to the outside of the house. "All that decorative busyness. He'd say it was too folksy."

"You're probably right about that," Grace said.

"Come on in," Candace said, without warmth, shifting the cat to one hip and propping the screen door open for Grace.

"Thank you so much for meeting with me." Grace followed the woman inside.

Candace gestured to a set of white wicker furniture that creaked loudly when Grace sat down. On the walls were, presumably, Ms. Shreveport's own creations: a row of Impressionistic paintings of none other than the cat she was holding at the door.

"Those are mine." Candace noticed Grace's gaze. She pointed to the signature in the bottom corner of one. "I sign my works Candy Port."

Grace cringed but tried not to show it. What on earth had her brother Mick ever seen in this woman?

"Mick and I met at a bar," the woman announced, as if she sensed Grace's bewilderment. "The Conch. Down in Key Largo. To this day, I don't know what he was doing down there, but I'd just run off from my husband."

"I see," said Grace, though she didn't really.

"I was drunk off my ass, and Mick danced with me. It was fun. He's loads of fun to drink with. Of course, we ended up in bed, at the Largo Lodge. Cute place—I've gone back a few times with my girlfriends."

"My brother says you drunk-dial him every couple of years," Grace broke in. "And as recently as this past spring."

"Yeah, he's not exactly on my speed-dial, if you know what I mean, but when you get to thinking hard about where your life went wrong, you know, he's one of the first people I think of."

"But you've done well for yourself." Grace couldn't help herself.

"Oh, I do fine. I'm in a few crafty galleries here in town, right there with the mosquito huts and the yard art. But I'll never be a real artist. I'll never be recognized. That's Mick. He took it from me."

Grace felt her temperature rising and worked to control her response. "And how did he do that?"

Candace laughed haughtily. "I can see Mick's his usual uncommunicative self. He hasn't told you a damn thing, has he? Listen, you want something to drink? It's a long story, and you've had a long drive."

As much as Grace wanted this woman to spill whatever sordid story she had roiling around inside her, the thought of liquor on her empty stomach made her blanche.

"I'll do you one better," Grace said. "I'll take you to dinner. Earn your story that way."

Candace was delighted. She popped to her feet. "Let's go to the Orange Spot. It just opened up. They have a vintage Wurlitzer. You'll love it."

The Orange Spot indeed featured a vintage Wurlitzer in its dining room, along with a collection of other old-fashioned musical machines, including a group of mechanized monkey musicians. Grace polished off her halibut, which had been cooked in a brown paper bag with shallots and hazelnuts, and let Candace do the talking.

The woman's list of grievances against Mick was long. According to Candace, it was she, and not Mick, who first had the idea for Mick's now legendary Sea Series, inspired by the turquoise waters in the Florida Keys. Grace let Candace prattle on about this even though it was fairly obvious that Mick had in fact been down in Key Largo searching for inspiration. He'd clearly found it, but he'd also picked up this leg biter and brought her home as well.

"I'm also the one who introduced Mick to the New York art scene," Candace informed Grace, emphasizing the point by shoving an olive from her martini into her purple-lipstick-ringed mouth.

"Come again?" Grace countered. "Mick met the gallery owner Peter Swanson at an opening, and the man loved his work. Everyone knows that story."

"I introduced him to Peter! You know how shy Mick can be. A real introvert, that one. He wouldn't have approached Peter on his own!"

The woman did have a point, but the facts flew in the face of things. "But Mick had already established himself in New York well before you say the two of you met."

"I did it!" Candace insisted. "Mick owes his success to me."

Grace switched gears, sensing an alcohol-fueled opportunity. "That must make you really angry, Candace," she said. "If someone I cared about used me like that, I'd want to kill him."

Candace downshifted her anger. "But I didn't torch his studio, if that's what you're driving at."

"Oh, a little fire ... happens all the time!" Grace said. "Maybe you only wanted to destroy his art. Maybe you didn't think anyone would be there. How would you know that? You haven't seen Mick in years!"

"Oh, I've seen him...."

"You have?"

"He didn't even recognize me! At his showing in West Palm Beach. I drove over there to get a look at those big monstrosities he's making now. And there he was. Bastard didn't even recognize me."

"Well, did you talk to him?"

"No. He didn't recognize me...."

Candace sort of shut down after that. She quit talking and eating, though she continued to drink. Grace paid the exorbitant bill and helped the woman home. As she tucked her into a living-room chair, Grace turned around and said, "Candace, you live in paradise. A lot of people would be jealous of you, but you waste your energy being jealous of my brother. Why don't you let that go? Enjoy life. Collect a few seashells."

Grace thought she heard Candace call her a bitch once she shut the door.

Grace spent the night in a simple but clean motel, thinking it best to drive fresh in the morning. She'd prefer a nice B&B on the beach, but after the splurge on dinner with Candace, she needed to reel in the spending.

The next morning she stopped into one of the galleries in Sanibel and found a whole section of paintings signed Candy Port. She perused them with a cold eye, looking for Mick's influence and not finding it. The woman's work showed marginal skill, but it had a certain "outsider art" appeal, as she roughed in her subjects' eyes, making them seem more childlike and lost than they would be had she stuck to the representational. There was certainly something there, that spark of intuition, perhaps, a way of seeing the world. But it was held back; something kept it restrained even here on the canvas. The woman's own limitations were omnipresent.

Still, Grace found herself especially captivated by the images of children and animals, which lost the sinister feel of the other depictions and seemed to reveal the artist's lingering sense of wonder. Grace remembered Candace had a cage of parakeets just beyond the front room of her house, and of course there was that cat, who was clearly her closest friend. But the children? She had not seemed to be a woman who would admit children into her life. But in a painting that gave her pause, there were two imps staring over a fence that Grace recognized as the one framing the artist's yard. The kids must be her neighbors, Grace surmised.

The painting was priced at three hundred and fifty dollars. The frame alone was worth that, as it was vintage wood and customized to echo the fence in the painting. It set the painting off nicely. Obeying some instinct she couldn't even name if she tried, Grace bought the painting.

On her way back to Miami, she decided that Candace was indeed capable of having set that fire, even if her intention had been to destroy the art instead of kill Mick.

Chapter 5

Suspect number two was right up the coast in Fort Lauderdale, so Cat didn't have to travel far to interview him. This was a man Mick referred to as "Chester the Molester," but Cat planned to address him as "Dr. Canon."

His wife answered the door. She was a diminutive woman with an old-fashioned permanent, her natural gray color and lack of cosmetic surgery—unlike many a Miami oldster—revealing her age to be upwards of eighty. On her feet were solid orthopedic shoes.

"You're here to see the Professor?" She looked Cat up and down as if she distrusted her on the basis of looks or maybe age alone. "He's in his studio." She left the door open for Cat and began walking down a long hallway that opened to an indoor atrium filled with plants and canvas-stacked easels.

Dr. Canon was sitting on a stool, legs akimbo, staring at a half-finished canvas, a lit cigarette dangling from one hand. He did not respond to the sound of their footsteps on the tiled floor.

"Chester, darling," his wife said, raising her voice, suggesting he was hard of hearing. "That lady detective is here to see you. The one who called."

At that, Dr. Canon turned and spied Cat over the top of thick reading glasses. What little hair he had left on his head had been combed back neatly with some sort of hair cream. There was a pack of cigarettes in his left shirt pocket. He was wearing a tropical cabana shirt and white loafers with trouser shorts. He looked like a very old-school Florida cracker. Cat thought about the mug in her Uncle Mick's dream, the one Rose dropped.

"A lady detective, eh? Well, why don't you sit down." He motioned to a hardback chair across from his canvas.

"I'll bring you some sweet tea," said his wife.

"That'd be lovely, Louise," said Chester, with a touch of real feeling that surprised Cat. This was the man her great-uncle characterized as "genuine only in his capacity for evil."

"I'm here to talk to you about Mick Travers," Cat prompted.

That drew a blank look, so she continued. "You had it in for him when he was a student in the MFA program at Columbia."

"Who's that, you say? Travers…" He put a finger to the side of his head as if mentally thumbing through a Rolodex of names. Cat wasn't sure she bought the act.

"You must forgive me," said Dr. Canon with a broad, apologetic smile. "I'm a professor emeritus now. I actively taught in the program at Columbia for more than forty years. So I've had thousands of students come through my studio classes in that time. The names alone don't register."

Cat's face flushed with frustration. He certainly wasn't going to make this easy for her, and she wondered if he were in fact putting on a show.

"Mick Travers," Cat said. "He's quite well-known in the art world now; his work has been featured in *Art in Our Time* and elsewhere. He was honored at Art Basel. He was your student in the mid-Seventies, back when he was in his twenties. You, ah, didn't think he had any talent."

Dr. Canon chuckled, shaking his head. "You just described a good twenty percent of the crowds of students I've seen over the years. Columbia's a top program, as I'm sure you've discovered in your research." He set his cigarette in a glass ashtray and picked up the brush that was teetering on the edge of his easel. As if bored by Cat's line of questioning, he began to dab at the painting, bits of maroon paint over what resembled a muddy field.

Cat cleared her throat. "Well, maybe you'll remember this: You opposed him for the National Emerging Artist award, but one of your rivals in the department submitted his work anyway. And Mick Travers won. Proving you wrong."

He slowly set the brush back down on the edge of the easel, picked up a towel, and used it to wipe paint off his hands. "Oh, all right... Now I think I remember that guy. Boy, that takes me back... I must have been in my forties then, not even tenured yet.... Sure. Some painting with pink splashed over it, and they called the kid a genius! What passes for genius in the art world is enough to make you puke most of the time."

"But why single him out?"

"Well, he must have had some talent, obviously," Dr. Canon said. "He can thank me for making him tougher. After me, he was ready to handle whatever came next. From what you say, he's done well. So I'll take my Teacher of the Year award now."

Cat let out a breath. She couldn't believe this guy was actually claiming to have tortured her uncle for his own good.

"So you've held no grudge against Mr. Travers?"

He chuckled again. "Grudge? Lady, I barely remember the guy."

Louise came in with glasses of sweet tea on a tray for them both. She set it down on the table next to Dr. Canon and disappeared again, her orthopedics issuing a soft shuffle across the tiled floor.

"Why do you ask, anyway?" He handed her one of the glasses of tea. It was terrifically over-sweetened, and she could feel the sugar as if it had been injected directly into her veins.

"Someone burned down Mick Travers's studio," she said. "And his assistant died in the fire."

Dr. Canon's face fell. "Geez, that's some rough stuff. And it wasn't an accident?"

"It looks like arson."

"You don't say."

Cat was quiet a moment, sipping her tea.

"Boy, I wish there was something I could do to help."

Cat reached into her coat pocket and fished out her business card. Amazing Grace Private Detective Agency, it read, and included the number for her cell phone. "If you think of anyone who might have wanted to see Mick Travers dead, please don't hesitate to call. This could be anyone—a fellow grad student, perhaps."

"'Amazing Grace,' eh?" he replied. "I wouldn't have figured you for a bible thumper."

Cat set her unfinished tea back on the tray and left him to his painting. She marked Dr. Canon as a "possible suspect" in her notes.

———

Suspects three, four, and five lived in New York, so Cat and Granny Grace planned a trip together to knock on those doors in person.

By the time she returned from Fort Lauderdale, Cat was exhausted and ready for a dip in the pool behind Ernesto's place, but there in the driveway was a cop car. Sergeant Alvarez, Cat guessed. She'd wondered how long it would take for her to circle back around in their direction. So far they'd been denied access to the evidence, autopsy, and lab reports, and Cat wasn't happy about that. Alvarez had been too busy to talk with them but seemed to be casting a tight net around Mick. Every time Cat or Granny Grace talked to someone in Miami who knew him, Alvarez had already been there to question the person. But she hadn't spoken to any of the suspects on the list that Mick had drawn up.

Cat opened the front door to find Alvarez, Speck, and Santiago. They were talking with a frowning Mick.

"Oh, good," said Alvarez. "The grandniece is here, too." She looked back at Mick. "If your sister shows up, I can talk to you all at once."

"She's out of town," Cat informed her.

"She wasn't supposed to leave Miami," complained Alvarez. "Make a note of this," she instructed Santiago.

"She'll be back tomorrow," Cat explained. "She's over on Sanibel Island, interviewing someone who might have wanted to kill Mick."

"Who's that?"

"Someone you would have interviewed already if you weren't so focused on my great-uncle."

Alvarez raised an eyebrow. "Are you sure Mick's the target? Has anyone tried anything in the past few days?"

Both Mick and Cat were silent. Cat noted that Alvarez was now addressing Mick by his first name. So maybe she was beginning to see him as more than a suspect.

Alvarez tapped a pen against her clipboard. "We've been watching your beach house, Mick. Twenty-four-seven since the fire. Nothing's going on. It's quiet as a church out there. So maybe nobody's after you."

Mick looked up at her, surprised. Cat was, too, that they'd committed police resources to watching Mick's beach house. But maybe they were doing it to keep an eye on Mick as well. They'd already searched his place top to bottom for evidence linking him to the arson.

"So I gotta figure, we've got a few choices here," Alvarez went on. "One, the killer's biding his time, of course. Laying low till the dust settles. Then he goes after you again, Mick."

"That's a likely scenario," Cat interjected.

"Great," said Mick. "So I'm looking over my shoulder the rest of my life."

"Two," Alvarez continued, "you're the killer, Mick, and your move out of the beach house was a ploy to throw us off."

"Why would I want to kill Donnie?"

Alvarez leaned in toward Mick. "Because he was better than you?"

Mick didn't even flinch. "He might have been. Or just different. Art is not a contest. I don't know why everyone thinks it is. But there's room for everyone. Donnie had a different expression than I did. I liked having him around. We inspired each other."

Alvarez leaned in closer to Mick. "It didn't burn you up inside to see his paintings in your studio? To see what he was doing? To see that he was beginning to attract attention?"

Mick stared at her. "I liked having him there."

"But you knew he'd been contacted by Gallery 120. The one gallery in town that never showed your work."

"He was? Well, good for him."

"Why didn't that gallery ever show your work?"

"I don't know," said Mick, running his hand through his red-and-gray hair. "They didn't like it, I suppose."

"You didn't know Donnie'd been approached by them?"

"No, I didn't."

"That he was thinking of leaving your employ? Going out on his own as an artist?"

"No."

"Well, why do you think he didn't tell you?"

"I don't know…" Mick was quiet. Then he clapped his hands together. "Good deal, Donnie. You did it. I just wish you'd lived to see it—" Mick choked up. "Are we done here?"

"Far from it," Alvarez said.

Cat butted in. "Can't you see you're upsetting him?"

"I can," said Alvarez. "But you're a detective, aren't you? People put on acts all the time."

Cat gestured at Mick, who'd got up and was pouring himself a drink. His eyes were watery even though up till now he'd been sober. "Sure, he's acting."

Alvarez sat down. "He doesn't have an alibi," she said softly, so only Cat could hear. "How well do you know him, anyway? You and your grandmother, his sister. You live in Seattle. That's about as far as you can get from here without leaving the continental United States. That doesn't exactly say 'family ties.'"

Cat didn't know how to respond. She flashed on the dream of Mick's she'd slipped into, how he poured gasoline over Donnie and lit the match. But then she remembered her grandmother's words, which echoed something Cat's father had always said, too. *A dream isn't evidence.*

"He's innocent," she said to Alvarez.

"If you're right, and Mick didn't kill Donnie, then that brings us to another possibility."

Speck, who looked like a fresh recruit with his baby face and new buzz cut, spoke up. "The victim was the intended target."

"That's right. We're investigating Don Hines's past, trying to find out if anyone bore a grudge against him."

Cat groaned inwardly. She'd actually brought up this point to Granny Grace, who clung to her hunch that it was about her brother. Cat wondered if her grandmother couldn't see the forest for the trees.

"As far as I know, he didn't have a single enemy," said Mick, slumping back down in his chair. The ice in his drink tinkled.

"If someone wanted Hines dead, we'll find him," said Alvarez.

"Unless we find him first," said Cat.

"You people," said Mick. "Why is life always a contest?"

Santiago, whom Cat thought was kind of cute in an abstract way, cleared his throat. "You're forgetting the other possibility."

Cat looked him in the eyes, wondering if he was thinking what she was thinking.

"What's that?" Alvarez quizzed him, as if she already knew the answer.

"Neither victim was the intended target," Cat put in.

"That's right," said Santiago. "The paintings were."

"This would make what my grandmother and I are doing even more valuable."

"And what's that?" Alvarez asked, her tone dubious.

"We're interviewing people who had a grudge against Mick. Maybe one of them wanted to destroy his work. That's a fairly stepped-up brand of jealousy there, but maybe they didn't bank on Donnie being in the studio. It does have the mark of an amateur."

"Any information you gather, I'd like to know about it," said Alvarez.

"Sure," Cat agreed. "But we need copies of the evidence reports. And the autopsy and lab reports. Your department hasn't been cooperative."

"You'll get them," said Alvarez, rising to leave. "But as soon as your grandmother returns, I want to know what you've got."

Cat stuck out her hand. "Deal."

They shook on it.

"Now," Mick broke in. "Can a man get a little quiet in his grief? I've got some serious drinking to do."

They left him alone.

Chapter 6

Mick wasn't sure anymore what to do with his hands.

His life up until the fire had followed a certain rhythm. It was an unpredictable one, with hours that weren't set, as his art-making couldn't be relegated to set times of the day. Sometimes he'd work through the night on a painting, afraid he'd lose the vision if he didn't get it down in one flood. Other times, he'd take several days off, drive down to the Keys to remind himself of the way nature itself paints with color and water and reflection. It was a place that never ceased to give him something new to see.

But now he heard no call from the Keys, and every time he looked at a blank canvas, he saw was what was left of his friend, that charred tree stump of a man, that piece of gnarled bacon. Donnie.

If he were athletic, maybe he'd go shoot hoops, or pump iron. Music usually gave him some solace. He and Donnie used to play one of the thousands of tapes or records Mick housed in that old studio, but they'd been melted by the fire. All he had was the stuff he kept at the beach house, old 45s he'd been given by his own grandfather. They were scratchy, though, and the songs were mostly too patriotic for his current feeling, a lot of John Philip Souza with a smattering of political speeches thrown in.

There was always the business of art to attend to, even though Mick paid for a contract agent/publicist. He was given a reprieve from the appearances for a while because of the fire, but he did need to talk over his business with Beverly, who was a smart, jovial publicist often distracted by her other, more important clients.

But that wouldn't take much time. Mick was supposed to be making art. His livelihood depended on his work. And not only was he not painting now, but the entire collection of art he'd stored in the back of his studio no longer existed. This, Beverly informed him, had reduced his potential net worth by several million dollars.

If only he'd updated his insurance, as Beverly had kept reminding him. It had been on his list, but he kept getting sidetracked. So his settlement would not include his last ten years' production as an artist.

But Mick tried to put distance between that loss and himself. Even if he had updated his insurance, it wouldn't have compensated him for what his art might have earned on the open market. Not that the market itself wasn't fickle and arbitrary. There were so many collectors these days speculating in the art trade, buying and selling paintings as if they were stocks. Some influential blog critic could declare his style dead. He was already seeing interest in his work wane. Besides, his paintings often sold for wildly different prices, depending on who sold it, where, and to whom. Mick understood from years of beating his head against its multicolored, glittering walls that the art world is essentially a Wild West of capitalism, and entirely unregulated.

He and Beverly were sitting in her home studio, which had a view of her tightly manicured garden, a white dolphin fountain flanked by bougainvillea, its pale yellow pistils hovering between vivid purple petals. He'd seen an army of Mexican laborers attack her garden on a regular basis with leaf blowers, rakes, and electric trimmers. Mick as always became distracted by the patterns the shadow of the trellis made, perfect diamonds on the wide St. Augustine grass.

"But there's a bright side," said Beverly with a wry twinkle in her eyes. "What paintings are left will probably double in value. I mean, once word gets out that the supply has diminished."

"That's a morbid thought," Mick scolded her.

"Sorry, Mick," she said, squeezing his shoulder. He knew she was holding back on saying "I told you so," as she'd been after him for years to update his insurance and find a proper art-storage facility rather than keep the canvases in his studio. But he used them as reference pieces, often needing to go back to study an old painting to see how he'd previously handled one aspect or another or to remember the landscape of his mind at the time of whatever painting he had created.

The "I told you so" hung in the air, without Beverly having to say it. She sat down at her computer. "Still," she said, "It's a good thing you're as tuned into the business side of things as you are, Mick. A lot of other artists would be worse off. Most don't even have insurance."

She tallied the damage. Fortunately, half his work had either been purchased outright, was in rotation in a gallery, or was in one of the lesser, smaller-city museums that had acquired it for their permanent collections. His recent opening in West Palm Beach had been well attended and critically lauded, despite the waning interest, so he'd had a slew of requests recently from galleries. Those paintings had been spared. But he'd lost the other half of his life's work, which left him feeling curiously numb. Maybe even lighter, as the personal loss took away at least a splinter of the guilt he felt about Donnie's death. He was glad he himself hadn't come away unscathed.

Beverly opened up a database of his artwork that wasn't complete, but that wasn't her fault, as Mick didn't pay her for documentation, and she wouldn't do that anyway in the smidgen of her time that Mick could afford. So this was a list he was supposed to have catalogued, and he hadn't kept up with it. She gave him a printout that was broken into two sections. The first listed the paintings lost in the fire. Some of these were accompanied by digital images, but most were listed only by name, date, and description. The other section listed his surviving paintings and where they might be, whether gallery or private collection. Most of these didn't have images either. It was a forty-three-page document. Mick found himself doing curious math in his head, as Donnie had been forty-three, exactly twenty-five years Mick's junior.

A page for every year of my friend's life, thought Mick.

Back home, Mick gave a copy on a thumb drive to Cat, who'd asked for it after Sergeant Alvarez had left.

His grand-niece was sitting cross-legged on the couch, poring over a bunch of files from the Miami PD, and he knew the autopsy report was in there. Part of him wanted to read it, and part of him didn't. He felt undone by his conflicting feelings, so he said nothing and slumped into a chair.

"I just learned the fire decreased my net worth," he announced, but he was staring at the reflection of the sun bouncing off the water in a birdbath outside. Nonetheless, he felt Cat look up at him.

"Harsh," she said. "The paintings? In your studio?"

"Yup."

"I'm sorry."

"Don't be."

"Okay. I'm not." There was a pause, and then she added: "I think most art is ridiculously overpriced anyway. I mean, don't take this the wrong way, Uncle Mick, but eighteen thousand for that big red splotchy thing you painted?"

Mick laughed. He should be offended, but on the contrary, he suddenly felt like he'd never loved his grand-niece more. He thought about that dream of hers he'd walked into the first night in Ernesto's place, the one with her Ranger lover dude or whoever he was, and the pool of blood.

"The Big Red Splotchy Thing," he said. "That's what I should have titled it."

"Sorry."

"Don't be," he said again. "It *is* a big red splotchy thing."

They both laughed, the laugh relieving the tension in Mick's head a bit.

"I've got the autopsy report here," she said, motioning to one of the files in front of her. "Do you want to see it?"

"I don't know. Would you look at it if it were for that Ranger guy who got himself shot in front of you?"

"Yes. I did look at his autopsy report, if that's what you're asking."

"But why? I mean, you were right there, Cat."

She looked away. "I don't know," she finally answered. "I guess the whole thing seemed unreal, so I wanted to make it real. I wanted to see it in cold terms."

"Did it help?"

"Yes. And no."

"Give it here."

She reached over toward him, offering the slim manila folder. He took it.

It was very clinical. He let the language wash over him, words and phrases like *carbon monoxide poisoning* and *rigor mortis.*

"So the smoke killed him before the fire got him," Mick said, feeling himself choke up.

"Yeah. He probably died in his sleep."

Mick felt his eyes water. "That's good. Better than what I imagined."

"Yeah."

"Once I went to hear this monk speak," Mick said. "He talked about immolating monks, the ones who set themselves on fire. It's the most painful way to die."

"I never knew that."

"God, it's unfair. And it won't get any fairer or make any more sense no matter how much time passes."

"I know how you feel."

He looked up, about to lay into her because there was in fact no way this spit of a girl who'd only lived a fraction of his existence could know how he felt. But he bit his tongue. She was looking at him, as if she were really seeing who he was.

"I thought you might've killed Donnie. At first. That dream you had…"

"I wondered about that. But you haven't turned me over to Alvarez." He meant it as a joke, but neither of them laughed.

"Well, I couldn't. I mean, I keep blowing Lee's head off in my own dreams."

He remained quiet.

"Besides," she continued. "You're dreaming it all wrong. That can of gas in your dream? That wasn't the accelerant. If you were guilty, I'd think you'd dream it the way it actually went down. So why can't you give an alibi?"

"It's complicated," he said, looking away. And then, both to change the subject and because he really wanted to know, he said, "Tell me about your Ranger."

Cat swallowed. "He believed in American freedom as something that needed to be protected. He came from a long line of military men, too, and he wanted to do them proud."

Mick gazed at his niece. Pris had said the loss was really hard for Cat to bear, that she'd loved the man, but it was submerged beneath a blanket of control. The girl seemed to be whitewashing her grief, convincing herself she hadn't loved that boy, and yet here she was, practically canonizing him.

"Really? I mean, what is he, like Captain America or something?"

Cat looked up at him, surprised. "Yeah, he kind of was."

"Well, so were you going to marry him? I mean, superhero and all."

Cat stood up and sat back down on the couch, where she'd been sitting when he came in. Her movement caused a stack of papers to fall to the floor, but she ignored them.

"Why do you ask me that?"

"Because you're talking about him like he's a character in a movie."

Cat stared at Mick, her arms crossed over her chest.

"You'd never have married that guy."

"I'll never find out now, will I?" Cat said, her face getting red. "I don't know!"

"There we go," said Mick, pointing a trigger finger at her. "Bingo."

"The possibility ended when he died. I don't know what I would have done. But he had to be so goddamn *brave*, jumping out there in front of me to save my life—" Cat broke into tears. "Stupid bastard," she whispered.

"You're angry," Mick said, stating the obvious, which he felt needed to be stated. "But you didn't kill that guy."

"It's my fault he died!"

Mick was silent for a few beats, letting that one reverberate around the room.

"You no more killed Lee Stone than I killed Donnie Hines. You're lucky that guy didn't get mowed down in Iraq, sweetheart. Here's the deal. There's no guarantee. Life is kind of meaningful, in small moments, and then you can just up and die without warning. It's cruel, but that's how it goes." He felt his words came from a place of wisdom inside himself that he rarely tapped into in a verbal way, usually reserving it for expression through color and shape.

"Yeah, well, I'm done with romance, Uncle Mick. That's it for me. I can't do it."

Mick laughed. "None of us can do romance, Cat. But you can't be done with it. It's one of the few things we've got down here to make sense of a world that doesn't make a lot of sense."

"Well, what about you? You're alone."

The word hit Mick like a punch in the chest. He *was* alone. That's exactly why his alibi was shit. And Donnie's death made him feel much lonelier. "Eh, I'm old, sweetheart. Romance is for you young'uns."

"What a cop-out."

Mick felt rightfully called to the carpet. "It's tough, when you're old and busted. Set in your ways. And a dreamslipper, to boot."

"That's what I'm talking about. This damn curse."

Mick figured Cat was relishing the chance to speak of their dreamslipping in such baldly negative terms, what with his sister out of the picture. Pris would never allow anyone to call it a curse. He knew from experience. She was his big sister, after all.

"Once," Mick began, "both Donnie and I fell asleep in my studio. We'd both been on a roll, the two of us painting like fiends. Maybe we fed off each other's energy, who knows? But I slipped into one of his dreams. It had been so long since I'd slipped into anyone's dreams of any consequence, Cat. A lot of the girls I, uh, date don't dream about much. You'd be surprised by how mundane people's dreams can sometimes be, if the people are pretty shallow. Anyway, Donnie's dream was like walking into a painting. The man dreamed in fractal images: crystals forming, strange, perfectly symmetrical shapes that repeated themselves infinitely. It was glorious. I didn't want to leave."

"You loved him," Cat said softly.

Mick felt himself smile. She was right. "Oh, I wouldn't know what to do with a man's body, and I never thought of Donnie that way, but yeah. I loved him." He sniffed, feeling a cry well up in his chest, but it was his nature to stifle it, so he did.

"But Donnie didn't die because of your dreamslipping. Like mine killed Lee."

"Whoa, is that what you think?" Mick said. He walked over and sat down next to her on the couch.

"How can I not? The killer in my case followed me out to Seattle and shot him."

"But she was trying to kill you, right? And he was there."

"He saved my life."

Mick nodded. "And Donnie might have saved mine, in a way. Since I let him live in my studio, I stopped sleeping there. I mean, except for that one night when I slipped into his dream."

"I used to slip into Lee's dreams, across thousands of miles."

"Really?"

"Yeah. They were like PTSD dreams. From when he was in Iraq. He kept reliving something, over and over again."

"Whoa."

"He couldn't save this kid. They'd strapped a bomb to the kid, and Lee tried to save him but failed."

"So he saved you instead."

Mick let Cat sit with that one a bit. She stopped chewing on her bottom lip. "He figured out I was a dreamslipper, in the end."

"No kidding." Mick had not seen that one coming. No one on Earth knew he could slip into their dreams.

"And now he's dead. The only person in the world—I mean the non-dreamslipping kind—who knew what I could do. And he's dead."

"Did he accept it?"

Cat smiled. "He said, 'That's a pretty neat trick you've got there with the dreams.' But he'd been in a coma, Uncle Mick. And then he died."

Mick didn't know what to say.

"So what do I do with this?" Cat asked, her eyes imploring. Mick didn't have an answer for her. He wished his sister was there. Pris had an answer for everything.

"I don't know. But you can't stop living. And living means loving."

There was a knock at the door, so Cat got up to answer it.

"We need to take Mick in for questioning." Mick recognized the voice. It was Sergeant Alvarez.

Cat protested, "But you've already questioned him."

"We have new information." Alvarez stepped inside and motioned for Speck and Santiago to escort Mick, who knew what this was about. He'd been waiting for it.

———

They put him in a room without windows, or at least that's what it looked like, but he figured the glass that appeared blackened was one-way glass, so they could see him, but he couldn't see them. That's kind of how he felt about the situation. He had no idea what Jenny had told them.

Soon Sergeant Alvarez walked in and sat down. "We know you were having an affair with Don Hines's girlfriend."

Mick did not respond. If he hadn't gone to see Jenny already and witnessed what a wrecked state she was in, he would have been surprised.

"She was no longer Donnie's girlfriend," he said. "They broke things off a month ago."

Alvarez raised an eyebrow. "Is that so?"

"Yes. And I was not having an affair with her."

Alvarez tossed a photocopy onto the table. Mick recognized the image.

"Then why was this on Donnie's cell phone? He received it the night he died."

He winced, realizing Jenny had sent the photo after all. He'd pleaded with her not to send it.

"Because Jenny was mad at Donnie. She wanted him to hurt. And she was jealous of my friendship with him. So I guess I had to hurt, too."

Alvarez glared at him. "What exactly are you saying? The photo's some kind of fake?"

Mick flashed on a moment from that awful night, before he went to the party, before he found out that Donnie was dead. Jenny's call for him from the bedroom, saying her zipper was stuck... His fingers on her back... The way she swayed into him.

"A frame-up would be more accurate," he replied.

Alvarez snorted. "You were fucking your best friend's girlfriend. Maybe the two of you killed Donnie."

Mick clenched his fists. "What, to get him out of the way? Why would we have to do that?"

Alvarez was silent for a moment, and then this: "Why don't you tell me what happened that night between the hours of nine and half past midnight?"

Mick swallowed hard, but his throat was dry. "Jenny called me, said she needed my help, that she was going to surprise Donnie, propose getting back together with him."

"And why did they break up?"

Mick grimaced. "Donnie kissed someone else at a party, and Jenny caught him."

"So Donnie was a player."

"I wouldn't call him that."

"Of course you wouldn't."

Mick shrugged. "Donnie really liked people. Everyone he met. He never discriminated, never talked bad about anyone else, and he'd give you the shirt off his back. He was the friendliest guy I've ever known. He could seem kind of clownish, but people loved him. Sometimes too much. And Donnie couldn't resist loving them back."

"And the night of the fire?"

Mick remembered. Her back was so soft, and she pressed her ass into his crotch. Then she whispered, "I've seen you look at me, Mick."

He'd let his hand trace down her back, down to the curve, felt her flex and arch backward.

But then he stopped. Pushed her away. He knew what she was doing. "You're just trying to get even."

She grabbed her phone, let her dress drop in front, and took a selfie with Mick there behind her.

Mick knew then that she wasn't just trying to get even; she was trying to destroy his friendship with Donnie. He lunged for the phone.

"Forget it, Mick!" She threw the phone into a drawer and stood in front of it, her arms crossed.

He knew he could take her. He could throw her aside, grab the phone, and smash it against the wall. But he'd have to hurt her, and something in him stopped him from that. This was dangerous ground, and he knew it.

"Jenny," he said. "I know Donnie hurt you. But this is… This is low."

"Get out!" She took off her witch boot and threw it at him. The pointy toe caught him in the chest.

"Don't send the photo," Mick said.

"Maybe I will, and maybe I won't!" She threw her other boot at him.

So he left.

He told this to Alvarez.

"And that's it? What happened after that?"

"I went to a bar and got drunk. Then, to please my sister, I stumbled over to the Art Basel party but didn't make it past the hotel bar. And Donnie got burnt to a crisp."

"Have you reached out to Jenny Baines since then?"

"I tried, but she threw me out."

Alvarez sighed. "Wait here." She picked up the photocopy and left him alone in the room again.

Then a few minutes later, the door opened, and in came Jenny with Alvarez, Santiago, and Speck. They sat down at the table, Alvarez at the head and Speck and Santiago in the middle, flanking Jenny. Santiago set a few bagged pieces of evidence in front of him on the table.

"Ms. Baines—Jenny," Alvarez began. "Tell us the nature of your relationship with Mick Travers."

Jenny cleared her throat. "Mick and I used to be friends. Because of Donnie."

"You never slept together?" Alvarez said.

Jenny looked right at Mick and said, "I wouldn't sleep with Mick if he paid me. A lot."

Mick didn't respond. Her anger sounded like a thin veneer covering over a wound that would never heal. Her eyes didn't look mad to him, just very sad. Her thick mascara had stained her face where it ran from her tears. She smelled of weed.

"Let's have the evidence," Alvarez said, motioning to Santiago. He passed the topmost white bag to her, and she opened it and retrieved what Mick recognized as Donnie's cell phone, perfectly intact.

"This was in Donnie Hines's car," Alvarez said. She gazed at Jenny. "He always left it there, didn't he?"

Jenny nodded, tears welling in her eyes. "Otherwise, he'd lose it in his studio. Drop it in a paint can. He did that once…"

"We found the selfie you took, Jenny. It had been viewed. But you already know that, don't you?"

"Yes," she whispered.

"We have his cell-phone records," Alvarez said as gently as she could. "We know you talked to Donnie before he died. You were the last person to talk to him."

Jenny broke down. "Please… I didn't mean…" She covered her face with her hands.

Mick felt his anger like a flame lit deep in his belly. "What did you say to him?"

"I want my lawyer," Jenny said through sobs. She attempted to dry her eyes on her sleeve.

"We're going to hold you," Alvarez informed her. "And yeah, you might want to get that lawyer. You wanted to hurt Donnie the night of his death. Maybe you went too far."

With that, Speck rose and gently placed handcuffs on Jenny, whose body was wracked with sobs as he escorted her out.

Mick didn't know what to say.

Alvarez turned to him. "She didn't try to get the phone out of his car even though she knew it would incriminate her. What do you think her last words to him were?"

Chapter 7

Grace walked in to find her granddaughter and Mick sitting in the living room, talking. Cat still had her purse slung across her body, as if she'd just come in. Mick had the rental car keys in his hands. Grace had hoped they'd help each other somehow with their shared grief, which was part of the reason she'd taken the Sanibel trip and dawdled along the way. They'd obviously been out somewhere together.

"We have some big news on the case," Cat said.

"So do I," said Grace. "But there's something in the car I need you to help me with first."

They followed her outside, where a good-sized painting was jammed in the rear seat of Grace's rental car. It was covered in cloth, so she didn't unveil it to them till Cat carried it into the house, where Mick propped it on one of his sawhorse easels in the lanai.

"Good Lord," remarked Mick. "You bought one of Candy's paintings. Why, Priscilla?"

"I wish you'd call me by my legal name," Grace complained. "And I'm not sure why I bought it. Something told me to. I'm sure the reason will reveal itself in time. Isn't it lovely, though? It's one of her best, I suspect."

"Which isn't saying much," Mick said.

"I should think you'd be more charitable," Grace reprimanded. Her brother could be entirely too critical of both himself and others. It was his Virgo temperament.

"I really like this one," Cat said, the response on her face genuine. "It's about something. These kids, their world on the other side of the fence. It's like the artist wished she could step back in time and join them."

Grace clapped her hands together. "Oh, Cat! I agree."

"It doesn't challenge anything," Mick put in.

"It doesn't have to," said Grace.

"But we can't take it back with us," Cat said. "On the plane. When we go home."

"We'll give it as a gift to Ernesto," Grace said, right as the idea came to her. "He'd like it. And doesn't it fit well in his cottage?"

"I'll give you that," said Mick. "Art shouldn't match your couch, but this one does."

"Oh, stop it," said Grace. "You're such a snob, Mickey."

"Now listen to what's going on with the case," Cat insisted. She and Mick filled Grace in on what had happened with Jenny Baines.

Grace was surprised to hear of the development. "Do you think she could have killed Donnie?" She directed her question at Mick.

"No," Mick said. "At least not directly."

"We were talking about that when you came in," explained Cat. "Mick thinks whatever she said to Donnie Hines, plus the selfie she sent, drove him to drink more than his usual that night."

"Of the two of us, I'm more the drinker," Mick said.

"Yes, I know." Grace shook her head at Mick.

Grace closed her eyes for a moment, imagining the scene they'd described to her, especially Jenny's desire to hurt Donnie. She pictured Jenny hanging up on him. Then Donnie throwing his phone in the car and heading up to the studio, where he would have found Mick's just-opened bottle of Bushmill's. He drank too much and went to lie down on the cot. As a diabetic, his body wouldn't be able to handle it. He wouldn't have heard the arsonist. The fire didn't wake him up; he'd died in his sleep.

"So what did you find out about Candace Shreveport?" Cat said.

"She signs her paintings *Candy Port,*" Grace said, pointing to her stylized curly-Q signature. "But that does not an arsonist make."

"Have you eliminated her as a suspect?" Mick said.

Grace could tell from his tone that he hoped she had. "No," she said. His face fell.

"I swear to God, if that woman killed Donnie—"

"Don't say anything you wouldn't want to have come true." Grace stopped him and motioned to the living room, where Cat had set up a sort of temporary office. "I see you got the files from the Miami PD."

"Yes," said Cat. "It took a bit of bargaining, however. I said we'd share our own research with Alvarez and her team."

"Good work, Cat. It's always better when people work together, isn't it?"

Her granddaughter gave her a begrudging nod.

Grace was glad Cat was losing some of her territoriality. If she had let more people help her on that Missouri case, they might have caught Anita Briggs sooner... Ah, well. That was Grace's own judgment creeping in. She'd have to let that one go.

"And you?" Grace prompted her little brother. "Have you found your way to the canvas again?"

"No, I haven't. But seeing Candy Port's masterpiece here made me realize something."

"What's that?" Grace asked, pleased that the painting was having whatever effect it was meant to have.

"Well, that and my heart-to-heart with Cat here. If all I see when I stare at the canvas is Donnie, then that's what I should paint."

With a newly determined flourish, he turned and disappeared into the lanai, shutting the double glass doors for privacy. He pulled the curtain shut.

"Let me make you some tea and a snack," Cat said to Grace, leading her to the kitchen counter delicately by her arm. "You must be exhausted from your trip. And I'll catch you up on things here."

"I am." Grace sat on a bar stool. Her back was kinked up from the drive, which a bit of yoga outside on the sundeck would cure, but first she needed that tea and snack. She listened intently as Cat filled her in on her visit with Chester Canon and their conversations with Alvarez. When she got to the part about investigating whether Donnie was the intended victim, Grace perked up.

"Wonderful," she said. "Let them spare us that legwork, since it most likely won't turn anything up."

Cat filled a teapot with hot, boiling water from the kettle and then let it steep as she cut fruit and cheese for a snack. Grace was famished and snuck a piece of plum and bit of goat cheese off the tray.

"I agree with Alvarez on the possible scenarios," Grace said. "But my hunch is that someone either wanted to kill Mick or at least hurt him, by torching the place where he makes his art."

"And you think this Candace could have done that?"

"What did the evidence report say, Cat? Was it the work of an amateur?"

"It seems so. I'll let you have a look yourself." Cat went over to the couch and picked up the file. She carried it over to the counter for Grace, who opened it.

"What is this? Six-point type? Fetch me my reading glasses, would you, doll?"

Cat handed Grace the red Art Deco frames she'd brought with her from Seattle.

"There, that's better." Grace read down the page, turned to the second page, and then announced, "Here it is. *'Ease of identification of accelerant despite obvious opportunity to hide it suggests the work of an amateur arsonist.'* Oh, for goodness sake."

"You just read the part about the Coleman fuel, didn't you? That's how I finally decided Uncle Mick is innocent. In his dream, he used a can of gasoline to set the fire." She set two teacups down and poured them both a spot from the pot.

"The arsonist brought in his own accelerant. Camping fuel. Something Mick didn't have on hand. He ignored the flammable liquids Mick already had there in his studio."

"The mark of someone who's never done this before," Cat said.

"Exactly," said Grace.

Cat laughed. "It sounds like our arsonist did an online search for 'How to Commit Arson.' Maybe Mick's wrong. Maybe Jenny did do it."

"Or Candace," Grace said. She couldn't get the woman out of her mind.

———

While the police tried to find more solid evidence against Jenny Baines, Grace decided it would be best to follow up on some of the other people on Mick's "hate list," as they'd taken to calling it. So the two sleuths planned a quick trip up to New York, where the next three lived.

Cat had never been, but Grace had been there many times. She'd lived in the Big Apple for a few years in her thirties. It was the Sixties then, and she had experimented on numerous fronts, using her dreamslipping ability to become a sort of mystic within a band of hippies centered around Washington Square Park. She told this to Cat on the train, which Grace insisted on instead of the plane for a change of pace, and ease of the journey, as they could get up and stretch their legs—even practice some yoga—more readily on the train. Grace wasn't sure she could keep up this pace and wondered if she should have waited a few more days before embarking on another trip.

But it was too late for second guesses, and she'd never been one to dwell on the past, even the recent past.

"I once met Jack Kerouac at a party," Grace announced. "But honestly, I didn't find him very interesting. His girlfriend, on the other hand... Now there was a gal."

Cat laughed. "Only you, Gran. Half the time, I don't know whether to believe you or not."

"Oh, my dear, everything I tell you is the unvarnished truth."

"Now let me see... His girlfriend was blonde and from the country, as I had been. We compared our strict religious upbringings. She was Protestant, but unlike regular people, whom we called 'squares' back then, she didn't hold me at a distance for my Catholic upbringing. Though it probably helped that I was busily trying to shed it."

"So how did you use your dreamslipping with them?"

"Oh, I was a bit of a charlatan, I'm sorry to admit." Grace smiled, enjoying the opportunity to tell Cat a story she'd never heard. "Several of us girls would share an apartment, you see, so I had occasion to slip into their dreams. I gleaned details about their lives from those dreams, and I would use them in my work with tarot cards. People were amazed. They thought I was psychic."

"Well, aren't we?" Cat asked. "In a manner of speaking."

Grace shrugged. "I prefer to think of it as 'spiritually in tune.'"

"Too bad you never slipped into one of Kerouac's dreams."

"Oh, heaven forbid. Have you read that man's writing? I agree with Truman Capote's assessment. 'That's not writing,' he once said. 'That's typing.'"

Cat couldn't stop laughing. "Granny Grace!"

"Enough of this chatter," said Grace. "Let's see what the view's like from the dome car."

Once they arrived in New York, Grace wished for a moment that they weren't on a case but rather there for a weekend on the town. How the two of them could cut a rug if they had the chance. She'd love to show Madison Avenue to her granddaughter, take her to a Broadway show, tour the Met... The city still sparkled, still held for her the allure of so many possibilities, so many people to meet. It pulsed with excitement, even now, despite the digital billboards and the yawning absence of the World Trade Center towers.

But they had work to do, and that meant talking with the rest of the top five on Mick's hate list, starting with a graphic artist named Norris Grayson. Norris had been a student in the same program as Mick, and like Mick, he'd dreamed of making it as a painter. But he had not enjoyed the same success as Mick, so he did what a lot of creative types do, and that was figure out how to find work that paid but approximated art. Grace was eager to speak with Norris, as he seemed to be the most likely person to have written the Letter to the Editor printed in *Art in Our Time* that was supposedly penned by "Mick in Miami."

Norris worked for a PR firm in Midtown Manhattan that was tucked down a narrow hallway, ironically, thought Grace, past several small art galleries.

A secretary—they still employed them? questioned Grace—led them down another narrow hallway within the offices of Sturdiman Fullman Grayson, or "two man son," as the firm had been nicknamed. Norris greeted them with a wide, bleach-whitened smile and a brisk, vigorously pumped handshake.

"Sit, sit," he commanded. "So? You're here about some artist I went to school with?"

"Not just some artist," led Grace. "Mick Travers. The most successful one of your class."

"Travers! Of course." There wasn't a trace of bitterness in his tone. "That old hack. Is he still making art?"

"He's not only making it," Grace said, letting her eyebrow arch for emphasis, "he's showing it regularly here in New York. You might have caught one of his shows, maybe even right here in this building."

"You don't say," Norris replied, his gaze distracted by Cat, whom Grace had to admit, did look rather fetching in a green skirt suit and heels. The suit emphasized her narrow waist and swelling hips, but the ruffles on the blouse gave the illusion that her bust line dimension echoed that of her hips, which it did not.

"Have you?" Cat prompted him. "Caught one of Mick Travers's recent shows, that is."

"Nope," he snapped. "Can't say that I have." He was bald, and he'd smartly chosen to shave most of his hair once the pattern baldness had carved a crescent onto his dome. Grace could see the beginning of a five o'clock head shadow over the tips of his ears.

Not particularly forthcoming, Norris would need a bit more nudging if this thirty-minute window of his precious time weren't to be wasted.

"Tell us what you remember about Travers as a student," Grace prodded.

Norris blew out his breath and ran a hand over his nonexistent hair. "Not much, honestly. That's ancient history now. Boy. I guess ... I guess you could say he was overrated. He got a lot of attention, and some of us—many of us—including some of the professors—didn't think it was deserved."

"Are you sure that wasn't sour grapes?" Grace asked, trying not to sound defensive. "His talent was validated by independent judges back then. And it's been validated many times by the entire art world since."

Norris chuckled. "Hey, sure, lady. I'm telling you what I remember. I've got no stake in it either way. I'm happy with my success. I've got a gorgeous wife—look, she used to model." He turned around one of the photos perched on his desktop to reveal a woman twenty years Norris's junior with the photogenic smile of a pro. "I've got a couple of bright kids, both on the honor roll. I'm a partner with the firm. I'll be retiring soon. I bet that's more than you can say for Mick Travers."

Grace laughed softly. "Well, an artist never really retires. But what of that? You're not a real artist. I'm betting you don't even have much of a hand in the actual art for any of these ads anymore." She gestured to the framed advertisements for hair care products for men, which seemed screamingly ironic, considering Norris's shining dome.

"Oh, I steer the artists in the right direction," Norris said with a smile. "And that's okay by me. You see, years ago, I realized that I'm

54

the idea man. I'm full of them. I let the grunts carry out my vision. But I'm the one with the vision. They couldn't see past their own color choices."

Norris stood up and wandered to the window to take in his commanding view, which Grace realized they were supposed to admire—not for the view itself, but for the fact that he had one. "Yeah, that's what most artists are these days anyway, this Travers fellow included. Grunts. They're just copying each other."

Cat picked up on his tangent. "I thought you said you weren't much interested in art, that you hadn't seen any of Mick Travers's shows."

He spun around on his heel. "Oh, I'm speaking in generalities. I do see a show every now and again, as part of this fundraiser or that. Hard to avoid when you're someone like me."

"And what do you think of Travers's work?" Cat asked.

"His work?" Norris smiled. "I think it's rather large, don't you?"

———

The next two people on the list were still making art at least part of the time, but neither had the success that Grace's brother enjoyed. Grace and Cat decided to tackle them together again.

Norris had been an interesting pickle. Toward the end of the interview, he swore he had not written the letter that appeared in *Art in Our Time*, though he did cop to reading it and enjoying the problems it must have caused for Mick.

Next up were two artists, both in their sixties and eking out moderate livings.

The first was a woman named Annie Lin who painted haunting white horses in an abstract style that reminded Grace of Louise Bourgeois's spiders. Lin's work was quite possibly as good as the celebrated artist's. Success in the marketplace had only marginally to do with talent. Grace had seen this to be true: So many forces out of the artist's control could determine what society called "success," which was, for an artist, recognition and sales.

Annie Lin greeted them at the door of her studio with a wide, genuine smile, her chin smudged with white paint. Her hair must have been jet-black at one time but had gone white. She wore it in a tight bun at the back of her head.

"Please come in," she beckoned them, motioning toward a couch Grace recognized from an IKEA showroom. The loft had otherwise been taken over by houseplants, which had clearly been given free range to stretch and grow under the wide warehouse windows, past which Grace could see a billboard advertising Depends undergarments beside the railway for the El.

Her paintings, in various states of completion, stood on easels distributed throughout the large live-work space. Grace was excited to see that one of Annie Lin's newest horses did not have a head. She made a mental note to ask about it when the time was right.

Grace approved of the woman instinctively and immediately, from her wide-legged trousers and boat neck, striped shirt to the Buddha statue perched high atop a shelf in the open loft. She was a bird of a woman, and she moved with deliberation, repositioning a pillow before settling herself on a chair opposite them, her legs tucked under her as if in preparation for lotus pose.

Speaking of lotus, Grace noticed a yoga mat in a far corner of the loft, surrounded by candles, incense, and more plants.

"You're here to discuss Mick Travers," the woman politely said. "I almost turned you down. I realize I don't have to talk to you— you're not the police, after all. But I have nothing to hide. And you've piqued my curiosity about Mick. He and I used to be ... close."

"Yes," said Cat, who was sitting on the edge of the IKEA couch, her legs crossed. Her green suit and heels had been visually more at home in Norris's office, Grace noted.

"We understand that you and Mr. Travers ..." Cat continued, as if searching for the right words. "... used to date."

Annie laughed. "Sure, call it dating," she said. "But that's not what we did back in art school. Not really."

Grace liked this woman even more with every passing moment.

"Such bohemians," Grace put in.

Annie's facial expression seemed to give back the same sense of approval that Grace felt. Grace warmed to Annie's gaze.

"You know something about this?" Annie asked her. "Where were you in the Seventies? Mick and I were right here. This was the center of the universe back then."

Grace smiled. "Well, I've got about a decade on you, which doesn't matter much now, and maybe it didn't then, either."

Cat interrupted. "So tell us about you and Mick."

"We screwed pretty much constantly," Annie replied, looking Cat straight in the eyes.

Cat sputtered a bit with her response. "Th-that sounds kind of ... intense."

"It was," she said. Then she cocked her head at Cat, as if noticing something. "Wait a minute... You know Mick, don't you?

56

Personally? I hope you're not doing him. You're far too young, even considering Mick's, ah, shall we say, maturity level?"

Grace was impressed with Annie's perceptiveness. "That would be rather taboo, since he's her great-uncle. My brother."

Cat tossed Grace a surprised look. They had been keeping their relationship to the subject of the investigation a secret from their suspects. But Grace's intuition told her to trust this Annie Lin. So she gave Cat a wink. Cat returned it with a dubious look.

Annie raised an eyebrow. "Oh, I see..." she said. "I hope my frank assessment of my past relationship with your brother wasn't too inappropriate."

Grace shook her head. "On the contrary. You exhibit an attitude I find refreshing."

Cat cleared her throat as if to say she wanted to get on with the questioning.

"Annie," Grace said, "were you and Mick ever at odds? I ask because he seems to think you despise him."

"I did," Annie said, looking past the two women and out the window beyond. "For too long, I did. But then I realized it was a waste of my talent and energy to harbor so much resentment toward another human being. Mick was terrifically flawed, and he made some bad calls where I was concerned. But I've let it go."

"Are you sure about that?" Cat asked. "Because Mick says you sent him ... a strange package ... last year."

"The broken record," Annie admitted.

"Yes."

Grace remembered her brother's description of the package, which was a padded envelope filled with the broken pieces of a vinyl record. Fleetwood Mac's *Rumours*, she thought it was.

"That was an artist's joke," Annie explained. "I used to tell Mick he sounded like a broken record, the way he'd go on about the primacy of art. And when I was painting back then, during MFA school, I used to glue pieces of broken records into my work. So it had two meanings. I guess both were lost on Mick if he took it the wrong way."

"Everything looks suspicious after a fire," Grace said. "Mick lost his friend and studio assistant, Don Hines."

Annie frowned. "Mick must be devastated."

"Yes," said Grace.

"I wouldn't mind seeing Mick," Annie said suddenly. "It's been... Gosh. I think it's been thirty years. Maybe the next time he has an opening in New York, I'll go."

"It's been a long time," Grace agreed.

"Do you have an alibi for the night of the fire?" Cat asked.

"I doubt it," Annie said. "I'm usually here, painting."

"I see you're losing your horses' heads," Grace said, gesturing to the painting that had caught her eye when they'd entered.

"Yes," said Annie, beaming. "It's good of you to notice."

"A gorgeous movement," Grace replied. "I think of the knight in a chess set. And Caligula. Not to mention the horse's head in *The Godfather*."

"That's imbedded in it for sure," Annie beamed. "Pun intended."

Riding down in the freight elevator in Annie's apartment building, Grace was taken aback when Cat accused her of flirting with their suspect.

"Excuse me?"

"You seem to be developing a girl-crush on Ms. Lin."

"I was merely bonding with our suspect," Grace said. "It's something you should try sometime."

"Bonding," Cat replied. "Right."

Grace let the sarcasm go for now, though sometimes she had to resist the urge to take her granddaughter down a peg or two. Their next interview wasn't till tomorrow, and in the meantime, they meant to visit some of the galleries in town showing Mick's work to see what else they could find.

Grace had always admired her brother's talent, and it thrilled her to see his work in some of the top galleries in New York. Winston Price Gallery gave his Conch Series prime real estate in their main window, facing the vibrant Chelsea neighborhood. Its prominence was such an impressive sight that Grace stopped to take a photo with her phone. Mick complained that he wasn't showing in as many galleries as he used to, but in every gallery that showed his work, it held a prominent position. Grace enjoyed her cachet as the older sister of a celebrated artist, and they tolerated her picture-taking. It seemed to rub off on Cat as well, who dropped her attitude toward modern art for the day, chatting up the gallery owners and uncovering a few anecdotes about what Mick had been like in his early days.

"He used to have a beard," said Greta Stein, who owned the Painted Stick Gallery in SoHo. Grace remembered her brother's facial-hair period. "He would show up to an opening with food stuck in it. It was clear he hadn't showered, and his clothes were a mess, full of paint. But New Yorkers embraced him. They thought he was delightfully eccentric, the unkempt artist. You could get away with that, back then. Now everything is business, business."

In Greta's gallery, Cat paused longer than normal at a triptych on a back wall, not heavily trafficked and near where Greta kept her overflow stock. Grace noticed her lingering and came to find out what held her in sway.

It was one of Mick's vaguely representational pieces, and the subject was a young girl, likely no more than eleven or twelve. There were three images, joined together. The girl had long red hair and tanned skin and was sitting on the edge of an armchair. Her legs were open to the viewer's gaze in a manner that forced a sort of visual invasion of the girl's space in each image, though her body language was slightly different in each. She wore shorts and a sleeveless T-shirt, budding breasts visible beneath the shirt, and no bra underneath.

The look on her face seemed to accuse the viewer of ill intent toward her and plead for help at the same time. And yet there was a resigned sexualized feel about the painting, as if the girl had given in to being used, and then merely discarded. The images disturbed Grace immediately. She heard Cat sniff, and turned to find her granddaughter getting choked up.

"Are you all right, my dear?"

"Her eyes," Cat said, gesturing to the girl's face, hidden in part shadow but her eyes staring blankly from each image. They were hazel eyes, washed out and sad, as if they'd seen far too much already.

"Yes," Grace remarked. "Haunting."

"I've seen a digital of this, in Mick's database," Cat explained. "He's not the best recordkeeper, so it's just this one." She motioned to the first of the three images in the triptych. "But seeing it in person, especially three like this, is a lot more … evocative, I guess is the word."

Greta approached them delicately from behind. "Mick has forbidden me from selling this piece," she said. "But everyone is affected by it. I get offers … maybe now he'll be willing to part with it."

"Do you know when he painted it?" asked Grace.

"Recently," Greta said. "Within the past few years. It was in Mick's studio, but I don't think he's shown it anywhere else. I saw it there when I came down over Thanksgiving and asked if I could try to sell it for him. He said it wasn't for sale. But I convinced him to let me include it in his last show here."

With that, Greta turned to greet a well-heeled couple entering the gallery. Cat and Grace decided to get an early dinner at a Japanese restaurant and head back to their hotel.

———

That night Grace did not have any strength left to prepare her mind properly against slipping into Cat's dreams, and slip she did.

Grace at first was fused with Cat's consciousness in the dream. As Cat she walked into a room where the girl from the painting they'd seen that afternoon sat on the arm of a chair, as she had been in the painting. A fire blazed behind her, crackling and spitting and threatening to engulf the girl, but she seemed unable to move. On the floor next to her was Donnie Hines's burnt corpse. The girl stared at Cat and then began to mouth something, her lips moving but no sound coming out. Cat moved closer, and Grace let Cat break away from her so she could observe her granddaughter from outside. The girl's lips kept moving, but what she said was unintelligible.

"Tell me how to help you," said Cat. "Say it. Out loud."

But the girl kept moving her lips soundlessly. The fire raged on, close but remaining in the background.

"I want to help you," Cat insisted.

The girl shook her head as if in slow motion: No-o-o-o-o-o. Then the girl began to shiver as if suddenly chilled. Cat took off her jacket and went to the girl to put it over her shoulders.

"They're hurting me," the girl whispered.

"Who's hurting you?" Cat said. "Tell me."

Then the girl's voice sounded like a man's. "You're hurting me," she said, and her eyes went black.

"No," Cat insisted. "I wouldn't hurt you."

"You are," the girl said.

"No!" Cat screamed, stepping away from the girl.

Grace couldn't hang back any longer. She went to Cat and said, "It's just a dream, Cat. And you didn't hurt that girl."

"Granny Grace," Cat said, grabbing onto her frantically. "I didn't mean to hurt anyone. I'm dangerous. Cursed."

"You are not," Grace said. "Now wake up."

It must have worked, as Grace popped out of Cat's dream. She drew on her robe and knocked on the door adjoining their hotel rooms. "Cat? You all right?"

"Yes, Gran," she heard Cat say, and then the door opened.

They sat, and Cat began to talk about St. Louis, Cat's first case, in a way they hadn't before. Cat was upset about a girl named Wendy she'd met when undercover in the Plantation Church.

"She felt so betrayed by me," Cat explained. "And she didn't even know the half of it. She had no idea I was using her dreams in my investigation."

Grace felt Cat's pain acutely. "All you can do is try. You weren't trying to hurt Wendy. You were trying to save that little girl.

You were focused on Ruthie, Cat. So you missed what Wendy needed. You're only human."

"But I'm afraid, Granny Grace. I'm afraid I'll hurt someone again."

Grace chuckled softly. "Well, you probably will, Granddaughter. We all hurt each other some of the time. It's unavoidable. Unless you want to live in a bubble."

Then she held Cat's face in her chin. "And you'll get hurt, too. That's part of what you're feeling here, isn't it? Your own strength, yes, and you have to be responsible about it. But you're feeling your own vulnerability, too. You're still hurting because you miss Lee."

Cat began to cry, and Grace held her.

—

The next day, it took the entire morning for them to journey to the suburbs of New Jersey to find their last interviewee, who owned a small house out where, Grace was sure, there'd be no there there.

And it took them forever and a day to arrive, too. They rode the subway to a bus station and took the bus into New Jersey, where they had to be picked up at a park-and-ride by the artist himself, who looked like the suburban grandfather he was.

Clive Smith, Jr., drove them past the usual travesty of fast-food restaurants and chain stores in his Honda Civic, and Grace found him unusually reticent. It had taken every trick in the book to get him to agree to the interview at all. Grace had the sense that she had simply worn the man down over the course of several phone calls and emails, and that he only agreed to meet so she'd leave him alone.

"Are you retired, Mr. Smith?" she asked. "And by that I mean from the web-services company you worked for, not from art."

"Yes, I am," he replied, without going further.

"Tell me about your family," she said, putting an overabundance of cheer into her voice.

Clive cleared his throat. "Are you here to investigate my family?"

"Well, no. I was making small talk."

"I think Clive here isn't the small-talk type," Cat interjected.

"Got that right." His voice sounded irritated. "I'm driving around here with two white women in my car, both of whom say they're here to investigate me. That's not exactly the kind of scenario that lends itself to small talk."

"My apologies, Mr. Smith," Grace said.

There was a long silence in which Clive Smith neither acknowledged nor accepted her apology. Cat and Grace let him drive without interruption, and soon they were in an older subdivision, the houses nearly identical to one another and built sometime in the late Sixties. The Smith residence was a rambler with a tightly manicured front yard. Smith led them through his front door, where an enthusiastic collie greeted them, followed by a woman in her thirties carrying a baby on her hip. Both mother and child shared Smith's likeness.

For the first time, Smith's stony countenance softened as he greeted his family at the door and introduced everyone. The woman was his daughter, Tabitha, and her baby was named Ru. They migrated to a playroom off the dining room, and Smith shepherded Grace and Cat into the living room. He did not offer them anything to drink.

He sat in an imposing leather armchair that Grace surmised was his favorite, and she and Cat took the couch. Steepling his fingers under his chin, he said, "Now then. What would you like to know?"

Pent up from the long journey to see him, Cat and Grace fired questions at him rapidly. He answered in as short a manner as possible. They were getting nowhere till Cat asked him this one: "What did you think of Mick's grad-school masterpiece? *Pink Splash*? The one that won him that national award."

Smith's face broke into a look of utter disgust. He rolled his eyes. "Some masterpiece," he said. "Mick did what every white man does who wants to make it big. He's the Elvis of the art world."

"Because the piece dealt with racial identity," Cat prodded.

"Racial identity! That's a laugh."

"You didn't think the work had merit?" asked Grace.

"No, I did not," said Smith. "Only inasmuch as he lifted his ideas from black artists of the time whose work deserved recognition but who would not get it because they were black.

"But that doesn't mean I wanted to kill the man. I could care less what happens to him, honestly. I've had nothing to do with Travers since Columbia. I see his work every once in awhile by accident, browsing through a magazine or something, but other than the ever-persistent, low-grade resentment I foster toward a racist culture, I have no beef with that man in particular."

"Do you remember anyone who might hate him enough to hurt him in print, so to speak?" asked Grace. "There was a letter in an art magazine. You might have seen it when it came out. It was made to look like Mick wrote it, criticizing a professor who supported him, but he didn't write it."

"I don't recall any letter like that. A lot of people were jealous of the attention he received. We'd bitch about it over beers, that kind of thing. But I don't think any of them have carried that around this long. You do realize it's been forty years, don't you?"

Grace felt deflated again by the man's words, but her granddaughter seemed to rise to his challenge.

"That's long enough to build into something pretty ugly," she said. "Especially if someone's looking at heading into old age without the artistic success they feel was their due. How are you on that front, Clive? I've never seen your face on the cover of *Art in Our Time*. Mick's been on several times."

He gave a bitter chuckle at that one. "You're like a dog with a bone." He shook his head. "Look, you're not going to find what you're looking for out here. Sure, I regret not having become the artist I dreamed of becoming, but that's life. I married a wonderful woman, God rest her soul, and I regret losing her to cancer more than I regret not becoming a big-shot artist."

He gestured toward a photo on the mantel, an old wedding photo taken in the Seventies. Clive had exaggerated sideburns and an afro. The bride was voluptuous and must have known it, for she'd chosen a form-fitting dress that hugged her curves.

"I'm sorry," said Cat. "When did she pass?"

"Two years ago," he said, his voice trembling slightly. "After our thirty-fifth wedding anniversary."

Grace felt her phone buzz in her pocketbook. "She was quite the looker," she said. "How many children do you have?"

"Oh, just the one." His gaze redirected to the room beyond, where they could hear his granddaughter exclaiming with delight over something her mother was showing her. "Have you got everything you need, ladies? I'd like to spend some time with my family, if you don't mind, and I need to take you back to where you can catch a bus."

They rose to leave although Grace hadn't felt the trip gleaned enough information to clear Clive of suspicion. She peeked at her phone in the car and noticed a call from Mick, who only called her when it was urgent. She listened to the message.

"Pris," he said, his breathing hard, "someone torched my beach house."

Chapter 8

C at wondered now if Granny Grace was right, that someone wanted Mick dead.

She reflected as she surveyed the remains of his beach house that the killer had twice missed the mark, which could mean murder didn't come naturally to him. Or her.

Mick's beach house was located in far South Dade, further south than where O.J. Simpson famously lived. And it was tiny, with only one bedroom plus a sort of indoor/outdoor porch with louvered glass windows that everyone in Florida called a "lanai." The house was too small for Mick to work on anything other than small roughs or prototype sketches for his oversized paintings, which is why he was hardly ever there except to sleep or when he wanted to sit and stare at the water. But it was beachfront property, set on a narrow strip of land on Biscayne Bay.

The knotty pine walls and floors must have gone up like fireplace kindling, as there was nothing left of them. Cat could see the sand beneath the floor joists. What she and Granny Grace had been able to piece together so far was that the Miami PD had stopped its twenty-four-seven watch on the place even before Cat and her grandmother had left for New York. But Mick hadn't been back except to pick up a few things here and there. He'd visited the beach house earlier that day but had been sleeping in Ernesto's cottage when the fire occurred. This time, the only victim was the building itself.

Alvarez, who'd been speaking with the forensics team combing the site, trudged across the sand to Cat and her grandmother.

"We haven't charged Jenny Baines," she informed them. "And she's looking less guilty for the first arson since she was in a jail cell at the time of this fire. We're likely going to let her go."

Cat nodded, thinking about her grandmother's theory about that night, how the revenge photo Jenny took likely contributed to Donnie's death in a roundabout way even if she hadn't actually set the fire. "That's assuming the two arsons were committed by the same person."

"True," said Alvarez. "But we're not sure we could make the charges stick. I suppose Mick could try to press charges against her for defamation, since she confessed to faking the photo, but that's a long shot, and he'd have to be pretty crude to want to do that. Jenny's clearly suffering. We, of course, don't have a recording of their conversation, but it's likely that her last words to Donnie were pretty bad. Still, there's no hard evidence linking her to the arson."

Granny Grace said, "And you don't have anything on Mick."

Alvarez gazed at Cat and then at her grandmother. "No, we don't. But we'll look at him for this one."

Cat knew they had to, especially since Mick was likely an insurance beneficiary, but it irked her anyway. Her great-uncle had already gone back to the cottage, badly shaken.

Alvarez excused herself and returned to the forensics team. Cat turned to her grandmother, speaking out of earshot of the others. "Could any of the people we met with in New York have made it down in time to set this fire?"

"I was just trying to work out the math myself."

"We met with all three of them in the daytime."

"You can get a three-hour non-stop flight from New York to Miami." Her grandmother stepped delicately over the burned ruins in her canvas espadrilles. "It's practically a commuter zone, what with all the northern snowbirds. That's why they call it the sixth borough of New York."

"So this fire doesn't eliminate any of them as suspects," Cat observed. "They're estimating it was set around midnight. That would have given both Annie Lin, whom we met on Thursday afternoon, and Clive, whom we saw on Friday morning, just enough time to reach South Dade and set the fire at the beach house."

"And dear Norris had even more time," said Grace.

They were quiet in their mutual frustration at having eliminated no suspects.

"Let's find out if any of them traveled," said Cat.

She and Granny Grace went back to the cottage and got to work. Granny checked the passenger lists at the airlines for the three New York suspects but came up blank.

Disguising herself as one of his clients, Cat called Norris's office to see if he was available for an urgent meeting. Chatting up his admin, she discovered that Norris was in fact in Miami.

"Miami, eh?" she said, making her voice sound aggressive. "I'm not far from there myself right now. Tell me where he's staying, and I'll drop by."

The admin gave a nervous cough in response. "Oh, well, Mr. Grayson took his wife for their anniversary. He didn't want to be disturbed with any business matters."

"The account's in jeopardy, so I'd say that's important enough to disturb Grayson," Cat spit back.

"Would you like to speak to one of the other partners?"

"Would Grayson like me to speak to one of the other partners? Or wouldn't he rather handle this on his own?"

"You're right. Let me find that hotel name for you... He's staying at the Biltmore. Special occasion, you see."

Cat informed her grandmother, who suggested it was time to loop in Sergeant Alvarez. Cat agreed and did the honors herself.

Within an hour, Cat, Grace, and Alvarez descended upon the Biltmore, where a stunned and angry Norris Grayson effected what Cat took to be a self-righteous act. Rising from a lounge chair in his swim trunks beside the Biltmore's famed Grecian pool, Norris sputtered his outrage at being disturbed on his anniversary.

"I told you everything I know about Mick Travers in New York!"

Alvarez stepped between Norris and Granny Grace, who bore the brunt of his ire. "Calm down, Mr. Grayson," she said. "You're under suspicion of arson, and we need you to cooperate and answer some questions."

At that, Norris's wife, who'd been ensconced on the lounge chair next to his, softly but firmly said, "Could we take this somewhere less public?" Cat followed her gaze toward the coiffed, slick hotel guests staring with interest at the spectacle. Norris's wife tightened her beach cover-up for emphasis and gestured to a door beyond a faux Greek statue. "There are private meeting rooms inside."

Cat was only too happy to oblige, as she was still wearing pants and a blazer, and the close Miami noontime sun was making her sweat. She welcomed the blast of air conditioning as they stepped into the hotel proper and filed into a swanky meeting room.

"Now then," said Alvarez, "tell us how you got to Miami without having your name added to any passenger lists."

Norris's wife broke in. "That's my father's doing, I'm afraid. This trip was a surprise for us, so it's in my father's name—the plane tickets, the hotel reservations."

"But with the Homeland Security precautions these days, you'd have to give your real names," Cat challenged.

"It's under the VIP Club," his wife said. "We didn't have any problems. They simply took Norris as my father's guest. His name is Stephen Dunnavan, if you want to look it up."

Cat felt this was too convenient, even if true. And what was this preferential treatment from Homeland Security? It figured that those with enough money and influence could avoid the scouring of security checks.

Her grandmother turned to Norris. "So you've been here at the hotel the whole time? Who can vouch for you? Do you have an alibi for last night?"

"I've been with Debbie," Norris said. "We had dinner here at the Biltmore. Room service. You can check with the hotel staff."

Debbie linked her arm with Norris's. "I haven't let this man out of my sight since we landed. It's rare that I get to drag him away from work like this."

Cat flipped to the notes she'd taken when they conferred with hotel staff before ambushing the Graysons. "According to staff here, you had room service delivered around eight. But your hotel card was swiped to let you back into the room at one thirty. That's the exact window of time that would allow you to set the fire."

Debbie laughed, tossing her hair. "Oh, come now. Norris and I were at the Cuban guitar concert in the hotel lounge. It ended around that time. You can check with the other guests, the staff..."

Regarding them warily, Alvarez asked, "When do you plan to return to New York?"

Norris answered. "I've got an important meeting next Monday. But we'll be here till then. Not that we welcome another visit from any of you."

At that, Cat, Alvarez, and Granny Grace left the two and made for the hotel desk.

Several staff members confirmed that the Graysons were in attendance at the concert. Cat maintained that Norris could have slipped away from the concert, set the fire, and returned. But her suspicion wasn't enough, especially when they checked and found out that Stephen Dunnavan's name had indeed been on the VIP clearance for the Graysons' flight from New York to Miami, and the Biltmore reservations were under his name. Cat confirmed Dunnavan's identity and that he had a daughter named Debbie.

If it came down to it, Debbie would either claim spousal privilege and refuse to say anything or else voluntarily back up her husband's alibi in court. But would she really, Cat wondered, if she knew her husband were guilty? It was worth pursuing.

—

Angry at having to leave Norris to his Biltmore excesses, Cat was a little irritated to find Ernesto waiting for them back at the cottage. He politely sat on the front porch though he had a key and could have waited for them inside. She was beginning to feel that his presence kept interrupting their work.

"How are my señoritas enjoying the sunshine?" His lilting tenor preceded him through the doorway. Cat saw her grandmother's eyes light up at the sight of him. They greeted with an intimate embrace and the customary Cuban-style kiss on both cheeks.

"The sunshine, we find divine," her grandmother said in answer to his question. "The heat, not so much."

"I heard about the fire. How's Mick? He must be in shock."

"He's pretty shaken," admitted Cat. She'd been surprised not to find him home but figured he'd gone to a bar.

"I'm worried about the three of you here," Ernesto said.

"I'm worried about your cottage's future as a bonfire," said Cat. She'd been thinking about it ever since they left the ruins of Mick's beach house.

"Oh, that's no matter," said Ernesto. "It's your safety I would like to ensure. I have other rentals. Let me move you to another."

"That only works as long as our arsonist doesn't know your properties," said Granny Grace. "And doesn't follow Mick."

"He hasn't so far," Ernesto pointed out. "Come to think of it, your arsonist has not been successful. One might even call him bumbling."

"Assuming Mick is indeed the target," said Cat.

On their way to the Biltmore, Alvarez had let them know they hadn't turned up anyone with a grudge against Don Hines or anyone with the motive to kill him. Cat thought of that now. "The chances that Don Hines was the target keep dwindling. But I think we should look again at whether or not the target was Mick's art."

"His art!" Ernesto said. "Why would someone wish to destroy his art?"

"Jealousy, revenge…" Granny Grace suggested. "The arsonist might not have realized there'd be someone sleeping in the studio. It's kind of a peculiar quirk of artists, sleeping in their work spaces."

Ernesto kept pressing. "Still, I think we should move you. I have a place in Brickell, an apartment, that I don't rent publicly. It's for family who come from out of town."

He made a handsome living in the financial-services industry as a registered investment advisor, and his properties were one of his many investments. He also invested in art, Cat remembered.

"Oh!" Granny Grace exclaimed, putting her hand on Ernesto's shoulder. "I nearly forgot. We've got a gift for you."

"Please, there is no need." Ernesto let himself be shepherded into Mick's makeshift studio in the lanai, where Candace Shreveport's masterpiece still sat on a sawhorse easel.

"Voila!" said Granny Grace, bracketing the canvas with her hands as if she were Vanna White.

"What's this?" Ernesto took a pair of sleek reading glasses out of the pocket of his suit and put them on so he could examine the work in detail.

"It's not the hand of a master. But there's a levity here, a lightness of being. It's these children. They inspired her." He dropped his gaze to the artist's signature. "Candy Port, eh? I do not know this artist."

"Well," said Granny Grace, "let's just say she's germane to the case."

"As an art investor, I would not have advised you to purchase this," he admonished with a smile. "But I understand the impulse to see value where there isn't any, speaking strictly in terms of the market."

Cat flinched a bit at Ernesto's response. She cast a glance at Granny Grace, who didn't seem at all put out by his criticism.

"I will always think of you when I see it," he continued. "Let's hang it. It suits the living room, don't you think? The beach poster I have there is dated now. I haven't changed the décor in here since the Nineties."

Cat drifted off to her room to do more research, letting them hang the painting together. Her grandmother's flirtatious laughter carried down the hallway to her room. Cat felt a pang of loneliness. She remembered Lee making her breakfast the first morning they were together after she'd moved to Seattle. When she dressed and joined him at the dinner table, breakfast was already made, and there was a daisy in a vase in the middle of the table.

"Where'd you get that?" she asked. "You don't have a single plant in here, let alone a garden."

Lee grinned at her. "No, but my neighbors do."

"You stole it?"

"Borrowed."

"It's not like you're going to give it back..."

Granny Grace appeared in the doorway, breaking Cat's reverie. "Ernesto wants to take us to dinner. You game?"

Cat stretched. "Oh, I think I'll let you two have a date without your third wheel."

"You sure?"

Cat could tell her grandmother was still reluctant to leave her alone. But she really didn't want to be a tagalong. "I want to get a jump on this research."

"Have it your way, stick-in-the-mud." Granny Grace looked beautiful in a shift dress and colorful wrap, for covering her shoulders when the trade winds kicked up in the evening. "Ernesto's moving us to his Brickell place tomorrow," she added.

In the quiet of the cottage after they left, Cat booted up her laptop and went to work studying the paintings that had been destroyed during the fire. If they held any clues, she did not uncover them. Part of the problem was that it seemed incomplete—some of the paintings weren't accounted for, and not all the ones that were had digital images. But by the time she fell asleep, still fully clothed, she felt she was becoming an expert on his work.

Chapter 9

Mick drove hard, praying that his Fiat would make it across Alligator Alley without any issues. All he could think about was that if Candace Shreveport killed Donnie, he'd wring her pudgy neck.

He'd been too angry to say anything to his sister and niece. He could barely think straight, and he thought of that saying, "seeing red." It had never happened to him before, but now he understood that the saying was literally true. As soon as he noticed that the conch shell was gone and put together what that meant, he saw red.

The shell came from Bahia Honda, where he and Candy once spent a rum-soaked afternoon. Swimming just off shore, she'd stepped on something jagged, dived down to retrieve it, and come back with the shell. It was larger than what you'd stumble across lying on the beach and perfectly intact, a true find.

He admired the shell, made studies of it in his sketchbook that very day on the beach. It became the basis for his Conch Series, and Candy gave it to him to keep.

"My heart's in this shell," she'd said to him, and for a while, he believed her. "As long as you have this shell, you have my heart."

The shell had been in his beach house, sitting on a steel Army-issue bookcase. The bookcase had survived the fire, but Mick noticed the shell was gone. There was soot atop the bookcase in the spot where the shell had been. So whoever set the fire took the shell first.

He knew it was Candace, and she was such an awful wretch to carry on her bitterness this long, long enough to still hate Mick, long enough to set that fire in his studio that killed Donnie.

He'd be putting her out of her misery, really. "You're not so big, Mick," she said the last time she drunk-dialed him. "You're small where it counts, no matter how big-ass your paintings get."

And this gem: "I never loved you anyway. I told you what you wanted to hear. Like every other woman in your life."

He drove like a madman, ignoring the speed limit and the growing darkness. In the sherbet-colored dusk, he saw wide-winged birds swooping across the Everglades.

Once he'd gotten lost on a hike that turned into a slog through the 'glades. He kept slogging that night though his feet were wet in his boots. He remembered trying not to think about the rather large carcasses of birds and boars he'd seen earlier in the hike and was deeply relieved when he spotted car headlights in the distance. He followed them till he came to a road, which eventually brought him back to his car. That was Christmas Eve, two years ago, he realized. He'd spent it alone.

But he would rather be alone than shackled to someone like Candace.

Finally, the Fiat rumbled into Sanibel. He knew her house; she'd inherited it from her mother. Mick had had dinner there once, made small talk with the old bird of a mother who died not long after of heart disease. He hated the gingerbread Victorian design of the place, the narrow rooms and hallways.

He banged on Candace's door, not caring that it was late, her porch light off. He banged until he heard a cat meow and knew Candace was up.

"What in the h—" She came to the door, tying her robe closed across her belly.

He grabbed her by the shoulders and pushed her into the house.

"Mick!" she said, pulling her cell phone out of her robe pocket. "You get out of here! I'm calling the cops."

"You aren't calling anyone." Forcing her to sit down, he grabbed the phone out of her hand and tossed it across the room. It skittered under a wicker chair and broke apart when it hit the baseboard. The noise startled her cat, which ran out of the room.

"That's my phone, you asshole! Get out of my house!"

He hauled off and smacked her across the face, knowing as his hand hit her that he'd spiraled out of control, that he had crossed a line, and that he was hitting both Jenny Baines and Candace Shreveport in one go here.

She got quiet.

"Where's the shell?" he asked.

She didn't answer.

"The conch shell, Candy. I know you have it."

She folded her arms across her chest. "I don't know what you're talking about."

Mick laughed. It looked like fifty miles of bad road had been laid atop the woman he once got a hard-on from just looking at. He remembered flashes of a dream of hers he kept inadvertently slipping into back when she'd moved into his beach house. Something about being the prettiest ballerina, the one other girls envied. Not for her dancing, but for her looks. At the time he thought it was kind of sweet and sad, but now it seemed indicative of where Candace had gone wrong as a human being.

"You're old, Candy."

"So are you."

She was right, of course. He could turn the mirror back onto his own flabby middle, his graying hair, the wrinkles creasing his forehead.

"Mick the Dick," she hissed.

"At least I'm not a murdering sack of shit."

"Murder? What are you talking about, Mickey Travers? I'm no murderer."

"You took the shell, Candy. From my house. I know you have it. So that means you set the fires. You killed Donnie."

Candy kicked him in the shin, and it hurt like hell. He resisted the urge to smack her across the face again and only felt mildly disturbed by how strong that urge was.

"Is that how you treat a woman, Mick? You abuser!" She began to cry, and he deeply resented her tears.

"What happened to you?" He meant it.

"What happened to you?" She reflected the question back to him in a way that really hit the mark.

He sat down, put his face in his hands. "I don't know."

She made a run for it, out the back door, but he took off after her and grabbed her robe from behind, sending her sprawling to the floor. They struggled there on the floor of her kitchen, the linoleum sticky and laden with crumbs, till Mick gained the upper hand. He tied her to her kitchen table with the sash from her robe.

"You can't do this to me!"

"Oh, yes I can."

With that, Mick set out to find the shell. He swiped knickknacks off shelves, turned over unfinished paintings, and emptied the contents of every drawer.

As he rifled through her house, Candy screamed at him from the kitchen. "You don't belong here, Mickey! I hate you! I wish you had died in that fire! You're the biggest asshole that ever held a brush!"

He finally found it in the bottom of a hat box tucked away in the back of her closet. It was his shell, undeniably, with two white barnacles flanking one side and a chip out of one edge. It had been the subject of his Conch Series, which appeared in catalogs and magazines throughout the world. He'd recognize it on a beach littered with hundreds of shells.

He stomped back out to the kitchen and shoved the shell in her face. "Is this worth killing for, Candy? Eh?"

She broke into a laugh. "Is that what you think, Mick?"

He stood there, staring at her, listening to her infernal laughter.

"You think I wanted that shell?" she howled. "You can keep your damn shell."

"Then what?" he asked, at a loss, his voice breaking. "What did you want?"

She looked at him, her face reverting to the face he knew years ago, open and full of a longing he could never fill.

"I wanted us, Mick. In that beach house. You promised me we'd stay there forever. But it was always your place. Yours alone. You filled it with your art till there wasn't any room for me anymore, and you pushed me out. And now look at you. Your art's so big, there'll never be any room for anyone else."

Mick felt tears drip out of his eyes. "But a fire, Candy?" he asked, his voice hoarse.

Candace's voice came from far away. "I wanted to burn you down, Mick. That's all. I didn't want you to have everything anymore. You've had enough."

Mick heard someone behind him, and he turned to see a police officer, someone he recognized. Santiago, the one who worked with Alvarez. They must have put a tail on him after he left the beach house.

"That's a confession," Santiago announced. "I'm calling it in."

Mick slumped down next to Candace, buried his face in his hands, and wept. He watched through wet eyes as Santiago cuffed Candace and read her her rights.

———

When Donnie's parents arrived from Ohio, Cat was off somewhere else, and Pris was at a Buddhist temple nearby, where she'd been spending a lot of time meditating since the first fire.

Which meant that Mick had to deal with the grieving parents on his own.

He picked them up from the airport in his Fiat, which was not ideal, but he put the top up so their hair wouldn't get blown around, at least. He and Pris had helped them deal with the cremation and other details long-distance, for which Donald Sr. and Mary Ellen were grateful.

But other than grace and gratitude, what emanated from the elderly couple was deep, deep sadness, and it knocked Mick back with a force he hadn't encountered in some time. He couldn't let go of the overwhelming feeling that their son should be there instead of him. Small talk seemed like an insult, so on the drive from the Miami airport to the hotel where he was putting them up, he told them about Donnie's recent success as an artist and tried to convey in a genuine way what a talented son they had.

"I always knew he had the gift," said Mary Ellen. "Isn't that right, Donald?"

"That's right," Donald concurred. "I tried to dissuade him from what seemed like a hard row to hoe, but his mother here, she wouldn't stand for it."

Mick searched his memory bank for anything Donnie might've said about his parents, but he didn't come up with much. Then he remembered something.

"Donnie got an idea once he said came from watching you make bread."

"Is that so? My bread?"

Mick looked at Mary Ellen in his rear view mirror. The couple had opted to sit together huddled in the tiny back seat, and they were holding each other's hands.

"Yeah, it was the way you kneaded the dough. He traced the pattern out on canvas once. I don't know if you ever saw it—a piece called *Dough Ties*."

"Oh, I'd love to see it."

But then Mick regretted mentioning it, as he realized the piece was lost in the fire. He decided to change the subject.

"I'm glad you'll be here for the wake," he said. He and a bunch of other artists, with the help of the gallery owner, who was a fan of Donnie's art, were planning a sort of "celebration of life" event in honor of Donnie's passing.

"Well, we'd have of course preferred a Christian burial in our home town," Donald said. "I don't quite know what to do with my son's ashes—" At this, the old man choked up. Mary Ellen offered him a tissue from her purse and patted his arm.

Mick was silent. Sometimes you had to let a man grieve.

He drove up I-90, glad for their sake the traffic was light. There was a cool breeze blowing off the water. With Christmas around the corner, Miamians had decked out every spare corner of their domiciles with season-appropriate ephemera. Even after the twenty years he'd called South Florida home, Mick still thought the juxtaposition of snowmen and reindeer against a backdrop of tropical flowers and sunshine was odd. Seeing it through the eyes of Donnie's parents, it seemed practically surreal. And South Floridians weren't known for their restraint, either. He passed a gated compound where an inflatable Santa Claus wearing a Miami Heat jersey was posed in a jump shot, hanging from a basketball hoop over a three-car garage.

Mary Ellen cleared her throat. "They certainly have the Christmas spirit down here, don't they?"

Mick was caught between the desire to laugh and weep. He bit his lip and nodded.

When they arrived at the hotel, he helped them check in at the front desk and then carried their bags to their room, which he'd arranged with the hotel staff to set up beforehand. He'd taken down the bland hotel art and put up three of Donnie's paintings that had been on loan in a gallery on South Beach. Mick had retrieved them, hoping his parents would want to take them home. They were some of the man's finest pieces, and looking at them now, Mick could see that his friend had hit his stride with the fractal imagery. These looked like delicate crystals that, given time and space, would grow into infinity.

"Please call me if you need anything," he told them. "Have a rest, and when you're ready, I'll drive you to the mortuary."

Surprisingly, it was Donnie's father who recognized the work around the room.

"That's his art," he said, putting on his reading glasses and walking over for a closer look. "My, my."

Mary Ellen followed her husband. She placed her hand on the painting, and then it was her turn to cry.

Mick closed the door, leaving them alone.

As he turned into the cottage driveway, there was Pris, walking back from the Buddhist temple, a serene smile on her face. She wore oversized Jackie O glasses and a wide-brimmed hat. His sister at seventy-eight still had flair.

"Hello, my dear," she said, kissing him on the cheek.

"Did we achieve enlightenment?"

"Enlightenment is not to be achieved. It just is."

He smiled, and then dropping the smile, he said, "Mr. and Mrs. Hines are here."

Pris saw that his Fiat was the only car in the drive. "Oh, Mick. You didn't make them ride in your little roadster, did you?"

"I had no choice. Cat took your rental god knows where."

"Isn't it time you traded up?"

Mick had an immediate reaction against that idea. The Fiat had been with him for decades. He'd nursed it through several clutches, a rebuilt engine, and a total body overhaul. He couldn't get rid of it now. It was practically family.

He told this to Pris, who shook her head as if she pitied him.

"Well, for heaven's sake, Mick. Did you at least offer them lunch? They must be famished."

He hadn't thought of that. "No."

"Well, let's give them a chance to regroup, and then we'll head over to that café I like on Coral Way."

They did just that, and Mick was relieved to have Pris's energetic, skillfully conversational presence there as a buffer. The four of them made it through a meal without anyone crying, and by the time they walked back to the building, Donald turned to Mick and said, "Let's visit the mortuary tomorrow, if you don't mind, Mick. Mary Ellen and I—we need some time today."

Mick was glad to give them space. He had a lot to do to get ready for Donnie's celebration, and he was working on a new painting as well.

The next afternoon, he switched cars with Pris at her insistence and took Donnie's parents to get the ashes. The mortuary was a large, clean, beautiful place, a bit of old Florida elegance, if you could forget that it was a house for dead people, that is. The attendant, a cute young thing in a skirt suit and actual pantyhose, something Mick hardly ever saw anymore, offered to show Donald and Mary Ellen the crematorium. They declined. "Only the, ah, ashes, please," said Donald.

What was left of Donnie was presented in a white ceramic urn, as generic as they come. Mick was sure if he got the full tour, he'd find a whole rack of them in back.

As they drove, Donald held the urn in his hands. The couple were sitting in back again, and they whispered to each other for a while. Mick turned on the radio at a low volume to give them some privacy.

"Say, Mick," Donald finally spoke up. "Is there somewhere here we could put some of these ashes? Somewhere Donnie liked to go."

Mick didn't even have to think about it. "I'll take you there," he said, pulling a u-turn.

As he drove, Mick remembered the first time he'd taken Donnie to this place. He'd promised him it was the most beautiful spot on earth, and Donnie was surprised to find they were heading into the belly of the Everglades and not to the beach or the Keys. Like a lot of people who were new to Florida, Donnie's only association with the Everglades was its air boats.

The heat of the city gave way to a lush coolness as he made his way into the River of Grass, as some called it. Mick knew it was no longer a functioning ecosystem, as it had been damned to the north and blockaded on all sides by the modern engine of progress. The only reason it continued to exist at all was because it fed the Miami aquifer, which supplied South Florida with water. But it was still the largest stretch of wetlands left in the country, and the word "swamp" did not do it justice.

After a long stretch of quiet, he steered into a parking lot and motioned for Donald and Mary Ellen to follow him down a path over a hummock and then across a boardwalk that led to a platform high above the glades.

It was approaching dusk, just as it had been the first time Mick brought Donnie to that place. The sky looked as if an artist had rinsed out her pastels in a tray of water, with robin's-egg blue mingling with bits of lavender and fiery orange and rose cast from the setting sun. It was quiet, so quiet, that Mick thought he could hear the river of grass sighing beneath their feet.

Here the largest birds in North America glided across the glades, their wings outstretched and casting strong shadows on the still blades of swamp grass: snowy egrets with bright yellow beaks, great blue herons, ibis with curved orange beaks, as if they'd stepped off an Egyptian hieroglyphic. Occasionally one cried out, its call echoing across the still river of grass.

For miles in every direction, that was all there was: slow-moving water, grass, birds, and sky. Mick had the sense here that nature would go on, that it was and always would be, and that it was he, a human being, who had a shelf life. Rather than feeling limited or depressed by this, he found it liberating.

When he and Donnie came here, they rarely talked. They'd bring sketchbooks, water, and snacks, and they'd sit for a long time, drawing, quietly working in each other's company. Mick knew that Donnie came here by himself sometimes, too, and it made him glad to know he'd given the place to his friend like a gift.

Donald had the urn in his hands. He motioned to Mick to take some of Donnie's ashes and spread them. "This is for you to do," he said. "And you can have some of him to keep if you like. We'll take the rest home to Ohio."

Mick realized his face was wet where tears had slipped down his cheeks. He dried them on his shirt sleeve, lifted the lid on the urn, and scooped out some ashes. Leaning over the railing, he let what remained of his friend fall from his hand and become part of the wide river of grass.

Chapter 10

Grace understood now why she'd been unable to get Candace Shreveport out of her mind. With her confession and the conch as evidence, Alvarez booked Candace for both fires. The woman had experienced some sort of psychic break after her confession and could only scream or cry or otherwise carry on about what a bastard Mick was, how he should have died in the fire. It could turn out that Candace took the murder rap but successfully plead insanity. She certainly was putting on a good show with it, if it wasn't in fact genuine.

Relieved of the burden of Mick's case, Grace allowed herself to be squired by the dashing Ernesto Ruíz. After the commotion of Candace's arrest died down, the three of them were still living in the man's cottage, as their proposed safety move to his Brickell apartment seemed no longer necessary. Not that Mick was satisfied. In addition to preparations for Donnie's wake, her brother had begun to look for a replacement studio, a live/work unit like the one he'd lost to the fire.

Ernesto took her to a restaurant that was as much outside as it was inside, and this was the case year-round, apparently. One of the tropical city's enduring charms, in Grace's opinion, was the opportunity to dine al fresco. This place, near Ernesto's office in Brickell, had been fashioned between the wide, branching trunk of a banyan tree, which sheltered diners from the sun and provided a romantic canopy.

"I often come here for lunch," Ernesto said once they were seated. "But just soup then, or a baguette sandwich. Tonight, we celebrate."

"Celebrate? That seems a bit strong, considering. A man's dead, and this Candace woman will probably spend the rest of her life behind bars. Not that she hadn't already created a prison for herself...." Grace let her words trail off.

Ernesto held up his hands. "Of course, darling. Forgive me for not being more sensitive. You are right."

Grace put a hand on his arm. "With you, old friend, every meal is a celebration."

Ernesto gave her his five-thousand-watt smile, squeezing the hand she'd placed on his arm. "Remember when I took you to the Argentinian restaurant?"

"Remember? How could I forget? I was a vegetarian at the time. And you bring me to a place with no menus. The waiters came out carrying platters piled with nothing but meat!" Grace gave him a playful slug on the shoulder.

Ernesto laughed. "They thought you were being rude until I took the proprietor aside and explained."

"Oh, and then it was a carb fest after that. It's a good thing I wasn't off gluten back then."

"But what lovely ravioli they made! Ah, I can still taste how fresh. The spinach it was stuffed with, it was bright green. They must have made it to order for you."

"What was the name of that place, Ernie? It was a treasure, but if I remember correctly, it had a queer name."

"Zuperpollo."

Grace easily translated in her head. "Crazy chicken? That sounds more appropriate for a fast-food restaurant."

"Yes, I agree. But you have to understand the Argentinian mindset. Do you remember the sign? It was a chicken wearing a costume…"

"Yes! Like a superhero! It's coming back to me now."

"The sign, it was irreverent, but the food, they took very seriously. It is a pity you could not taste the meat. The memory lives with me still."

"And the singing!" Grace recalled how at the end of the evening, several generations of men gathered on stage and sang old songs, some sad, some seemingly silly, at least from what she could pick up with her limited Spanish. What a good time they'd had that night.

Ernesto stroked her hand beneath the table, and she enjoyed the feel of his touch. The two of them reminisced on old times for a while, and then their food arrived. A converted meat-eater at this point in her life, Grace had chosen seared tuna with mango relish and star fruit. Ernesto had ceviche, a nice cold dish for a warm night. They drank an Argentinian wine in honor of that restaurant from so long ago.

Neither was interested in dessert, and by this point, Ernesto had found Grace's knee under the table. He squeezed it with a delicate but insistent grip that sent a shiver into her thighs. Grace remembered what a lovely physique the man had. He was shorter than she and built like a fire plug. Perhaps this had worked against him in his early years, but he was still solid muscle well into his seventies, and he had a stamina she admired, and in fact had taken full advantage of.

He drew close to her at the table after the waiter whisked away their dishes. "So tell me about Mick's case. Are you making progress?"

"Oh, Ernie," said Grace. "Let's not talk about that business tonight. I'm having far too lovely a time."

He nodded and smoothly changed the subject. She could imagine him doing the same with his clients. "Would you like to see my office? I have some new acquisitions, a sculpture in particular I think you'd want to see."

"And you still have that Herman Miller couch, I trust?"

Ernesto gave her a smile that was modest on top, with mischief underneath. "Yes, I do."

An hour later, the two were spent. Sprawled on the aforementioned couch in various states of disarray, they let their breathing return to normal.

Grace traced Ernesto's lips with her finger. "You know you're really very good at pleasuring a woman, Ernie. You should teach others your gifts."

"If you are referring to that epic—as the kids say—orgasm you had while my head was between your legs, I must say you are the one who should teach others."

"Oh, well, I have, as a matter of fact. Didn't you know? At Seattle Community College, back when I hit forty. It was a continuing ed class. 'Climaxing at the Climax of Your Life.'"

Ernesto laughed, slipped his hand up under her hair, and brought her mouth closer to his for another kiss.

Once he released her, she continued. "I didn't know as much back then. Imagine, calling forty the climax of your life!"

"Maybe you should offer to teach it again."

"Only if you co-teach it with me." They both laughed.

"Oh, I have no special technique. Only a deep love of women." He stroked the inside of her thigh. "I love their fullness. Look at the way your hips swell here..." he circled the sides of her hips. "And as you've aged, the fullness grows. I have looked forward to seeing what time brings with each visit."

"You are quite the flatterer." Grace felt herself glowing in the aftermath of their sex. As always, she took note of the moment, reflecting inwardly, knowing how blessed her life was. But then Mother Nature tugged at her, so she excused herself to use the bathroom.

When she returned, she asked, "So where is this sculpture? Or was that merely a pretense to re-introduce me to our friend Herman Miller here?" She patted the enormous leather couch that had served them well.

Ernesto had dressed while she was in the bathroom. "Let me show you."

He walked in sock feet to a far wall, where he flipped a switch, illuminating a large glass cabinet. In the center was a piece she'd never seen before, but she recognized the artist. It was a Garrison DeGrant.

"How did you get it?" Grace went to the sculpture, drawn by the bright gold leaf applied in an uneven, deliberately rough manner over what appeared to be a set of primitive wings. The gold caught the light as she moved, reflecting it in glints. As Grace drew closer, she saw that they were wings, but they were oversized, as if too large for the figure beneath them. And the figure was a woman. She bore her wings as if they were a burden.

"She is tragic, no?" Ernesto said. "An angel is supposed to be idyllic, but here, he has shown the cost of being divine. It's so much to bear."

"It's exquisite," Grace breathed. "But Ernesto, the price..."

"It is an investment. DeGrant's place in the art world is secure." He turned to a hidden panel on the wall, opening it. "As is my collection." He punched in a code, and Grace heard a voice announce, "*Disarmed.*"

"Please," he said, motioning her toward the glass case as he opened it. "If you'd like to touch it, by all means."

Grace reached in, surprised that the gold felt warm to her touch. The medium beneath it was smooth stone that had been chiseled by DeGrant's fine hand. She felt a strong vibration from the piece, as if the angel herself wished to shed her wings and walk away from them.

"It's wonderful, Ernie." Grace yawned, suddenly feeling her age.

"Why don't you come home with me," Ernesto offered. "We have an understanding, and I do not wish to disrupt that. But it would be nice for us both, I think, to sleep in each other's arms."

Grace could not resist.

———

She stepped out onto a balcony, her bare feet aware of the edges where the sun-bleached pink paint was flaking off in chunks. Over the edge of the balcony wall, she could see the ocean, pale turquoise capped by white waves. Down below was the street, a row of Fifties-era cars lined up, kids playing around them.

Grace recognized this place, though she'd never been. It was Havana. She must be dreamslipping with Ernesto—a consequence of letting her guard down with him. He was dreaming of his childhood in Cuba. He'd come over in the Mariel Boatlift, in his forties, she knew.

She spotted a speck in the distance, a black dot in the sky. But someone was calling from inside the apartment. "Ernesto ... Ernesto..."

Grace stayed with him as he turned and went back indoors. There was an altar on top of a very old TV, also Fifties era. A striped cloth had been draped over the top of the TV, and a row of candles spread across. Dog-eared cards depicting Catholic saints. A shot glass full of water. Faded purple flowers.

But Ernesto's attention was on the TV screen, which zig-zagged in wavy lines. He picked up the pliers that were sitting to one side of the altar and used it to turn a spoke sticking out of the TV, where a dial had been lost.

"A veces se puede recoger de los canales de los Estados Unidos," Ernesto said, to no one in particular. The room was empty. He said it again, this time in English. "Sometimes you can pick up channels from the United States."

The pattern zig-zagged and then stuck on Bozo the Clown. But as soon as Ernesto set the pliers down, the zig-zag pattern resumed, rendering Bozo in black-and-white slices. Ernesto threw the pliers across the room. They disappeared down a hole in the floor. He bent over the hole, but it was a dark, bottomless pit, giving back nothing.

Then a man in a suit came to the door, a man from the U.S. who seemed to be taking the census. "Is your mother home?" he asked, in English.

Ernesto slammed the door in his face.

A group of men were now set up in the middle of the living room, gathered around an apparatus. A pile of moldy potatoes spilled from a gunny sack. They appeared to be distilling alcohol from the potatoes. Ernesto watched for a moment, but they paid him no attention, so he went back out to the balcony.

The dark speck in the sky was closer now, and Grace could see that it had wings. They were large and glinted in the light, as if covered in gold.

Ernesto watched as it flew toward him. Soon Grace could see it was the angel, the DeGrant figure. But she was magnificent in her sleekness and strength. She bore her wings as if made for them. Her feet were talons. She swooped down and picked up Ernesto, the nails of her talons piercing him. Grace cried out, feeling the pain of it. The blood dripped down from Ernesto's body and dispersed into the sea.

The figure flew a long way across the ocean, clutching Ernesto.

Finally, land came in sight. A vast highway, cars swarming like bugs. She set him down in the center of a lane. He ran to the edge of the lane. Cars nearly nicked him as they sped by. He waited for an opening and then dove to the far lane, and then the shoulder.

There on the side of the highway was the winged figure, but now she appeared to be a middle-aged woman, shaped like an apple and wearing a faded apron. Her wings were too large for her, and they weighed her down.

"Mamá," he said, running toward her.

85

But then the scene switched, and Ernesto was hugging Grace's brother Mick. Grace found this interesting, since in real life, the two were not close. Mick always seemed uncharacteristically brotherly and overprotective about her liaison with Ernesto.

In the dream, Mick pushed Ernesto away, sat back on his heels and laughed, pointing at Ernesto. "You're no angel!"

Ernesto, and Grace as well, felt an enormous weight. He turned to the right and caught a glimpse of black feathers. The wings. He was wearing them.

Under their weight, he fell to the ground. Mick stood, laughing. Ernesto could feel the gigantic wings growing back there, crushing him down. He couldn't breathe. He yelled. Grace gasped, coming out of the dream.

Ernesto had awakened next to her. He was still yelling, clawing in front of him, his eyes wild.

"Ernesto," Grace said calmly. "You had a nightmare."

Recognition flooded across his face. "Maldito," he cursed. "That was...." He ran his hand over his thinning hair, at a loss for words.

"...A real doozy," she finished for him. "You were yelling, you know." She would not let on any more than what could have been observed by anyone of the non-dreamslipping variety. But spooning Ernesto as he turned to go back to sleep, she wondered what the dream meant.

Chapter 11

While her grandmother was puzzling over Ernesto's dream that morning, Cat was trapped in a hoarder's house with a battalion of beagles underfoot.

Maysie Ray Duncan had thirty-three of her great-uncle's paintings. That is, if you could find them under the detritus accumulated over however many decades Maysie had occupied the cinderblock home. It was set down on a canal in a quiet section of Miami suburbia. The beagles, which seemed to number at least twenty, had the run of the place, and judging by the odor that hit the back of Cat's palate the minute she set foot inside, the dogs had quite possibly never been bathed.

Unable to shake the feeling that they'd missed something about that first fire at Mick's place, Cat was still investigating. Sure, maybe crazy Candace did set both fires. It was hard to argue with a confession. But Cat felt she owed it to her uncle to make sure.

She'd combed through a digital catalogue of Mick's art and decided she needed to talk to some of his regular buyers, people who made a point of collecting his paintings. One of them could have a grudge against him, she reasoned, or maybe they only wanted to destroy some of his work so the pieces they owned would go up in value.

Which is how she got to Maysie Ray Duncan, apparently one of her uncle's biggest fans.

Behind a tower of newspapers dating back to the Sixties, Cat found a piece with Mick's tell-tale signature on it—a wide M followed by a scribble followed by a cursive T followed by more scribble.

"Oh, that's *Blue Shift Number Seven*," said Maysie with delight. "One of my favorites! Number Nine must be nearby. I wanted to get Number Eight, but I was outbid. Imagine that."

Maysie wore a velvet housecoat over a long silk dress. Her arthritic feet were stuffed into velvet-trimmed slippers. Her face was made up as if she were about to do a curtain call. Her hair was wrapped in a silk scarf tied above her painted-on eyebrows, the fringe falling down over her forehead.

"When was the last time you purchased one of Mick's pieces?" Cat asked, trying not to topple a tower of washed-out dog food cans.

"Let me see… I attend so many of the gallery openings, you know," she said, as if wanting credit for her society status. "I suppose it was three or four years ago. I like to get them before they really make it big."

Cat had to hand it to her; that was some shrewd collecting. If Maysie put Mick's work out to a gallery or auction house now, she'd surely see a huge profit.

"Do you sell the work you acquire?"

"Oh, heavens, no!" Maysie shrieked, reaching out to stroke *Blue Shift Number Seven*. "They're my babies. Even more than you guys, eh, Melvin?" She picked up one of the beagles and kissed him square on the mouth. Melvin seemed unfazed by the gesture.

"So you've kept them all."

"Of course!"

Cat told Maysie about the fires in Mick's studio and beach house, and the woman broke down and wept, clutching her chest. "It's horrible, my dear! That poor man. His precious things."

Cat left Maysie's house gasping for fresh air. That had been a bust, but at least her mental picture of who collects art these days got more rounded out.

She debated going further with the next set of collectors on the list. Part of her wanted to head back to the cottage for some hermit time to research more online. She'd recently made a connection with someone at *Art in Our Time* who said she could get access to the archives, which could tell her who wrote that letter defaming Mick to his beloved professor way back when. But it would mean another trip to New York, which was costly. She and Granny Grace weren't earning any money of course on Mick's case, and while they'd had a slew of lucrative ones after Cat made her name on the Plantation Church murder, she was conscious of spending more than she earned.

But the next person on the list was someone Mick said dickered with him on the price of his paintings to the point of aggression, wearing her uncle down till he'd parted with an entire series for less than half its market price.

Jerry O'Connell was also prominent in the Catholic church there in Miami, rising to the level of deacon, which is where devout men could fuel their energy without the formality—and personal sacrifice— of the priesthood.

Cat hadn't been to church since Lee's death, not even with Granny Grace's friend Simon, who was openly gay and had introduced her to the tolerant church she favored in Seattle. Every time she thought of going, she pictured Lee lying there with blood pouring out of his head, and she became too angry at how arbitrary and senseless God could be. It didn't matter that her Catholic upbringing had taught her that "God works in mysterious ways." She didn't buy that Lee's death could constitute anything "working" in the world. To her it showed that nothing worked.

So she had two reasons to head back to the cottage instead. But then she thought about her grandmother's warning that she not get too caught up in online research to the detriment of her "boots on the ground" sleuthing, and she turned her rental car in the direction of the suburban neighborhood near Coral Gables where Jerry O'Connell lived.

His house was a peach-colored compound with a white coral-rock roof, like the houses around it. The white coral rock was popular because it deflected the intense Miami sun. She had to notify him of her arrival through an intercom at the end of his driveway, and he activated the gate to let her in. A circular drive lined with tall palm trees led to a door festooned with audacious pink blossoms, pinwheels of frangipani. The door opened before she could lift the knocker, which was shaped like a seashell.

"Good afternoon," O'Connell bellowed at her. An Izod shirt stretched tightly over the wide girth of his stomach. Cat wondered vaguely for a moment if the alligator thought he'd be eating well. Shaking her head to dispel the judgmental notion, she gripped O'Connell's outstretched hand and stepped inside.

The foyer was cool and adorned with a crucifix encrusted with seashells. It was the most beautiful crucifix she'd ever seen, and she had trouble taking her eyes off it.

"Stunning, isn't it?" O'Connell said. "It was made by one of the boat people you don't hear about. Not from Cuba. This one was Bahamian. We send them back, you know."

"Like Elián?" Cat asked, as Elián González had yet to fade from the Miami memory. The boy who was sent back to his father in Cuba after landing ashore in Florida had practically sparked a revolution.

"No," O'Connell said, a bit more sternly than Cat felt was warranted. His voice put her on edge. "Not like Elián. This Bahamian artist? Dominic St. Claire is his name. His type lands in Miami pretty regularly, and without the fanfare of an Elián. Unlike Cubans, Bahamians can't claim political asylum here. So they get sent back, if they're caught. And they're usually caught."

"How did you come by this piece?"

"It's not a 'piece,'" he corrected. "It's a holy crucifix. And I bought it from him at a church sale, when he was staying with my parish. We tried to help him stay, but we failed. Economic hardship in your home country is not sufficient reason to be granted asylum, as it were."

"I'm sorry."

"You should be," said O'Connell. "We should all be." He turned on his heel and walked down a hallway toward a sitting room that was lit with sun streaming in through floor-to-ceiling windows, not to mention what flooded in from above through skylights.

"Here are some of Travers's paintings," he said, gesturing toward a far wall. "I have the whole series, but they wouldn't fit in this room. That would be too overwhelming anyway, so they're spread throughout the house. Let me know if you want to see them all."

At that, he sat down in an armchair, opened a box on a table next to him, and brought out a pipe. Cat watched as he filled it with tobacco, lit it, and began to puff.

"Well?" he asked. "What are you looking at me for? Didn't you come to see the art?"

Cat felt flustered. "I was hoping to talk with you," she said. "I-I'm interested in who acquires Mick—I mean Mr. Travers's art."

"Whatever for? I thought whoever set fire to his studio had been caught."

"She has. I mean, yes. But there are some lingering questions."

"Well, if I'd known that, I probably wouldn't have agreed to this," he said. "You're here, aren't you? So, ask."

She cleared her throat. "Mr. Travers says you badgered him pretty relentlessly in order to acquire the Seaweed Series at such a bargain."

"That's one way of looking at it," he said. "Are you going to stand there while we talk, Miss, or are you going to have a seat?" He gestured toward a chair.

Cat sat, burning with irritation. "And what"—she crossed her legs and set him with a hard look—"exactly is the other way of looking at it?"

"Art's priced too damn high. So I talked Travers down to something more reasonable."

"Did you do the same to Dominic St. Claire?"

O'Connell chuckled. "No. I did the opposite. He'd priced the crucifix at twenty-seven dollars. A measly twenty-seven dollars! I gave him a hundred for it."

"So you're like the Robin Hood of art."

He didn't respond to that one. Cat pressed further: "Mr. Travers isn't super rich, you know. His house isn't even as nice as ... well, yours."

O'Connell softened a little. "Oh, come on. He's not a showy artist, I'll grant you that, but he's not hurting, either."

"Would you say you resent artists like Mick Travers?"

"I suppose."

"They make you sick?"

"In a manner of speaking."

"Why collect their art?"

"I like the challenge of not playing the game with them, of talking them down in person. We remove the façade of the art world, the gallery, and the list price, and it's just me, standing there with a checkbook, saying I'll buy their art, but for my price. Besides, I like looking at the art once I get it home."

Cat listened to what he was saying, but she heard an entirely different truth underneath his words. She leaned forward. "Doesn't it make you feel proud of yourself?"

"No. When it's in my home, it's art for art's sake." He grinned at her and puffed on his pipe a few times for emphasis.

"I don't think so," Cat said. "I think the art is always something else for you. You can't look at St. Claire's crucifix without feeling your righteousness."

O'Connell didn't respond at first, and then he tapped out his pipe on the side table. "I think we're done here."

He led her back through the entry way, past the St. Claire crucifix, which made Cat think of something. She paused before he shut the door behind her and said, "A real Robin Hood would have given St. Claire a lot more than a measly hundred bucks for that crucifix. You got a deal and declared it charity."

Cat marked Maysie Ray as "not a suspect" but put a question mark next to Jerry O'Connell. At that, she called it a day. The wake was planned for that evening, and some of the people on her list would be in attendance, giving her an opportunity to talk with them unofficially, when their guard would be down and she wouldn't have to cajole them into an interview.

———

Donnie's parents pitched in with the setup at the gallery, much to the surprise of the gallery owner, Bryson Hughes, who had been the first in Miami to feature Donnie's work. Helping out seemed to make them both feel like they were part of something connected to their son, Cat observed. They kept a polite distance from Rose, however, and Cat wondered if they were uncomfortable with her being transgendered. Rose's outfit for the evening had a Morticia Addams look to it, though the campiness was toned down a bit. She was hanging back, looking left out, so Cat asked her to help set up the hors d'oeuvres. They prepared a fruit, wine, and cheese spread, as the celebration was to resemble an art opening, except for the part of the program that would be a more personal tribute to Donnie Hines.

Cat noticed that Rose kept checking her cell phone, but Cat couldn't tell if she was looking for the time or for a message. After the third check, Cat touched Rose on the arm and asked, "Nervous?"

"Irritated," Rose said. "Roy Roy was supposed to be here, but he's not. And I haven't heard from him, either. I can't believe that gangsta would stand me up today."

"Maybe he's just running late," Cat said, but Rose did not look reassured.

As the guests came in, Cat mingled, making note of who was there. Old Maysie Ray arrived with one of her beagles decked out in a harness identifying him as a service animal. "I need him for my nerves," she explained to Cat. After a delighted examination of the art on display, Maysie sauntered over to the food table, where she wrapped up sizable portions in napkins and stowed them away in her voluminous handbag. Cat noted that Maysie put herself down for two of Donnie's works. Bryson was generously donating the proceeds from the sale of Donnie's art to the Everglades Foundation.

Cat recognized in the crowd the electric-razor performance artist she and Granny Grace had interviewed soon after the studio fire. There was also Kazuo Noshihara, the pocket-lint artist, who must have flown back from Japan for the occasion. He and Granny Grace bowed to each other and launched into a deep conversation.

"When I die," Noshihara said, "I wish to have everyone gather in a gallery in which the art has been removed from the walls."

"Kazuo," Granny Grace beamed. "That's very Buddhist of you."

Cat overheard but steered clear of this conversation, and she managed to control herself from visibly rolling her eyes.

To Cat's surprise, Jerry O'Connell made an appearance, and she cringed to think that he would have the stones to dicker with the gallery owner over the cost of any of Donnie's art at a time like this. Still, she had to admit he was a suspect in her mind based mainly on his lack of personal character.

As she was sizing up O'Connell from across the room, Grace touched her arm.

"Cat," she said. "I'd like to introduce you to the Langholms, Carrie and Kristoff. They're clients of Ernesto's."

Cat shook the hands of a refined couple who seemed to exhibit the confidence and style that great wealth supplies. When Cat mentioned she was from St. Louis, Kristoff exclaimed, "I love doing business in the river city. So much brick! I believe every single thing in St. Louis built before 1960 was constructed out of that gorgeous red brick."

"Except for the bridges," Granny Grace added. "Brick wouldn't do for those."

"I stand corrected," said Kristoff, a twinkle in his eye. Then he switched gears. "How is Mick holding up?"

"Oh, he's doing quite well, considering," said Grace. "He's over there if you'd like to speak with him." She motioned to where Mick stood near Donnie's parents.

"I'll introduce you to the parents of the deceased," Cat said.

"'The deceased'?" said Kristoff. "My word, girl. You sound like a cop."

"I studied criminal just—" Cat began but then stopped herself, remembering that she didn't want anyone at the wake to know she was a private investigator.

Carrie put her hand on her husband's arm. "Now, Kristoff. You promised to be on your best behavior."

"You're right, love," he said to his wife. And then to Cat: "We own one of Don Hines's pieces. A real up-and-comer that one was. It's a shame."

"Did you know him well?"

"We talked with him often at gallery openings," Carrie said. "We like to mingle with creatives, don't we, Kristoff?"

"It gives our rather dull existence more luster," said her husband.

They reached the other side of the room, and Cat introduced the Langholms to Donnie's parents. Carrie and Kristoff graciously expressed condolences to them.

"Your son was an enormous talent," said Kristoff. "Carrie and I own a few pieces, and we're planning to purchase several more tonight."

"Yes," said Carrie. "It will help keep his memory alive."

It was the perfect thing to say to the two grieving parents. Almost too perfect.

Cat felt a tap on her shoulder and turned to find her Uncle Mick escorting a woman wearing two-inch patent leather heels under a dark Gucci suit. Her salon curls pointedly stayed put as she constantly turned her head, looking around the room as if noting who else might be in attendance.

Cat shook her French-manicured hand, and the two exchanged pleasantries, but it was clear that the woman had more important networking to do.

The woman dropped Cat and Mick as soon as she saw the Langholms, and Cat circled back around to her grandmother, whom she steered in the direction of Jerry O'Connell. She wanted her grandmother to size him up for her. Of course, she hadn't exactly told Granny Grace that she was continuing to investigate the case. But she planned to, as soon as she had gathered more information.

"It's good to see you again, Mr. O'Connell," Cat said as politely as she could muster. "May I introduce you to my grandmother, Mick Travers's sister, Amazing Grace."

He shook her grandmother's hand. "And are you as devout as the name suggests?"

"If by devout, you mean deeply committed to matters of a spiritual nature, then yes. But if by devout you mean toeing the line according to patriarchal Judeo-Christian tradition, then no."

"I see." He began to pull on his whiskers.

"My granddaughter tells me you're quite the collector."

"That I am. And you? Do you collect art, or are you merely associated with it via familial tie?"

"Oh," said Cat. "My grandmother is what you might call a long-time acquirer and appreciator of art."

He followed up, asking about her most prized pieces, and Cat took the opportunity to leave them to their conversation.

She slipped across the room to where Rose de la Crem was flirting with one of the bartenders. Once Rose had a white wine in one black crocheted-gloved hand and had turned her back to the bartender, Cat asked her if she'd heard from Roy Roy.

"Yes. A text. He's running late."

"How are you holding up? I should have asked earlier. I mean, Donnie was such a good friend."

Rose looked down at the glass in her hands. "Oh, nothing this drink won't cure, once it's multiplied by about eight more of them right after this one."

Cat didn't know what to say. She glanced over Rose's shoulder at one of Donnie's paintings. "It's lovely to see his work here."

"I know!" exclaimed Rose. "I wish Donnie himself were here to see it. That's the thing, isn't it? Most artists are more famous after they're dead. Maybe I should up and die. It's just what my career needs. Of course, my own boyfriend probably wouldn't show up for my funeral."

Cat didn't know what to say to that, and probably sensing her discomfort, Rose said, "Forgive my morbid sensibility, Kitty Cat. I'm emotional tonight."

Cat flinched at the nickname. "Kitty Cat" was what Lee used to call her.

"Did I say something else wrong? I'm so sorry. I should go stand in a corner and drink this thing."

"It's okay, really. It's just—that's what a friend used to call me."

Ernesto appeared, gave them cheek kisses, and offered the red wine in his hand to Cat. "I noticed you weren't drinking anything. Forgive my presumption, but I sensed you might need fortification."

"You're right, Ernesto," said Rose. "I'm upsetting her."

At that, Rose left them alone.

"Rose is a … troubled soul." Ernesto sipped what appeared to be brandy. "Anyone who changes his sex must be."

Cat bristled at the comment. "Well, that just isn't true, Ernesto."

He looked contrite. "Oh, I did not mean to give offense. My apologies."

His response took the edge off her feeling toward him. She did not want to argue sexual politics at the wake, especially when she was supposed to be investigating. So she segued into teasing him instead. "I should ask you, Mr. Ruíz, what exactly are your intentions with my grandmother?"

"Oh, I intend to give her memories of her trip to Miami that will eclipse this sadness and tragedy." He waved his drink at the crowd, indicating the wake.

"That's a tall order," Cat said. "But I'll note my grandmother's perfectly made bed this morning. As if she'd stayed out all night!"

"Scandalous," said Ernesto, chuckling. "And also none of your business."

"Sorry," Cat said, taking an apologetic sip of the wine he'd given her. "I couldn't resist."

"That's one of the differences between our generations, chica." Ernesto winked. "We old ones always resist such things." And then, changing topics, he said, "Will you return to Seattle soon, now that the case is solved?"

"Oh, we're not in a hurry or anything," she said. And glancing around to make sure the coast was clear, she added, "Besides, I'm not sure it is."

"Excuse me?"

Cat regretted divulging her hunch. "Oh, I'm just kidding."

"Well, if the investigation does go on, that means I am blessed with your grandmother's presence a bit longer."

Cat resisted telling him more. "I better check on my uncle," she said, excusing herself from Ernesto's company.

Mick was standing by himself in front of one of Donnie's pieces. Cat caught herself looking at the painting deeply, really understanding it in a new way. And that surprised her. Gray crystal fractals emerged from the white canvas center and radiated outward and off the edges of the canvas as if to suggest that they would never end.

As she moved closer to her uncle, she realized tears were streaming down his face. She touched his shoulder. "It's a stunning piece," she whispered.

"Yes," Mick said. "It really is."

"He painted that the night of our first date," said a voice behind Cat. She turned to find a middle-aged Goth with black lips and raccoon eyes. She looked as if she'd toned down a bit of the Goth appearance for the wake, the many holes in her ears empty of adornment.

"I was blown away by Donnie," the woman continued, stepping on clunky platform heels closer to Mick. "Such a pure soul. His art—it was like things I'd only seen when I was ... tripping."

"I remember how excited Donnie was," Mick said. Cat thought his voice sounded conciliatory. This must be Jenny Baines, she realized.

"He'd been going to that club hoping he'd run into you again. And there you were. And you liked him, too."

"I told him my Goth name at first."

Mick laughed, tears in his eyes. "Donnie came home bragging that he had a date with Dark Moon."

Jenny held out her hand to Mick. "Thanks for inviting me. I would have understood if you hadn't."

Mick took her hand, and then, motioning toward Cat, he said, "Jenny, this is my grand-niece, Cat. Cat, this is Jenny."

"Nice to meet you, Dark Moon." Cat shook her hand.

Bryson asked those gathered to sit, motioning to rows of folding chairs in the middle of the gallery. Jenny floated toward the back. Cat noticed Mick quickly dried his tears on his shirtsleeve. She reached into her purse and fetched him a tissue, which he took. They remained in the rear, standing, and Granny Grace sidled up to Cat.

"See that glamour puss in the third row?" her grandmother whispered.

"Mick introduced me," Cat whispered back, "but she had more important people to see."

"I bet she did. That's Serena Jones. She's a neighbor to the Langholms, on Star Island."

"Star Island!" It was the most exclusive island in South Florida. "Where'd she get that kind of dough?"

"You ever hear of La Luz beauty products?"

"Yes," Cat said. "They're everywhere down here."

"That's her. She's someone else you might want to talk to, by the way."

Cat did a double take in her grandmother's direction. "What?"

"As you continue to investigate."

Cat dragged her grandmother further away from the crowd. "What makes you think I'm investigating?"

"Oh, please. I wasn't born in a barn, you know. Wait, I take that back. Actually, I guess you could say I was—"

"Don't you think it's a good idea?"

"Yes. But that Jerry O'Connell—he's not the one. You don't like the sanctimonious types. But sanctimony is not a crime."

"Will you help?"

"Of course. I was waiting for you to ask. But let's not be rude. We're at a wake, after all."

Following her grandmother back to the cluster of chairs, she noticed Sergeant Luisa Alvarez, who must have just come in, sitting near the back row next to Ernesto and Rose de la Crem. Rose had saved a seat next to herself, likely hoping that Roy Roy would still make it.

"...Donnie had a vision that was informed by a love of science and nature," Bryson was saying. He showed early examples of Donnie's work on slides, and then he traced Donnie's artistic path using the paintings hanging in the gallery around them.

It was Mick's turn next, and Cat saw Granny Grace give his hand a squeeze before he walked to the front of the room. Mick told the story of how he met Donnie when the man applied to be his assistant.

"I was very lucky to have someone with his experience helping me," Mick said. "I liked him right off, but I didn't realize we'd end up becoming best friends." Mick choked up a bit, and Cat felt the urge to hug him but stayed by Granny Grace's side.

Rose spoke through tears. "I never once felt judged by Donnie," she said. "Not as an artist, and not for being ... who I really am."

Donnie's parents had not planned on speaking, but his father stood.

"Donnie and I weren't very close here in his middle age, my old age," he said. "But you have helped me know who he was, as an artist, and to feel closer to him. Thank you so much, for loving my son and for sharing your memory of him with us." He choked up, and his wife rose to take his hand.

It was at that point that Roy Roy chose to make his entrance.

The door burst open, and in walked a white man, or more accurately, Cat thought, a white *boy*, wearing a black nylon track suit with neon green high-tops and a matching hat. Trailing after him were two similarly attired young men, also white.

"Yo yo yo yo yo," said Roy Roy, presumably the ringleader. The entire room turned in his direction.

97

"What?" he said, as if he hadn't just interrupted a wake. "Why you all looking at me like that?"

Cat glanced at Rose, whose gloved hand was poised over her mouth. She looked as if she either wanted to die, or kill her boyfriend. Probably both.

Chapter 12

Mick was sitting in a high chair, and he had a sense that the pink fuzzy boots on his feet were his favorite item of clothing, and quite possibly the most beautiful things he'd ever owned. His mama was standing above him, waving a fudge pudding Popsicle in front of his face. "What a pretty baby," she cooed at him. "Now give mama a kiss, and she'll give you a treat!"

He puckered up his lips real good. He wanted that pudding pop. In came Mama's face, her cherry red lipstick bleeding into the cracks around her mouth. Mick could smell the cooking sherry on her breath. It made him worry that she was going to have one of her spells. The smell of sherry always accompanied Mama's spells.

She relinquished the cherished pudding pop, and Mick stuck the gooey lovey dove treat in his mouth, letting the fudge slip down his throat. He was in heaven. His mama loved him.

But then she turned into a pink bird like the ones in the white cage in the parlor and began flying around the room. She swooped down and took his pudding pop from him, devouring it in her beak. He began to cry.

Mama the bird cackled. He threw a rattle at her, and she flew up and then straight for his eyes. He screamed from the pain and struggled to pry the bird off his face. But he was only a baby, so everything he did felt thick and awkward. He fell down out of the high chair, and then blood dripped out of his eye. He tasted it with his tongue, his own salty blood mingling with the taste of chocolate still in his mouth.

Finally he wrested himself free of the bird and broke its neck in his hands. He could see with only one eye, but he cried again. He hadn't meant to do it.

But then the pink fuzzy boots came alive as wriggling caterpillars and were crawling up his pants legs. He jumped up and down and tried to get free of them, even stripping off his clothes. He was naked and noticed he did not have the dangling piece of boy flesh he knew should be there, and that's when Mick Travers realized he had slipped into one of Candace's dreams.

After all these years.

He woke with a start, looking for her in the room. But she wasn't there. He walked down the hallway to Cat's room, and it was empty. So was his sister's. They must still be out at that woo-woo yoga thing on the beach, he told himself, but he suddenly felt afraid. Why had he slipped into Candace's dream? It was a recurring one, a variation on a dream of hers he'd slipped into when they lived together.

It was these dreams that both made her more interesting than some of the other women with whom he'd shared a bed and also made her more dangerous. Her nightmares had always been overwhelming and weird like this and always featured her mother, whom Mick had met in person and couldn't figure for a child abuser, so why the attack dreams?

Now Mick wondered if Candace had maybe killed her own mother, like the bird in the dream. But where was she? She'd have to be nearby, but as far as he knew, she was in a jail cell downtown.

He grabbed a decorative boat paddle off the wall in the foyer and went to inspect his makeshift studio in the lanai. As he opened one of the double glass doors, he heard something fall. His heart pounding, he flipped the overhead light on and raised the boat paddle.

"Candace," he called. "If you're hiding out in here, it's time to come clean."

But there was no one in the room. He realized a paint can set precariously on the edge of an easel was what had fallen. He'd left the lid off, but, luckily, the paint was dry, so there was no mess on the floor to clean up. He was alone.

And the rest of the house was vacant as well. Mick sat down in the living room, puzzled. This had never happened to him before.

Then he got an idea. He went outside and walked the perimeter around the house, checking the cars to see if Candace could be sleeping inside one of them. But they were empty. The neighborhood was as quiet as it could be, with only distant highway noise to be heard.

He began to panic and felt himself sweating. Suddenly everything seemed topsy-turvy to him. He jogged as far as he could, peeking into every car. Nothing.

About seven blocks away from Ernesto's cottage, a cop car pulled up, and the officer inside asked him what he was doing.

"Sorry, Sir," Mick said, flustered. "I'm looking for someone. I thought she was out here."

The officer shined a flashlight in Mick's face. "You been drinking? We got a complaint from the neighbors that someone was casing the cars out here."

"Nope," Mick said. "Just looking for someone. Sorry, Officer. I thought she'd be out here."

"And who is that?"

Mick smiled, shaking his head. "My attempted killer."

"Excuse me?"

"Yeah, I'm Mick Travers. The artist someone tried to set fire to. Twice."

"Oh, I know about you, Mick. I think I saw your killer, too, when they brought her in. Is that who you thought was out here?"

Mick gave an embarrassed laugh. "I guess so."

"Oh, man. Don't worry. She's locked up tight. We'll throw the book at her, believe me."

"Sure you will," Mick said. "Sorry to cause any trouble. I'll head home now."

"Good idea," said the cop.

Mick returned to the cottage, but he couldn't shake the feeling that everything had flipped upside down on him. The fabric of reality had unraveled, and he didn't know why.

It took him a long time to go back to sleep, which was a shame, as he really needed it. He hadn't been getting much since Donnie died.

As soon as he hit the REM cycle, he realized he was dreamslipping again.

"Such a pretty girl," her mama cooed. She was sitting in front of a mirror, with her mama standing behind her, brushing her curly blonde hair. Mama's hair was tied up in curlers with a bandana over them. Mama's hair was naturally straight, while Candy's was naturally curly. She didn't need any curlers, and this made mama jealous sometimes, but she was being nice right now, brushing Candy's hair, making it fluff out around her face like a halo.

"Some day a boy will ask you to marry him," Mama said. "And you'll wear a veil trailing over your pretty hair, and you'll walk down the aisle, and he'll be there. Your husband. A man to love you forever, like your daddy loves me."

Mick couldn't stand it anymore, so he forced himself to imagine Candace in the real world, in some jail cell, and he tore himself away from her. He was so fused with Candace's consciousness, however, that this took some struggle. It was as if he could hear the ripping sound as he separated his mind from hers. But it worked. He was out.

There was nothing to do but watch as little Candace sat in the chair, her mother brushing her hair. The moment seemed frozen in time.

But then everything shifted. Now Candace was about the age she was when she lived with him, and she was wearing a wedding dress. There was a dream version of himself here, too, waiting for her at the end of the aisle. But they were in a life-sized painting, and Candace's mother was a giantess, standing there, her brush poised over Dream

Mick's head. She painted a smile on his face, and painted his hand extending toward Candace.

"No!!!" Mick yelled. "You can't trap us here."

But neither Candace nor her mother could hear him. For once he wished he'd paid more attention to his sister's advice to hone his dreamslipping skills. There wasn't much he could do now but watch the painful show.

Candace's mother spoke, but her words came out as if in slow motion, and her voice sounded deep and echoey, as if her tremendous size had altered the sound waves carrying her voice. "All ... you have to do..." she boomed, "is be pretty for him..."

"You're lying, Mama," Candace said, but she was putting lipstick on as if she still wanted to believe it. Dream Mick took the lipstick out of her hand and began to draw with it over Candace's face.

"Be pretty for me," he kept saying over and over as he painted her face with the lipstick. Mick watched his dream self, painfully aware that his characteristic painting gestures were captured well by Candace's imagination.

Things shifted again, and they were at Coral Castle, a real place in Homestead, Florida, that Mick had taken Candace to once. The story of the castle was that some quirky Latvian midget—Mick mentally corrected himself—little person, built the castle by hand out of large slabs of limestone coral rock, and locals claimed he'd used supernatural powers to achieve such a feat. It had been featured in a couple of Billy Idol music videos, which explained the sudden look of an Eighties rock video that Candace's dream had taken on. Mick shook his head, feeling judgmental that even in her dreams, Candace couldn't come up with her own original material.

She was wearing a bikini, and he recognized it as the red one she often wore down in the Keys in those days. Just the sight of Candace in that bikini used to fill him with lust. But the body in the bikini was the one Candace walked around in now, in all its middle-aged splendor, the pouchy belly, the cellulite, the sagging breasts. But in the dream, Candace carried herself with great confidence, strutting around in that bikini as if she still looked like she had in her late twenties. She was still strong, with nice, defined calf muscles, and her ass was larger, which to him was not a bad thing at all, and it was the same general shape, which he'd always admired. Her big blue eyes were the same, too, large and too expectant, like a baby bird's. Something about the way she moved began to awaken his lustful impulses...

Till he stopped himself, shaking it off. This woman wanted to kill him, after all.

Candace began to giggle. "Silly Mick," she said. "I didn't try to kill you!"

"You didn't?" he heard himself say before he realized he'd voiced his thought and it would be futile to speak.

But Candace startled, as if she'd heard him. She hid behind a rock carved into the shape of a moon. "Mick?" she asked, peeking out carefully. "Are you butting into my dreams again?"

"Candace?"

"Mick! You get out of here! You're invading my privacy!"

"Can you hear me?" He moved toward her.

"Yes. Now get out of here."

He moved closer, unsure what he was doing. "Can you see me?"

She laughed. "No, Mick. I've never seen you. But I always know you're there."

Mick woke up screaming, "Ah!" His sheets were soaking wet from apparent night sweats. Once his breathing slowed down, he got up and turned on the shower.

Standing in the cooling stream, he tried to make sense of what had just happened.

But he could not.

Chapter 13

Grace firmly believed that you couldn't stay too much in your head on any investigation. Besides the need for "boots on the ground" work to interview witnesses and suspects, she also knew that the best ideas came to an investigator when she wasn't actively working on the case.

That's why she insisted Cat accompany her to a class called "Midnight Moonlight Yoga."

Of course, it took some convincing. Cat wanted to stay home with her face glued to that laptop of hers, as if it held the answers. But Grace had persevered, which is why the two of them were standing in mountain pose on the beach beneath the full moon and open stars.

Yoga on the beach was an unparalleled experience, in Grace's opinion. One didn't need a mat—simply slide your hands and feet into the soft sand and root yourself that way. Out there, part of the elements, a yogi could feel her connection to nature without the barrier of buildings and concrete. Grace breathed in the salty air, detecting hints of spice on the trade-wind breeze. What a wonderful place Florida was, she thought, that you could practice yoga on the beach in winter.

Their teacher, Spiritfire, was a master yogi who had traveled through the earth's chakras, from points in India to South America and beyond. It had never occurred to Grace that one could travel through the earth's energy centers. She made a mental note to do so before she died.

Spiritfire led them in a series of what he called "moon salutations," a variation on the poses usually done in honor of the sun. Grace enjoyed the movement as her stiff joints became lubricated. She was aware of Cat next to her, being a good sport and giving the movement her full attention. It had been a while since the two of them had done yoga together. Grace always felt a preternatural connection with her yoga partner, even if the two of them had their own solitary practices.

Grace breathed ujaiyi breath, synchronizing her breath and movement, and as she did so, she heard Cat's breath slow and ground itself the same way. *Good*, thought Grace. But then she took her attention off Cat and centered on her own heart chakra, as that was what she needed to do to get to the core of this case. There was so much swirling, intense emotion in it: Donnie's horrifying death ... Candace's dramatic break ... Mick's paintings ... the envy of those artists who hadn't made it as he had ... whatever cord pulled taut between Candace and Mick...

And there Grace sensed the cord between those two being pulled even tighter, as if in a game of tug o' war. She felt an assurance within that Candace hadn't set that first fire. But then who did?

As she moved to Spiritfire's lovely, liquid voice, she searched the energy in Miami, under the intense full moon, for something. They transitioned to a back-bending series, and Grace prepared for the heart-opener that was camel pose by squeezing her inner thighs, lower abs, and glutes. Then she arced backward, working to keep her core strong and supportive while bending her spine backward, reaching to the moon with her heart.

And there, holding that pose, it was as if an energy whispered to her. She closed her eyes to hear it better, tuning it in. The energy was dark and red, vibrating to some frequency that wasn't positive. She thought she heard the sound of large wings beating. Her eyes flew open. Breathing hard, losing her ujaiyi breath, she carefully extracted herself from the pose and took a resting pose on her knees, her hands in her lap. The place where her heart chakra should be ached.

Spiritfire came over to her and whispered, "Are you okay?"

She nodded. "I need a minute."

"Ustrasana, camel pose, can reveal so much," he said. "And it's not always pleasant."

She nodded again, rubbing the space that ached. It was an emotional ache, not a physical one. And it had to do with whoever set that first fire. The energy there was intensely negative, not accidental.

As she came back to her breath and to the class there on the beach, she decided that Cat should take that trip to New York to pore through the *Art in Our Time* archives, and soon.

After class, Cat's eyes seemed shinier, the worry lines in her forehead relaxed. "That was incredible," she said, brushing sand off her yoga pants. "I'm glad you got me to go."

"You're welcome," said Grace, but she must have looked uncharacteristically worried herself, as Cat asked, "What's wrong? Did something happen during that camel pose? You seemed bothered by it."

Grace could still feel the remnants of the ache. "There's something really nasty at the bottom of this case." She let out a sigh. "I think you should go to New York. Find out who wrote that letter."

Cat agreed, but they spent some time discussing finances. Grace preferred to trust that the money would come, but Cat was much more conservative, owing to her own mother's influence. Grace was secretly proud that her daughter, Mercy McCormick, had raised Cat so well. But sometimes Mercy's conservative streak could be an obstacle.

The matter of money was still being quietly debated when they arrived at the cottage to find Mick still up, which was not itself surprising since he kept irregular hours. But he was sitting in the living room with a disturbed look.

"What's the matter?" Grace sat next to him.

"Everything." Mick ran a hand through his hair. "Cat, what was that you were telling me about dreamslipping with Lee, over thousands of miles?"

Cat washed out her water bottle in the kitchen and set it on the drying rack. "Yeah, his PTSD dreams," she said to Mick, a shadow crossing over her face. "I was in Illinois, at the Plantation Church, and he was on the East Coast."

"Oh, God," Mick said, burying his face in his hands.

Grace tugged on his shoulder. "Mickey, tell us what's going on. Did you dreamslip while we were out?"

"Yes," he said, shaking his head. "Into one of Candace's dreams. A recurring nightmare, like the ones she had years ago, when we lived together. Damn, I thought she was here. Then I thought maybe she was outside. But she's not. She's locked up in jail, downtown."

Grace was excited by this. She stood up and began pacing. "Extraordinary!"

Cat sat next to Mick. She patted his back. "I know how freaked out you must be."

"Freaked out doesn't even begin to describe it."

Grace saw a pattern of dots like constellations in the air in the room, and she traced them. She spun on her heel as she realized what they meant.

"I think maybe our dreamslipping grows stronger when the three of us are together."

"But we were out on South Beach," countered Cat.

"Yes, but we've been here together, dreamslipping in each other's dreams and engaging in energetic activities," she said, waving her arms at the two of them. "I think we kick up each other's powers a notch."

"Okay," said Mick. "But why Candace?"

Grace smiled, walking over to Mick. She placed her hands, the bangles on her wrists jangling, on his knees and leaned her face into his. "Because you once loved her. And maybe still do."

"Who am I, Patty Hearst? That woman tried to kill me."

"No, she didn't," said Grace.

Mick looked at Cat in a way that signaled he hoped she'd come to his defense, but she didn't.

"She destroyed your beach house, Uncle Mick, but we don't think she set the first fire."

"Have you two lost your minds?" Mick said, his hands clenched into fists.

"Think about it," Grace said. "Cat has had long-distance slips twice: The first being Lee, whom she loved, and the second was a girl named Wendy, whom she also loved and felt a good deal of guilt for betraying."

"What does that have to do with me and Candace?"

"Mickey, she's the only woman you ever lived with. The two of you had a relationship for several years—tumultuous, admittedly, but an on-again, off-again thing means there's a lot of passion at stake. You want to tell me that was just sex? You seem to have been able to get that anywhere."

Mick was silent for a while. "Fine. I loved her. But not anymore. I can barely stand that woman."

"There's a thin line between love and hate," Grace said, but Mick did not respond.

"But she didn't kill Donnie," Grace added.

"Yeah, that's what Candace said in the dream."

"Whoa, what?" Cat asked. "She declared her innocence in the dream?"

"Yep."

Grace began to pace again. "Interesting! Candace's consciousness might be struggling against the psychic break. Maybe she's telling the truth in the dream. We might get her to tell the truth in real life."

"But not too soon," said Cat. "We want the real killer to think she's taking the rap."

They agreed.

"There's one more thing," Mick said. "Candace seems to know I'm in her dreams."

Grace couldn't believe her ears. "How do you know?"

"She said she could hear me, but not see me. She said something about always knowing I was there."

Grace looked at Cat to see if she could back up what Mick had said from her own long-distance experiences. Cat nodded. "I was able to communicate with Lee in his. I was able to sort of get him to let go."

Grace had never been prouder of her granddaughter than in that moment, though she understood now the depth of her granddaughter's loss. He was the sole person in the world besides her family members who knew about her dreamslipping, and now he was dead.

"Cat, you've been the most amazing apprentice," Grace told her granddaughter, feeling her own eyes tear up. "The pupil surpasses the teacher."

Cat hugged her in return.

Grace also felt a surge of hope about Mick. He'd only used his dreamslipping as another tool in his artist's toolbox, but here he was helping them solve the crime despite himself. It showed true progress, spiritually speaking.

Mick cleared his throat. "Hey, ah, listen. Here's another thing. I heard you talking about a trip to New York when you came in, and I know it's expensive to be running around working on what's basically my case, but without pay."

Grace demurred. "Oh, but Ernesto is letting us stay here."

"He's been very generous," Mick said. "But I have not."

"You've been in shock," said Cat.

"Please," he said, looking at his grandniece. "Don't make excuses for me. I'm done with Ernesto's charity, for one. I'm going to find a new studio and live there."

He stood up and took Grace's hand. "Secondly, you're both on my payroll, starting now. I want to find the bastard who killed Donnie. If it's not Candace, then let's find out who it is."

Grace tried to protest, but Mick held up his hand. "Don't even try. I received an insurance settlement for the first fire, and there will be more to come with the second. So don't worry about ol' Mick."

Chapter 14

The offices of *Art in Our Time* were near Times Square, which blinded Cat with its audacious display of flashing advertising. She swirled around, taking it in, excited to be in New York for a second time, and so soon, and this time without Granny Grace as chaperone.

Jacob Reiner, the assistant editor who'd scored her access to the back archive, greeted her at the front desk. Cat had to walk around the lobby sculpture, which depicted Michael Jackson with a monkey on his lap. It was constructed out of white porcelain, with gold trim, like the angel statuettes her Grandmother McCormick kept in a locked china hutch, but this was life-sized.

Noticing the expression on her face, Reiner said, "You've never seen that before, have you?"

"No," said Cat. "But I wish I could un-see it now."

Reiner nearly choked on his laugh. "That's a Jeff Koons!"

"Great," said Cat.

"You have no idea what that means?" he said, incredulous.

"Should I?"

Jacob smoothed down his turquoise tie. "Some people would say, yes. But I guess I find that refreshing. Most people try to sound impressive in the presence of that piece."

He led her to his office, which was only half an office that he shared with a woman who looked to be about twelve wearing a suit made out of see-through plastic. Thank God she was wearing a slip under that suit, Cat thought. She could hear the plastic squeak as the woman pecked at her sleek silver laptop.

Jacob angled his head in the woman's direction. "That's our intern, Jacinta."

Cat sat down in a chair next to his desk.

"So," he said, "How is it that the grand-niece of one of our most acclaimed artists can't identify a Jeff Koons when she sees one?" His voice had taken on a vaguely flirtatious quality.

"I think you just answered your own question," Cat said, laughing. "I'm his grand-niece. Do you even know who your great-uncle is?"

Jacob smiled. "I do, but he's dead. Actually, I had two. Both dead."

"Did you know them?"

"Not really," Jacob admitted. "Family reunions, that sort of thing."

"Well, mine's always lived in Miami. We visited him once, but he and my mother aren't close. He's not very close with anyone in the family, actually... But my grandmother loves him dearly." Cat stopped, aware that she was for some reason telling her family history to a stranger. "Anyway, where's the archive? I don't have a lot of time, and judging by what you said on the phone, it's probably going to be a chore to find what I'm looking for."

"Right," said Jacob. "Which is a letter to the editor submitted to the magazine back in the Seventies."

Cat opened her bag and took out a photocopy of the microfilm version of the letter in the magazine, which she'd found in the Miami Public Library. "This letter, to be exact," she said. "I was very encouraged when you said they kept such good paper records back then, that you might have the original."

"Yes," said Jacob. "But you're right about what a chore this will be. And the archives aren't here. They're in a warehouse in New Jersey."

Cat felt peeved about wasting more time. "How do I get there?"

"I'll have to drive you."

"You have a car here in the city?" Cat knew enough about New York to know how expensive that would be.

Jacob snorted. "Not on an assistant editor's salary," he said. "But I've got the company car." With that, he opened his desk drawer and grabbed a set of keys.

It was ten a.m. when they exited the parking garage, and Cat had a sense that the traffic was light for New York. She wondered what it would be like to live in such a big city, with so little green space. At least in Seattle you didn't have to go far to feel like you were in nature again.

Jacob was a steady driver, and she enjoyed the look of his side profile. He had a large, prominent nose, and she found those to be sexy on the right guys. Jacob was the right kind of guy for it, with his olive complexion, brown eyes, and black hair. They'd hit it off easily on the phone, and he seemed to find either her or her case intriguing. She reasoned it might be a bit of both and wondered if he'd done his homework on her. She'd certainly done her online research on him. He was from a Jewish family but didn't eat kosher. He'd graduated magna cum laude from The New School for Social Research. His thesis had been on the impact of graffiti art on schoolchildren's early art consciousness.

"So what's it like, hanging out in Miami with the art celebs?" he asked.

Cat shrugged. "Probably not too different from hanging out in New York with the art celebs. I mean, isn't that what you do at the magazine?"

"When they don't keep me chained to my desk," he said. "It's not exactly a nine- to-five job. I get to attend an industry function maybe every other month, if I'm lucky."

The traffic through the Jersey Turnpike slowed to a crawl, but soon they were free. Cat recognized some of the landmarks from the drive she and Granny Grace took with Clive, that artist who went to graduate school with Mick, the one who in Cat's opinion had a legitimate bone to pick with the art establishment for its racism.

"Do you know the artist Clive Smith?" she asked.

"It sounds familiar, but I'm not sure."

"African American," she said. "Mixed media. I'm not good at describing these kinds of things, but his work is kind of ... sculptural? Like a lot of Mick's, the paint builds up like it's caked on."

"The process painter? Kind of mid-list, I think."

"Mid-list?"

"More of a publishing term. You know, not quite there, but not undiscovered, either."

"Yeah," said Cat. "That's him. What do you mean by process?"

"Oh, he's kind of into chance operations." When this elicited no recognition from Cat, he further explained. "He sets up a pattern in his painting and then lets the process break down organically."

Cat thought about the paintings she saw in his house, which at the time had looked like nothing so much as a field of raised dots on blue. Now she remembered the dots weren't uniform but rather like cupcakes that had been poured by hand, each one coming out different. There were splatters of paint in between. She told this to Jacob, who smiled. "You got it, sister."

Clive wasn't really a suspect in Cat's book, but there was nothing to rule him out other than his own insistence. She thought Clive's beef about the art world was a lot more personal than he had let on, and she had a feeling Mick was included in that.

They drove into the parking lot of an aluminum-clad warehouse building surrounded by a barbed-wire fence. "Have you been here before?" Cat asked Jacob, and he nodded.

"Just once. I was looking for the original art for a vintage ad we ran in the Sixties."

He took out another set of keys and slid one into a rusty lock. "Behold," he said. "You're about to be transported to a bygone era."

Dust motes swirled in the shafts of sunlight let in by clerestory windows. Jacob threw a series of light switches on the wall, flooding the warehouse with light.

"All right," he said. "We're looking at these dates on the end caps." He pointed to a yellowed index card taped to the side of one of the metal bookshelves. This one said, 1922-3, AD COPY, so they walked down to another section. It took them about fifteen minutes of tracing around, as the rows weren't always sequential, before Cat spotted it. "Here it is. 1973-5, LETTERS TO THE EDITOR."

They spent a good hour digging through the boxes of letters, Cat surprised by how many there were, but Jacob not so much. "You should see my email inbox," he groaned.

The letters were an interesting lot, she had to admit, and the most interesting ones were the ones that had never been printed. They bore huge red Rejected stamps. There was one from a housewife in Mobile, Alabama, that requested the magazine "stop printing those lascivious nudes." The writer went on to catalogue every nude appearing in the magazine for the past three years, each page noted, and the nude described in almost lurid detail. Cat read it aloud to Jacob, the two of them roaring with laughter.

Soon Cat's stomach was grumbling, and they hadn't yet found the letter Cat was looking for. "Let me take you to lunch," Jacob offered. "Some of these strip malls out here hide amazing mom-and-pop restaurants."

He took her to a place called Star of India that had a buffet. Cat was no food critic, admittedly, but she'd never had Indian food this good before. The place seemed to be run by a family, the mother in a beautiful orange sari working the cash register, and her daughters waiting tables. Cat could see an older gentleman in the kitchen banging well-seasoned pots around.

As Cat dug into a helping of curried chickpeas, she asked Jacob, "So are you a frustrated artist? I mean, is that what you *really* wanted to do?"

Jacob again nearly choked on his laughter, and this time on his food as well. "You're so to-the-point," he said, but his face was glowing, and it seemed to come out as a compliment.

"I didn't mean for it to sound like you shouldn't want to do what you're doing."

"To answer your question," he said, wiping his face with a napkin, "no." He elaborated: "My parents always subscribed to *Art in Our Time*. I grew up reading it. But that wasn't the only magazine. We had the *Atlantic*, too, and *Harper's*. But it was art I loved to read about most."

"And you never wanted to make any of it?"

Jacob laughed. "I never progressed beyond stick figures. No. Talent. Whatsoever."

Cat smiled. Jacob's honesty, not to mention his rare lack of ego, made her like him even more. He paid the bill and told her not to worry, he'd get reimbursed for it, and then they headed back to the warehouse.

About fifteen minutes into their search, Jacob cried, "Eureka!" He produced a postmarked envelope and the letter he'd retrieved from inside it.

Cat took it delicately, examining every square inch. Emblazoned with the words ACCEPTED in bold blue all caps, the letter was on watermarked bond typing paper, and it had been typed on an electric typewriter. She could tell that by the level lettering and the faint smudge left by the ribbon along the edges. It was signed *Mick in Miami*, but it wasn't her uncle's handwriting, of course. There could still be fingerprints on the letter, she thought, especially since it had been so well preserved in the archives. The paper hadn't even yellowed. And perhaps she could have someone analyze the handwriting. But she needed more.

She turned over the envelope, and a clue jumped out at her: the postmark. The cancellation read *Apr. 29, 1974*, and around the circle instead of Miami it said, *Ft. Lauderdale, FLA.*

Cat immediately thought of Chester Canon, who'd had his house in Fort Lauderdale back then as a summer home. After retirement, he'd given up his New York apartment and moved there permanently. April twenty-ninth was probably Columbia University's spring break. That's when he sent the letter, Cat realized. No other suspects had ever lived in Fort Lauderdale. The postmark should be New York, Miami, or even Sanibel. Chester would have had no reason to conceal the letter's origin to that extent. It merely needed to sound authentic enough to publish.

"Why do you think this was published?" Cat asked Jacob.

"Oh, art MFA programs are always political. You know, people say academia kills art. I'm sure the editor back then snapped this up. People love gossip, and here, disguised as a confession from an art student? That's gold."

Cat was ready to head back, but first she had a hunch about something she wanted to follow up on. It would require a detour, and taking Jacob into her confidence more than she would normally. She looked into his big, brown, trusting eyes and decided to risk it.

"How'd you like to meet Clive Smith?"

"Uh ... sure."

Cat still had Clive Smith's address in her phone. She gave Jacob directions, and they were at Clive's front door twenty minutes later. The artist himself answered the door, the look of surprise on his face soon replaced by suspicion.

"I'm sorry to bother you, Mr. Smith," Cat said, putting some heft into her voice, "but there's been a new development in Mick Travers's case, and I need to ask you a few more questions."

"I thought they caught the killer," he said. "I read it in the art news."

"They did," she said, partly to put him at ease and partly to keep the facts a secret. "But there's been a new development I'd like to discuss with you."

"And who are you?" he asked, looking pointedly at Jacob.

"I'm an editor at *Art in Our Time*," Jacob said, holding out his hand. "And I'm a big fan of your work."

Clive's face softened at that, and he opened the door to them. "Very well," he said. "Come on in."

Once they were seated in the living room, Cat began. "Mr. Smith, I want to ask you about that letter again, the one in the magazine."

Clive looked at Jacob. "Is that why you're here?"

Jacob gave him a nodding shrug.

"What about it?" Clive asked.

"We've found the original, in the magazine's archives," she said. "I know you didn't write it."

"Fantastic detective work," Clive said sarcastically. "Now you best be going."

"There's just one thing," Cat said. "I know nearly without a doubt who wrote the letter. But it contains details about the curriculum in that professor's class that the author wouldn't have known. You were in that class, though. You would have known."

"But you said I didn't write the letter."

"Yes, but you gave information to the person who did."

Clive was quiet. He sighed heavily, looking out the window at the backyard, where a robin pecked at a worm. "I swear. Mick Travers is not worth this."

"You know something," Cat said, her voice gentler. "Tell me."

"All right," he said. "Listen, I'm not a drinking man normally, but I could use one right now. You two want a glass of whiskey?"

Cat looked at Jacob, who shrugged in a gesture of "Why not?"

"Okay," she said.

Clive disappeared into the kitchen and came back out with three tumblers of whiskey on a tray. He gave Cat hers first, then Jacob, and then he sat down with his between both hands, as if it had the ability to warm him.

"One night we were at this pub near campus. Everyone except Mick. Annie Lin, Norris, a bunch of first-years, too, but they didn't really know what was going on."

Clive took a pull on his whiskey, closed his eyes briefly, and then went on.

"We were pretty drunk, and as usual, the subject of Mick came up. Chester Canon was there, and he seemed to enjoy the way we raked Mick over the coals for this or that. He fanned the flames, totally breaking out of his professorial demeanor, telling us what a phony Mick was, what a hack."

Clive set his drink down. "In retrospect, I wish I'd left at that point. It wasn't healthy, what we were doing. We were jealous of Mick, so we egged ol' Canon on, taking glory in having our anger at Mick validated. Then at one point, Canon got onto the subject of how Mick had been championed by Professor Altair. He thought Mick was all that and a bag of chips, you know what I'm saying? And Canon couldn't stand having Altair best him on that Emerging Artist Award. So he cooked up this scheme to make it look like Mick had betrayed Altair, in public."

"And you went along," Cat said, "giving him details to put in the letter."

"Yes, we did," Clive said. "Canon's the one who typed it up and sent it, though. I never thought he'd actually do it, till I saw the letter in print."

"And how'd that make you feel?" Cat asked.

"I'm not proud of this," Clive said. "And I've worked hard to successfully distance myself from it. But I have to admit, I took some pleasure in it at the time."

Cat felt ashamed for the man, but sad for him, too.

"So if you've got the killer," Clive said, "there's no connection between the letter and the fire after all."

"That would be the logical conclusion," Cat said.

"But you know Canon sent it anyway, don't you," he said.

"Yes."

As they rose to go, Jacob commented on the paintings on Clive's wall, the ones Cat had thought of earlier during their drive.

"I think your work is some of the finest example of process painting," Jacob said.

"Why, thank you, son," Clive said.

"But these are from the Eighties, aren't they? It looks like you're still active." Jacob gestured toward paint visible on Clive's hands. "I'd love to see what you're working on."

Clive's drawn face broke into a genuine grin. "Oh, I'm dabbling in my old age here, but I'll show you."

They followed Clive down a narrow hallway to a room that opened up to double ceiling height, with skylights added for natural light. Cat realized it was the garage, converted into a studio.

On a bank of easels were paintings that looked no different from the ones they'd seen in the living room. Cat was amazed at how well Jacob hid his disappointment, though. He asked Clive questions about the way he layered and how often between layers. Then as they turned to leave, Jacob stopped, Cat nearly bumping into him.

"Oh, my God," he said, walking over to a grouping of strange sculptures along one side wall. "Are these new?"

Clive came over, sounding apologetic. "Oh, those are for my grand-baby, Ru. She loves them."

"They're astounding!"

Cat watched as Jacob examined the sculptures, which to Cat looked like what you'd get if you crossed an old-school Fifties-era wooden child's toy with an African statue. One had red spikes coming out of its head, but when Jacob touched them, they were soft, likely made of silicone.

"That's so Ru doesn't hurt herself," Clive said. He seemed actually bashful about these pieces. Cat was amazed at the change in his attitude.

"They really are great," Jacob said. "Do you mind if I take a few pictures?" He took his phone out. "We have this blog... These would be great on there."

Clive looked flabbergasted. "Okay," he said, as if he were still thinking it over, or maybe he couldn't believe his sudden good fortune. "Sure."

Chapter 15

C andace was wearing an orange prison jumpsuit, and her gray roots were showing. Mick felt an unexpected pang of sympathy for her as she shuffled over to the table where he was sitting. A guard hovered nearby.

"I'm sorry," he said, which is how Pris told him to start the conversation. Back in their cottage kitchen, he'd protested, saying he had nothing to be sorry for, but then Pris told him he should say it anyway, that it would take the wind out of Candace's sails and improve his chances of getting some answers from her.

"What are you sorry for?" Candace scoffed. "I'm the one who set the fires."

That hadn't seemed to work, so Mick shifted to his sister's second suggested concession. "I forgive you," Mick said, though he followed it with an involuntary cough. It was hard for him to say these things to Candace. Even if she didn't set the first fire, she'd still destroyed his home. And his burning anger toward her felt like it would never run out of fuel.

Candace glared at him incredulously, her arms crossed in front of her chest. "Did you get religion or something? Shit, that would be the day, wouldn't it?" She roared with laughter.

"Candace," Mick said, reaching across the table to try to hold her hand. He noticed her nails had been bitten to the quick.

"Don't touch me!" she screamed.

The guard tensed, stepped forward.

Mick motioned to him to stay back. "I'm fine, really."

"Why are you here?" she demanded.

"I-I wanted to see you," Mick said. "It's been so long, and…" his words failed him. It was times like these he wished he could paint a picture to illustrate the feeling.

"Aw, did Mickey miss me?" she taunted. "You want a lick of your Candy?"

He winced. The phrase came out of their lovemaking play so many years ago.

This script of Pris's he was following wasn't getting him anywhere, so he dropped it, clearing his throat and starting over the way he should have when she'd sat down.

"Candace, look. I know you didn't kill Donnie, so quit being a damn martyr."

Her eyes went wide, and she began to shake her head. "No, no, no, no, no! You don't get to say what the truth is. I do."

"You're acting like a crazy woman, C. And this isn't you. Come on. You're better than this."

She fixed him with a look that seemed perfectly lucid. "My lawyer says I'll be charged with first-degree arson for your precious beach house, Mick. Even though you weren't even living there! And since you're so beloved by the art world, I'll probably get the max, which is thirty years. I'm fifty-seven, so that means I'm locked up till I'm practically dead anyway. Might as well 'fess up to both crimes. It'll make me famous."

"You stupid, vain, competitive woman," Mick spat out. "You know Florida carries the death penalty, right?"

She stared at him, blinking.

"That's right, the electric chair. You killed an upstanding man in the prime of his life because you're jealous of the man you were really trying to kill. They'll think you're a monster. And you set fire to a building that a whole bunch of other artists lived in, too." Mick laid it on as thick as he could, even though he was pretty sure even Florida, as enamored as it seemed to be with frying folks, wouldn't seek the death penalty in her case. But he needed her to think so. "You know my studio was right next to a school, and they were having parent-teacher night? Oh, they'll fry you, honey, like a piece of candied bacon. This is Florida, remember? They'll take a lady killer and strap her into Old Sparky toot-sweet."

She continued to stare at him as if realizing she was a kid playing a grown-up game.

"You don't want to die for this, C. Besides, if you go down for the crime, we never catch the real killer."

She kept staring and began to bite one of her fingernails.

Mick let out a heavy, emotion-laden breath. "You would have liked Donnie. Remember how you and I used to watch brown pelicans, diving into the waves? Imagine if you painted the arcing motions of their flights. Yeah, that's Donnie. A real talent."

"Not like me," she finally said. Her voice was dull.

"Is that what this is about? You feeling sorry for yourself because you haven't made it big? Well, neither had Donnie. He was my assistant."

"I know that."

"And you've got an eye, Candace. I never told you that, but I should have. You just needed to get out of your own way."

"Oh, what do you know about it? You hardly even looked at my work." She uncrossed her arms and leaned forward, staring at him with those big blue eyes he used to wish he could get lost in.

"My sister bought one of your pieces. It's hanging in the place where I'm staying."

"Your sister's too loyal to you."

"That's probably true. But that's not why she bought your piece. She liked it. She had a feeling about it."

"You just feel sorry for me."

"Right now, Candace, you're right that I feel sorry for you. But that's not it. I don't want you to waste any more time than you have."

Candace's eyes started to fill with tears, but Mick could see her resisting the emotion.

"What if I didn't set the first fire?" she said in a very quiet voice, and staring across the room, avoiding Mick's gaze.

"Then we'll figure out who did," he said. "And we'll see if we can get them to go easy on you about the beach house."

Candace met his gaze, and the tears slipped down her cheeks. "I never thought this would be my life, Mick. Alone, you know..." She stopped, choking up.

He reached for her hand, and this time, she didn't pull away.

"I know," he said. "I know."

She wiped her tears on the sleeve of her orange jumpsuit. "I'm not like you. Making art wasn't the only thing I ever wanted."

"You wanted me to make a home with you," Mick said. "But I'm no good for that. I'm so sorry."

"It's okay," Candace said, removing her hand from his. Her voice was so quiet, it was almost a whisper. "I know I was never as good as you."

He didn't know what to say, and her words made his eyes fill with water.

"I think I need some help," Candace said, biting her nail again. "This is all ... too much for me."

"Maybe we can get your sentence reduced," he said. "I mean, you weren't trying to kill anyone."

"Yeah," she said. She looked resigned.

He sat there for a moment longer, but there was nothing left to say. Soon, the guard said "Time," and Mick got up to leave.

"One last thing," Candace said, her voice going hard again. "I'd appreciate it if you'd stay the hell out of my dreams."

The guard gave Mick a knowing look, as if to convey his sympathy for her apparent derangement. Little did he know, thought Mick.

—

121

He returned to Ernesto's cottage after that hoping to hear from his real estate agent about touring live-work lofts. He was eager to get out from under his sister's friend's charity and start painting for real again.

But when he stepped in the door, Pris and Cat were embroiled in an intense conversation about Cat's findings in New York. He overheard the mention of Chester Canon's name.

"Don't tell me Chester the Molester is your primary suspect now," he said.

His sister and Cat greeted him with hugs, ignoring his comment.

"How'd it go with Candace?" His sister had an expectant, hopeful look.

"She recanted," he said.

His sister clapped her hands together. "Good work! Do you believe us now?"

Mick shrugged. "Deep down, sister, I guess I always knew Candace didn't kill Donnie. Now what's this about Chester?"

Cat stepped in and explained what she'd learned in New York.

Mick felt incensed, but this time he resisted the urge to hop in his Fiat and tear up the highway to Fort Lauderdale. "You think this leads him to the murder?"

"It certainly points to an above-average obsession with you," Cat said. "In person, Canon played it off well, acting as if he barely remembered you. But it's clear you got under his skin. That might have festered over the years, as you became more and more successful."

"If he killed Donnie, I swear I'll…"

Pris reiterated what he already knew. "Don't do anything rash."

"So what's your next move?" he asked the two of them.

They exchanged glances. "We want to reach out to Alvarez," said Cat. "We bring her in, and we'll go after Canon."

"I want to be there when you do," said Mick.

"Understood," said Cat.

Mick picked up his laptop and disappeared into his room to check his email. His real estate agent had sent him several links to live-work lofts. He clicked on the first one. It took him to pictures of a brand-new building with stainless steel appliances in the kitchen section of the loft. Instead of the old corner windows he'd had in Brickell, this one had two cement walls, with only the third wall to let in natural light, which would have to come through windows that didn't look like they opened. There was a view of the neon lights of South Beach. It looked like the kind of place some yuppie would live in, a young stockbroker or software engineer who wanted to feel hip, not a real artist. It disgusted him, so he closed the browser window and opened the next link. It wasn't any better, and neither were the other three.

His old loft hadn't been updated since the Fifties. It had the original appliances, a large Frigidaire with a chrome handle and a mammoth stove he had to light every time he used it. The palm tree that had stretched to the top of the loft had come with the place, and all he'd had to do was add a little water whenever he thought about it, and it thrived. The windows were old and rickety, but he had a bank of floor-to-ceiling corner panes, the middle ones louvers that opened with a crank handle on each end to let in fresh air.

He couldn't picture himself in any of the lofts his agent suggested, and he couldn't picture Donnie in them either, or Rose de la Crem.

At the thought of Rose, he realized he hadn't seen her since the wake and her public embarrassment, courtesy of Roy Roy. Mick missed her. Where had she gone? The fire had closed the Brickell down, since it was no longer secure with half its end wall burned away. He dug into his jeans pocket for his cell phone, which was an old-school version that only took and received calls. It didn't text or surf the Internet, as he found that business distracting. He thumbed through, looking for Rose's number. He finally found it under "Rosie," which was strange, since she didn't answer to that name. He got her voice mail.

He felt awkward leaving a message and was tempted to push End Call, but he didn't. "Hi, uh, Rose. This is Mick. Just, uh, wondering how you're doing. I haven't seen you, uh, since the wake."

She called back several hours later, after he'd had a frustrating conversation with his real estate agent, and after Cat and his sister had announced that Sergeant Alvarez—this time without her usual posse—was coming for dinner. He'd protested but was overruled by the two strident women.

"Mickey!" cried Rose. "I'm so glad you called. Where are you now? Did you find a place to live?"

Mick told her what he'd learned.

"You're lucky you can buy something," Rose said, her voice flat. "There's shit to rent out here. I'm staying at Roy Roy's place for now."

So they'd made up after his scene at the wake. Mick was sorry to hear that. Leroy was not Mick's favorite person. Rose's on-again, off-again boyfriend with the bleach-blond hair and pierced nose, a Roy tattoo on each forearm, had seemed to show up at the Brickell Lofts only long enough to relieve his itch for Rose, as well as score some cash.

"It's to tide him over," Rose would shrug off when questioned.

"I'm sorry, Rose," Mick said, in apology for her homeless status but thinking he was sorry for her shitty boyfriend situation as well. "Is there anything I can do to help? After all, it's my fault. The fire was meant for me."

Upon hearing Rose's name, Pris motioned to Mick from the kitchen, where she and Cat were cooking up a storm. His sister held a wooden spoon stained yellow from saffron. She waved it at him. "Invite her to dinner," she said. He did.

"Oh, you know me, social butterfly that I am..." Rose sounded coquettish. "But for you, Mick, I'll break my plans."

"Great, you do that," he said, playing along. "Looks like we're eating soon, so let me give you the address."

Dinner turned into a grand party with Rose, Alvarez, and Ernesto as well joining them for dinner. Rose turned out in a black-and-white polka-dotted cocktail dress cinched at the waist with a wide belt. Her face was made up in a way that exaggerated her lips as wider and more bow-shaped than they really were. She looked like a drag queen doing Fifties pin-up girl, and Mick felt charmed by the effort, especially considering the dark circles he could detect under her eyes, beneath the heavy makeup.

Ernesto had been the first to arrive, and he and Pris had disappeared into her room for awhile for conversation and who knows what else. Mick tried to stay out of his sister's private life, but he frankly didn't like her liaison with Ernesto and wondered how Pris could keep it casual over so many years. Ernesto's smooth ways rankled Mick. But far be it from him to pass judgment on Pris's choice in men. Now Ernesto eyed Rose with the look of a connoisseur of women, but he didn't seem to quite know in which category Rose belonged. Even this smidgen of confusion in Ernesto pleased Mick greatly to see.

"Mick, how goes the search for a loft?" Ernesto inquired politely.

"If my real estate agent could grasp the concept that not everyone wants something new and within walking distance of South Beach, it would be going better," Mick replied.

Ernesto nodded. "You like—what is the word? Vintage."

"Well, most things are better with age," quipped his sister.

"What about Hollywood?" Rose suggested, and Mick nodded. He did like the little town north of Miami and went up there every spring for their blues festival.

At that moment the doorbell rang, and Mick guessed it must be Sergeant Alvarez, which is how he greeted her at the door. "Well, if it isn't Mick Travers," she said. "The one who destroys perfectly good confessions."

"Oh, we'll have time to get into it after dinner," said Pris, flocking to Alvarez as if she were an honored guest. "What'll you have? My granddaughter here makes a mean margarita."

"Oh, nothing for me," Alvarez begged off.

Cat announced that dinner was ready. The guests ooh'd and ah'd at the food, and Mick was impressed that Cat and Pris had done such a good job of preparing it all: mango salsa with mangos from Ernesto's cottage garden, yellow rice and black beans, and tostadas with either chicken or tofu.

"You said on the phone that this wasn't a social call," said Sergeant Alvarez. "I'm curious about what else you've got, now that your brother here blew the state's case against Candace Shreveport."

"Believe me, I didn't want to do it," Mick said. "But it turned out to be the right thing." He felt even more certain about that now, thinking back on how desperate Candace had looked, how ... innocent. He and Grace had already talked to Alvarez about getting her charge reduced to second-degree, but she would definitely face some jail time.

"We might have had trouble getting that first fire to stick, even with the confession," Alvarez said. "The second fire was set using turpentine and some other art supplies you had at the scene, by the way. Which Candace would have known something about, being an artist. It doesn't match the method of the first fire."

Mick thought Alvarez looked gorgeous tonight, her curvaceousness no longer hidden by her uniform. Her hair was swept up, revealing lovely lines from her chin to her collarbones. It made him want to sketch her, and more, though he tried to squelch the thought, realizing she was probably a good twenty years his junior.

"So what's this new development? It better be good, because we've got nothing on the first fire now. We're checking on Norris some more, though. I still don't like that guy."

Pris glanced at Cat and Mick. "Oh, I suppose Rose and Ernesto won't mind if we talk shop."

"By all means," said Ernesto.

Rose scooted her chair in. "Are you kidding? This is better than TV."

At that, Pris told them what Cat found in New York, with Cat filling in any details she left out.

Alvarez listened intently, asking questions the whole way. Then she narrowed her eyes at Pris and said, "I'll take that margarita after all."

It'd been close to forty years since Mick had seen the smirking, bloated zeppelin that passed itself off as Chester Canon's face. But the letter the man had apparently authored and sent to *Art in Our Time* was burned into Mick's memory, and it popped into his head now as he gazed at the piehole from which Chester Canon spoke.

I actually had Edward Altair as a professor while earning a master's in fine arts. He made my class study his Pastoral Series, and after that moment, I lost respect for him not only as a professor but also as an artist. His work is derivative, obscure, and plain. His technique is undeveloped and sloppy. His slight attempts at visual humor feel dull and forced. It is, quite frankly, an embarrassment as an artist that his works receive any gallery space at all. This magazine shouldn't waste its ink on such a hack.

Signed,
Mick in Miami

Pris had pointed out to Mick the letter's circular reasoning and badly constructed sentences, and since Canon was known as a skilled writer who often penned art criticism for academic journals, Mick realized he must have gone to great lengths to try to make the letter sound as if it had been written by Mick.

All of them—Cat, Pris, Alvarez, and Mick, along with Speck and Santiago—were standing in the foyer of Canon's residence as Canon blustered about what an intrusion this was, who the hell cared about something that happened a lifetime ago, and what gave them the right to barge into his home in the middle of the afternoon?

Mick listened, but it was as if the sound of Canon's voice was reverberating down a long tunnel. Forty years separated him from the moment that letter printed in *Art in Our Time* hit the newsstands. It was forty years in which he'd heard nothing from Edward Altair, nothing in response to Mick's calls and letters attesting to the truth, swearing he did not write the letter. Altair never responded, and Mick never knew if he believed Mick had written the letter or not. It was maddening to Mick, even now. He had to stifle the urge to punch Canon in the face.

The women—without Mick's input, he noted—had decided that since Canon was Cat's suspect, she should lead the charge.

"Professor Canon," Cat said, "we do have a warrant."

At that, Sergeant Alvarez stepped forward, producing it. She was back in uniform again, the vision of her in a dress lingering in Mick's head nonetheless. Because the professor had lied to Cat about the letter's authorship with apparently nothing else to lose, the judge had granted the warrant to search his home for anything that would link him to the fire that killed Donnie.

At that, Alvarez signaled for Speck and Santiago to begin searching the premises. Mick noted that Canon seemed to be alone in the house.

"Is there somewhere we could go for a conversation?" Cat prompted him. The man shut his fat lip at the sight of the warrant and seemed to be in a daze.

"I have nothing to say without my lawyer present," he said.

"We know you wrote the letter in *Art in Our Time*," she told him.

"I have nothing to say without my lawyer present," he said again.

Mick couldn't take it anymore. "Why'd you do it? Do you really hate me that much?"

Canon glared at Mick as if struggling against whatever logic was telling him to keep his mouth zipped. "Hate you?" he finally said. "I barely remember you."

Cat stepped in. "Then why'd you lie about writing it?"

"I didn't write it."

Mick butted in again. "Why can't you admit the truth for once in your huge, phony life?"

Canon laughed. "My life's phony? What about yours? Masquerading around as a genius. We shouldn't even have granted you that degree. It wasn't earned."

Mick reached into his pocket and took out the Polaroid he'd been carrying around. Rose had snapped it with her retro camera one day when they were horsing around in the studio. It was Donnie, both thumbs up in the air, a goofy grin on his face. Mick shoved the photo in Canon's face.

"This is Donnie Hines. The man you killed when you were trying to burn me down."

Canon refused to take the photo in Mick's outstretched hand.

"I did not set that fire."

"Where were you the night of December eighth?" Cat asked.

"I'll have to check my calendar."

"Do that, please."

"Look, my wife's not here, and she handles our calendar."

"Where is your wife?" Cat asked.

"In Jacksonville, visiting family."

"Why aren't you with her?"

"I wanted the time to paint. And, if you must know, I don't care for my wife's family."

Mick was still having trouble not punching Canon in the face. And Mick realized he still had the photo of Donnie in his hands, that he'd been staring at it. He put it back in his pocket.

Pris had been uncharacteristically silent through the proceedings. She stood behind Cat and Alvarez, watching Canon's every move, as if sizing him up. Mick caught her eye, and she gave him a sympathetic look.

"It must have been hard," Pris suddenly said, directing her comment at Canon. "To deal with those students year after year. I'm betting you never wanted to be a teacher. But it paid the bills. How many sabbaticals did you get, over the course of your tenure?"

"Only four," Canon said, without missing a beat.

"Four years in forty," Pris said, clicking her tongue at the end to put a fine point on what a shame it was. "Well, you work a decade and get a year off. But I guess that's better than most folks get."

"Unless you're a full-time artist," Canon said. "Like Mick here."

"Well, we can't all be as lucky as Mick, now can we?" Pris agreed. "Did you get much painting done, during the school year? Or was it strictly a summertime occupation?"

"Oh, a dedicated artist manages. Spring break, summer, winter break. Long weekends."

"It's surprising that you'd waste one of those precious spring breaks on that letter to *Art in Our Time*," Pris said.

"Oh, for Pete's sake," Canon said. "It was a stupid prank. I was a relatively young teacher back then and hadn't yet earned tenure."

Mick could kiss his sister. She'd led Canon right down her rabbit hole.

Cat cleared her throat and added, "If you'd have been found out, you might not have been granted tenure."

Canon put his hands in his pockets as if to convey his nonchalance. "Try to prosecute me for it if you like. I'm sure the statute of limitations on whatever crime it is to fake a letter to the editor has run out by now. And I'm a professor emeritus and for all intents and purposes retired. So you can't hurt me there, either."

"I think we're more interested in how far you were willing to carry this lifelong obsession with Mick," Cat countered.

"Lifelong obsession? That sniveling little hack irritated me when he was in graduate school, but that's the end of the story. I wouldn't call that a lifelong obsession."

"Well, we're standing here in the middle of the winter of 2013, discussing it," Cat pointed out.

Mick was conscious of the deputies rifling through the rooms of the house while he and the others remained in the foyer. Canon had refused to invite them into the living room.

"I'd rather discuss any other topic under the sun," Canon said with a sarcastic laugh.

"Sir," Speck interrupted. "We need access to your garage."

"Fine." Canon pulled a set of jingling keys out of his pocket. "Follow me."

The four remaining in the foyer were silent a moment before Alvarez looked at Cat and Pris and asked, "So do you two want him for this or not?"

"No," said Cat.

"Yes," said Pris.

Cat and Pris gave each other questioning looks.

Alvarez shot one at Mick, as if he could break the tie, and he shrugged. He honestly didn't know if Canon was capable of arson. The man wasn't exactly light on his feet. It was hard to imagine him setting a fire in a locked, occupied building. But it was an amateur arson job. Maybe Canon hired someone? A student? That would be ironic.

He wanted to hear what his sister and grand-niece thought, but Canon soon reappeared.

"Your flunkies are wrecking my garage," Canon said, rolling his eyes. "Gee, I hope they find something useful back there. I can tell you one thing, though. There aren't any donuts."

Mick groaned inwardly. It was this sensibility that explained why Canon's art wasn't more successful, he thought.

"Well, have we run out of things to say?" Canon leaned against the table in the foyer and whistled, as if waiting for the bus. He checked his watch.

Mick regretted his decision to accompany the three women on this trip. At least he could stop off in Hollywood on the way back to check out an apartment building that looked promising, more his speed. He'd driven his Fiat up alone, and Cat and Pris were in the rental car.

Speck and Santiago returned with a couple of boxes of evidence total, from both the garage and the rest of the house. They would take it in for further analysis. Mick peeked inside one of the boxes as they loaded it into the police cruiser and saw a canister of Coleman fuel. He didn't figure Canon as the camping type.

Chapter 16

At first, Grace thought Mick moved too quickly on the fourplex he'd found in Hollywood. But then she realized it wasn't the speed with which he purchased the building; it was that he'd done so entirely without her input. She'd hoped their recent closeness would mean he'd at least show the place to her—and Cat—before he agreed to buy it. But no.

And that hurt.

She nursed the wound as they moved into the place, which did turn out to be a great buy. It was a mid-sized apartment building housing four units that had been converted into live/work lofts. Built in 1957, the structure still retained its original character, with many of the features Mick had admired in the Brickell Lofts. So he'd bought the entire building outright directly from the seller, paying cash. He moved into one unit himself, rented another out to Rose de la Crem, reserved a third for Cat and Grace, and was looking for a tenant for the fourth. He'd purchased it from an elderly woman who could no longer adequately take care of it and was moving herself into a retirement home in Boca. She'd apparently given Mick a deal, and in exchange, he agreed to help her sell off what she didn't need and move into her place in Boca.

Grace's brother had done well, quite well, in fact, without her. She was proud of him for that, but she'd enjoyed how closely they'd been working on the case and had developed a notion that he might be persuaded to move to Seattle.

His purchase of the building put the kibosh on that.

So Grace turned to other concerns. For one, she was trying to figure out how she could sleep close enough to where Canon lived to slip into his dreams.

Standing there in the foyer of his house, she'd had the strongest sense that he was guilty of more than the letter forty years ago, and she needed to find out if the wall of guilt included the fire that ended Donnie's life. Canon was as bitter as a mustard root in winter, and she believed him capable of murder if pushed far enough. Mick's Palm Beach show might have tipped the scales, as it were. While Canon might have written off Miami's urban, Latin America-focused art crowd, Palm Beach was home to an older, more established clientele, the sort of people whose approval Canon undoubtedly craved. It had to have eaten Canon up inside to know that Mick was the toast of that crowd while Canon himself painted in relative obscurity in his studio an hour south of there.

Cat thought differently, of course. She'd chalked up Canon as one of the frustrated "those who can't do, teach" variety.

"His type, I saw a lot of in college," Cat said. "These were the teachers who'd never really made it in actual law enforcement." She was open to the possibility of his guilt but had shifted her focus back to Mick's paintings and was continuing down the list of his many patrons.

Grace didn't envy her the task, especially since it involved a bit more highway driving now that they were living in her brother's building in Hollywood.

Ernesto had protested the move, apparently loath to let Grace slip away so fast, but honestly, Grace was relieved to get a little distance from him. As much as she enjoyed his company, she was beginning to feel smothered. He'd taken to showing up at the cottage unannounced and assuming that her Friday nights would be spent with him. Furthermore, he was a bit too nosy about Mick's case. She regretted letting him listen in the night they had Alvarez for dinner.

Canon had produced an alibi the day after their ambush, claiming to have been at a gallery opening at the Lowe Art Museum on the campus of the University of Miami the night of the fire. The interesting thing about his alibi is that it actually put him nearly an hour closer in proximity to Mick's studio than he would have been at home in Fort Lauderdale. The Brickell Lofts were minutes from the Lowe. Alvarez and her team were questioning Lowe attendees that night to verify Canon's presence at the party and determine any gaps. Canon's wife, of course, maintained he was with her the entire evening at the Lowe and that they drove home at nine thirty.

Grace distrusted automatically any backed-up alibi—or destroyed alibi, for that matter—based on a spouse's words. Either way, they were meaningless. A spouse could not be compelled by law to testify against his or her married partner. Of course, many of them *volunteered* to testify against their married partners, but this was usually out of spite or vengeance and couldn't be trusted any more than a backed-up alibi could.

If only she could get inside that man's head and see what was there.

A few nights after the revelation that both Cat and Mick could slip into other people's dreams from a distance, Cat delicately asked Grace if she were jealous. After all, it was something they could both do, but she could not.

"Not at all," she'd replied, and she meant it. She had never found jealousy to be a useful emotion, so she learned to starve it years ago, and it had practically died of malnourishment. Besides, she had trained herself to make as much use of her dreamslipping ability as she could, to hone it and put guardrails around it so that she could call it a true gift instead of a liability. Of this she felt an earned pride, and she tried to pass on her knowledge, at least to Cat, since Mick wasn't very interested in honing his. And of course her own daughter Mercy, Cat's mother, didn't have the gift, as it seemed to skip a generation. Grace's own mother didn't have it either, but Grace's grandmother had.

But now, with Canon living at least a good twelve miles away from any hotel or other place of lodging, Grace reasoned that having a traveling dreamslipping gift would definitely come in handy after all. She wondered how she could forge a connection with Canon across a distance.

She sat cross-legged on a yoga mat she'd set in a patch of sunlight. "Ohm," she intoned, letting her mind empty completely, or as completely as was humanly possible. Then she placed Chester Canon into the emptiness. She heard his sarcastic laughter, felt again that overwhelming sense of his layers of guilt. It wasn't pleasant. But she got no further, and taking a nap didn't help, either. She not only didn't slip into Canon's dream but failed to slip into anyone else's.

Of course, she was alone in the building. Rose was off with that man she called her boyfriend; Cat was interviewing someone who owned some of Mick's art, lived in Miami, and had been in attendance at Art Basel; and Mick was meeting with a gallery owner.

Grace realized she didn't know Canon well enough. She was still calling him by his last name in her head, as if he were her teacher or someone she were citing in an academic paper. Now that she and her clan had moved up the coast to Hollywood, they were only twenty minutes away from Chester's house. She decided to pay him a visit.

This time his wife answered the door. Grace hadn't met her before, since it had been Cat who interviewed Chester the first time, and the woman had been visiting family during the ambush. Mrs. Chester Canon was a treasure in her hand-knit crochet vest over a blouse that tied in a large bow at the neck, and of course the orthopedic shoes.

"Can I help you?" The woman's tone was polite but skeptical.

"You must be Mrs. Canon," Grace began. "I'd like to—"

"Who is it, Louise?" Chester's voice behind the door was gruff.

"It's an older lady."

Chester appeared behind his wife. "You again? I'm beginning to feel genuinely harassed."

"Please," said Grace. She put her hand to the door to stop Chester from closing it on her face. "We're all … of an age, aren't we? I promise I'm not here to interrogate you. I'm here to visit. I've brought pastries." She held up a basket of guava turnovers she'd picked up from the delightful Cuban coffee walk-up window down the street from Mick's new building.

The prospect of a visit lit a spark in Louise's eye. "It seems rather rude to turn her away."

"This woman wants to send me to the electric chair," Chester bellowed, his face too close to his wife's. "For murder, Louise."

"Now, Dr. Canon, I want nothing of the sort," Grace said. He moved her hand aside and slammed the door.

This was going to be harder than she thought.

She took one of the guava pastries and bit into it, enjoying the ooze of cream cheese and sweet guava over the light, flaky crust. It was a lovely day, just right for a stroll, so she decided to check out the neighborhood. There were no sidewalks, but the streets were quiet, and she felt safe.

"Good afternoon," she said to Chester's neighbor, an older woman with lovely white hair peeking out from under a wide sun hat. She was kneeling near a bed of goldenrod and adding bark mulch to the soil.

"Good afternoon," the woman said in return, flashing Grace a wide grin.

"Would you like a pastry? They were meant for my hosts"— Grace gestured toward Chester's house—"but it seems I'm an unwanted guest."

"Ha, that doesn't surprise me," the woman said, slowly moving to stand. She removed her gloves, stowing them in the pocket of her vest, which also showed a tiny shovel and a packet of slow-release fertilizer peeking out. "Don't mind if I do." She reached for a pastry.

"Dr. Canon isn't one for socializing?" Grace prompted.

"That old cuss?" The woman replied between bites of pastry. "Keeps his poor wife locked up with him all day, waiting on him hand and foot while the undiscovered genius paints."

"How are they as neighbors?" Grace asked.

"Oh, fine, I suppose." She gestured toward a rather solid wooden fence between their properties. "'Good fences make good neighbors,' and all that." The woman polished off her pastry and wiped the crumbs from her hands. "Of course," she added, "Frost had something more to say about that, didn't he?"

Grace smiled and picked up the thread of the poem to which the woman was referring. "'*Before I built a wall I'd ask to know ... what I was walling in or walling out.*'"

"'*And to whom I was like to give offense,*'" the woman finished.

"Yes," Grace said, enjoying the camaraderie of speaking to someone of her own age and culture. As much as Grace loved her granddaughter, she knew Cat wouldn't get the Frost reference. It came from a different time.

"Do they still teach Frost these days? I'm Evelyn, by the way." The woman offered her hand.

"Nice to meet you, Evelyn. I'm Grace," she said, giving her a warm handshake. "Oh, and Frost? Perhaps as period lit. But they don't seem to value memorization any more. It's a rare person under thirty who can quote anything that isn't set to music."

"Boy, that's the truth!" Evelyn swiped off her hat and wiped her forehead with the back of her hand. "Would you like to come inside for some lemonade? I don't use too much sugar. Like it tart."

"That's the best way to have lemonade," Grace said. "I'd love to."

Evelyn's house was much homier than Chester's, and it was filled with plants and cats. Evelyn invited Grace to perch on a stool in her kitchen and set a glass in front of her on the counter. Lemon rinds floated between the ice cubes, and the lemonade was perfectly tart, indeed. A plump tabby jumped up on the counter, and Evelyn picked him up and cuddled him.

"Pitsel! You know you're not supposed to do that!"

She set him down on the floor and shot Grace a coy look. "I'm not very good at disciplining them."

"Oh, don't apologize to me," Grace said. "Felines don't take it well anyway."

Evelyn sat on a stool opposite Grace in the kitchen nook. "How do you know Chester Canon? Or is it Louise you were here to see?"

"I know them both," explained Grace, quickly fabricating a cover story. "I ... was an administrative assistant in Dr. Canon's office at Columbia. I got to know him and his wife that way. I'm not sure why he's so grumpy this morning, however. He said something about me disturbing his time to paint."

"That figures," Evelyn said. "All that man does is paint and smoke. But who's even heard of him? I think he sells one painting every five years or so. I like Louise, though. If you're lucky, he'll go out for a drive soon. He does do that, come to think of it. Drive around, he says, for inspiration. Judging by how blurry his paintings are, he should probably slow down. A walk would serve him better. Besides, he could use the exercise."

Grace laughed in spite of herself. She liked Evelyn's frank manner.

"Do their children ever visit?"

"Children? Oh, yes. I guess they do have kids. There's a young man, a lawyer, I think. CPA? Some sort of profession. And a girl, a dancer."

"A dancer?"

"Yes. She's the apple of that man's eye. I mean no swipe against Louise, as he does love his wife, but he practically twinkles when his daughter's around. She was a little princess growing up, you know, a ballerina with the pink tutu, the whole nine yards."

"And she's still a dancer? It wasn't a passing adolescent fantasy?"

"Oh, no. She's managed to turn it into somewhat of a career, though I'm not sure she has the hunger, you know?"

Grace did know. It was the lack of hunger she saw in Chester as well. It was as if he wanted to be an artist more than he actually wanted to paint.

"You're in luck!" Evelyn pronounced. She was looking out the window. "Did you see that big boat of a car that passed by? That was Chester's. He's gone for a drive. Time to visit Louise. I'll come along as a buffer."

"Oh, I don't want to put you out," Grace said. "You've been so gracious already."

"Don't worry," Evelyn said with a wink. "I'll split as soon as she lets you in. Then you can have the private conversation with her you're looking for."

Grace smiled. Ah, if only it were always this easy.

The ruse worked, and thankfully, Evelyn didn't mention the bit about Grace having worked as an administrative assistant at Columbia. Maybe she hadn't believed that line, but no matter. In a few minutes, Grace was sitting in a sort of knitting room with Louise, who seemed nervous to have her there, but curious about Grace nonetheless.

"You don't really think my Chester's a murderer, do you?" Louise fretted. "I mean, he can be a bit of a boor, but he wouldn't hurt a fly."

"Oh, don't you worry about that," Grace said. "I meant what I said about a visit."

Louise relaxed.

"Evelyn mentioned your children," Grace said, motioning to a wall of photographs that seemed to track every year of their school pictures.

"Yes," said Louise. "That's Davy. He's a CPA now, lives in Atlanta. And here's Sarah. She's a dancer in New York with Merce Cunningham."

"Merce Cunningham! You must be so proud. Of the CPA, too, of course."

"Very. Davy's financially in better shape, though."

"Well, a dancer in New York…"

Louise piped up. "Oh, I worry about her so much! I'm a bit traditional, I guess, but I wish she'd come back here, get married, and settle down."

"With grandchildren, I suppose?"

"Yes."

"And your husband? What does he think?"

Louise paused, looking as if she were afraid to contradict him. "He believes in her … a little too much."

"Is she good?"

"She's good enough for Cunningham's troupe, but she's last in line there. I don't believe she … stands out."

"Well, it certainly takes all kinds, with varying levels of commitment. We can't all be Merce Cunningham, after all. Some of us are needed to make up his troupe. That's our place."

Louise warmed to Grace's words immensely. "Would you like more tea?" she asked, but Grace declined, her bladder already singing "Anchors Aweigh."

"If you don't mind, I'd like to visit the ladies' room."

Louise instructed her toward a guest bathroom in the hallway. But on her way back, Grace got a glimpse of Chester's atrium studio. "Louise," she called out, "Would you mind if I took a look at your husband's latest work? I've always been an admirer."

"Not at all! Go right on in."

Grace coughed a bit in reaction to the smell of cigarette smoke, which she reasoned would be worse if the place weren't filled with plants thriving anyway in the sunlight spilling into the atrium. Louise's doing, no doubt.

But what drew Grace's attention were the paintings.

She recognized them as coming from her generation. They were abstract expressionist, with echoes of the greats: Pollock, de Kooning, Rothko. What was startling to her was that Chester was not like Clive Smith, who was still painting today the same way he had forty years ago. No, Chester wasn't like that. Rather, he was painting anew; this was fresh work; he had progressed in his artistic technique and style. But it still referenced another era. They gave Grace a feeling of the familiar, and a wistful sense of something lost to the past. It was the same way she'd felt when talking to Evelyn, both of them quoting Robert Frost.

There was a great mass of muddy brown caged in by a primitive line that was neither circle nor square but more organic. She touched it, the paint still wet and coming away from the canvas on her hand. She could see the ridge lines of her fingerprint in the painting now, and she felt terrible about it, so she looked around for a brush. There was one balanced on the edge of the easel, next to a cigarette stubbed out in the easel tray. She picked it up and began to brush out her fingerprint.

"So you're a budding artist now, too?"

It was Chester.

Grace spun around, flustered. "Oh, what you must think of me," she apologized.

"Indeed," he said. His face grew red, and she felt a tirade coming on.

"Chester!" Louise exclaimed from behind him. "I thought you went for a drive."

Chester turned on his wife. "Do you want me to be hauled off to jail, Louise? Is that it? You invite this snoop into our home, into my studio?"

"Why, Evelyn knows her!"

"Evelyn? What does our neighbor have to do with this?"

Grace broke in, setting her voice as calmly as she could. "I can explain—"

"—I don't need any explanations," bellowed Chester. "I need you to leave."

"I will at once," Grace said. She walked out as quickly as she could, Louise trailing after her, a look of utter confusion on her face. Grace took her hand. "Thank you so much for your hospitality, Mrs. Canon."

Chapter 17

While Grace continued to pursue Chester Canon as suspect number one, Cat couldn't shake the feeling they were missing something big. The whole time she and the others were standing there in Chester Canon's foyer, she felt they were wasting time—that the real killer was off somewhere, slipping further away from them.

She kept coming back to the paintings that were destroyed in the fire. Over and over she looked at the ones that had surviving digital images, hoping something would trigger, but nothing did.

She'd gone as far as to make Mick review them with her, but that didn't get her any further on the case although she enjoyed the time to bond with him. He taught her about the techniques he used over the years. He also taught her the meaning of words and phrases she then used when she interviewed the people who bought his art. Mixed media. Resin. Woodblock print versus lithograph. Latex versus oil.

She'd spent the better part of the past week, once they'd settled in Mick's new building, interviewing buyers of his art. There was the Miami Dolphins quarterback who collected art as an investment and because he liked the look of real art in his manse. But he wasn't a true appreciator of art. He wasn't sure which of his paintings was Mick's till he opened a document listing his possessions for insurance purposes, which noted where the piece was in his tremendous house, its dimensions, and its estimated value.

Then Cat met an architect, a woman, who said she'd once slept with Mick, which made Cat feel awkward, but at least the woman seemed age-appropriate for her great-uncle. There was a stockbroker who had Mick's pieces in storage because he was getting ready for an extensive trip abroad; a commercial airline pilot who had Mick's art in condos he owned throughout the world; and the head of an Internet startup who hung the art in his corporate offices.

None of them stood out to her as suspects, so perhaps it was a waste of time. But she didn't want to sit around trying to poke holes in Canon's alibi. The closer she stayed to Mick's art, the closer she felt to the killer.

And she'd said nothing to anyone about this, but the closer she stayed to Mick's art, the closer she felt to God.

He was talking to her again.

It had been a long time.

She was aware that this so-called voice of God could be a trick her mind played on itself. It was always a male voice, after all, for which she gave herself a bit of feminism-fueled grief. And she was aware that it was probably her intuition or inner wisdom or higher self or any number of other phenomena that were perfectly acceptable explanations for what was happening.

But none of that really mattered. For Cat, the "voice of God" worked as a label for the spirit or energy or whatever she felt in communion with during these moments. And right now, it—or he, as it were—was giving her a consistent message: *Follow the core of the passion.* She understood that the "core of the passion" was the art itself.

After Lee died, it was as if her connection to God had died with him, her line to the divine disconnected. In its place was an engulfing static noise of pain. But now the pain had receded some, like the tide in Seattle going out to reveal anemones and hermit crabs and bright green sea grass. And Cat felt an import to this case that she hadn't felt since she followed that girl Ruthie back to St. Louis last year. She sensed that the fire was about something much larger than Mick and the petty jealousies of a few wannabe artists. *Follow the core of the passion.*

But of course she knew she could be wrong, the voice of God notwithstanding, and Granny Grace's theory that there was more to Canon's guilt than they'd already uncovered held huge sway with Cat.

It was into this crossroads in the case that Jacob Reiner, her new friend in New York, intruded. Or rather, stumbled.

Cat was sitting on the balcony of Mick's new building, an umbrella shading her laptop from the sun, when her cell phone rang. The number ID'd as Jacob's, so she answered it, thinking maybe he had somehow come across more information about the letter Canon wrote.

After exchanging slightly awkward greetings, there was a pause as Cat waited for the purpose of the call. Sounding nervous, Jacob said, "So … I have too much vacation. I never take any, and they're telling me I have to use it by the end of the year here or lose it. So I figure I'll take a trip to Miami. I've never been."

Cat closed her laptop and sat up. She didn't know what to say, and she sensed that Jacob was hanging on her response. This was a bit of a shock to her, but then she traced back in her mind's eye their interactions and could see the friendliness and attraction, even amidst her focus on the case and her Great-Uncle Mick.

Still, she felt fear at dating right now. She didn't want him to distract her from the case, and she was still entertaining thoughts of a life free of romantic entanglement.

But the God voice in her head reverberated clearly: *Say yes.*

"Hey, that's great, Jacob," she replied. "I'm still here, working on the case. Maybe we can hang out."

"I'd love that, Cat," he said.

The word "love" gave her heart a shot of fearful adrenaline. They made plans to connect once he was set up at a hotel on South Beach, which was far enough away that she didn't feel the pressure that he was flying down there to see her, but she wondered if he was anyway.

A bit later, Sergeant Alvarez called Cat to let her know that the guests at the Lowe had confirmed Canon's attendance at the opening that night.

"Of course this confirms that he was in the vicinity of the crime and therefore could still have committed it once he left the party," Cat said.

"Agreed. He was definitely at the party the whole time. Folks say he and his wife left early, though, around nine thirty. He could have started the fire afterward."

"Or met up with someone he paid to do it."

There was a pause, and then Cat asked, "What about the evidence confiscated from his home?"

"The Coleman fuel we found is the same as what was used to set the fire," said Alvarez. "But it's also incredibly common. I've got some myself at home."

"But Canon's not a camper."

"He maintains it's left over from his kids. That's certainly plausible. We don't have enough to charge him."

"My grandmother's looking into his background some more," said Cat.

"Well, good luck to her. We've done all we can. Looks like we've hit another dead end."

"I'm still looking at the art," Cat said. "I've talked to more buyers."

"Find anything?"

"Not really," she said. "But I could use some help. I've got a database of some of the paintings that were lost in the fire. Mick didn't keep the best records, so most of what was lost we don't have images for, only names, dates, and descriptions. But hey, I'm surprised he has this much documented. I could send it to you and your team."

Alvarez agreed, and they exchanged FTP information so that Cat could upload the hefty database of images to the Miami PD network. Then they signed off.

Cat sat on the balcony a moment, staring out at the water far in the distance. It was a nice perk that came with the old building, this view of the water. It was far away, and the beach itself wasn't a short walk by any means, but Cat thought her great-uncle had made a sound financial decision in purchasing the building. It had good bones and loads of charm. That was the thing about Mick. For all the talk of his genius and great creativity, it could be that what led him to such a solid career was his practical business sense. He'd paid off his debt to Columbia University as quickly as he could, never lived extravagantly, and had a good reputation with gallery owners. He wasn't very tech savvy nor was he the best recordkeeper, but for his time and age, he had done a better-than-all-right job of running what was essentially his own business.

———

Cat took Jacob to an outdoor restaurant set on a canal that Granny Grace had introduced her to. It was casual, the kind of place where they brought you a bucket of beer on ice and set it in the middle of the table. A man played an instrument that looked like a smaller version of an accordion, which Granny Grace called a "bandeón." They ate chicken with rice and beans, or arroz con pollo, with plantains as an appetizer. As they dined, people drifted past the table selling their wares: a brightly feathered electronic bird in a cage, a single red rose. Cat was relieved when Jacob passed on the rose.

He was as interesting a date as he had been a research companion in New York. She learned that he had two siblings. As he told stories about his sister the nurse and his brother who was trying to break in as a fashion designer, Cat felt the old yearning for siblings she'd endured as a child.

"It sounds like you get along very well," Cat observed.

"Oh, sure," said Jacob. "I mean, there was rivalry when we were younger, especially between my brother and me. But we're really good friends now."

He shifted gears, putting the focus back on her. It was something he'd done smoothly throughout their interactions, so they felt like a give-and-take, with neither Jacob nor she dominating the conversation.

"But what about you?" he asked. "I used to envy only children when I was a kid. They never had to share their toys, and their parents had more money to spend on them."

"I'd have traded that for built-in friends any day," Cat admitted.

"So it was lonely?"

Cat thought about how solitary she felt, especially as a teen, struggling with her gift for dreamslipping. She would have loved being able to talk to a sister or brother about it. If it weren't for Granny Grace, she wouldn't have had a soul who understood.

But she didn't tell any of this to Jacob, of course. "It could be, at times," she said instead. "But I grew up in one place, St. Louis. A nice, mid-sized city. I'm from the South Side, which was clean, safe, and working class—at least most of the time I lived there."

"And white, I bet."

"True," said Cat.

"I've never been to St. Louis."

"That doesn't surprise me. Most New Yorkers avoid the vast middle section of the country. You've probably been to L.A., though."

He flashed her a wide grin. "That I have."

"Would you ever live anywhere besides New York?" she asked. "L.A.?"

"Los Angeles is a place where people go to chase their dreams, not knowing that a dream is just a dream," he said.

"Do you really believe that?"

"Believe what?"

"That a 'dream is just a dream'."

"Yes, I suppose. A lot of people in L.A.—they're basically playing the lottery with their life. The odds of making it big are so slim—"

"—So don't even try?"

"That's not what I mean. Of course you should try. But you need to be capable of a realistic assessment of yourself. Take my brother, for example. He knows he's got an eye for special-occasion wear, you know, wedding gowns, ball gowns, tuxedoes, that kind of thing. But he's not so good at casual wear. He knows this and is trying to both maximize what he's good at and get better where he's weak. But I don't see a lot of rock star and actress wannabes in L.A. doing that. In fact, some of them are utterly unaware that they simply lack the talent."

"Don't you think most people just need to get out of their own way?" said Cat. "I mean, look at Clive Smith. There he was, quietly making those brilliant pieces for his granddaughter. It was pure joy for him, no pressure to be great art. And that's why it succeeds where his super-serious art failed."

"You aren't kidding, Cat. Did you see the blog article? It went viral. It put Clive Smith on the proverbial map."

"Really? What happened?"

"It was one of my most popular posts. Social media blew up over it, and now Smith's getting calls from galleries all over the city."

"Well good for him," Cat said. She picked up her bottle of beer. "Let's toast to his success."

When she brought Jacob back to his hotel, he paused in the car, taking her hand and stroking it with his thumb. "I'm really enjoying getting to know you, Cat."

A panic shot through her, and she realized what a mistake the date had been.

"I lost someone," she blurted.

He let go of her hand. "A boyfriend?"

"Sort of. Yes. Someone I knew when I was a kid, and then again recently. It's complicated."

"I'm so sorry," he said. "Truly."

She was quiet.

"That must have been very difficult."

"It was."

"Do you want to talk about it?"

"Not really."

"Do you want a drink?"

"I had a beer with dinner."

"I'd noticed that. But I mean a real drink." He added: "In the hotel bar. *Not* my room." He emphasized the "not," but the specter of his room and what it represented made her feel more panicked.

"I think I better go," she said. "I'm sorry."

With that, Jacob squeezed her hand, said, "Good night," and got out of her car.

She went home and fell into bed but couldn't sleep no matter how hard she tried.

The next day, she felt terrible. She cursed herself for listening to the voice in her head and for thinking it was God instead of a sign that she was losing it.

She must really be losing it.

Cat immersed herself in the investigation and did not hear from Jacob the whole next day.

Granny Grace, who was busy with some strange "project," as she called it, involving Chester Canon, was not too preoccupied to notice something bothering Cat.

"How was your date?" she asked.

"It wasn't a date."

"This is the man you met in New York? Who happens to be in Miami all of a sudden?"

Cat had tried to downplay the situation, but nothing got past her grandmother.

"We're just friends." Cat continued to stare at her laptop screen.

Grace sat down next to Cat on the chaise lounge she'd claimed as her command center. Cat's papers fluttered around her.

"You know you can go at your own pace," Grace said. "If it doesn't feel right, don't do it. Nobody's rushing you. This guy, if he's meant to be a good connection for you, it'll keep. Till you're ready."

Cat slowly closed her laptop. "I kind of ditched him. I couldn't help it. I panicked."

"That's understandable. But it's been more than a year, Cat. You can't cloister yourself forever."

"I—" Cat stopped. It was hard to put into words what she was feeling. "I feel guilty, because I'm really attracted to him. I want … him. And I need to let go of something bound up inside me. But that's it."

"Not very Catholic of you, I'm afraid," joked Granny Grace.

"I know. Mercy would not approve."

"But your mother's not here. The only thing to worry about is dear Jacob's feelings. I suspect, however, that a guy who lives in New York and came down to Miami to see a girl who lives in Seattle but is from St. Louis isn't looking to get married to her, at least not anytime soon."

"Granny Grace," Cat said. "God forgive me, but I don't even want to, um, fall asleep with him. No dreams."

"You'll get no judgment from me," said her grandmother. "And as for Jacob, I mean, hmm… I don't know of any man who'd say no to that."

The following day, Cat got up the nerve to call him.

"I want to see you," she said. Before he could answer, she rushed headlong into the speech she had prepared. "In your hotel room. I think we have great chemistry, and I want to explore that. But that's it. I can't do more right now. You're here for another week or so, we have a great time, and you go back to New York. Maybe we keep in touch; maybe we don't. It doesn't matter. But right now, we have this. If you're interested. If not, it's okay."

There was a long pause, and then Jacob let out a breath. "Wow."

Then another pause and another breath. "Jesus," he finally said. "Yes. I mean, wow. You're gorgeous, I'm totally into you, and if we have a mind-blowing experience and I never see you again, I might be totally heartbroken, but I will still have had this. Are you kidding? Yes. Get over here right now. Before I drive up there."

Cat was laughing. "Considering I'm rooming with my grandmother, that's not such a good idea."

"I'm waiting for you, Cat."

She hung up, packed a small bag, and drove down to South Beach.

He opened the room to his hotel and presented her with a single red rose.

"I wanted to get one for you at the restaurant the other night, but I sensed that would freak you out. Now I know why. But here, red is for passion as much as it's for love."

She thanked him, took the rose, and inhaled its scent, dragging the soft petals across her lips.

He'd ordered Champagne through room service. But Cat didn't need or want a drink. She offered him her hand, and he took it, stroking her skin with his thumb as he had that night. This time, she didn't panic. She let the feeling sizzle there, burning her with desire. She liked the way his lips parted and his breath quickened as he touched her. His hand traveled up her bare arm. She put her hands around the back of his neck, bringing his face to hers, and kissed him hard. He responded, enfolding her in his arms. Her hand went for where he was hard and made it harder.

"I'm not wearing anything under this," she whispered, and he moaned, reached down for the hem of her dress, and bringing it up over her head. Then Cat turned around and took him in, pushing back against him as her hands gripped the dresser in his hotel room.

They stayed in his room all day, ordering room service when they were hungry. When it was time for them to sleep, Cat left.

Chapter 18

Mick understood Cat's need to keep working other angles in the case, but taking her around to see his best patrons was not something he relished doing.

Two lived on Star Island, an entirely private island accessible off the causeway but gated to all but residents and their guests. It was a place he'd been to several times before, but he never felt as if he belonged there. On the contrary, it was a game he played, in order to sell his art. But Cat wanted to talk to Serena Jones and the Langholms, and Mick was her only way in.

The drive out on the causeway was lovely, though. The gorgeous water would appear to be the shade of a green glass bottle if there was sea grass beneath the shallow waves or run bright turquoise if there was not.

You couldn't even drive onto the island unless a resident called you in, which is what Jones did for them when they stopped at the guard booth. They parked in a large circle drive, and Mick explained to Cat that the mansion next door, which dwarfed this one considerably, belonged to the Langholms.

Jones's house was faux Mediterranean style, like a lot of houses in Miami, probably built when the island was first constructed in 1922. But it had apparently been gutted and rebuilt inside, as it was now a large open-concept white palace filled with art. Mick was flattered to see she'd hung his paintings in a prominent place, in the dining room above a fireplace that must be completely unnecessary there in the tropics. Jones's housekeeper, a stout Hispanic woman wearing a cap and apron, a sight that always struck Mick as an Old World gesture there in Miami, led them to where Serena Jones was exercising with a trainer. They worked out in a bright, sunny room with floor-to-ceiling windows overlooking the water and South Beach beyond. Serena wore boxing gloves and hit her trainer's focus mitts at his urging: "Jab left. Right hook. Uppercut."

Mick and Cat waited for them to finish the sequence. Serena was firmly out of her twenties and into her thirties but appeared to be maintaining pretty good ground, Mick thought. With the time to work out in the middle of the afternoon, a personal trainer at her disposal, and possibly a personal chef as well, the only thing she had to fight was the aging process itself.

Her trainer threw her a towel and politely exited out a back door as Serena guzzled a bottle of Perrier and walked toward them.

"Hola, Mick," she gushed, allowing him to kiss both cheeks, Miami-style.

"And this is your grand-niece, I understand," Serena held out her hand to Cat as if meeting her for the first time, but Mick distinctly remembered introducing them at Donnie's wake. Ah, well. It wasn't like Serena to remember the little people.

As was customary in Miami, Serena asked Cat, "Prefiére hablar Español o Inglés?"

"Inglés, por favor," Cat replied. "Y gracias."

"De nada," Serena said and then slipped into English. "You wanted to see Mick's art?"

"Yes," said Cat, sounding to Mick as if she weren't sure where to start, or perhaps Serena's wealth was making her nervous.

"Come this way," Serena said, and they followed her back into the dining room, where he'd seen a glimpse of the pieces on the way in.

Meanwhile, Cat found her footing. "How did you come across his work, initially?"

"Let me see ... it was at a party, here on Star Island." Serena glanced at Mick. "You remember, right?" He nodded. To Cat, she explained, "My neighbor has a very boring life in large-scale commercial real estate, you know, development projects? So when he plays, he likes to surround himself with creatives. He throws these big parties and invites artists, writers, film people—all sorts, really—to stay the weekend."

"The guests stay overnight?"

"Yes, it is safer that way, with the drinking that goes on." Serena laughed.

Cat nodded.

"Anyway, so I was admiring this really great piece that Kristoff had—"

"Kristoff?"

"My neighbor, the one throwing the party."

"Got it." Cat remembered Carrie and Kristoff Langholm from the wake and was hoping to get to see them as well but wanted to play it cool around Serena.

"So I was admiring this painting that was like nothing I'd ever seen before. I mean, your uncle! His work, it grabs you, you know? It nearly knocked me off my heels. And I was wearing like four-inch heels that night, you know what I'm saying? And then Kristoff says, 'Well, if you want to meet the man who painted it, he's right here.' And there you were, Mick." She squeezed his arm. "Such a funny guy!" She turned back to Cat. "Your uncle said, 'Hello, ma'am. I'll be your artist for the evening.' Like he was part of the hired entertainment or something. So meta!" Serena nearly choked on her Perrier, she was laughing so hard. Mick felt his face grow red from embarrassment.

They waited for her to take a recovery sip of water and calm down. "Ah..." Serena said. "I just love artists."

"Where did you end up buying his work?" asked Cat.

"Right here," Mick said. He'd forgotten to tell Cat.

"Yes, he came to my house to show me a few pieces," Serena said. "I wouldn't have minded going to his studio, but Kristoff insisted he could get Mick to make a house call. That Kristoff, he's so persuasive."

"The fire that killed Donnie happened in Mick's studio," Cat said.

"I've lost most of my life's work," Mick added.

Serena slumped down in a nearby chair as if the news took a personal toll on her.

"Qué terrible!" She shook her head. "I mean, I was so sorry about Donnie. I bought one piece before he died, because I was told it would be a good investment some day. At the wake, I bought several more, of course... But Mick, I did not realize you lost so much that night. Your paintings!" She clasped her hand over her mouth. "Most of them are gone?"

"Yes," said Mick.

"What hap—" Serena began to ask, but then she stopped. "Are you here because of the fire? Because I need my lawyer present if so."

"Oh, don't worry," said Cat. "They've already charged someone with the murder. I'm helping Mick file a claim on his lost art. It's the least I can do."

"Damn, that must be a huge loss, Mick."

"It is. But I'd give it up to get Donnie back." He was thinking about Serena buying up his friend's art after his death. A cold chill ran up his spine as he wondered if he'd be worth more dead than alive as well.

"Of course," Serena said, her face solemn.

"Serena, can you get us over to see Kristoff?" Cat asked. She was following Mick's script, which was to start with Serena, the more accessible of the two, and then use her to get in to see Kristoff. Even though Mick had been at a party at the Langholms' before, he didn't feel he had the kind of relationship with them that would allow him to pick up the phone and propose a visit. The Langholms were the type who *got in touch with you*, and only if they needed you for something, such as serving as creative entertainment for a party.

"My neighbor? I guess..." Serena gazed out the window as if in the direction of the Langholms' much larger house, but her grounds were landscaped in order to block the neighbors and afford sweeping views of the water. "If he's not traveling. He travels a lot. If not, Carrie might be home."

"It'll help Mick put a price on his collection," Cat assured her.

Kristoff Langholm was not traveling, as it turned out—they'd caught him between business trips, as he'd just come back from a small town near Baton Rouge and was headed somewhere in the Northwoods of Wisconsin next. And he agreed to have them over.

He greeted them warmly, kissing Serena on both cheeks and taking Cat's hand to his lips. He grasped Mick's hand, holding it a little longer and pressing it with his other hand.

"It was a lovely wake you gave at Bryson's gallery," he said.

Mick thanked him with a nod.

Kristoff wore a linen suit, just right for the tropics, and slip-on driving moccasins. Likely easing up around Pris's age, he had grown old in a distinguished manner, with a good shock of thick gray hair and the barest sign of a wattle. His eyes reflected the blue of the water in the bay and his voice had a reedy quality Mick always liked.

Cat seemed to respond to the man's charms. Well versed in the ways of the world and well traveled, Kristoff smoothly dominated any gathering. His work was mainly domestic, but he traveled abroad for pleasure. His wife soon joined them for coffee, which a servant also in uniform poured in the least intrusive manner possible.

"Serena tells us you're fond of entertaining," Cat said, sipping her coffee.

"We have been in the past," his wife, Carrie, said. "But Kristoff here seems to have lost interest."

Serena added, "Yes, that's right. You haven't hosted in a long time."

"Oh, we've been so busy." Kristoff shrugged it off. "It's these development projects in small towns these days. Everyone's rediscovering their Main Streets."

"Ever think about retiring?" asked Cat. "Forgive me for saying it, but you seem to be nearing retirement age."

Carrie laughed delightedly at this. "Yes, Kristoff. Tell us about your plans to retire. You are of the age. And then some, I'd say."

"Now, now, ladies," he said, setting down his tea. "A man who loves what he does never retires."

"You sound like Mick here," Cat said. "I'm sure my great-uncle will die with a brush in one hand."

Mick bristled a bit at Cat's cavalier manner, tossing around the idea of his death so soon after Donnie's. He felt that chill up his spine again.

"How have you been, Mick?" asked Carrie. "We've been thinking about you. The wake for Don Hines was lovely, memorable. What a way to honor him."

Mick had barely uttered a thank-you when she continued.

"Oh, but that rude intrusion at the end! Who *were* those men? How did they get invited?"

Mick felt a flash of protectiveness for Rose. "Friends of friends," he said, shrugging it off.

"You just can't be too careful these days, can you? Donnie's death itself is evidence of that. Some wonder why we live on Star Island, behind the security wall. But I feel safer here than I have anywhere." She motioned for the maid to take the trays away.

"You've had a terrible run of luck, Mick," added Kristoff. "I was horrified to hear of the studio fire. And then the beach house! What a shame."

"I'll be okay," Mick said. "All things considered." He realized he wasn't doing a great job of holding up his end of the conversation, but he wished he were anywhere else in the world right now. He noticed through an open archway that the Langholms had also purchased some of Donnie's art at the wake.

"You're probably still in shock," Kristoff said. "It was a terrible tragedy."

"It was," said Cat, saving Mick from a reply. "And the arsonist—Mick knew her personally. So that's hard to take."

"Indeed," said Kristoff. "You must feel so betrayed."

"They hadn't been close in many years," Cat explained. "I'm not sure that makes it any better, though."

"Don't blame yourself," said Kristoff, reaching over to touch Mick on the shoulder. "You aren't responsible for what happened to Don Hines."

"Yes," added Carrie. "It's so easy to blame yourself for things you can't control. But you mustn't. You've got to resist that."

Mick didn't like where this conversation was going. It felt too personal for his relationship with the Langholms.

Thankfully, Cat turned to Kristoff, steering the conversation in a direction that better served their mission. "Serena says you're the one who introduced her to Mick, and I know you also collect his art. Did you know that most of his work was destroyed in the first fire?"

"That's right, old boy," Kristoff said. "I've toured your studio. You kept so much there."

"That's why we're here, to get a better idea which pieces might be in private collections. But maybe we're trying to get back what Mick lost, you know?" Cat broke down, and Mick for a second didn't know if she were faking it or not. She gave a pretty convincing performance. "My poor uncle…" Cat put her hand on Mick's arm. "He hasn't painted since the fire."

"You poor thing," said Carrie, offering her a handkerchief.

Serena reached over and touched Cat's arm sympathetically.

Kristoff cleared his throat. "Carrie and I are proud to think of ourselves as stewards of your work, Mick. That will never change. And please, know that your work is in good hands."

At that, he stood up. "Paint, Mick. Whatever you lost, it's in *you*, not on the canvas. It'll come back."

Chapter 19

Conditioning, Grace called it. The spirit becomes fringed around the edges sometimes, if you're not paying attention, if you're not taking moments to re-center. But if properly oiled, massaged, cared for, there was no limit to what the spirit could do.

She had an inkling that connecting with Chester Canon even across a comparatively short distance was going to be as grueling spiritually as running a marathon would be physically. So she prepared accordingly.

After that day when Grace met Evelyn, talked with Chester's wife Louise, and then was thrown out of the professor emeritus's house, she'd been working to tune her spiritual vibration to his. She was absolutely certain that there was more there, some great guilt, and she needed to know if it had to do with the fire that killed Donnie. The guilt seemed raw to Grace, either a fresh wound on the psyche, or freshly peeled open again after years of scarring.

She'd found a new Buddhist temple there in Hollywood, and she liked it better than the one she'd been attending down in Coral Gables near Ernesto's cottage. This one was bright and gay inside, and they welcomed her warmly, allowing her in to meditate whenever she wanted, and for however long she wanted. Grace helped out in the kitchen a few mornings to return the good karma. The meditation there had been good. She remained open to whatever would come, unbidden, and just like she had on the beach that night during Midnight Moonlight Yoga, she felt the dark, red energy at the core of this case, heard the beating wings. But at the Buddhist temple she'd been able to contain it in space, visually speaking. She'd watched it vibrate red and anguished without having to feel it as pain in her heart chakra. The wings, though, kept beating.

Grace had also stepped up her yoga practice, twice daily. Cat joined her a few times, and Grace could feel her energy as they quietly moved through their poses. Cat had progressed well in her own practice; it delighted Grace to see Cat's foot finally rise up above her head like a crown in standing bow. Grace was drawing on the energy of both Mick and Cat in her life, meditating on the strings—or ley lines, whatever you wanted to call them—connecting her to these two people she loved. These two people who, through some miracle of light and magic or maybe even genetics, shared her gift. She was counting on their energy to magnify hers, to allow her to slip into Chester's dream the way they had with Candace and Lee, across a distance. Grace's would be targeted and deliberate, and with a particular end in mind.

Grace was aware that it could take several nights of such dreamslipping before she gleaned any information about Chester's guilt. But in this, she could be patient.

The first night, Grace placed sage on her pillow to cleanse her mind of anything that might interfere. As she went to sleep, she imagined her own energy being made stronger by Cat, who slept behind a bamboo screen on her side of the studio, and Mick, next door in his own studio. She went through a series of breathing exercises, and then lay down to sleep, tuning her mind to that man in his big house twenty minutes away.

At first she slipped briefly into Mick's dream, which seemed to take place on a boat that looked like his beach house. Candace was swimming past a porthole outside. Candace smiled and waved before turning into a pelican and flying up into the sky.

Then Grace bounced into Cat's dream. Anita, the woman who killed Lee, was calling Cat a liar, but Cat was fighting back in this dream, telling Anita she was the one who had missed the truth.

Grace was so pleased with the content of these dreams that she nearly forgot her objective. But Cat's dream came to an end, and Grace concentrated all three of their dream energies on Chester. Slowly, she began to perceive the shadows of something from him.

They were distorted, angled, without concrete form. Voices. Many, many voices. Women, some of them so young they sounded like girls. Men, both boyish and practically middle-aged. And then colors. Like paint, in splotches and streaks and swirls. Drips of color. Shapes, abstract, formless. Grace had the sense of Chester turning off lights, making things dark. Squeezing, stamping down. She couldn't breathe; it was too much. She was cast out; she woke up.

Lying there in the moonlit room, Grace felt only this: That she had been a bright-hot spark of creativity that Chester had somehow extinguished.

She relinquished the dream's hold on her while hanging onto enough of it to ponder its meaning. Grace was one of those rare individuals whose buoyant spirit persisted even in the presence of sad, depressing realities. It was a quality for which she was thankful, especially when she saw how much others, like Cat and Mick, struggled to dispel dark feelings.

She thought back to that lunch with Donnie's parents, a sweet couple but relatively limited in the wide spectrum of life's experiences. But now that she reflected on the conversation, she realized Donnie's mother, Mary Ellen, had given a rare insight that day, one that was relevant to the case against Chester.

They'd been discussing Donnie's lack of an art-school pedigree.

"Do you think it held him back?" asked Donnie's father of Mick, who shook his head and said, "Many of the greats never went to art school."

At first Grace thought Mick was being polite, that it was the right thing to say to the grieving parents, but then Mary Ellen said this: "I have to admit, I was selfishly glad when Donnie quit school. I'd never seen him so miserable. His professors were as mean as snakes."

"How so?" asked Grace. "Surely they had to toughen them up for what they'll endure out in the real world."

"Oh, you must think I'm being an overprotective mother," Mary Ellen demurred.

"Not at all. Please, it sounds like you have a story."

"Well, it wasn't even Donnie who bore the brunt of it. It was the other students. During a critique session in front of the other artists, one professor said a student's painting obviously showed he harbored homosexual tendencies. This was back in the early Nineties, you know. Things were different then. The student left, but Donnie kept in touch with him. That student never painted again."

Donald steered the conversation in another direction, and Grace obliged, but the anecdote now made her reflect on that shadowy dream of Chester's. She prepared her mind—and this time, her heart, too—to receive it, whatever was Chester's burden from all of the students who must have crossed the thresholds of his classrooms over the years.

This time, the voices became audible. They were a swarm of vision and desire, of reaching and stretching and wanting to express something in their hearts and minds. Not all of them were altruistic. Some were about money and fame, and some were about the sexual conquests that would come to them as celebrated artists. Grace felt her spirit descend into Chester's, and she was laughing at them at first, a bitter, cackling, dismissive laugh. Fusing with Chester's consciousness, she felt a blanket contempt for these students; there was no distinguishing the genuine visionaries from the ones who just wanted to get laid. There were so goddamned many of them, every year, like a bunch of yippy dogs snapping at her heels. She wanted to kick them back where they came from. They were competition; they were the enemy. She thought bitterly that if any of them would actually buy art, or patronize museums instead of selfishly wanting to be great artists, there would be more opportunities for people like her, people who'd put in the time. Where would these sniveling snots be in twenty years? Would they stick with it? Not likely. So it was up to her to teach them a lesson.

Grace as Chester stood at a podium in a room full of their paintings. Thousands of drippy, messy, sloppy paintings. The ones that weren't that were too clean, too technical, too ordered. Then the students filed in, thousands of them. Hippies with dirty feet poking out of leather sandals, Andy Warhol wannabes in hipster clothes and gelled hair, the frat-boy types defying their parents, the shy girls in worn cardigans, the affirmative-action scholarship kids, the dykes and homos and cross-dressers and pierced goths and Jewish rebels and the ones who weren't even born in America and could barely speak the language. She loathed every last one of them.

Suddenly some of her students began to cry. Others called her names. A group in the corner drafted a letter to make a formal complaint about her to the dean of the art school. A scattering of women inexplicably tore off their bras and lit them on fire with cigarette lighters. Then someone got a keg and passed out beer. A fistfight broke out. Another group of students played Twister. A few were practicing jiu jitsu in the middle of the room, where they'd cleared away the chairs. A couple near the front, real teacher's-pet types, kept pestering her with questions about how they could improve their technique.

Into this chaos, Chester's daughter danced into the room, with Mick as her partner.

Grace as Chester didn't like the sight of that, not one bit, but she/he was transfixed by the plaintive dance. Mick looked like himself, which is to say not exactly the dancer type. And the daughter—Grace had seen her pictures on the wall behind Louise when they were chatting. The girl was attractive in a generic sort of way, blonde with a pert nose and light freckles on her cheeks. She moved prettily. That's it: She was a pretty dancer, nothing more. No passion, no greatness. Grace felt Chester's recognition of this like a slicing pain in the chest.

Mick lifted her atop Chester's podium, and the students who were still paying attention became upset. "Hey, she's stealing our show!" said one. "Who's the ballerina?" complained another.

"That's my daughter!" Grace yelled at them, Chester's bellowing voice coming out of her mouth.

Mick, distracted by a blank canvas on a far wall, drifted over to it and began to paint.

The bra burning got out of hand, someone having lit a painting on fire, and the flames spread around the room. Grace went with Chester, still fused to his consciousness but beginning to slowly tear herself away from him. Chester lifted his daughter down from the podium. It was as if she were a little girl again, nestled in his arms. How sweet the world was back then, when everything was only possibility, for him and for her.

She reached up, cupping his ear with one hand as if to whisper a secret. "Daddy, when will I be famous? I want to be a star, like Mick."

She pointed to Mick, who was hard at work on his best-known piece, one of the Conch Series paintings, oblivious to the fire and chaos around him. It pained Chester to know that his daughter had said "like Mick" instead of "like you, Daddy."

"Someday," Chester lied to his daughter. "Someday."

The flames grew stronger.

Grace peeled herself away from Chester as he ran out of the burning room with his girl in his arms.

It wasn't necessary to save Mick in this dream, Grace knew, for this was Chester's concoction. But she was curious to see his version of Mick, so she went over to her brother at the canvas.

There was the first painting in the Conch Series taking shape under Mick's brush, exactly the way it looked in the gallery where Grace had seen it in Chelsea. It was glorious, a true shining example of Mick's talent, and probably his finest piece. So Chester acknowledged that at least in his own dream.

It must have ended then, as Grace popped out of that world before she was ready. She found herself awake as the first light began to stream into the room.

Grace spent the day speaking to Chester's former students, but this time, she asked them questions about the way he taught. Since they had already been introduced, she called Clive Smith, Norris Grayson, and Annie Lin first. They painted a consistent portrait of Chester's classroom tactics, which included bullying and making unfair, often blistering comparisons between one student and another.

Annie Lin described it this way: "Chester seemed to choose one or two mediocre students every year and hold them up as geniuses." She scoffed. "In our class, it was this girl from the Midwest who painted nothing but Fourth of July parades. A real Thomas Kinkade type, let me tell you. It was ludicrous. But Chester actually compared Mick to her once. I'll never forget it. 'Mick, you'll never have the fine sense of color that Miss Waters here has,' he said. I saw that muscle in Mick's jaw— you know the one I'm talking about. I saw it spasm. He must have been gritting his teeth. The rest of us were happy to have Mick taken down a peg, sure. But that Beth Waters sucked."

To round out the evidence, Grace enlisted Cat's help in tracking down more former students who weren't connected to the case.

A few of them had nothing but good things to say about Chester Canon. Grace guessed that these had been the ones he'd singled out for praise. Everyone else reported the same scenario.

After Grace's last phone conversation, Cat announced, "Here's something else. Canon's father was an art critic."

Grace read the series of profiles Cat had bookmarked on her laptop. His father had a reputation for brutality. He'd singlehandedly killed a number of budding artists' careers back when critics like him held more sway over public opinion.

Late that afternoon, Grace called Professor Canon's house, and he answered.

"I'd like to take you to dinner," she offered.

Recognizing her voice, he replied, "And what makes you think I'd consent to dinner with you?"

Grace was prepared for this. "Two reasons. One, I know without a doubt you didn't set that fire in Mick's studio. And two, I know what kind of teacher you were, Professor Canon. And I don't think you can go to your grave with all that guilt."

He sputtered a bit, obviously caught off guard. There was a long pause. Then this: "No dinner. Just drinks. The Blarney Stone, five minutes from my house. Eight sharp. And leave Louise out of this. She'll think I've gone for a drive."

"Agreed."

Grace met him there as planned, and despite his obviously distressed state, he gave her an appreciative once-over as she came in and sat down, which was understandable, as well as she was able to turn herself out.

She ordered a gin and tonic. He had a glass of bourbon in front of him already.

"So let's hear it," he said. "You've been talking to my former students, getting the dirt on me, I presume."

"It wasn't difficult. Approximately one in ten thinks you're the bee's knees. These must be the ones you chose to praise."

He smiled wretchedly.

"The other nine, however..."

"Crybabies who didn't get their parents' love."

Grace squelched the urge to slap his smug face.

"Don't try to cast them as prima donnas," she asserted. "Your classroom methods obviously left a lot to be desired. What awful games you played, Chester! What a waste. It's a good thing you had tenure."

"Is that it? I don't even know why I'm here..."

"You're here because of Maggie." That was his daughter's name.

He didn't respond. "Is she happy?" Grace went on. "Maggie. Is she happy?"

"No."

"Do you know why she's not happy?"

Chester took a swig of his bourbon. "Are you seriously here to counsel me on the father-daughter relationship, lady? I don't even know you."

Grace regrouped. Chester was a tough nut to crack. She thought about the dream, how he recognized Mick's achievement.

"Chester, I'm going to stop asking you questions and tell you how it is."

"Oh, I'm on pins and needles. Enlighten me, sister."

"First of all, you are a mediocre talent."

Chester clenched his glass, and for a moment Grace feared he might actually strike her.

"What you should have done was embrace your role in life as a guide for others to discover their talent or the limitation of their talent, and to either be okay with that or transcend it."

She took a sip of her gin and tonic and then continued. "But instead, you verbally and emotionally abused whole classes of students with your sick, twisted games. So many years and so many classes, and what do you have to show for it? The ones you couldn't break, like Mick, went on to do great things despite you. Of course, some of the mediocre ones got further than they might have if they hadn't been falsely propped up by you, so maybe you deserve a bit of credit for their success. But not at the expense of those you harmed."

Chester was very, very quiet, and his face was expressionless. Grace figured most likely no one had ever spoken to him like this before.

"The worst is your own daughter." Grace let the words sink in a moment before continuing. "I can't believe you, Chester. You're doing to her what your own father did to you, and there's no excuse for that. Pushing her the way you do, when you know she doesn't have what it takes."

"How do you know she doesn't?" He glared at her across the table.

"I saw her dance, when I was in New York," Grace lied. "She dances like someone who's only doing it to win her father's love."

"Get out of my face." Chester pushed away from the table. "I should've known better than to have anything else to do with you."

Grace reached across the table in a spur-of-the-moment gesture and grabbed his hand. "I know you'd do anything for her. You love her like no one else you've ever loved."

He stared at Grace's hand on top of his, but he did not pull away. Then, letting out a low groan, he motioned for the waiter to set him up with a second drink.

"Well, you're right about that. That's the smartest thing you've said yet."

There was a pause as the waiter brought Chester another drink.

"Do you have a daughter, Grace? I'm not talking about a son. I mean a daughter. It's a whole different ball game, a girl. I should know. I've got both."

"I do," she said.

"Look, I don't want you to pity me as somebody who got beat up emotionally by his asswipe of a father. I mean, you pegged him, that's for sure. And maybe in the beginning I was doing it for him. But that wore off pretty quickly. For most of my career, I painted for myself, not him. But when Margaret was born, it was for her. I wanted her to look up to me."

Grace gave him a generous smile and patted his hand. Finally, he was telling the truth. But what an emotionally blunted man he was. "I don't want to sound like a therapist here," she said. "But Maggie undoubtedly looks up to you for a whole lot of reasons that have nothing to do with art."

"That's what Louise always says."

Grace nodded, wishing more husbands got into the practice of listening to their wives. "All right, back to the questions," she said. "Does painting make you happy?"

"Of course it does."

"Then it doesn't matter how successful you've been. You enjoy it, you don't need to make a living at it, and you have a certain following."

He was quiet, chewing on that. Then he thought of something else. "Maggie tried to tell me she wanted to quit dancing the last time she came to visit."

"But you wouldn't let her say it."

"That's right."

"Would you love her any less if she gave up dancing?"

"Of course not."

"Then tell her."

Chester smiled. It was the first genuine smile she'd seen grace his face, not a hint of sarcasm about it. Then he became serious again. "It's a funny coincidence, but I had a dream about Maggie last night. At the end of it, she told me she wanted to get married and have kids, like her mother did."

Grace nodded. So that's how the end of the dream had turned out, she thought. That's what happened after she tore herself out of Chester and went to see Mick.

Chester was shaking his head. "You're a hell of a woman, Amazing Grace."

"So I've been told."

He took her hand, which was still resting on the table near his. "If I weren't already married, I'd haul you off and make a decent woman of you."

Grace laughed, happy to see some of the old-school charm revive in this bitter old man. "Oh, I think I'm more than decent without your help," she said playfully, unable to resist. She squeezed his hand and let go.

He nodded, smiling for the first time. "And so is Louise."

Chapter 20

Cat was doing what she thought was an admirable job keeping this thing with Jacob casual. Which is not to say they didn't treat each other with care and respect. After that first day spent in his hotel room, they'd gone to the beach together and to dinner, and they'd enjoyed each other's bodies again and again. The difference for Cat this time was that she was enjoying her interactions with him in the present instead of having to figure out what their relationship meant for the future.

And even though he was only in town for a short time, she didn't feel she should be with him every moment. In fact, she sensed that Jacob wanted this vacation for his own reasons, too, that he needed time to figure out something that had nothing to do with her. For that reason, she was glad again that she'd made the decision to keep their liaison casual, as he might have made the mistake of focusing on her instead of whatever it was he needed to figure out down there in Miami, away from his New York life.

It was during one of these moments of space between her and Jacob that Cat decided to pay a visit to her great-uncle Mick in his studio next door. Truth be told, she missed having him around now that they were in separate units. As unpredictable as he could be, she enjoyed his perspective on life, so different from her grandmother's, or from her own parents', for that matter. Getting to know him better here in Miami made her regret that her family was spread so far apart, with sparse visits in between. There was so much more you learned about people by being a part of their daily lives.

So she planned to bring him takeout from the Indian restaurant they both liked there in Hollywood. When she rang his bell, he opened his door still wiping paint off his hands with a rag.

"Come on in," he said, leaving the door open for her and grabbing one of the bags of takeout.

They set up on his kitchen bar counter. She'd purchased two mango lassi drinks, as Mick said he was easing up on the bottle, and she didn't much like to drink that early in the day anyway.

As they dug into the samosas and tandoori chicken, she asked, "How was it with Donnie's parents, overall? I know you were kind of freaked out."

"It was strange, for sure," Mick admitted. "But better than I thought." He told her about the day they spread the ashes, how perfect everything was.

Cat warmed to hear him talk about that place in the Everglades and how he and Donnie used to go there. Watching him there in the kitchen talking and sipping his lassi, Cat realized that Mick was doing much better these days. He still looked sad, and she could tell he was still grieving, but he seemed to be doing so now from a place of strength. She realized she and her grandmother were part of that, and she felt a pang of sorrow knowing that eventually, they would have to leave him. What would Mick do then? The only person in his life now was Rose de la Crem, and her life tended to be a bit transitory, her finances and her art career insecure, not to mention her romantic life.

As they finished up lunch, she asked to see what he was working on. He'd erected several giant easels in the middle of the room. All Cat had seen so far were the canvas backs of his new works in progress.

"Sure," he said. "You might even recognize them."

This further piqued her interest. He led her around the easels and lifted a drop cloth.

Cat gasped. Her uncle's painting referenced in obvious ways the dream of hers that Mick had slipped into a few days after the fire. She recognized Anita's face, albeit an abstracted version, but it was Lee's killer nonetheless. And there was a lot of red in the painting, signifying the blood coming out of Lee's head. Lee wasn't identifiable, but the work was unfinished, with canvas showing through parts of it, the brushstrokes rough.

"Oh, my God." She began to breathe heavily, remembering that terrible day.

"It's upsetting you," Mick said. "Sorry. I didn't mean for that to happen."

"It's okay," she said, calming down. She forced herself to look at Anita. "I've never"—she paused, looking for the right words—"I've never had anyone capture my innermost life like that. It's startling."

"I'm really sorry," he said. "I can't seem to get your dream out of my head. It wants to come out on the canvas."

"Right," Cat said. "I can understand that."

"You okay?"

"Yeah," Cat said. "But now I'm kind of wishing we'd had something stronger than mango lassis with lunch."

They laughed a little. Then gazed at the painting in progress.

"Do you want me to paint over it?" Mick asked.

"No," Cat said. "I don't think so. But I'll let you know if I change my mind."

Something occurred to her at that moment, something so obvious she couldn't believe none of them had considered it before. And there she'd been, circling around Mick's destroyed paintings, but for the wrong reasons.

164

"Uncle Mick," Cat said, placing her hand on his arm. "You've done this a lot, right? Painted what you've seen in people's dreams?"

"Off and on, over the years, yeah. But most of the time, that's not what I paint."

Cat felt the case open up before her. "I need you to look at those paintings again, the ones destroyed in the fire, and tell me if any of them came from dreams."

"Why, Cat? What are you thinking?"

"I'm thinking you might have painted something that the arsonist didn't want anyone else to see."

They went through the list one by one, Cat marking anything that Mick said had a connection to a dream.

Out of the more than two hundred paintings destroyed in the fire, thirty-two had been inspired by dreamslipping. Mick had digital images for nineteen of those, which was lucky, Cat thought. But this still amounted to a search for a needle in a haystack.

"I think we need to get a projector and blow these up really big. We can go through them in detail," Cat said. "But I want to wait for Granny Grace. She'll notice things we won't."

"Yes, she will," said Mick.

Cat peered at her uncle, wanting to ask him something but not quite sure how to phrase it.

"What?"

"Sorry. I…" Cat swallowed. "What's the deal with you and my grandmother, anyway? You live on extreme opposite ends of the country."

"I like Miami. She likes Seattle."

"But is that it? I mean, you're both dreamslippers. And you're the only other dreamslippers I know."

"Look, Cat." Mick paused to sweep their takeout detritus into a large barrel he used as a trash can. "Your grandmother is my older sister. You wouldn't know this, being an only child, but older sisters are as bossy as they come."

"That sounds kind of childish."

"Well, it is. I admit that. Which is why I invited the two of you out here for Art Basel."

"Granny Grace was so excited to see you," Cat said, feeling wistful about the days before the fire. "She went out and put together a whole wardrobe for the tropics. We wrapped up our cases and didn't take on anything new. I've never seen her like that."

Mick frowned. "I'm sorry the two of you got dragged into this mess instead."

"Oh, it's okay, Mick. I think it's been good for us. Both."

He smiled. "Your grandmother wasn't always so enlightened, you know."

"Really?"

"Yeah, she made some mistakes with her dreamslipping, early on. And one of them cost me a lot. But that's all you need to know, Cathedral."

Cat prodded him to tell her more, but he refused.

"I think I can get a projector from the gallery where we held the wake," Mick said, changing the subject.

"Sounds good," she said. "But you know, Uncle Mick, I'm a private investigator. I'll find out your Granny Grace story eventually."

She laughed with him as he shooed her out the front door.

Chapter 21

Mick set the projector up in his studio. The three of them examined each of the nineteen paintings for signs of anything their arsonist might not have wanted shown on one of Mick's large, public canvases.

The collection spanned the many decades of his career, from one he painted in graduate school that contained fragmented images from a dream of Annie Lin's to a stray cheerleading pom-pon that cropped up in a recent painting. That one came from a woman he'd slept with whose age was too embarrassing to admit to Cat and his sister. Suffice to say she was still young enough to be dreaming of her high-school glory days.

The three of them went through the paintings slowly, Cat and Pris quizzing him about each one. He racked his brain to remember the original dreams that had inspired the paintings. They analyzed every piece of imagery in every painting, Cat sitting with her laptop and searching for words and phrases online as they flipped through the slides.

There was a fire engine with the number five emblazoned on it in gold that Cat and Pris got excited about for a moment but then couldn't take further.

Next was a trash can tucked into the corner of a painting. Cat fixated on it for a good hour or so, or at least it seemed that long to Mick. She could make out the name of the waste-management company on its side, Sauvey Systems. She searched the web for any crimes connected to that company but didn't turn up anything significant. They moved on, but Cat made a note to have Alvarez check it against the police database in case any dead bodies had been found in a Sauvey Systems dumpster.

When they came to a painting of his titled *Red Shift Sunset*, Pris said, "That red..." and walked up closer to the projected image. "There's a number here."

"Yeah, I sometimes scrawl numbers into the top layer of paint. It's kind of a thing I do."

"Did the number come from a dream?" Cat asked.

Mick thought about it, hard. He barely remembered the dream that had inspired the painting, which he'd completed several years ago. At the Brickell Lofts, he rarely ever slipped into the other artists' dreams. He wasn't sure why; maybe it was because the walls in the old warehouse were so thick, or because he'd got better at shutting dreams out by that point in his life, with advice from Pris. But there was one that slipped through, and this was it. He was certain it belonged to one of the short-term residents, a young guy, fresh out of art school, who didn't last long before he'd moved on to a regular day job. Harry, that was his name. He was from California, and the sunset in the dream looked to have been over the Mojave Desert. But the numbers, they were Mick's.

"Nope," he said. "That's my locker number from high school."

He hated to disappoint Pris and Cat, and even more than that, he hated that their art-review project wasn't yielding anything worthwhile. What they had at the end of a long evening spent on those nineteen paintings was exactly nothing.

Pris paced the room, and Cat flipped over on Mick's couch so that her feet dangled over the back of the couch and her head hung from the seat. She stared at painting number thirteen, still projected on the wall.

"Looking at it upside-down isn't making this any better," she said.

Mick felt frustrated and drained by the whole case. It had been such a roller coaster ride for him, first wanting to kill Candace, thinking she was responsible, and then having to dredge up those old feelings about Chester Canon. And it turned out that neither of them was guilty, at least not of killing his friend.

"I don't see how this is getting us anywhere," Mick said. "If you're right, and the killer torched the studio to destroy one of these paintings, then he must have been paranoid. Because we're looking at them, and nothing's standing out."

"These paintings have been a dead end since the beginning," Cat said. Her face was turning red as the blood rushed to it.

"There must be something we're missing..." said Pris.

Mick walked over to the painting on his easel, the one inspired by Cat's dream. He lifted a lid off a can of paint sitting nearby, picked up a brush, dipped it once, curled the brush sidewise to catch the drip, and then began dabbing it onto the canvas. It was red paint, which was always thinner than other pigments. It went on bright, almost pink, but would dry much darker.

Working a bit freed his mind, although he was conscious of Pris and Cat in the room with him.

He thought about the two hundred or so paintings he'd lost, some of them without even a photograph left due to his own negligence. He wondered why Pris hadn't said how Buddhist that was, how clean he should feel now that half his life's work no longer existed.

And how strange it was that the sum of who he was as an artist now belonged to other people. The only paintings he himself now owned were works in progress, his unfinished stumblings around after

168

the fire: An abstracted image of Donnie all burned up, like a piece of human jerky. This unfinished painting from Cat's dream. Everything else was spread throughout the world, in galleries, houses, a few middle-grade museums.

And he thought of something.

He set the brush down and turned around. "We're looking at the wrong paintings."

Cat righted herself on the couch. Pris stopped pacing.

"We're looking at the paintings that no longer exist," he said. "But what if the painting is still around, and our arsonist doesn't know that?"

There was a long silence. Mick could practically see his words hanging in the air, like someone's textual art.

"That's good, Mick," said Pris. "This is an amateur, after all. What if he failed?"

"We need the other database," agreed Cat. "The one of the surviving paintings." She scrambled to find it on her laptop.

They made quick work of the new list of paintings, and Mick identified another twenty-six that had been inspired by dreams. Of those, twelve were accompanied by images.

Cat called Sergeant Alvarez again, and explained their theory. "He could have assumed it was in Mick's studio, since it was well known that Mick kept his work there. But it might not have been there. It could have been sold, or on loan."

Mick wasn't able to hear what Alvarez was saying, but it sounded as if she were skeptical, or else growing weary of their dead-end case.

"I know, I know," said Cat. "You're right. But just look at the remaining digital images, at least. I'll even flag the ones that, um, look promising."

Mick figured those would be the dreamslip paintings.

After Cat did some whiz-bang stuff on her laptop to transfer the images to the Miami PD, the three of them turned their attention to the new crop of twelve paintings.

The first three they were able to eliminate easily, as they were part of Mick's most abstract stage, and they contained little that was discernible. He'd merely been inspired by the color and texture of those dreams, which hadn't contained much substance anyway.

The next one gave them pause, as again it contained a number that seemed to be a serial number. Mick couldn't remember what it was at first but then realized it was the serial number for his Fiat.

The two after that they analyzed for a good half hour each but couldn't find anything in them to research further.

The next six paintings didn't yield much either, though they certainly gave Cat plenty to search on, everything ranging from the name of an old-fashioned soda company to the time 2:21, which was prominent in the painting Mick had titled *When It's At.*

So they reached a dead end. Again.

Mick looked over Cat's shoulder at the full database of surviving paintings. "If it's here," he said, "it's probably one of the paintings I don't have an image of. Sure wish I'd done better on the documentation side."

"Here, Uncle Mick," said Cat, offering him her laptop. "Take a look at the descriptions."

He tried reading her tiny screen, but the words were jumbling together, and he hated the glare. So he walked over to a drawer and fished around till he found the printed copy on forty-three pages that Beverly had given him after the fire. *One page for every year of my friend's life,* he remembered.

He sat back down, flipping through the pages with Pris staring over his shoulder.

"Find the ones that might have been sold or loaned out right before the fire," Cat said.

As soon as Cat said that, he flipped the page to where there was a description of a piece called *Three Views, One Girl* that he remembered letting his old friend Greta take back to New York with her two weeks before the fire. If Greta hadn't been in touch with Beverly about his inclusion in a show at the Painted Stick so she could help publicize it, this painting would have been on the other list all along.

Pris leaned in over Mick's shoulder. "Mickey."

"Yes, sis?"

"The painting in that gallery in New York—what was the name of it, Cat? The one with the girl. The one you won't sell."

"The Painted Stick," said Cat. "That's the name of the gallery. Greta is the owner's name."

The mention of it gave Mick chills even though he was staring at the description already.

Cat seemed to know what Pris was onto. "Is that a dreamslip painting, Uncle Mick?"

The image of the redheaded girl flashed in his head. He remembered the dream that had produced it. He'd fused with someone who desired that girl, and he hadn't liked the feel of that at all. So he'd popped out of his dreamer's consciousness and then out of the dream entirely. The girl stayed with him, though, so he painted her. He painted her to rid himself of her.

"Yes," he said.

"Why won't you sell it?" asked Cat. "Greta told us you wouldn't let her sell it."

Mick saw the girl in his mind's eye again. "I don't know," he answered. "I feel like she shouldn't be sold."

Cat and Pris looked at each other. "That has to be the one," Cat said. Pris agreed.

"I'm thinking the same thing." Mick felt terror clench his stomach. Why did he have to paint that girl? He'd known it even as he was painting her that he shouldn't have, that he should have let her go. "That would make sense," he said, the logical part of his brain working the details. "I sent the triptych to Greta in New York right after Thanksgiving, right before the studio fire."

He told them about dreamslipping in some stranger's dream, someone who desired the girl, how wretched it made him feel, and that he'd left the dream.

"Where were you, Mick?" Pris asked. "When you slipped into that dream."

Mick tried to remember. Everything before and after the fire was a blur... And there it was. "At a party on Star Island."

Cat asked, "Was it at that patron's house—Kristoff Langholm?"

"Yeah," he said. "But there were probably thirty, forty people there that night."

Cat went into the kitchen and got a sheet of paper and a pen. She thrust them at him. "Write down the name of everyone you saw at that party. Everyone."

Mick sat staring at the white page in front of him. He jotted down *Kristoff and Carrie*, followed by *Serena Jones*.

"I wish we had a copy of that painting," Cat said to Pris. Mick resented the way they sometimes discussed his case as if he wasn't there. "Maybe Greta used it in promotional materials," Cat continued, popping open her laptop again.

"Most likely not," said Pris. "Since Mick didn't wish to sell it. Remember? It was in the back of the gallery, marked 'NFS.'"

Mick cleared his throat. "Well, you know, I could call Greta and ask her to send a photo from her phone. She is my friend, after all."

Pris and Cat looked at him in amused surprise. Then the three of them burst out laughing, glad to have something break the tension.

Mick called Greta, who was in her gallery, thankfully, and not busy. She was curious about the request but sent the image to Cat without too many questions. Mick's phone was too old-school to handle digital images. Cat did some techie magic to get the image on her laptop and then projected it onto the wall.

And there she was, in triplicate. His wan heroine, his redheaded lady-child. She wasn't yet eighteen, as he'd tried to capture in the budding quality of her breasts under a white tank top. She had an unnatural thinness about her as well, as if slightly malnourished. The whole time he'd painted her, he felt as if he wanted to save her. That was the attempt in painting her, to save her and rid himself of her haunting eyes at the same time. But he felt strongly now that he had failed. And in his failure, he'd simply failed her.

"What if it's her," said Cat, suddenly. "There's nothing in the painting that seems searchable—no numbers or codes or passwords of any kind. Maybe it's the girl herself."

"Perhaps she's missing," said Pris. She ran her hands over her bare arms, as if suddenly cold. "I don't like the way this case feels."

"Neither do I," said Cat. "This is ramping up into something else. We need to be more careful."

"You're right, Cat," said Pris. "You know it's not my nature to say this, but I'm not sure whom we can trust."

Mick felt his hands grow clammy, the pen slipping where he was still writing the names of the people who were at the party that night. "What about Rose?" he asked.

Pris put her hand on his shoulder. "Tell her no more than she already knows."

"The same goes for Ernesto," Cat said to Pris, pointedly.

"I suppose you're right." Her voice was reluctant.

"He was at the party that night," Mick said, eliciting surprised looks from both of them. He wrote *Ernesto Ruiz* on the paper in front of him.

"Well, they are his clients," said Pris, as if to explain.

"Was Jerry O'Connell there?" Cat asked.

"Who's that?" replied Mick.

"He bought several of your paintings," said Cat.

The name still wasn't ringing a bell.

Cat cleared her throat. "He talked you down in price for them."

"Oh, that guy." Mick remembered Jerry, a sly piece of work, that one. "I can't recall if he was there or not. It doesn't seem like it would have been his crowd, but you never know."

"What about Chester Canon?" Cat said. Mick figured she was running through the suspects.

"Nope."

"Clive Smith?"

"No, although with his recent meteoric rise, he'll probably be on the next invite list."

"Annie Lin?"

"Negative."

"Norris Grayson?"

"Nein."

"Maysie Ray Duncan?" Pris put in, her tone light.

Mick cracked a smile. "Hardly."

"I should think Ms. Duncan would be a delight at a house party," Pris countered.

"Tell that to Langholm," said Mick.

There was a long break in their conversation as Cat typed notes in her laptop, Pris gazed at the triptych projected on-screen, and Mick wrote down more names. *Pennington James*, he scrawled. That was the name of a friend he sometimes met for drinks and to shoot the shit. He was there that night, too, as were a few other artists. *We were the cheap entertainment for the evening*, Mick thought somewhat bitterly, although he'd swallowed his aversion to such things years ago, and that's how he stayed in business, as it were. But would any of these artists be twisted enough to hurt the girl? His imagination was already running through the kinds of trouble a young girl could find herself in. He couldn't imagine any of his artist friends capable of such things, but then people like that hid their crimes well. What a bloody awful thing he'd somehow got mixed up in, and all he'd ever wanted to do was paint.

Tina Wright came next. *Samantha Forrester*. Those were the artists he knew, but there were other people, Langholm's wealthy set, who were also there. The main guests. Not entertainment, but people there to be entertained. He closed his eyes, pushing himself to remember. A judge wearing a bolo tie, as if South Florida were Texas hill country. He couldn't remember his name. An owner of an educational software company who used to teach back in his "poor" days, he'd said. *Philip Peters.* Mick remembered that because he called him "the man with two first names." A few women, maybe friends of Carrie's. One hit on Mick; she'd seemed to be the type to pour money into a male gigolo. Not his speed, so he'd avoided her. *Danielle something.*

And so it went. He filled the page with names, half names, and descriptions when he couldn't come up with anything else. Then he turned it over to Cat, who was busy texting the triptych image to Sergeant Alvarez.

"Let me know if you need any help with the investigation," Rose said. She was sprawled underneath the sink in his studio, trying to fix it. "I mean, not that I have any idea how to do that."

"Well, at least you know your plumbing," he said.

Rose laughed. "That's a funny thing to say to me, considering."

Mick had been referring to the fact that Rose learned the plumbing trade from her father. But then he got her meaning.

"You can really snake a pipe," he said, keeping the joke going.

"You're a real wit, Travers. Now get down here and give me a hand."

Mick crouched down beside Rose, who lay on her back, her face underneath the pipes.

"Grab the sealant," she instructed.

Mick looked around on the floor beside them, feeling dumb.

"White canister," she said. "Green lid."

He found it and handed it to her.

He watched her hands, somehow both delicate and strong, dab an applicator wand into the sealant, stroke it around the mouth of both pipes, and then firmly connect them.

"Now hold this for me," she said, taking his hands and sliding them into the place where the pipes connected.

She relaxed backward and smiled up at him, his face inches from hers.

"That's it?" he asked. "Just hold it?"

"Yep."

"How long?"

She put her hands behind her head and laughed. "As long as it takes." She closed her eyes.

He liked the way her chin dimpled below her bottom lip, as it was at that moment. What would it be like to kiss her there? He sighed, and her eyes opened again.

They looked at each other for a long moment.

Mick felt the air change, felt himself lean in to kiss her.

But then he realized what he was doing.

And he pulled back.

"Isn't this long enough?" he asked.

It was clear that his pulling back was like a slap in the face for Rose. She closed her eyes again, but this time her lids were crinkled in pain. "Yes," she said. "You can let go."

Mick scrambled to his feet. He helped her get out from under the sink.

"You need to keep the goosenecks clear," Rose said. Mick thought she was returning to their earlier line of jokes, but then he realized she was talking about something under the sink.

"And don't skimp on the fixtures," she said, her voice noticeably strained. He saw there were tears in the corners of her eyes. "If you ever have to replace these vintage sinks, go upscale."

She turned to the sink to test it, running the tap. "There you go. Good as new."

"Rose," he said. "I—"

"Don't go there, Mick." She washed her hands in the running water. "Because we both know you wouldn't"—she grabbed a towel to dry her hands—"go there."

"Rose."

She turned to face him, still holding the towel.

"Would you." She said it like a statement, but to Mick it felt like a question. One he couldn't answer.

"I don't know." He met her gaze. "I'm sorry."

"It's okay." She tossed the towel onto the countertop. "I'm used to it. How do you think I ended up with Roy Roy?"

That one hit Mick in the gut. He didn't know what to say. There was a long, awkward pause, and then he said, "You're a genius with these household repairs, Rose. How much do I owe you?"

"Oh, more than you can imagine," Rose said. "But for the sink, don't worry about it. Just remember this if I'm ever late on rent." She sniffed. "Not that I ever plan to be late, but you know, the best-laid plans..."

Mick shook his head. "I'm not worried about it. You've already helped me out a ton fixing this place. And thanks for showing it yesterday." He was trying to get a renter in the other unit, and she had shown it to a prospect while he was busy at the marathon projector session with Cat and Pris.

"Don't mention it," Rose said, adjusting the strap on her overalls. "But seriously, what's happening on this case? Are we ever going to get justice?"

Mick sighed. "I don't know. It's taken a weird turn."

"Really? What's going on?"

He stopped himself, remembering his pact with Pris and Cat that they would keep the details to themselves.

Rose got the meaning in his silence. "Fine. So, what am I now, a suspect? Please. I just fixed your damn sink, Mick."

"I'm sorry," he said, feeling that nothing he said would be right.

"Whatever." She picked up her toolbox and left, shutting the door hard behind her.

In the quiet of his studio, Mick walked over to the unfinished painting that was inspired by that dream of Cat's. He remembered the shock on her face when she saw it. So much trouble, he thought. He reprimanded himself for what suddenly amounted to cheating, taking others' ideas and making them his own in his art. Was it ethical? He thought about Candace telling him basically to butt out of her dreams. And he thought of the haunting look in the girl's eyes in the triptych. And of his own limitations, just now with Rose.

Mick picked up a large brush, dipped it into a can of black paint, and crossed out the painting. Then he began to fill in with black everywhere the cross lines weren't. Soon, he'd covered the canvas in nothing but black. The painting was gone.

This gave Mick an idea, an even better idea, he suddenly saw, than what had been there before.

And he went to work.

Chapter 22

W"e'll be sticking together on the case from now on, not splitting lists of suspects," Grace told Cat.

Her granddaughter groaned. "Everything will take us twice as long."

Grace would not be moved. The signs were telling her they needed to be together from now on. "I feel strongly about this," she said.

"All right," Cat said. "But if you want to be cautious, let's dig up as much as we can about these suspects before talking with them."

Grace went along with that plan, although it cut against her instincts. She preferred to meet them face-to-face first without an impression pre-formed by public profile. Then she'd fill in any blanks afterward.

First on the list were the Langholms, of course, since they were the hosts of the party that night. Grace had liked Kristoff, finding him to be a witty and intelligent collector with a wry sensibility. She remembered how warm he was with Mick at the wake and couldn't imagine Kristoff capable of arson and murder. Then again, many a guilty party in her experience had seemed unlikely at first. So she would have to reserve judgment about him. Cat went to work digging up what she could on the couple.

Then there was Serena Jones. Grace took that one on herself, curious as she was about the woman's rise to fortune. The official story on her web site claimed she was second-generation Cuban, so Grace started there.

Mick wanted to help, so Cat showed him some public-access databases and a few other research tools and told him to snoop into the backgrounds of the other artists at the party. After some choice complaints from Cat about Mick's dinosaur of a laptop, they left him to his research.

Grace's laptop was sleek and relatively new, and she had it even before Cat came into her life with her constantly wired techie attitudes. She knew more about how to dig for information than her granddaughter gave her credit for, and in a day or so, plus a visit to the Miami Public Library, she'd discovered that Serena Jones wasn't who she pretended to be.

Luckily, Grace had spent some time at Donnie's wake talking with Serena, and the woman took her call and agreed to a visit.

This time, three of Donnie Hines's pieces graced the space above the fireplace in the dining room where previously Mick's paintings had hung. Grace and Cat were admiring again Donnie's fantastic crystals when Grace heard Serena's heels clicking on the terrazzo floor behind her.

"I couldn't resist," Serena said, gesturing toward the paintings. "It was so emotional, the wake. I know better than to get out my credit card at a time like that, but no matter. It's a good investment nonetheless."

"These might have already increased in value," said Cat. "Did you see the write-up in *Art in Our Time*?" There had been an obituary and favorable remarks about his work in the January issue, which had hit stands in advance of the New Year.

"No, I did not," Serena said, looking pleased. Then she affected a slightly more businesslike demeanor. "Have a seat." She motioned to a grouping of armchairs to one side of the dining room, in front of a window through which Grace could see a stone fountain spurting water dyed fuchsia, the color of the La Luz logo. To Grace it looked as if the fountain were spouting a sports drink. They sat, and then Serena asked, "So what can I do for you ladies today?"

Grace cleared her throat. "Well," she said. "We've actually come to speak with you about a highly delicate matter." She looked pointedly at the maid, who brought them two tall glasses of water with lemon and sprigs of mint. "I was hoping for a private conversation."

Serena looked surprised. "Very well... Mariana, please, leave us for a few moments. Close the door on your way out."

The maid did as instructed, Serena took a sip of her water, and Grace again cleared her throat. A few minutes after the door to the dining room clicked shut, Grace said, "Angie Ramirez."

Serena dropped her water glass, which shattered when it hit the floor. "Miss Jones, are you okay?" called the maid from behind the door.

Serena recovered, leaned toward the door, and said, "I'm fine, Mariana. We'll leave the mess for later." She kicked a few pieces of glass with her designer heels, Christian Louboutins, Grace noted.

"Where," she said slowly, leveling her gaze at Grace, "did you hear that name?"

"I understand the desire to remake yourself," Grace said. "You know, I wasn't born 'Amazing Grace.' But to this day, I can't get my own brother to stop calling me Priscilla. I guess the past can never be fully excised."

Serena sat back in her chair and stared out the window at the fuchsia fountain. "You have no idea how hard it is to make it as a Mexican-American woman," she said quietly. "Still. With Hispanic politicians and everything."

"So you moved to Miami and reinvented yourself as Cuban, which as I understand it, is as good as white. Here, anyway."

Something seemed to break in Serena. "Fucking racists," she spit out, kicking a piece of glass across the room for emphasis. "The whole lot of them, with their constant claims to European ancestry. They do everything they can to separate themselves from Mexicans. Which means natives. Indians. Mestizas, like me."

"Yes," said Grace.

"Luckily, my father was white. So I pass."

"You're practically a pillar in the Cuban-American community here. That's impressive, considering you grew up poor in a small border town."

"Like you, I do my research."

"Touché."

There was a pause, and then Grace pressed a bit further. "Who else knows your real story?"

"No one."

"Not anyone back in Del Rio?"

"No."

"But now we know. It's not hard to find out the truth, if you know where to look."

Serena bent over and picked up a piece of glass, and Grace tensed. "I don't know why either of you would want to blow my cover." She looked at the shard of glass as if it were a precious work of art.

"Think of what it would mean to those Mexican-American girls like you if they knew you came from the same place they did."

Serena clasped the glass in her hand angrily. "It's my job to pave the way? Bullshit. I don't owe anybody anything."

"She's right," Cat broke in. "She doesn't. It's not her job to be a trailblazing member of her ethnic group." It had been their agreement that Cat play the good cop in this scenario, should things get out of hand.

At Cat's words, Serena relaxed her grip on the glass, but Grace could see blood beginning to drip from her hand.

"I'm not Angie Ramirez anymore," Serena said. "I stopped being her long ago. It's like I've created a fictional story for myself, and it has become non-fiction." Her laugh was bitter. "You know, when I was a girl, I thought they had the labels backward. I thought the word 'fiction' sounded like it meant truth, reality, and that the books that were full of stories should be the ones called non-fiction."

"I understand the logic," said Cat.

Then Serena thought of something. "Why are you here? To out sad little Angie Ramirez? I don't think so."

"Someone tried to kill my brother," said Grace. "And I'm trying to find out who. Lies usually come in batches, and I discovered that you had a tremendous one."

"I hadn't realized his killer was still on the loose. Well, you can't think I had anything to do with it. Really."

"We're following our leads," said Grace. "But maybe you'd be willing to help us out with a few things."

Serena looked to Grace like she wanted to turn them both out of her home, but of course now she couldn't do that. "So you want to blackmail me now? Hold this Angie Ramirez thing over my head?"

"We wouldn't dream of doing that," added Cat. "It's not our way. But we need some information, as well as your discretion."

"Fine," Serena said. She took a napkin off the tray beside her and pressed it into her bleeding palm.

Cat continued. "That party at Kristoff Langholm's house in September. We need to know who else was there. And anything you can tell us about them. Including the Langholms themselves."

"The party was a while ago. I don't really remember. And the Langholms... You've met them. They're a wealthy couple who collect art. They're my neighbors. That's all there is to tell."

"Take your time," said Cat, offering her card. "Something might come up."

"Why do you want to know about that party?" asked Serena, taking the card in the hand that wasn't wounded.

"It's part of our investigation," Grace said. "We can't say more."

"Are we finished here?"

Grace and Cat nodded, and Serena rang a bell on the tray. Her maid appeared at once.

"Show these ladies out," she commanded. "And then clean up this mess." At that, she rose and stalked out of the room, slamming the door behind her.

Grace smiled at the maid. "Mariana, this is really our fault. You should let us clean it up for you."

"No, no, no," said Mariana. "I will take care of it."

Grace bent and began picking up shards of glass.

"Señora, no," insisted Mariana. She politely but firmly patted Grace on the shoulder. "I will take care of it."

"All right," said Grace, rising to her feet. "Say, Mariana, I have a question for you if you don't mind." Grace fetched her phone out of her bag, called up the triptych of the girl, and showed it to Mariana. "Do you recognize this girl?"

Grace thought she caught a flicker of alarmed recognition in Mariana's eyes, but then the woman's face went hard again. She shook her head, her lips pursed as if she were willing herself not to speak.

"You recognize her?" Grace responded. "Tell me. Who is she?"

"No lo sé," Mariana said. "I do not know."

"You don't know, or you won't say? Where have you seen her?"

"I cannot say…" Mariana said, backing away. "Por favor, leave me to my work."

"Please," Grace said. "We need to know who she is."

"You recognize her, but you don't know her name," said Cat.

Mariana clutched her broom to her chest and backed further away.

"Where did you see her?" Cat asked.

Mariana took a deep breath. "Lo siento, but I was mistaken. I have never seen that girl."

Grace and Cat could got no further with Mariana, so they left.

———

When they arrived home, Sergeant Alvarez's squad car was parked out front. Grace looked at Cat, who shrugged and said, "I sent her the databases and the image of *Three Views, One Girl*. But I wasn't expecting a visit. Maybe she turned up something…"

Encouraged by this, Grace sprinted up the steps to Mick's door, and finding it unlocked, went inside.

Immediately she sensed that the mood in the room was wrong. Mick looked scared and confused. Speck and Santiago were slipping Mick's behemoth laptop into a large plastic bag.

"What's going on here?" asked Grace, searching Alvarez's face for answers.

But the woman's stern expression gave back no trace of the camaraderie they had recently shared on the case. "Your brother here is under investigation for possession of child-abuse material."

The words hit Grace with the force of a cannonball. She reeled backward, clutching at Cat behind her.

"Wh-what?" Grace struggled to regain her composure, as well as her balance. She felt her granddaughter propping her up from behind, which was good because Grace was having trouble getting her knees to obey her brain's instructions.

"What's going on?" asked Cat. "What evidence do you have? You know that's not Mick."

181

"I don't *really* know you people," Alvarez countered. "And the evidence came from you, Cat."

"The painting," said Grace, finding her knees, her balance, her self. "The one Cat texted to you."

"The girl depicted in Mick's art, if you want to call it that, has appeared in child-abuse material known to law enforcement."

"But his paintings aren't pornographic," Cat protested.

Alvarez looked as if she were weighing in her mind how much to tell Cat. "The girl, what she's wearing, the chair she's sitting on—all of it appears in photographs that are, that we know have circulated for years. So it stands to reason that if Mick's painting those details, he's got the kiddie porn."

There was a moment of quiet in the room, as if everyone were letting that information sink in. And then they all began to talk at once.

"But I had no idea, I didn't mean..." said Mick.

"Don't say another word," Cat said to Mick.

"We need to take you down to the station for questioning," said Alvarez.

"Mick's innocent," Grace heard herself add to the fray.

The next few moments were a blur. The deputies combed through Mick's studio, bagging and tagging anything that might have been used to house or transmit images. They asked for his passwords. They asked if he used any online or cloud storage providers or clouds. They also sifted through every box and drawer for printed photos or anything else that could connect Mick to child-abuse material.

Grace saw the spasm in Mick's jaw working. She went over to him and touched his shoulder.

"I didn't mean anything by the painting," Mick said, his voice weak.

"I know," Grace said. "You had no idea."

Cat was visibly angry, Grace could see. The girl clenched her fists at her sides as the officers ransacked Mick's studio.

"Are you arresting him?" Cat demanded.

"We're taking him down for questioning," Alvarez replied. "After that, it depends on what we discover. This is a very serious charge."

"You won't find anything more than what Cat sent you," said Grace. "And that doesn't make much sense, does it? That Cat sent it to you?"

"Maybe she wanted to out her sicko of an uncle," said Alvarez.

"That's not why I sent it!" Cat yelled. "You're making a huge mistake."

Grace searched for something she could say to Alvarez to explain why her brother painted a girl who had appeared in child-abuse pornography, but there was nothing that would make sense. So she remained silent.

"Mick, due to the nature of the potential charges here, I'm going to have to bring you in in handcuffs."

Grace detected a strain of empathy in Alvarez's tone. She focused on that to control her own panic. She did not want to see her brother dragged off like a criminal.

"You can't do this!" Cat yelled.

"On the contrary," said Alvarez. "I have to do this. It's my job."

Grace watched powerlessly as Mick was escorted outside, installed in the back seat of the cop car, and taken away. She reached for Cat, but her granddaughter was more angry than upset. Cat pushed her hand away and tried to appeal to Alvarez.

"You're making a mistake," Cat kept saying. "He's innocent."

Grace found herself at a loss for words.

Chapter 23

C at barged into Alvarez's office the next day with Granny Grace, who was weakly protesting, telling her that a calm head would prevail. Cat didn't have a shred of calm left at this point, and Granny Grace must have been too upset herself to push the issue.

"You haven't found anything, have you," Cat asserted to Alvarez. "Let my uncle go."

Alvarez sat behind her oversized desk, her index fingers steepled at her chin. "We need your uncle to be more forthcoming about where he found the 'inspiration' for his work of art."

That took the wind out of Cat's sails a bit. It meant they were switching gears, looking at Mick as some sort of accessory or accomplice. They couldn't get him on possession, so they'd try using him to bust whoever else they could.

Alvarez continued. "I mean, come on. It came to him in a dream? I really doubt that. Who is he protecting?"

"No one," said Cat. "Believe me. He's telling the truth."

"My brother's a very active dreamer," Grace added.

Alvarez laughed haughtily. "An active dreamer, huh?" She reclined back in her chair. "Don't take this the wrong way, but I am kind of tired of you people."

Cat allowed herself to breathe. Maybe it was even a yoga breath, not that she would admit that to her grandmother.

She spoke in a more measured tone now to Alvarez. "You've got nothing to hold him on, and he doesn't have any information about the child porn. But if you'll work with us on this, we might be able to help you track down whoever was involved in whatever material is known to law enforcement that depicts that same girl."

Alvarez crossed her arms in front of her chest. "So it really came to him in a dream? That's what he's telling us. 'She came to me in a dream.' Not a series of dreams, or God forbid something slightly more useful, like a recurring nightmare or a PTSD episode, but no. One lousy dream."

"Yes," Cat and Granny Grace said in unison.

"I don't buy it."

Cat held her hands out in front of her. "It's what we've got, because it's the truth."

"I don't think so," said Alvarez, standing up. "There's something you're not telling me."

Cat backed away. "We'd like to see Mick now."

"Fine," said Alvarez. "I'll take you to him. We're done questioning him, until he's ready to tell us more."

Cat and Grace followed Alvarez down a hallway lit by fluorescents to a small room where Mick sat with his impromptu lawyer, a defense attorney recommended by Mick's publicist, Beverly, who was unhappy about what this would mean for Mick's career.

Cat had assured her there would be no charges against Mick, but Beverly didn't care. "Once his name is mixed up in the press with anything having to do with child porn, we're done for," she said.

Cat shook the lawyer's hand. "Dave Sommers," he said. Grace shook hands with him next and then went over to Mick and embraced him.

"I can't believe this," Mick said.

Sommers cleared his throat. "They've got nothing against him. The child porn his painting references has been in circulation for a while, they believe, maybe even a long while. So it's not like anyone thinks Mick knows where the girl depicted in them is, or had anything to do with her appearance in them."

Cat and Grace both let out sighs.

Sommers continued. "And they didn't find any child porn in your uncle's possession. There's no crime here."

"Then let's go home," said Granny Grace.

"Just a minute," said Sommers. "They can't hold him, but I would recommend that Mick give the police more to show his innocence and cooperation, I mean, if you can, Mr. Travers. The details in the painting do exactly match those in known images of child porn, and that's been hard to explain. I mean, the dream thing is thin."

Mick looked at Cat and Granny Grace.

"Could you excuse the three of us for a moment?" Cat asked Sommers.

He appeared taken aback. "Sure ... I mean, anything you say to me is protected by attorney-client privilege, but I, uh, respect that this is also a ... family matter." He smiled politely and then left the room.

Mick spoke first. "I've never been in a position like this before. I didn't know what to tell them."

"What you told them was fine," Granny Grace said in a manner that struck Cat as overly cheerful. "Perfect, in fact."

As mad as Cat was at Alvarez at that moment, she realized the value in bringing in the resources of the Miami PD again on this case. An idea occurred to her. "I think the three of us need to agree on a story. A non-dreamslipping version of the truth."

"Truth is good," Mick said. "I'm not a very good liar."

"Great idea," said Grace.

"So tell them where you were when you had the dream."

"Okay," said Mick.

"Leave out the dreamslipping part. We'll use this to get Alvarez's help investigating who was there at the party. We want access to police databases. We need to know what they already know about this girl and where else she's appeared."

"And we need them to put some pressure on that maid of Serena's," added Granny Grace.

"Agreed," said Cat.

"But won't they want to know what I saw at the party? I mean, I don't want to have to make something up."

"Tell them you don't remember. Tell them you'd been drinking."

Cat felt Grace's hand on hers on the table. "There's only one problem here, Cat. We're going to point a guilty finger at Kristoff, since it was his party, and Alvarez will think it's likely he's the one who had whatever inspired Mick."

"Yes," said Cat. "And it was probably someone else at that party who happened to dream about the girl while spending the night at Kristoff's. But it's a risk we'll have to take."

"If Kristoff's innocent, that will be borne out soon enough," said Grace.

There was a moment of quiet as they fortified themselves to go forward. Then Cat motioned through the window for Sommers to rejoin them. Once in the room, Cat explained to him that they had a hunch about where Mick might have seen something that sparked the dream.

"Why didn't you tell me this before?" Sommers asked. He cast glances at Cat and Grace.

Mick stepped up to the plate. "I wasn't sure I wanted to drag someone else into this who might be as innocent as I am."

"And who is that?"

"Kristoff Langholm."

"The real estate magnate?"

"Yes."

"Jesus." Sommers reached into his briefcase and took out his audio recorder. "Let's start from the beginning. Tell me what you know."

Mick explained about the party and how he'd had the dream while sleeping overnight at Kristoff's place on Star Island.

"But you didn't see anything there? You didn't wander into his study, find something in his desk drawer, or a book on a shelf? Anything?"

"Not that I remember," said Mick.

"It was a party," Cat offered. "Everyone was drinking."

"How drunk were you?"

"The booze was free, and the bar was well stocked."

"I see. So you might have seen something and not realized it, in your state."

"I suppose that's possible. But I don't remember anything except the dream."

"Right. And quite a dream it was, as you've already explained."

Cat interrupted. "The police need to investigate everyone who was at that party."

"Sure," said Sommers. "Look, you do what you want. You can go talk to them about this party, and they might follow up on it, but there's not much evidence here to link either your uncle or Langholm to any child-abuse material. At the very least, however, it's a cooperative gesture. As long as fingering Langholm doesn't come back to bite any of you."

As Sommers wrapped up their session, Alvarez appeared in the doorway.

"You're free to go, Mick. We haven't found a thing. I mean, nothing beyond what the average citizen has bookmarked, if you know what I mean."

Cat did not want to know what Alvarez meant by that, but she noted that Mick's face reddened a bit.

"My client has more information for you," said Sommers.

Alvarez came into the room and shut the door, and Mick told her everything—or at least, everything they'd agreed to tell her.

Alvarez still didn't buy that Mick hadn't seen something concrete at Kristoff's, and the fact that he'd withheld the information about the party initially made her more suspicious that he was covering for someone.

But this worked to their advantage in a way, thought Cat. It made both Serena Jones and Kristoff Langholm strong suspects, as they were both patrons of Mick's, and Alvarez would think Mick would be reluctant to finger either of them.

"Let's work together on this," Cat said to Alvarez. "We'll bring you our research on the suspects so far, and we can map out a strategy."

Alvarez's demeanor was still wary, but she had softened toward them.

"All right," she said. "Let's see what you've got."

Sommers was dismissed, and the four of them got down to work.

On their way back home that evening, Cat checked her text messages while Granny Grace drove. There was one from Jacob: *There's a story breaking on Twitter that your uncle got hauled in for questioning for possession of child porn!!! Are you okay?! What's going on? Is it true?*

Cat flipped to her phone's browser and searched for the reference, and there it was. A Miami crime blogger had written up a short piece based on Mick's questioning, which had been recorded in the police blotter. And it looked as if the blogger had tried to increase his traffic by sharing it widely with anyone connected to the art world. There were already tweets shaming Mick as a "pervert." Cat noted with disgust that most of those tweeters spelled the word "prevert." A group of tweeters had already set up the hashtag #boycottmicktravers.

"Oh, my God," uttered Cat aloud. And then she wished she hadn't, with both Granny Grace and Mick in the car, and her grandmother driving.

"What, Cat?" Granny Grace asked.

"Ah, it's nothing. I'll tell you when we get home."

"Might as well tell us now, girlie," said Mick from the back seat. "Otherwise, we'll sit here imagining the worst. And after this, it can't get much worse."

"Yes, it can," said Cat. She reluctantly handed him her phone.

"Fuck me." Mick flipped through the phone till he'd seen enough, and then he tossed it to the floor of the car. Cat left it there, not particularly wanting to see it, either.

"Well, would one of you tell me what's going on?"

"I've become the almighty Internet's latest whipping boy," Mick said.

Cat explained to a bewildered Granny Grace, who was uncharacteristically clutching the steering wheel.

"I'm just famous enough to be damaged by this," Mick said.

They were silent the rest of the way home, and when they arrived, they retreated to their own private spaces for some solitude. Cat stuffed her earphones in her head, closed the partition around her bed, and lay down to try to forget the past couple days. She wondered where her God voice was now. Tuning in, she heard only silence, beyond the ringing in her ears.

She was almost asleep when she realized she'd forgotten to reply to Jacob. *Not OK*, she tapped out on her phone. *Not true.*

He replied immediately. *Can I see you?*

Not in the mood.

Not that. I mean, I want to help.

Risky.

Doesn't have to be. Let me help.

Cat sat staring at her phone, trying not to think about how much she wanted Jacob's arms around her right then. But she was too tired to drive back down to South Beach. It was almost as if Jacob heard her thoughts, as what came next was this: *I'll drive up there.*

My grandmother. Jacob knew that Cat shared the studio with Granny Grace.

It's okay. We'll be sleeping. That's how you'll know it's just that. Let me hold you tonight. OK?

OK.

Chapter 24

For the first time in his life, Mick wished he owned a gun.

Maybe he'd use it on himself.

If not that, then he'd have it in hand for the moment when he could look his arsonist/killer/child porn sicko/frame artist in the face and pull the trigger.

Because that's what he would most definitely do. The bastard who'd torched his life and hurt the redheaded girl like that deserved to die. But a gun wouldn't do it justice. No, the creep needed to die in a slow, torturous manner.

Mick sat down on the couch in his studio. He couldn't look up his public stoning on the Internet because his equipment was still at the Miami PD, not that he needed to see it anyway. He didn't have much for them to search through in the first place, and Alvarez wanted her people to comb through everything a second time to make sure they didn't miss anything.

To make sure they didn't miss anything.

He couldn't believe this was happening, that it wasn't some surreal painting he'd stepped into and was living. But it was real. He pinched himself to make sure. He was sitting there, in his studio, with the world out there now thinking he was a repugnant waste of human flesh.

He'd never live it down. His career might be over. What now?

And Sergeant Alvarez, of all people. For her to think that he was that kind of sicko... He remembered her smirk as she said that all they found was what "the average citizen" would have bookmarked on their computer browser. She and her cop buddies must have kidded around good at his bookmarks for *Chicks with Nightsticks* and *Broads with Badges*.

He knew she was too young for him, but hey, it wasn't a crime to let out a little steam that way. Then again, maybe it had reassured them he wasn't the pedophile sicko type. If there was one thing made clear by his taste in porn, it was that Mick Travers favored strong women of clearly and firmly adult age.

But still.

Mick pushed himself to his feet, went into the kitchen, and grabbed a bottle of whiskey that hadn't even been opened yet. He broke the paper seal and unscrewed the cap. Took a sip, right out of the bottle.

And began to cry. Heaving dry sobs while he stood there staring into the white porcelain sink he couldn't even fix himself.

When he was done, he went into the living room and plotted how he could get that sick bastard Pennington. Mick knew now it was his dream he'd walked in that night.

He'd had to describe the dream twice, once to his own lawyer, and then again to Alvarez. And the second time, with Alvarez grilling him, a specific detail had floated up from his subconscious.

A watch, an antique gold watch with a brown snakeskin band. He remembered the watch in the dream, on the wrist of whoever's dream he'd slipped into. It took him a minute or two while Alvarez told him why his story sucked and she knew he was lying before he realized where else he'd seen that watch. Pennington James, a middling artist who painted pictures of animals dressed as superheroes, never left home without it.

"This here's my grand-pappy's watch," Pennington always said, affecting a Southern drawl. Mick knew in fact the man had grown up in Pittsburgh.

Mick hadn't said anything to anybody else about the watch. He didn't know why, exactly. It wasn't that he thought he should protect Pennington. Mick knew him from a group of artists who liked to get together and drink, spending much of their time one-upping each other with insults, when they weren't comparing the relative dick sizes of their respective art careers. He'd never liked Pennington's art, truth be told. But they were friends. Not to the level that he and Donnie had been, but they were friends. How had Mick not seen it? Not once did he ever get a bad vibe about him. In a million years, Mick never would have thought Pennington to be the pedophile type. The man was a pretentious snob whose work wasn't as good as his opinion of himself made it out to be. But a creep who bought pictures of naked kids? And who might have even killed Donnie?

He never would have thought Pennington capable of either crime. But now that it was clear he'd been the one to dream about the girl, Mick no longer considered the man a friend. Far from it.

No, he didn't want to protect Pennington.

He wanted to kill the bastard.

Himself.

Maybe even with his bare hands.

———

Fortunately—or unfortunately—for Mick, the group of artists was meeting soon in honor of a holiday they unanimously liked to disparage: Christmas. So he went.

Mick braced himself for the evening with several shots of whiskey out of a new bottle to replace the one he'd downed the night of his questioning. He knew the evening was bound to be a roast with himself as the designated suckling pig, since a man questioned for possessing child porn made such a glee-inducing target. And that wouldn't even be the hardest part of the evening.

The Orinda Lounge was a slice of ol' cracker Miami, with its grimy red carpet, pizzeria lamps, and jukebox playing nothing but classic rock. "Hotel California" was blasting when he walked in the door, and the cadre of artists who'd already assembled at their usual back table bristled when he entered and sat down, clearly surprised to see him.

Barney Dent, a troglodyte of a sculptor whose pieces graced the lobbies of many a South Beach hotel, sounded the first note. "Mick, what gives? You more of a perv than any of us gave you credit for, or what?"

Mick was conscious of Pennington James, drinking a beer, his demeanor nonchalant. Mick wanted to lunge across the table, grab him, beat him senseless, announce, "There's your perv," and stalk out. But he knew better.

"Aw, it was a stupid misunderstanding," Mick answered. He knew the police hadn't released the details of his questioning, so he didn't have to explain the painting of the girl or any of that. Besides, it was better if his responses were vaguely suspicious. "They, ah, had me confused with some other guy. We got it cleared up yesterday. That's why I'm out."

"Well, that's rather boring," Dent replied. "But I guess I'm relieved to hear you're not any screwier in the head than I thought."

At that, the group pounced on Mick with the subtlety of kids going after candy thrown from a parade float.

"Say, Mick, if you're looking for the Toys 'R' Us, it's down the road. I think the chicks in there are more your type."

"Aw, Mick. It's so nice to see you. We weren't sure you'd make it since we hear there's big doings tonight down at the elementary school."

"If your art career doesn't recover from this, I hear they're looking for new recruits for the priesthood."

And so it went. He took it in with his face set to a mask of good-naturedness. They advised him to steer clear of nudes and to paint using models whose hair had gone gray. "I guess you ought never to apply for the Artists in the Schools program!" That one got a huge laugh.

Mick stuck around far longer than he could stomach, betting that Pennington would, too. And he did.

Soon it was only the two of them, and Mick acted drunker than he really was. He'd been alternating every gin and tonic with plain tonic water.

They laughed and kidded and told stories, getting back into each other's confidence. Mick waited for the right moment. There was no one else in the back room now, and the jukebox was loud in the front of the lounge.

"Boy, what a rap," Mick said. "Child porn. What's the big deal with that, anyway?"

"You're all right, Mick," Pennington said, moving in closer to Mick and lowering his voice. "Man, even if you did have a few, you know, pictures or whatnot, say they're a bit young-looking, what of it? It's just a picture."

Mick squelched the urge to grab Pennington by the neck and choke the hell out of him.

"Yeah, you sure? You okay with that kind of thing?"

"Oh, in the right context. Society's far too overprotective."

"Damn straight," said Mick. He took a fortifying sip of his drink, which he was glad was a real gin and tonic this time. "Say, you got anything I can borrow? I'm pretty cleaned out, you know, with what happened yesterday."

Pennington stood up, took out his wallet, and settled the bill. Mick reached for his own wallet, but Pennington waved his hand, said, "It's on me."

They walked outside, and Pennington turned to Mick. "You want to follow me? My Mazda's up there. You remember it."

Mick nodded, thinking back to a night when Pennington gave him a ride. His car had been in the shop, and Donnie had gone to Ohio.

Pennington lived in a newly constructed home, peach-colored stucco with tall square columns flanking the front door. Mick had never been there before. Pennington pressed a code into the security system to gain entrance. *"Disarmed,"* came the voice. Once the two of them were inside again, he rearmed it. *"Alarm stay,"* it said.

Mick was in, but getting out without Pennington would trigger an alarm. That wasn't good, but so be it.

Mick followed Pennington upstairs. Lining the stairwell were the artist's own paintings: a zebra in a Green Lantern outfit. A giraffe dressed like Superman. It struck Mick suddenly that he'd never liked Pennington's art because it looked like it could grace the cover of a children's book. Thinking about that in the present context nauseated him.

194

"Wait here a minute," instructed Pennington, pausing outside what looked to be the door to his art studio. Then he went in, and Mick stood outside.

There were sounds on the other side of the door. Pennington getting into his secret stash, Mick figured. Then he popped the door open.

"Entrez," he said with a flourish, gesturing with his hand as if whipping off his hat and bowing to Mick as he stepped inside.

It was a sizable atrium studio, which must have been custom-built with the house. Four skylights showed a fuzzy moon and city stars. On a low table in the corner, Pennington had placed a stack of color images, letter-sized, as if they'd been printed off from a computer.

"You can take them if you want," said Pennington. "I have the digitals."

Bracing himself, Mick rifled through the images, looking for the redheaded girl. He had to control his reaction to them. He felt his stomach churning and was afraid the few gin and tonics in his belly wouldn't stay there.

The worst part was, he had to look as if he liked seeing them.

"I prefer gingers," Mick said. "Got any of those?"

"Of course," Pennington said, his voice sounding delighted, as if he'd met a fellow connoisseur. "But if you wouldn't mind stepping outside? Just a precaution."

"Sure," Mick said. Again the sounds behind the door. A sound like metal sliding over metal. The click of a lock. A shuffling noise.

Then footsteps. Pennington opened the door, and Mick walked back over to the table.

Three photos down, there she was. But it wasn't like his painting. This was his girl, but the image was one of terrible violation, something he would now never be able to forget, and the girl was even younger than he'd realized. Something snapped within Mick, and he turned around and lunged at Pennington.

The man was a wimp, smaller than Mick and not in possession of the kind of build that one associates with physical labor. But he fought back with a wiry spite and was able to knock Mick over.

Only once, though. Mick hit him across the face, and Pennington fell. Mick dragged him to a chair. There was some duct tape there in the studio, which Mick had seen earlier. He used it to secure him to the chair.

He should put him out of his misery, Mick thought. Strangle him right here. No one would weep for a sicko like him.

"You look like you want to kill me," Pennington said, laughing. "Go ahead, Mick! It'll do wonders for your career. You're already a child molester. You can be a murderer, too."

"Where's the girl?" Mick asked.

"The girl? What girl?"

Mick grabbed the awful photo and smashed it into Pennington's face. "Her!"

Pennington gazed at the image. "Ah, so this is about her. Haunting little minx, isn't she? I've had the most delightful dreams about   her."

In one smooth maneuver that did not require any thought at all, Mick picked up a nearby paintbrush and shoved the pointed end into Pennington's ear. The man screamed. Blood dripped.

"Tell me where she is," Mick said. His rational mind, working behind the rage he felt, told him the girl was long gone, maybe dead by now, and that Pennington wouldn't be able to help him save her. But he wanted it to be possible.

"Where?"

Pennington cried, tears streaming out of his sockets. Mick kicked him, and he called out again.

"I-I have no idea! They're just photographs. That's it. Innocent photographs."

"This sick stuff isn't innocent, and you know it."

"I don't know anything about any of these kids," Pennington insisted. "Not even their names. Jesus, don't you know how this works?"

Mick tapped the brush sticking out of Pennington's ear, and the man screamed again.

"Stop! I can't help you! I buy this stuff online, and that's it. It's a hobby. Nothing to kill over!"

"Who'd you buy it from?" Mick demanded.

"It's just like regular porn, man. So what if they're a little young. You can tell they liked—"

Mick went for Pennington's throat.

The studio door burst open, and there was Sergeant Alvarez, her gun drawn.   "Stand down, Mick," she said.

But Mick couldn't stop. His rage was blind, red.

"Move away from him," Alvarez commanded. She moved closer, her gun out in front of her.

Mick did as he was told. Speck and Santiago appeared behind her, their guns drawn as well.

"Get this maniac away from me!" Pennington screamed. "He's a creep. That's his porn over there. I brought him up here to show him my art, and he took out those awful pictures."

Speck held a gun on Mick.

Santiago went for the stack of photos. "These are children."

Alvarez saw the picture of the redheaded girl on the floor near Pennington and stooped down to retrieve it. She looked at Mick, at Pennington tied with tape, and around at the room.

"You were trying to get him to talk, weren't you?" she said to Mick.

"Oh, he doesn't need any help talking. But I can't get anything good out of him. Not about that girl or where he got this shit."

"Don't listen to him!" Pennington yelled. "It's his! He brought it here!"

Alvarez grabbed the roll of duct tape and stuck a strip across Pennington's mouth. Mick loved her for it.

"Where does he keep it?" Alvarez asked, looking around the room.

"I don't know. He made me wait outside when he dug it out."

"Did you hear anything? Look around the room."

Mick looked. Metal sliding over metal, he remembered. There was too much ductwork in the room, he realized, and not all of it led to the heating vents. He walked over to an odd section of metal duct that seemed to have no purpose. He slid the duct aside easily, metal sliding over metal. But there was nothing there.

Further into the studio, though, there was another batch of ductwork that also didn't make sense. He slid that over, and there it was, a safe with a metal lock. But it needed a key.

Alvarez was peering over Mick's shoulder at this point and saw what was needed.

"Search his pockets for a key," she said to Speck. Pennington began a muffled protest behind his tape. Speck produced a ring of keys from Pennington's trouser pocket.

The third one they tried was a perfect fit. Inside was Pennington's personal treasure trove of sickery.

Alvarez took out her radio and called for a forensics team. "Cuff him," she told Speck. "We're taking him in."

"Do you want me to remove the tape?"

"Not the one on his mouth," she said.

"What about this guy?" Santiago gestured at Mick.

"We let him go," she said. "He's clean. We know this didn't come from him."

Mick felt the tension drain out of him. He turned to Alvarez. "How'd you get here, anyway?"

Speck put handcuffs on Pennington and led him downstairs.

"Check the other rooms in this house," Alvarez instructed Santiago. "When the team gets here with the supplies, start bagging and tagging everything you can find."

As he left the room, she turned to Mick. "I knew there was something you weren't telling us, Travers. So I had you followed. When my officer radioed in to update me that you'd entered James's residence, we heard the first scream. So I came here myself, and by that time it sounded like you were murdering someone."

"I might have if you hadn't shown up."

"Better shut up about that," she said, giving him a sympathetic look. "And I don't want to see you going rogue like this ever again."

She glanced toward the door to make sure no one else was within earshot, smiled, and lowered her voice. "Or else I'll use my nightstick on you."

Chapter 25

G race couldn't believe her brother Mick had turned into a vigilante. She gave him a good talking-to when his story came out. They couldn't have Mick going around like that, taking matters into his own hands.

Then again, she'd never been more proud.

Grace was looking forward to leaving this case behind soon. It wasn't that she didn't have plenty of experience with child victims. Besides Cat's first big case, with the mother and girl on the run, Grace had seen her fair share of innocence lost. The worst was when she'd gone undercover in a satanic cult in the Eighties. There wasn't much actually going on in terms of black magic or genuine Satanism, but they'd used the cult as a way to gain control of young people, whom they used to sell drugs and for prostitution, and that was as much evil as Grace could stand.

It appeared that Pennington James bought the images through the darknet, a kind of off-the-grid shadow Internet, where there wasn't a trace the Miami PD could follow. But at least James himself, who had been the source of the dream that caused Mick to paint the girl in the first place, would easily be convicted of possession of child-abuse material.

The police were still examining the evidence to connect him to the fire in Mick's studio. Grace had lingering doubts that he was the arsonist as well—if so, why did he ask Mick over to his home? And there was also the matter of that maid's reaction to the painting of the girl....

But now it was Christmastime. Everyone was taking a break from the case anyway, and Grace needed one herself.

She'd never been one for the Christian religious aspects of the holiday, but she relished a good winter solstice party, and that's what they were going to have, right there in Miami.

Grace enlisted the help of Cat and insisted she invite her friend Jacob, who'd been around more often than not ever since the night Mick had been taken in for questioning. She included Rose as well, who proved to have quite the flair for decorating. But then, given Rose's sensational outfits, that was hardly a surprise.

Auspiciously, a couple of hill mynahs set up roost in the tree outside Grace's window the day of the party, their boisterous calls filling the revelers with extra-special merriment. To Grace's amusement, Cat mimicked it perfectly: "wee-onk!"

Grace insisted they hold the party in the studio where she and Cat had been staying. She wanted to place two dozen candles set into seashells on the stairs leading to their room and then inside, throughout the apartment.

"Can't we put up a Christmas tree?" Cat whined. "It'll make the room smell like pine."

"Well, I happen to think a northern pine at this latitude is an environmental travesty." Grace couldn't help herself. "Think of its carbon footprint! And it'll take up space in a landfill afterward."

"But it won't be the same without a Christmas tree..."

Grace couldn't sway her granddaughter from her conventions, no matter how much she tried.

"How about a compromise, ladies?" Mick offered. "A tropical plant in a pot, and we decorate it like a Christmas tree. Then after the holiday, we plant it out front."

They agreed. Cat and Mick left to get the plant while Grace and Rose fussed with candles and seashells.

Grace was glad to see Mick's spirits lifted. Catching Pennington James must have taken a huge weight off him, even though his reputation still suffered.

"I must've caught a drunken glimpse of his porn stash at that party," Mick told Alvarez, and that stuck as the only logical explanation.

Speaking of the painting, Mick had Greta send the actual triptych down from New York, and it was in police possession as evidence in the case against Pennington James.

"Instead of pine boughs, what do you think of using palm fronds?" Rose asked.

"Bring on the fronds!"

Rose went outside to gather them in the yard around the fourplex, and Grace lit a candle to melt some wax into the shell so she could affix the candle to it, upright.

In her mind she ran through the list of tonight's attendees: Cat, Mick, Ernesto; Cat's new friend Jacob, who would be in town through New Year's; Rose and her boyfriend, Leroy; and Evelyn, Chester Canon's neighbor. Grace had invited Sergeant Alvarez and hoped she could make it as well. After that were a number of people she'd met in her previous visits to Miami, people she hadn't had time to catch up with properly.

Rose returned with an armful of tropical foliage, and the two of them spread it around the room. Then Grace set Rose to the task of making punch, and Grace herself began assembling the tofu pâté.

Soon enough, Cat and Mick came home bearing a small, potted hibiscus tree. Its tangerine flowers resembled umbrellas that would unfurl in full bloom, a decadent pistil of pollen beckoning from its center.

"Let's set it here, in the window," Grace said, beaming at her two lovely family members.

Mick and Cat carried the hibiscus together and set it down delicately. They stared at the tree for a moment.

"I'll go get the other swag out of the car," Cat said.

"I've got some bling upstairs to add to this thing." Mick winked at Grace and slipped out the door.

"It's perfect, isn't it?" Grace said this to Rose, who was stroking one of the soft blooms.

"It smells like tropical Christmas." Rose stuck her nose closer to the flower and inhaled.

Cat came in, her hands full of shopping bags, which she dropped onto her chaise lounge, now clear of paperwork related to the case. She reached into a bag and withdrew a box of retro bubble lights. Together, the three of them strung the lights onto the miniature tree. Once the lights had warmed, Cat, who said she had experience with these kinds of lights, tapped or inverted them to get them to bubble. Their effervescence made the room sparkle.

In came Mick with a canvas drop cloth he placed around the bottom of the tree as a skirt. He also brought down a box, which he offered to Grace. "Will homemade ornaments work for your solstice party, Miss Pris?"

"Oh, Mick." Grace took the box and reached inside. He'd fashioned the most delightful ornaments out of bits and pieces from his studio: a few spines of an old Chinese fan tied together with red velvet ribbon; a garland of driftwood and shells; a vintage toy car hung with glittery string. The four of them decorated the tree together, marveling over Mick's creations.

When they were done, they stood back to admire it, and Rose said, "We need a star." She looked at Grace and smiled. "I know you're not hot on the Jesus story, but that star of Bethlehem, it always makes me weepy to think about it, a beacon in the night."

"I'm not against those aspects, per se," said Grace. She thought about the church sermons of her childhood, the fire and brimstone and talk of sinning. "There's a reason they're always claiming it's the greatest story ever told. I think it resonates with us to think of God as not just a man, but a small baby in a manger. He's nothing but potential."

"I think I have an idea for our star," Rose announced. "Mick, come and help me." The two of them left.

"The studio looks beautiful, Granny Grace." Cat gave her a hug.

"It does, doesn't it? Oh, I do miss the old Victorian, and Seattle is quite lovely this time of year, when everyone hangs lights out so as to push against the rainy darkness. But the tropics for winter solstice? This is simply delicious!"

Grace glanced at the stove clock, which read 7:23 in retro flip letters. "We should probably get ready. And you still need to call your parents."

"Right," said Cat. She picked up her cell phone and went out to the balcony to have a private chat with them.

Cat hadn't been in touch with her parents much since Lee Stone's death, and Grace was worried that she was distancing herself from them.

Grace retreated to her own private section of the studio to change. She had chosen a peacock theme for her evening wear. She eagerly shed her casual clothes and slipped on a royal blue silk dress with a turquoise tunic over it. She'd indulged in a peacock "fascinator," as they called them, a jeweled number with feathers that she used to secure her hair back over one ear. She wished she had her grandmother's diamonds to wear as well, but of course those were in her safe back in Seattle.

Around the same time Grace finished dressing, Cat reappeared with a smile on her face. "Thanks for reminding me to call them," she said. "I hadn't realized how homesick I was for their voices."

"Wonderful," said Grace. "Now go get dressed."

Grace fussed with the decorations again, and soon enough, Cat came out in a red velvet dress with a tartan-plaid sash. "Exploring your Scottish roots?" Grace teased, and then told her how smashing she looked.

Rose and Mick resurfaced, Rose holding something delicately between her hands. "I got to thinking about the star of Bethlehem, and the wise men, bringing gifts of frankincense and myrrh. Well, we don't have any of that, whatever it is, but we have something better."

She moved her top hand to reveal a star crafted out of thick white paper stock backed by tracing paper. There were cutouts in the thick top layer of paper so that the lights from the tree would shine through the tracing paper, dotting the star with glints of light. It was a six-pointed star with beams emanating downward. She shook the star softly, and fine glistening grains of sand filled the beams of light like stardust.

"Did you use beach sand?" Grace asked. "It looks sugary, like it came from Bahia Honda."

"No," Rose said with a glowing smile and a wink at Mick. "That's Donnie."

———

A few hours later, the party was in full swing. Cat and Jacob played a card game with Rose and Mick. Grace was catching up with Ernesto, who cut a handsome figure in a dark suit and crimson tie, when Evelyn arrived, bearing a basket of guava pastries.

"I brought your favorite," Evelyn said, offering the basket to Grace.

Grace explained to a puzzled Ernesto how they'd met over an offering of the same.

"Grace here nearly had me convinced she used to work for that cretin Chester Canon." So Evelyn hadn't bought that ruse after all, Grace thought. But it certainly hadn't mattered.

"But I knew right away she was far too smart to work for a man like that!"

The three of them laughed.

"Let me get you a drink, Evelyn," Grace offered. "You stay here and chat with Ernesto. What'll you have?"

"Oh, I'll be fine with some of that punch, assuming it's spiked, of course."

Grace checked in with the card party on her way to the punch bowl. She noticed that Rose kept glancing at her phone, most likely anticipating word from Leroy, who still hadn't shown up. She nudged Rose and motioned for her to follow her into the kitchen.

"How's Leroy?" Grace asked.

"I wish I knew."

"He hasn't been in touch?"

"Nope. Not a word."

"Why don't you call him?"

Rose hemmed and hawed. "I don't want to nag him."

Grace flashed angry. What kind of boyfriend would think that about an important evening like this? "Nonsense. Give him a call."

Reluctantly, Rose dialed him on her cell phone. Grace turned her back to the punch bowl and made a show of dishing up Evelyn's punch to give Rose privacy.

"Where are you, Roy Roy? You promised you'd be here. Don't think you're going to show up at the end this time, with your boys in tow." There was a pause, but Grace couldn't hear Leroy's side of the conversation.

"What do you mean your homies are up in your crib? Well, I hope they're up in your grill, too. You knew this was important." Rose hung up on him.

Grace turned around. "Maybe it's time to let him go."

"It's past time," said Rose, her chin set hard. "I know that."

Something occurred to Grace. "Rose, may I ask you a question?"

The woman nodded.

"You have such good judgment when it comes to your friends. I mean, Donnie and Mick, others I've met..." Grace paused, unsure how to phrase it.

"You wonder why I don't apply that to my love life?"

Grace nodded, feeling instantly regretful that she was butting in *and* offending Rose all in one go here.

"Donnie was special," Rose said. "We ... you know ... once. He's one of the few men who wanted me for me. I wasn't a fetish for him, or a curiosity... or a charity case."

"Oh," said Grace. She hadn't anticipated that.

"But he was in love with Dark Moon, or whatever she calls herself." Rose tucked her phone in her pocket. "Not that she deserved him."

Grace was quiet.

"And your brother." Rose shot a look at Mick across the room. "He thinks I'm a freak show."

"Oh, I don't think that's true," said Grace.

"No, it's fine," Rose said. "We're friends. Man, after what he's been through, I have nothing but sympathy for him. But if you want to know the truth, Miss Grace, it's this. If I weren't transgendered, your brother would have fucked me by now."

At that, Rose turned on her heel and went to rejoin the card party.

Finding herself uncharacteristically flustered, Grace poured another glass of punch and took a swig. Then she carried both over to rejoin Evelyn, who seemed unfazed by Ernesto's charms.

"With all due respect, Mr. Ruíz, why would I invest in art? I don't trust it. I've seen wildly inflated prices for pieces one week that no one will touch the next. There's no regulation. Did you read about that Brazilian banker who used art to launder his embezzled loot? An eight-million-dollar Basquiat was seized in the Port of Miami. The bill of lading listed it as valued at only one hundred dollars."

Ernesto appeared a bit flustered at Evelyn's brashness and, Grace suspected, her knowledge of the underside of the art world.

"Are we discussing money now? At a solstice party?" Grace dazzled them with her smile and presented Evelyn's punch to her with a flourish. "Evie, dear, let me introduce you to some of my family." She whisked her new best friend away from Ernesto, figuring he was a grown man who could take care of himself.

After introductions, the card game broke up, and Cat hooked her laptop up to a pair of speakers Mick had bought. She'd created a playlist for the party, and the song "Grandma Got Run Over by a Reindeer" began to play. Grace shuddered and cast a disparaging glance at Cat, who ignored her. Grace despised the song, deep down in her bones. She hung back as the rest of the crowd laughed and began to carry on. Grace hooked her arm through Ernesto's and squired him to the balcony.

"Horrid excuse for music," Grace said, shaking her head.

"Yes, well, it is Americana at its worst."

There was a pause as they gazed at the moon casting a beam of light on the waves far in the distance. Then Ernesto turned to Grace, swept his arms around her and said, "I've missed you."

"I've missed you, too," she said instinctively, though she realized she was only being polite. She'd been so wrapped up in the case that she hadn't had time to miss him.

"So you've caught the man who set the fire? And this has to do with pornography? Involving children?"

"Why, yes, I suppose you've summarized it nicely." Grace felt something new, something that had been pushing at the edges of her consciousness that she'd ignored before, but it was coming in stronger. She tuned into it.

"Terrible business that must have been," Ernesto said, as if he were inviting her to elaborate.

She resisted. That dark red energy at the core of this case began to pulse at the fringes of her vision, and again, she heard the wings beating. "Yes," she said, meeting Ernesto's gaze. He had deep brown eyes, sweet enough to make an old lady like her swoon. But right now she didn't feel herself swoon. She was thinking suddenly of Serena's false identity, and of that dream Ernesto had, the one with the winged figure, and of what Evie had said about art.

"Miami's such a strange place," she said, squeezing his arm. "It's populated mainly by people who've been forced from their homeland, and yearn to return."

"This is true for many, I suppose. But not for me. I would never go back to Cuba, not even if the U.S. took it away from Castro."

"America has been good to you, Ernie."

"Yes."

"You've forged incredible connections here." She folded herself into him, let him circle her with his arms. Then, nonchalantly, she asked, "What do you do for the Langholms, exactly? Mick says he's seen you at parties at their home."

She felt his energy shrink from her, as if he were drawing wings around himself. "Not very much, really. Minor investments, stocks, bonds…"

"Do you ever advise them on art? Or handle their acquisitions?"

"Oh, no," he quickly denied. "Not at all. Only boring financial transactions."

Grace sensed that Ernesto was lying. But why would he want to downplay any art dealings he'd had involving the Langholms? His secrecy on that point seemed suspicious, and she felt a cold chill down her spine as she realized that Ernesto had been there all along, asking questions about the case, nosing around in a manner that was more than merely polite or supportive.

The red energy pulsed at the corners of her vision, enough to make her head ache. She steered Ernesto back inside as the horrid song ended.

Chapter 26

C at found herself standing on the Golden Gate Bridge with the wind whipping her man's shirt and trousers against her skin. Wait, man's shirt and trousers? She looked down at her hands and recognized them as Jacob's. Cursing herself inwardly, she realized she'd slipped into his dream, against her better judgment.

As Cat and Jacob leaned over the edge of the bridge in a manner that felt too precarious, the latter thought about what had got her into this predicament with the former. The Christmas party, she remembered. They'd stayed up very late dancing and drinking and having too good a time. It seemed cruel to send Jacob home, so she'd let him stay.

Jacob hoisted himself up onto the bridge railing and then jumped.

Cat reacted instinctively, but she was trapped in Jacob's mind and body, so all she could do was ride along as they plummeted into the water below. But then Jacob's body began to slow down till it was practically floating in the air. The impact in the water felt like a jump into a swimming pool. It was as if she were in a Disney cartoon, with fish swimming by jauntily and a happy, soaring soundtrack playing. What was this? she wondered. Then the fish flattened out and with a curious cartoon pop, they became paintings. She was standing in an art gallery.

A man with an enormous fish face but sporting a suit and cane sidled up to her and said, "Journalism's dead, don't you think, my boy?"

At that, Jacob woke up, popping Cat out of his dream and unsettling her sleep as he turned over in the bed they were sharing.

"Jacob," she whispered. "You awake?"

"Umpf, yeah," he said groggily.

"Me, too."

"I had the weirdest dream."

"Yeah? What was it."

He cuddled into her. "I think it was about my uncle."

"Your uncle?"

"He wants me to move to San Francisco."

Cat realized this must be the thing she sensed Jacob needed to figure out down there in Miami, away from New York and his magazine job.

"What would you do there?"

"Work in his gallery. Take it over someday."

"That's huge."

"I know."

She didn't know how to respond. She didn't want to make this about her, not at all, but if he moved to San Francisco, he'd be in the same time zone and a couple hours away by plane from her in Seattle. The thought made her feel simultaneously excited and apprehensive.

"Could you leave the magazine?"

"I don't know. There's more money for me working with my uncle."

"And more future, too?"

"Yeah. I mean, journalism... Not exactly software development. Or health care."

"But your life in New York..."

"I know. I thought I'd never leave it."

She braced herself for him to say something about the two of them, about the proximity thing, but he didn't. Soon, he fell back to sleep.

She was awake, though, and reflecting on the evening. Ernesto had not spent the night, Cat noted, and her grandmother had claimed a migraine. Cat had never known Granny Grace to suffer from them.

Cat got up quietly, careful not to wake Jacob, grabbed her laptop, and set herself up on the chaise lounge. As much as she'd enjoyed the break for the party, she was eager to do whatever she could to help Alvarez and the Miami PD find out where Pennington got that material.

Cat knew something about the darknet from her criminal-justice courses. It was a parallel Internet to the obvious one, but with a great deal more encryption and security to protect anonymity. This was a good thing when it came to whistleblowers, political activists, or anyone else trying to remain anonymous for legitimate reasons. Anyone with a private account online was part of the so-called "darknet," as it was loosely defined as any content not searchable by a public browser. But these otherwise inaccessible, untraceable portions of the Internet were also a safe haven for illegal activity. Drugs, weapons, prostitution, even human organs—one could find anything through the darknet. It was notoriously difficult to catch lawbreakers using it, though.

Deeply involved in her research, Cat didn't hear Granny Grace until her grandmother was standing beside the chaise lounge.

"You're looking into the dark corners of the Web, aren't you?"

Up on Cat's screen at that moment was a video game she'd downloaded from a darknet site after consulting with a hacker friend of hers back in St. Louis, who verified that it didn't have any viruses.

"You've got to see this, Gran," Cat said. "It's called 'Sad Satan.' Here, listen." She offered Granny Grace her earbuds so the dissonant sound wouldn't wake Jacob, who was still sleeping behind the partition.

Cat let her walk through the first few scenes, which took about ten minutes. Having already played through it, she watched her grandmother's face as she made her way down the long, dark hallway. Cat knew the ominous sound of what was supposed to be her grandmother's footsteps were replaced by distorted music and then a growl.

Grace yanked out the earbuds. "Cat, this is really disturbing. Does it ever end?"

"Wait, you're just about to the part where it really gets weird."

"This isn't it already?"

"Just keep going."

And there it was. For a couple of seconds, a man wearing antlers appeared at the top of a long flight of stairs, the walls lined with the same antlers.

"Shut it off," said Grace.

"But it's almost over."

"I don't like this."

Her grandmother seemed upset, her forehead creased in worry.

"Sorry, Gran. It's kind of a darknet mystery. As far as anyone knows, this is the only game of its kind, and it's free. No one knows who uploaded it. It contains references to child abuse, but not in an exploitative way. Like whoever made the game is trying to caution or warn people. But then there's also this vague Satanic imagery, like that guy with the antlers—creepy, huh?"

"I really didn't like that," Grace said. Her grandmother pressed her hand to her chest.

"Are you OK?"

"Cat, are we alone?"

"No. Jacob's still here. Sleeping."

"After he leaves, I want to talk to you."

"Don't mind me," said Jacob, who appeared from behind the partition around Cat's side of the room. "I know when I've overstayed my welcome."

Cat watched her grandmother shake off whatever was eating her and brighten as Jacob appeared around the partition wearing rumpled shorts and a T-shirt, his hair standing out in crazy angles.

"You're not going anywhere till you've had something to eat," Grace insisted.

Cat, surveying the disheveled room and, feeling her own stomach growl, said, "I think we need to go out for breakfast."

They agreed, and after a subdued but friendly breakfast at a café nearby, Cat kissed Jacob goodbye. She wanted to ask him more about the dream but felt she already knew too much.

Cat expected Granny Grace to quiz her about Jacob after he left, or at least to have picked up on the dreamslipping, but her grandmother was focused on whatever was bothering her.

"I hate to say this, Cat, but I think Ernesto knows something."

It was as if she'd scratched her fingernails across a chalkboard. "What?"

"I don't know, maybe I'm mistaken. I hope I am. But I think he lied to me last night about representing the Langholms in their art dealings. And it occurs to me that he's been overly curious about this case from the beginning, as if he's been monitoring our progress to make sure we stay away from something."

Cat couldn't believe what she was hearing. She didn't like feeling suddenly as if she'd missed something about him.

"Are you sure, Gran?"

"No, but my feeling on this is too strong to ignore."

"Whoa. Okay. So what do you want to do?"

"I need your help getting a picture of what exactly he does for the Langholms."

Cat's pulse quickened. "The Langholms?"

"Yes."

"Okay," Cat said, "I've got this." She picked up her laptop and went to work. The Internet was like a gigantic haystack, but if you knew how to look for things, you could start to pull out the clues, straw by straw. After about an hour or so of digging, she found that Ernesto Ruíz had been the trader of record for a number of his clients who invested in stock. Her own grandmother's name was there, Cat was interested to find out, for stock purchases and sales he made on Granny Grace's behalf back in 2007, before the crash.

And there they were: the Langholms. They had been his clients for quite some time, in an on-and-off manner, and he wasn't the only financial advisor they engaged. There were many, it seemed. The Langholms had a complex financial life.

Cat presented her grandmother with the information, which was hardly surprising, as they knew that Ernesto counted both them and Serena Jones as clients.

"What about art-related transactions?"

"Nothing came up, but I can keep looking. There isn't much of a financial trail in the art world."

After more searching produced a blank for Cat, they decided to go down to the station and talk to Alvarez.

The sergeant greeted them eagerly. "I was about to call you in myself."

"Oh?" asked Granny Grace.

"We're not having any luck linking Pennington James to the arson."

Cat had known this was coming. She nodded.

"Mick will be disappointed not to have Donnie's murder solved," said her grandmother.

"That goes for all of us," Alvarez said, with a hardness to her voice. "The other matter is that the Feds are now involved."

Cat should have seen this coming, too, but she'd missed it. The darknet, Pennington's stash… It was only a matter of time.

"They'll want you to stay out of the case," Alvarez said. "But of course I can't stop you."

"Someone else torched the studio because they were afraid Mick saw something." Cat felt the case crystalizing before her. She cast a glance at Granny Grace and then at Alvarez. "We think Ernesto Ruíz might be involved, at least financially."

"Ernesto!" Alvarez said. "You're kidding."

Cat handed her a few printouts showing the stock transactions. "He advises Kristoff and Carrie Langholm. We think he's also managed their art dealings, but he felt it necessary to lie about that last night when my grandmother questioned him."

"Oh, the party…" Alvarez said. "I'm sorry I wasn't there. I just … well, maybe I wanted a break from you all. Please don't take offense."

"None taken," said Granny Grace. "We've been your cross to bear for weeks now."

Alvarez returned to the case. "So we've got Ernesto Ruíz, who's involved in art brokering. Was he at the party that night?"

"Yes. And there's more. There's a maid who works for Serena Jones. We showed her the image of Mick's painting, and she recognized the girl."

"When was this?"

"Before Mick went rogue and caught Pennington," Granny Grace explained. "We were following up on something I'd found out about Serena Jones, about her past. It's not connected to the case, but it gave me an excuse to show the image to her maid. I didn't think anything would come of showing her, but she acted as if she'd seen her image before. Undeniably."

"But then she clamped down," Cat added. "We couldn't get anything out of her."

"Let's get her in here before the Feds take over," said Alvarez. "I'll impress upon her what an important case this is."

It took some time, but that afternoon, Mariana Medina was brought in for questioning, followed by Serena Jones and a lawyer who looked as if he charged a hundred dollars a second.

They successfully barred Serena from the room, but the lawyer of course had to be present. Alvarez insisted Cat and Granny Grace join in as expert consultants.

"I'm sure you can appreciate the seriousness of a case involving murder and arson…" Alvarez began.

"Of which absolutely nothing links to my client," said the lawyer. "We're happy to help if there is anything relevant for Ms. Medina to contribute, but you'll have to prove that."

Alvarez held up her hand. "There's more if you'll allow me to finish." She gazed not at the lawyer but directly at Mariana. "The case now includes charges for possession of child-abuse materials."

Mariana's eyes grew wide. She seemed genuinely caught off guard, and that surprised Cat. She'd assumed the woman had seen the girl in examples of child-abuse material, and that's why she had reacted that way.

"I'm sorry to hear that," the lawyer said. "But again, unless there is something relevant to my client, I'm afraid you're wasting your time."

Alvarez continued. "Ms. Medina, these ladies say they showed you an image of a girl, in a painting. It was on their phone?"

No answer, so she prodded further. "You remember, don't you."

Mariana looked at the lawyer, who nodded.

Finally, she answered. "Yes, I remember this woman showing me the picture." She gestured toward Granny Grace.

"They tell me you looked as if you recognized the girl. Was that from other pictures you've seen?"

"No."

Cat felt frustrated that the woman continued to lie.

Alvarez pushed her. "Let me remind you that we need you to tell the truth. You don't want us to call you to the stand in court, have you swear on the Holy Bible, and then have to lie again there."

"I'm telling the truth," Mariana said. "I was not reacting to seeing that girl in other pictures."

Cat could feel Alvarez's breathing pick up next to her. "But you've seen the girl, then? In person?"

Mariana looked at her lawyer, who did not seem to know any longer what this was about.

"They already know, anyway," Mariana said, gesturing toward Cat and her grandmother. "Serena said so. They want to blackmail her with her past. After what she's accomplished! It isn't fair."

"Ms. Medina," Alvarez said. "I'm afraid you'll have to explain. I don't understand."

"It's Angie!" Mariana cried. There were tears in her eyes. "Angie Ramirez."

Cat broke in even though she was supposed to stay silent. "The girl in the picture is Angie Ramirez?"

"Yes. She dyed her hair red back then. Grade school. Even then she wanted to be someone else."

Cat explained Serena Jones's hidden childhood roots to Alvarez. And as she did, the same thought occurred to both of them, as they said in unison to the woman, "Did you know about the child pornography?"

"I don't know what that is about, or what it has to do with Angie."

"How do you know this … Angie, er, Serena Jones?" asked Alvarez.

"She is my cousin. She came back to Del Rio last year and asked me if I wanted to escape, to come away with her. But I had no skills. She wanted me to live off her, let her pay my way while I go to school, but I didn't want her charity. So I'm her maid. It's the only thing I know how to do."

There was a pause as they absorbed what she said, including Mariana's lawyer, who seemed irritated to have been out of the loop on this information. He remained silent, which, judging by his facial expression, did not come naturally to him.

"I don't understand," said Mariana. "Is this a mistake? I don't know anything about child porn. Please, I want to see my cousin now."

"Her parents…?" Alvarez asked.

"Addicts," the woman said. "Angie did not have a happy home."

"What about you? Couldn't your parents take her in?"

The woman looked away. "I didn't have a happy home either."

Alvarez was quiet a moment. Cat figured the sergeant was debating how much to divulge to Mariana Medina. Then Alvarez took a deep breath. "Ms. Medina, I am sorry to have to tell you this, but the girl in the picture they showed you is the same girl who appears in images of child-abuse material known to law enforcement."

Mariana's hand went to her mouth, and she shook her head. "No, it can't be. Serena said she got away…"

She broke down in tears.

They gave Mariana a break from the questioning and brought in Serena next, but only after she held counsel with her lawyer. They also ran some tests on the photographs to determine whether or not the redheaded girl could really be Serena Jones as Angie Ramirez.

"Ms. Jones, I can imagine how difficult this must be for you," said Alvarez once they were seated.

"I will cooperate as much as I can," said Serena. "But I hope you understand that my privacy has been seriously violated. That makes me a victim again, do you see that?"

"I'm very sorry, Ms. Jones," said Alvarez. "But I hope you understand that our intent here is to catch the psychopaths who took those pictures of you back then, not to mention whoever's still selling them."

Serena closed her eyes. "I cannot believe this. You can never escape, can you? It keeps dragging you back."

Alvarez placed a manila folder on the table. "These are the photos, Serena. You do not have to look at them. But you can if you want to be sure they are you. We've examined them using software, and we've concluded that they could be you, but you must have had plastic surgery. You'd also have to be wearing colored contacts."

Serena ignored the folder on the table in front of her. "All of that is true. I've had my nose and chin altered. And my natural eye color is hazel. My father was white, my mother born in Chihuahua. And my cousin told you I dyed my hair red when I was just a girl. That's when the photos—" She broke off.

"Thank you for that," Alvarez said. "I'm very sorry to ask you to revisit such a painful time in your life. And I hate to ask you this, but we'd like you to remove your contact lenses."

"Are you asking me to prove what I don't even want anyone to know?"

"I'm sorry," said Alvarez. An attendant brought in a plastic contact case, a mirror, and a bottle of saline solution and set it on the table.

Serena stared at them. "I can't do this."

Her lawyer spoke up. "Surely you're asking her to do too much."

"I'm sorry," Alvarez said. "But we need to be sure."

Slowly, Serena reached for the contact case, squeezed saline into the tiny cups, and then leaned over the mirror to remove her contacts. Her eyes went from brown to that washed-out hazel. Cat gasped, recognizing them from the girl in the painting—and in her dream that night in New York. She had seemed like a ghost girl, yet here she was. Cat felt admiration for her, to have recovered so much from the girl she had been, captured in those terrible photos and then in Pennington's dream and Mick's art.

After Alvarez took a few photos of Serena without her contact lenses, she waited while Serena put them back in.

"What can you tell me about how those photos … came into being?"

"With my parents' blessing," Serena spat out, still wiping saline from around her eyes with tissue from a box Alvarez retrieved from a corner of the room. "They needed the money. For drugs. They didn't care what those creeps did to me. 'It's just pictures of you, Angie,' my so-called mother said. 'Like you're a model.'"

Alvarez got Serena's whole story over questioning that took several hours. There wasn't much she could tell them about where the photographing took place or who did it. She said she believed she was drugged and raped at that time as well, but the truth of it had been hard for her to fully piece together, which she did through years of therapy sessions.

"I don't want a damned soul to know about my history," Serena said at the end. "Now I've helped you with these details, but I don't know what use they are to you. Those monsters back in Del Rio didn't have anything to do with the murder of Donnie Hines. And you'll never catch them. It was so long ago. They're long gone, maybe dead by now. I should know; I've gone back."

"Did you go looking for them?"

"Yes. I even learned to shoot. I brought a gun with me! I don't know what I would have done if I'd come across those pieces of shit. But I found nothing, the place where it happened had been demolished, a Taco Bell built in its place. I found nothing. Except my poor, half-literate cousin, who was still worth saving. You probably think I'm terrible for keeping her as a maid, but right now, that's what she can do. It's like she has to repeat her whole education over again, you know? Because the first time, she learned nothing in those barrio schools."

There was a pause as Alvarez let that sink in.

Cat took the opportunity to ask what she'd been wondering the whole time.

"How did you escape from Del Rio?"

Chapter 27

Mick spent an entire afternoon down at the Miami police station torturing himself with images of Serena Jones. She was a media darling, a real personality who'd been photographed in public throughout South Florida, at marketing events for her La Luz line of beauty products, at fundraisers and galas, and by paparazzi catching her out at the clubs with celebrities and other members of her nouveau-riche set. He saw now what he would never have been able to see before: the resemblance she bore to the redheaded girl in his painting.

He had to mentally alter her chin, nose, and eye color, but he could see it now. He wished he'd been able to see it before.

It made him wish he'd killed Pennington James. To think the photos that poor excuse for a human being had locked up in his safe were Serena as a young girl living through some unimaginable horror. At least he'd made it so that Pennington would never hear out of his left ear again. That was something. And the man's defense attorney had advised him not to press charges on Mick for it, as no jury in South Florida would likely convict Mick for what he'd done.

But there was no redheaded girl to save, because she'd already saved herself.

Mick was okay with that.

The thing was, after all the pain and suffering, he still didn't really know who killed Donnie.

Cat and Pris were looking into something having to do with Ernesto, and now the Feds were involved as well. Cat tried to explain to Mick about something called the "darknet," and listening to her talk about it made him feel really old and out of touch. His grand-niece had cozied up to the FBI agent from the Miami field office, and the two of them had geeked out on each other over the technology behind it all. Mick glazed over when they started flinging acronyms around. He didn't know his FTP from his PSP. At least he had FBI down.

He watched Pris making a valiant effort to ride the crest of things as well, and while she certainly fared better than he did and held her own in conversations with Cat and the others, he sensed she might be feeling her age, too, especially since she had a decade on her li'l brother.

Mick was glad they kept him around. He had to admit he liked using the computers the FBI brought in, as they were a dozen times faster than his own. Alvarez thought the FBI would come in and kick everybody out who wasn't official, but on the contrary, the agent leading the charge said he liked to have "all hands on deck."

Roger Strickland claimed to be a synesthetic, which, he explained to Mick, meant that the wires between his senses often got crossed. "The number five is red," he announced, by way of example. "But three is green."

Pris took to him, and Cat really bonded with him. They were, surprisingly, closer in age, as Strickland was some kind of boy genius who'd graduated from Quantico at twenty. Mick could sense that Cat saw in Strickland someone she could learn from.

But it was Cat, and not the boy genius, who came up with the prevailing theory they were now in a tizzy to prove, and that was that Kristoff Langholm was the biggest, baddest, child porn-distributing motherfucker that had ever lived.

Kristoff. Fucking. Langholm.

As Mick understood it, Cat first began thinking in that direction when her grandmother sensed that Ernesto lied about handling art transactions for the Langholms. Grace's hunch was correct; the FBI found evidence that Ernesto handled quite a few art transactions for them in a highly unregulated market, many of them now appearing questionable from a tax standpoint. After that, it was Serena Jones who became the linchpin in the case. And that damned tenacious woman didn't even know what kind of monster he was, or might be, if Cat's theory was correct. Serena thought of Kristoff and his wife Carrie as surrogate parents.

Mick heard the recording from Serena's interrogation, which wasn't on "tape," anymore, he noted, but on computer. He could see Serena's voice on the audio meter bob up and down as she talked. Strickland had him listen to it in case it triggered anything he'd forgotten to add, any details about Langholm. Mick liked that about Strickland, that he thought every detail could be relevant to the case. It reminded Mick of the way he used to paint, his chance operations, where any drip or smudge could become a new pattern or way of movement for his brush. Nothing was insignificant.

On the audio recording, Cat asked Serena how she'd escaped from Del Rio, and that was a curious story.

"There was this businessman who would come to town," Serena said. "He was so … cultured. Not like the thugs we knew. He was buying old buildings, pretty ones with fancy columns, beautiful old tiles, even chandeliers that were busted and forgotten. This man saw the beauty in them. He bought them from the owners and restored them."

"That was Kristoff Langholm, wasn't it?" Cat said.

"Yes. He'd be in town for long periods of time, sometimes with his wife, Carrie. I got to know them because I worked at the hotel, cleaning rooms. I was trying to escape, you see. I'd left my parents' house and was sleeping in the hotel, in the back with the other maids."

"The Langholms helped you?"

"Yes. They took an interest because I offered to help them first. I wasn't stupid, you know. I knew everyone wanted charity from them and that I would have to prove my value to get their help. So I showed them where the best buildings were. I'd been in them, as a kid growing up. I knew which ones were dangerous because their foundations were unstable. I knew which ones had fixtures and tin ceilings and those old-fashioned architectural features the Langholms were looking for."

"After that, we helped each other every time they were in town. I told them more, too, details about the people who owned them, which ones were involved in drugs, and which ones were just down on their luck. And they paid me money that I used to buy books, or clothes. I used it to further myself, and they took an interest in me."

"So they sort of adopted you?" Alvarez asked.

"No, not like that. More like, they took an interest. I've never lived with them. There's no charity here. They paid me for my services, and I made my own way in life."

"How did you come to be neighbors on Star Island?"

"When I graduated from business school, I asked them if they would introduce me into the Miami community. I had my plan already in the works. They encouraged me to create a new identity as a Cuban American, and I did. I launched La Luz. After a number of years of hard work, it really took off. It became bigger and bigger. The Langholms had this place on Star Island, I think it used to be a mother-in-law dwelling, actually, and they sold it to me well below market."

"They didn't try to out you or hold that over your head?"

"No! The Langholms have always been decent. Nobody knew about me till these two ladies showed up on Star Island with their *research*."

Mick noted that Serena said the word "research" as if she were saying "cockroach."

It was from this revelation that Cat came up with her theory that Langholm bought and sold child porn.

"It's the only thing that makes sense," she explained to Strickland, who resisted her idea at first. "Langholm was there when the photos of Serena were first made. He probably bought them. Maybe that's what he really does all over the country, buys and sells pedophilic material."

Strickland warmed to the theory. "Sure, sure. He's the clean one. He doesn't actually take the pics. He buys them from those who do, and then he redistributes them, making a mint."

At this point, Mick raised what he thought was the obvious objection. "But why show kindness to Angie Ramirez? Wouldn't that be risky?"

It was his sister who picked up the thread at that point.

"Angie's right that she had value," said Pris. "She gave the Langholms information, and she knew to charge for it. Maybe they admired her, saw her potential. But that didn't mean they'd destroy the images of her they'd paid for. Perhaps the Langholms are only motivated by money."

"Or maybe even they needed a child of sorts," said Strickland, staring up at the board. "Someone to love."

"How could a couple like that be capable of love?" asked Mick. "What we're saying here is that they killed Donnie."

"Did they see the painting of Angie Ramirez?" Strickland asked.

Mick thought about Kristoff's visits to his studio. There were two in the month preceding the fire, and Greta had retrieved the *Three Views, One Girl* triptych out of his seldom-seen back archive of paintings during her visit, and he agreed to send them to her gallery for the show. They were probably sitting out the second time that Kristoff came by.

And, come to think of it, when Serena Jones bought Mick's work after the party, Kristoff had insisted he bring a few pieces to her house on Star Island rather than having Serena visit Mick's studio. Maybe Kristoff didn't want to risk that she would see the paintings and recognize herself in them.

"Yes," said Mick. He told them how it was.

They broke for lunch, and Mick found himself in a conference room alone with Strickland, the two of them eating sandwiches.

"I sure do like what the Cubans have done to luncheon," said Strickland, who held out his sandwich in front of him, admiring the several layers of meat and pickles pressed between thin slices of toast.

Mick wolfed down his own pork concoction and had to agree. "Of course, it pales in comparison to what they've done with coffee," he said.

"Right-o." Strickland winked as he picked up a Styrofoam cup holding a café con leche and took a sip. Then, wiping his mouth on a paper napkin, he stared up above Mick's head at the wall behind, but it seemed as if he stared at something in his mind's eye. "The aboriginal cultures of Australia believe in something called Dreamtime. It's hard to describe this in English, as there are no words for it. It's not the past, exactly, but they do believe that the spirits of their ancestors are passed to them. It's not the same as dreaming…" He peered at Mick pointedly. "But it does call into question what we think of dreams."

Mick's back went up. He wasn't sure how to take this line of discussion.

Strickland continued. "It would be beyond a purely secular man like Langholm to imagine something like Dreamtime, don't you think?"

Mick nodded, unsure what to say. He sipped his coffee.

"He wouldn't have been able to account for your dream, for instance."

"No, he must not have."

"Curious thing, your dream, Mick. I've been considering it in the back of my mind as Cat sold me on her suspicions against Langholm. Dreams in our culture are entirely frivolous, for the most part. But I believe—and I'm in part doing some guesswork here, as I am outside aboriginal culture and can only form a hypothesis in a distant sort of way about them—but I believe they would not separate your dream that night from Dreamtime. They would think of it as part and parcel of the ancestor experience."

"That's pretty deep," Mick said.

Strickland chuckled. "Oh, forgive my academic obtuseness. Your grand-niece is a smart cookie, Mick. I'd love to steal her away to the FBI. But I sense she belongs with you and your sister. Something binds the three of you—I can see that clearly—and I think it has something to do with your dream."

Mick nearly choked on his cortadita. "Excuse me?"

"That dream you had at Langholm's, Mick—I don't doubt that you had it. But Cat, she exhibits an odd conviction about it. And for one so data-driven as she is? It got me thinking about dreams and how little we really know about them. They are the most powerful imaginative experience a human being can have. And everyone dreams."

With that, Strickland polished off his pressed sandwich, swept the wrappings into a trash bin, and exited.

Mick sat for a moment, stunned that another person had an inkling about his family's dreamslipping ability. He was glad that Strickland was on their side.

Mick rejoined the others back in the briefing room. Strickland was standing in front of an evidence board with the players and their connections marked. "We have one mission here, folks. Catch Langholm. But how do we do it?"

"Ernesto's the key," said Pris. Mick felt for her, having her companion mixed up in this awful mess.

"Let's bring him in," said Strickland. "In the meantime"—he looked at his technical team—"keep monitoring the chats like you have."

"What does he mean by chats?" Mick asked Cat. "Is that like the chatting you do online?"

Cat was happy to explain. "We think Kristoff uses this particular chat alias, and if we can connect it to an upload link for hidden pedophilic services, we've got him."

"Oh," said Mick, but he didn't really get it.

When they brought Ernesto in, Mick caught his eye and gave him a hard look. Pris looked upset but determined, her mouth set in a flat line. Mick squeezed her hand.

"You don't have to join in the questioning," he told her.

"I know," she said. "But I'll wonder if I don't."

With that, she slipped into the room. Mick followed, and so did Cat. Mick expected Strickland to protest, but he was solicitous.

"Come in, come in," he said to them. "Have a seat. Make sure you're sitting where you're most comfortable. I like to sit far from any air conditioning ducts myself." Mick almost laughed out loud at his quirky manner.

"Grace, darling," Ernesto said. "What is this?"

"I think you know," said Pris, who'd chosen to sit directly across from Ernesto. "That's why you've been following the case so closely."

Ernesto looked at her blankly. Mick wanted to punch his lights out.

"You're involved in this, aren't you? Through Langholm's art. Which you do handle, as it turns out."

Ernesto didn't miss a beat. "Grace, you must forgive my secrecy. But my clients always ... expect the strictest confidence. But involved in this? Mick's case? I should think you would know me better than that."

"I thought so, too, Ernie. But you're in this. I know it."

Ernesto glanced at Mick. "I am very sorry for the misunderstanding over your brother's ... predilections, as it were. But I do not see how that has anything to do with my business."

"My predilections? You asshole—" Mick couldn't control himself. He was seeing red again.

"Sorry, sorry. I didn't mean anything by that. It is not a matter to easily discuss, you see."

"You can't discuss child porn, but you can do business with those who sell it?" Pris challenged him.

Ernesto sputtered. "Eh ... how do you mean?"

Grace leaned across the table. "Your client. Kristoff Langholm. Do you look the other way, Ernesto? Is that it? His transactions are fishy, his need for anonymity suspicious. And you look the other way."

"I-I don't know what you're talking about."

"How much money do you make off Langholm, annually?"

"Off the top of my head, I am not sure. I would have to look at my records."

At that, Strickland broke in. "Records! Fantastic. I love good recordkeepers. Why don't you give us access to those records, Mr. Ruíz? The federal government insists, as a matter of fact. Here, my staff will escort you back to your office for the confiscation. But that's just what you've got in your own possession. We've already been in contact with the relevant banks, savings and loans, brokerage houses, credit cards, the IRS, you name it."

"Wait," Ernesto said. "I would like a lawyer."

"Certainly!" said Strickland. "I'm surprised one isn't already in the room with us, Mr. Ruíz. After all, a person's rights must be protected. But you probably thought this was going to be a friendlier conversation, didn't you? I mean, Ms. Grace here has been quite her namesake with you up till now, hasn't she? Gracious, if you haven't gathered my meaning."

Ernesto looked around the room, and to Mick he resembled a mouse, cornered by a cat and trying to find a mouse hole. Mick chuckled to himself, realizing that Ernesto *had* been cornered by a Cat, in a matter of speaking.

"I wish to say something," Ernesto declared.

"Wonderful," said Strickland, but with a softer tone. "Speaking is one of the greatest of God's gifts. It allows the truth to come out, connections to be made."

"You have to believe me, I don't know anything about the fire, or whether or not Kristoff was involved. And up until this mess with Mick Travers and the illicit material, I did not know there was any connection to that kind of illegal activity."

"Do go on," said Strickland. He picked up his pen and had it poised over a yellow legal pad.

"The Langholms—and I do mean both of them, and not just Kristoff, but Carrie as well—they have been my clients for a number of years."

Strickland put down his pen. "And I thought you were going to tell us something we didn't know."

"If you go looking for the financial trail, you will find … irregularities. Enough to convict me, perhaps. But you won't find anything against the Langholms."

"And what makes you so certain of the limitations of our abilities?"

Ernesto laughed, shaking his head. There was a sad, bitter quality to the man that Mick realized had always been there, underneath the facade of elegance.

Ernesto looked directly at Mick. "You think art is some kind of pure thing, with its aesthetics and meaning? I am here to tell you it is not. The money people of the world, the ones who run everything, behind the scenes—they use your pretty pictures to hide their ill-gotten wealth."

Strickland picked up the meaning. "Langholm uses art to launder his child-porn money."

Ernesto flinched. "I really didn't know where his wealth came from. I thought he was committing fraud through his construction projects. And he probably does. Victimless crimes."

Pris cleared her throat, attracting Ernesto's gaze. "That's what you told yourself, anyway."

"Please, Grace…"

Pris shook her head. "You're trying to convince yourself, Ernie. But your conscience prevailed. You've never interfered, tried to steer us the wrong way… I think some part of you wanted this to come out. You knew when Donnie was killed that there was something darker going on, and then when Mick stumbled into that pedophile nightmare, you wanted out. But you weren't courageous enough to be conscious about it, to come to us with the truth of your suspicions."

Ernesto looked down at the table. He didn't say the words, but Mick took this as a gesture to say, "I'm sorry."

Strickland took the reins again. "Mr. Ruíz, I need you to tell us for the record exactly how Kristoff Langholm launders his money through art."

Ernesto explained. Mick couldn't believe he had no idea this was going on under his nose, probably even involving his own paintings. Kristoff would hide his money in art, reporting the worth of the piece as far more than he'd actually paid for it when he resold it overseas. There were no rules in the art world, no checks and balances of a bank or financial institution. Art went from private collection to private collection, and the price could go up or down by millions of dollars arbitrarily, with amounts reported on receipts at the convenience of whatever the smuggler needed. Listening to Ernesto describe how it worked, and his role in it as a sort of "financial art advisor," Mick realized something.

When Ernesto paused, Mick said, "I think that's how Pennington James got the Angie Ramirez photo from Langholm. He traded it for his art, the night of the party." Mick remembered Pennington hauling in several pieces that evening, but he'd assumed the Langholms had purchased them in an aboveboard manner. That must have been why Pennington dreamed about the redheaded girl that night. She was fresh in his mind. There'd been a trade.

"I think Langholm used those parties for transactions, trades," said Mick. "And Pennington provided Kristoff with a fake receipt for the art, which he could use to hide his child-porn money."

"I do believe you're right, Mick," said Strickland, who then turned to Ernesto.

"Mr. Ruíz, thank you for your cooperation. I'm sure the prosecutors will take that into consideration when determining your guilt and sentencing." Then to Alvarez, he said, "Let's have a chat with this Pennington character."

Chapter 28

G race had to leave the room during the questioning of Pennington James.

It had gone on for a long time, Strickland and Alvarez working on James. At first he stuck to his story about only purchasing material through online sources.

But the two law-enforcement pros kept leaning on him, and they used the information they got from Ernesto. They bluffed, saying that they had James's tax records and had found discrepancies in the amounts he reported earning from his paintings and the paintings' values in the market.

"Tell us about Langholm," Alvarez said. "What do you have to lose? It's not like he's here, coming to your rescue or anything. We checked your phone records. You haven't reached out to him, so obviously, the two of you don't have that kind of relationship, do you? You must know better than to contact him for help."

At that, there was a long pause and James conferred with his lawyer, who did a lot of nodding as they whispered. Then he began to offer up what he knew about his chief source of pedophilic material.

"Look, Langholm's a smooth guy," James said. "The porn—it's digital. No need to ever meet anyone in person. But art—that's got to be handed off. It's a physical object. So he has these parties. I didn't need to get my porn that night, but why not? Kristoff knows I like the vintage stuff, little girls from the Seventies and Eighties, you know, and a lot of that's fuzzy in the digital versions."

He described the small gathering of men behind several layers of security under the cover of a large party raging in the very same house.

It was the idea that Serena Jones was at that same party, that she was in the house while these men bought and sold images of her as a young girl—that's what made Grace have to leave the room.

It wasn't that Serena was some fragile victim who'd been irreparably damaged. The woman was a survivor. She'd come through so much, and she'd done it on her own, using street smarts and strength.

No, what upset Grace was thinking that after what Serena Jones had been through, she still wasn't safe. No child or woman was, as long as men like these got away with their crimes.

Strickland wanted to bring the Langholms in, but he needed more than James's word against them. Serena Jones herself would torpedo any case against them, unless she could be convinced of their role in disseminating the material that had caused her such trauma as a child.

Grace insisted she be the one to deliver the news about the Langholms to Serena Jones. And she wished to do it alone, with no one else in the room.

It was the day after Serena's previous visit, and the woman was not happy about having to come back. "Is this going to be a daily thing now?" she asked sarcastically.

"I'm sorry, Serena," Grace said. "But there's been another … development in the case. I need to tell you something potentially upsetting." Grace got up and went to the corner of the room to retrieve the same box of tissue Serena used the day before on her contact lenses. While she felt compassion for Serena in this moment, Grace was also aware of her own choreography in setting the tissue as a prop with psychological import.

"I'm not a crier," Serena said emphatically.

Grace let that go. She cleared her throat. "This concerns your longtime friends, the Langholms."

Serena appeared genuinely surprised.

Grace took a deep breath. "We have reason to believe they have been involved in the … dissemination of the abusive material in which you appear."

"I don't believe it."

"We have evidence."

"I'd like to see that."

"My brother's paintings were inspired by something he saw at a party at the Langholm's residence."

"The night I met Mick?"

"Yes."

"Are you kidding me?"

"No. Do you remember another artist there that night, a man named Pennington James?"

Serena thought about it. "I think so. I remember his work. Zebras and giraffes, right? Dressed like superheroes?"

"That's right."

"Are you telling me that man had photos of me—as Angie?"

"Yes."

"But it's been like twenty years!"

"This kind of material lives a long time, it seems."

"My god." Serena clasped her hands together, her perfectly manicured fingernails done in the French style. "How do they get it? Online?"

"Yes. And, as it turns out, from a network run by Kristoff Langholm."

"What are you saying?"

"Pennington James was there that night to give his paintings to Langholm, who would use them to launder money. And in exchange, he received pedophilic material, including photos of you."

"Langholm ... had those photos ... of me?" Serena's voice was weak. She looked away, at the far wall. "All this time..."

She turned back to Grace. "I don't believe it."

Grace was prepared for this. There was a laptop sitting on the table. She opened it, cued up the audio interview with Pennington, and hit play. His words filled the room, describing the meeting at the party, and his preference for what he called "vintage child porn."

As the interviewed played, tears slipped down Serena's cheeks, but she didn't grab for the tissue. She let them fall.

When it was done, Serena said, "I need you to play that one more time."

Grace did as she was told. This time, Serena's body moved in sobs. She reached for the tissue.

"Tell me," Serena said, aggressively tearing the tissue in shreds, "exactly what we need to do to get them."

"Do you think it's Kristoff, alone?" Grace asked. "Or Carrie, too?"

"Everything Kristoff does, he does with Carrie's blessing, and more."

———

Grace was on a boat about a mile off Star Island, listening to the wire hidden on Serena Jones, as were both Strickland and Alvarez. A few Miami PD and FBI boats were on alert in the area and would respond if anything went sour.

After initial greetings in which the Langholms mentioned getting ready for a long trip to Italy, Serena launched into her agreed-upon performance.

"Carrie, Kristoff," she said. "Something terrible has happened."

"What is it, Serena?" asked Carrie, her voice sympathetic. "Have a seat, dear."

Serena must have been feigning having trouble telling them about her past, as there was a long pause, and then Kristoff prompted her. "Whatever it is, I'm sure we can fix it," he said cheerily.

"There's something I never told you about my past. In Del Rio."

"You can't tell us anything that would alter our opinion of you, love," said Kristoff.

"You're like family to us," Carrie assured her.

There was a rustling noise as Serena took out her phone. "When I was a girl, before I met the two of you, my parents sold me out to these disgusting people." She broke off, convincingly upset. Grace understood that Serena wouldn't need to pretend much, as this was a fresh wound. Probably some part of her wished this was the way it went down anyway.

"Serena, there's no need—" said Carrie.

"They did things to me, took pictures of me," Serena said through her sobs. "I was only twelve."

There were more rustling noises. Grace figured Carrie and maybe Kristoff as well were consoling her.

"But why tell us this now?" Kristoff said.

"Because..." Serena explained, "the pictures must still be out there. Someone ... oh, God. Someone painted them."

This was the part where Serena was supposed to show the Langholms *Three Views, One Girl* on her phone.

There was a long bout of silence, and then Kristoff asked, "Where did you get these?"

"I was just in New York, and those paintings were in the back of a gallery there. I couldn't believe it!"

"Did you notice who the artist was?" Carrie asked.

"Yes," answered Serena. "It's that Mick Travers. After the money I've spent on his work, to find out he's that kind of man..."

"There have been reports in the press," said Carrie. "There was even a boycott."

"But how did he get pictures of me?" Serena wailed. "That was so long ago. I thought this was in the past, dead and buried."

"I don't know," said Kristoff, his tone hard. "But I will get the piece and have it destroyed. Tell me the name of the gallery where you saw it."

"The Painted Stick," said Serena. Grace winced even though she knew the FBI had arranged for extra security on Greta Stein and her gallery, should the Langholms decide to act on the revelation that the paintings had not burned. The triptych itself was still in police custody.

"I don't want to cause you any trouble," said Serena. "I tried to buy the pieces myself, but the gallery owner told me they weren't for sale."

"It's no trouble, Serena," said Kristoff.

"Now, don't worry about it anymore," Carrie said. "Why don't you treat yourself to a spa vacation? Take Mariana. If one of the society bloggers sees you treating your maid to a spa trip, it'll make a good write-up."

Grace cringed.

"But what about the photos?" Serena demanded. "Those photos are out there somewhere. I want them destroyed!"

"That's likely impossible," Kristoff said. "Those images have been floating out there for twenty years, right? I wouldn't even begin to know how to track them down. But look, you've altered your appearance so much, no one will put it together that it was you."

"But *I* will know they're out there. Maybe I should go to the police with this."

"Not if you want to remain Serena Jones," Carrie said harshly. "You don't want that to come out in the press. You'll be nothing again, dear. Just Angie Ramirez, a little whore from a nothing town."

Even Grace clenched her fists to hear that. She and Alvarez exchanged pained glances. Strickland was all business, though, as if he expected it.

But Serena was a raw, open wound. And she went off script.

"I can't do this," Serena said softly, as if speaking to her wire. Then, louder: "Don't refer to me that way."

"I meant that's what people *will think*," came Carrie's voice.

"I know what you meant. You listen to me. Angie Ramirez was not a *whore*, Carrie. She was a girl … who was raped." There was a pause, and Grace could hear Serena taking in a breath.

"And you two might as well have been her rapists."

"Serena!" cried Carrie.

"My word, girl," said Kristoff. "What on earth are you talking about?"

"What happened to me back then was your fault."

There was a long silence across the radio that felt eerie to Grace. Strickland called for agents to close in on the Langholm residence.

And then Carrie said, "Serena, how can you say that to us?"

"I know what you are," Serena said. "You bought those terrible pictures of me. You've been making money off them for years."

"Serena, you don't understand," said Kristoff.

"We've been … like parents to you, Serena," said Carrie. "If it weren't for us, you'd still be trapped in Del Rio."

"Don't try to take my accomplishments away from me."

"But we helped you so much," said Kristoff.

"You owe us everything," Carrie snarled.

Serena smacked her hands down on something hard, causing static on the radio. "I owe you nothing! You're no better than those crackheads back in Del Rio who called themselves my parents. No— wait. You're worse. You had more choices than they did. And what do you choose? To make money off scum like Pennington James."

"Pennington James?" Kristoff asked. "I thought this was about Mick Travers."

"I don't know what lies the authorities have filled that pretty little head of yours with, but that's not true," said Carrie. "The sole transactions we've had with James concerned his art."

"You're the ones bankrolling it all. You're buying and selling child porn."

Kristoff was gasping for breath. "How ... how can you say such things? My dear, if you only knew what I've done for you..."

Carrie spoke, "Darling, there's no need."

"But she needs to know," said Kristoff. "I did everything I could to protect her.... I took ... great risks, even."

"Kristoff, no..."

"I thought I destroyed that painting, love," Kristoff said. "Up till you showed it to me on your phone, I thought the painting was long gone. I got Mick to come to your house so you wouldn't see it. I went out of my way to make sure it was destroyed."

"You set the fire," said Serena.

"Kristoff," said Carrie. "You're telling her too much."

"I did it for you. I recognized you in the painting, from all those years ago, and I knew you liked his art. I didn't want you to have to see it."

"You didn't set that fire for me," said Serena. "You did it so I couldn't trace the porn to Mick, and then to you."

Kristoff did not respond.

Strickland gave the order for agents to invade.

"Carrie," said Serena. "How could you?"

Carrie laughed. "Serena, we couldn't erase what those men did to you. It was already too late. What's done was done. You think you had it rough as a girl? Well, I had it worse. But I prevailed. There's so much darkness in the world, don't you see that? You can't fight it. You can't control it. So you might as well profit from it. Then you can afford to wall yourself off from it, just as we have."

"But you've *become* the darkness," Serena said.

Carrie cleared her throat. "Those pictures have been around for twenty years, Serena. You would never have known about them if it weren't for Mick's painting. There's no harm in a few photos being distributed through the underground. In fact, some people think it's better for men like that to have the images to look at so they won't actually need to prey upon children. So we're providing a service to society. We never imagined someone would use them as inspiration for his art and bring what happened to you out into public view. I mean, really. What is wrong with that Mick Travers?"

"We were so careful, Serena," said Kristoff. "We keep that world separate. I had to destroy the painting. It was the only way."

"You're both monsters. You don't deserve to live." Grace didn't like the sound of Serena's voice, which conveyed that a double murder was a viable option. She remembered Serena's story about going back to Del Rio to settle that score, how she'd learned to shoot.

"She's got a gun," Grace told Strickland and Alvarez, who both registered alarm.

Grace began to pray silently, appealing to the universal energy running through all things to show Serena a better way.

"Let's be reasonable," said Carrie. "It's been a very profitable business for us. Even you've benefited from it. Think about it. The money we've paid you over the years. It came from pictures like the ones of you."

"I can't believe this. Are you offering to cut me in?"

"Look how much I've taught you," Carrie said. "There's so much more you could learn."

"I don't want any more to do with you."

There was the sound of heels clicking across the floor. "Stay away from me!" yelled Serena. And then the gun went off.

Strickland had the pilot take their boat in to Star Island, where agents had secured the Langholm residence. An ambulance was already on the scene. Grace walked toward the front door, which was open, with agents filing in and out.

"Is Serena okay?" Grace asked. Strickland was speaking with someone on a radio. He and Alvarez pressed forward.

Inside, Grace was relieved to see Serena talking to a group of federal agents. Kristoff Langholm, in handcuffs and with two agents guarding him with guns raised, sat on the couch. Carrie was on the floor, a group of paramedics surrounding her like flies.

They loaded Carrie onto a stretcher. Grace could see she was wounded but alive. Kristoff stood up and motioned to the guards. "Please, I want to see my wife."

They nodded but followed him. Kristoff took Carrie's hand. "I'm sorry, love," he said.

"We shouldn't have tried to help that stupid girl," Carrie said. "That was our biggest mistake."

The agents nudged Kristoff, and he was taken outside to where an FBI van waited.

In his wake, Grace leaned over Carrie. "Tell me one thing. How is it that you and Kristoff made your relationship work for so long, with such darkness at its center?"

Carrie closed her eyes and then opened them again. She gave Grace a sinister smile. "We always wanted the same thing. Great wealth, to buy perfectly secure lives, so that nothing could ever hurt us. That's better than love, you know. Love fades."

———

Back at the Miami PD station, Cat was working with the tech team, and this much Grace knew: They were trying to monitor what they called "hidden services sites," which were sites offering illegal services such as child abuse material, drugs, and the like. Grace had heard about the highly encrypted, anonymous Tor network, which originally had been a Navy invention and was relied upon by activists and whistleblowers who had legitimate reasons for anonymity. Unfortunately, criminals were its heaviest users.

"Your whiz-kid granddaughter came up with the idea to use Flash code," one of the tech guys told Grace. "We think we can get some IP addresses this way. We might be able to break the whole Langholm network."

Grace saw Mick researching Pennington James online. She thought of that party again, and the fact that Kristoff hosted so many of them. He must indeed have an extensive network of people across the country to make as much money as he had. Situated there in Miami, he was probably the one who handled the art fraud and smuggling aspect of the business for the rest of them.

She realized they'd been interrupted in their investigation of the other men at the party, the Texas judge with the bolo tie and the other one Mick had jotted down, a guy with two first names. What was it? Philip Peters.

Grace went over to Cat and Strickland, who were bent over a computer monitor where Cat had been working, and told them her insight.

Strickland stood up slowly. "Get those names from Mick," he directed to one of his FBI assistants. "We've now got probable cause for a raid on both their houses."

What happened next was a whirlwind for Grace. It was as if two torpedoes had been set off simultaneously. One torpedo detonated in Denton, Texas, where Judge Reinhold Busch ran a server for hidden services on the darknet with suspected ties to a network involving the Langholms. The other blasted into Kalispell, Montana, where Philip Peters did the same.

Grace watched footage of the raids. In addition to the servers, which had not been scrubbed and still contained child-abuse material, they found caches of illegal firearms at both residences.

"Residences" wasn't even the right word to describe what amounted to compounds, as they were on sizable acreage with security fencing surrounds and watchdogs as an added deterrent. At the judge's compound, they found a collection of artwork that had been reported stolen from private collections and museums. At Philip Peters's place, they uncovered a studio he used to create forgeries of valuable artwork, with several pieces in progress.

Chapter 29

I t was New Year's Eve, and Cat's last night with Jacob.
They were having a quiet evening in a hotel room away from
the revelry, and away from her grandmother and great-uncle.
They'd decided to celebrate the evening on their own, a needed break
after spending so much time together the past month.

Jacob gave Cat a full-body massage lasting more than an hour,
with extra attention to the trouble spots in her neck and shoulders that
had come from tensing up about the case and bending over computer
screens for what seemed like days at a stretch. He demanded she remain
quiet while he worked, and every time she tried to say something, he'd
playfully reprimand her. "No talking, only sighing and grunting."

While he worked, she reflected on the case. There was a lot she
had learned about the world through it, and much of that wasn't pretty.
Cat grieved for Serena and hoped that she'd find some peace after what
amounted to a lifetime of betrayal and multiple forms of abuse, ranging
from that of her own parents to the deceit of her so-called surrogates.

With the news that Mick had helped bring an entire child-porn
network to its knees, he'd been somewhat vindicated in the press. But a
few members of the blogosphere—conspiracy-minded types—still held
out that Mick was some kind of pervert to have painted the girl in the
first place, that he and Pennington were child-porn buddies, and that
Mick had simply turned on his friend. Cat couldn't do anything about
that, and it frustrated her.

Cat remained astounded by her grandmother's skills as a
dreamslipper and was eager to continue apprenticing with her back in
Seattle in a more advanced capacity. If Cat could learn to target and
direct her dreamslipping like she did, there was no limit to what she
might be able to do.

For a cool minute she'd considered leaving the Amazing Grace
Detective Agency and entering the FBI. Strickland and his team were
awesome, and Cat felt the pull of that world of more sophisticated tools
and access to information. But in the end, she realized it wasn't her
place. She wanted to remain with Granny Grace.

On the whole, she was feeling more acceptance of herself as a
dreamslipper, and she ultimately had her grandmother, as well as her
great-uncle Mick, to thank for that.

Jacob finished with a feathery brush of his fingers across her
face, and she popped open her eyes and said, "Can I talk now?"

"Silly woman," he said.

Cat propped herself on her side, and Jacob lay down next to her. She reached across and tugged on his chest hairs. "You haven't told me what you've decided about San Francisco."

Jacob grinned. He grabbed her hand and squeezed it. "That's because I didn't want to freak you out. This is supposed to be casual, after all."

Cat's pulse sped up, but she nodded. She still wasn't sure what she wanted with this man.

He took a deep breath. "I'm going to give this gallery thing a try."

She smiled, recognizing that her heart leapt at the thought.

"Oh, good," he said. "You look happy. I was hoping that would be the case."

Cat rolled into his arms. "I don't know where this is going, but I would like to see you again."

"I feel the same way."

They made love with less urgency and more tenderness than they had previously, and when the clock struck midnight, they stood in the window watching fireworks go off over the beach. She kissed Jacob, and then they held each other a long time.

They fell asleep together, and soon Cat found herself slipping into one of his dreams, albeit with some guilt, since she hadn't resisted much. She was growing more curious about Jacob and liked the ability to see into him through his subconscious mind. What girl wouldn't use any trick up her sleeve? But she knew her grandmother probably wouldn't approve.

Jacob was standing on the Golden Gate Bridge again, but this time, Cat saw herself, way in the distance at the other end of the bridge.

"Cat!" he called after her.

Police cars with sirens flashing blew past Jacob on the bridge, headed in the direction of Cat at the end of the bridge, who became quickly engulfed in a flurry of activity: black FBI vans, police squad cars, FBI helicopters, police boats. And Cat disappeared.

"Wait!" he yelled. Then his uncle, his face once again shaped like a giant fish head, appeared next to him. "That's a dirty business your girlfriend's into, sonny. Why don't you stare at these pretty pictures instead?" At that, he opened his coat, which became the wall of his art gallery. And the scene morphed so that Jacob was standing in what must be his uncle's gallery in San Francisco. And in walked a woman Jacob seemed to recognize, an attractive blonde wearing high heels and a skintight cocktail dress showing off her hourglass curves.

Cat felt jealousy, and it was hers, not Jacob's. The feeling she had from Jacob could best be described as tortured. He seemed very much stirred up by this woman.

"You're a New Yorker," he said to the woman.

"And so are you, Jewish boy. But go ahead and shack up with some Catholic girl. She seems like she can read your mind. You guys love that."

His uncle reappeared, took off his fish head, and set it on the woman's body. "Is that any better?" she asked him.

"You're a fish stick," said Jacob.

"You're mad because I'm not kosher," she said before disappearing.

Jacob heard the sound of heels clicking on hardwood, and he turned to see Cat walking into the gallery. But Cat's dream self seemed not to see Jacob. She walked over to a painting on the wall, grabbed it, and threw it to the ground.

"Rubbish!" she pronounced. "Pornographic!"

"No, it's not," Jacob protested, but Cat in the dream didn't seem to hear him. "Burn it all!"

At her words, the gallery burst into flames, and Jacob woke with a start, ending the dream and popping Cat out of it.

He sat up in bed, his breathing rough.

"You okay?" she asked.

He began to laugh. "Yeah," he said. "I had the weirdest dream." He snuggled back into her and chuckled softly till he finally fell back to sleep.

Cat lay in bed and wondered at her strange gift. She didn't feel bad about the blonde woman at all. Whatever was going on in him with regard to that woman didn't have much to do with Cat. As far as the rest of what the dream revealed, she could lie there and analyze it if she wanted, but she was tired, and she wanted one last night's sleep with Jacob before returning to her bed in the Grand Green Griffin. She fell back to sleep thinking fondly of her room in Granny Grace's old Victorian.

Chapter 30

After most of the activity surrounding the Langholm case had subsided, Mick found himself back at the fourplex with a beautiful day beckoning outside. Pris invited him to go for a walk on the beach. Mick had been watching his sister in the aftermath of the case and knew she'd been to see Ernesto a couple of times. Released on an astronomical amount of bail, he had engaged the same lawyer who worked with Serena Jones. It was a contrast to how Candace's case was going down. She would definitely be doing some jail time for second-degree arson.

Unsure how to broach the subject, Mick stumbled into it. "So, uh, you okay with this whole Ernesto thing, Pris?"

His sister gazed out toward the water as they stepped from the wooden boardwalk and onto the sand.

"I won't ever be seeing him again," she said. "And I'm sorry about that, but I can't."

"You feel betrayed."

"Yes."

"You're angry."

"Yes, I am."

Mick was quiet for a while. Anger was not an emotion his sister showed often.

"It's something I'll have to work on," she added.

"I'm sorry," Mick offered. "I dragged you and Cat into this."

"Don't be," Pris said. "I lost a lover and old friend, and that is sad. But you and I, we're closer than ever. And Cat? She's reawakened. Look at us! We're a family of dreamslippers!"

Mick smiled, but what she said made him think of Strickland and the strange conversation over sandwiches. "Pris, I think Agent Strickland suspects our, uh, superhero power."

Surprisingly, Pris laughed. "He does?"

"Mine, anyway." He told her about their exchange.

"Well, he's an intriguing one, isn't he? I wonder if he ever makes his way to Seattle. I rather liked working with him, and so did Cat."

As they traced a path at the edge of the surf, Pris said, "Speaking of Seattle, you know we have a very exciting art scene. I've been so impressed with the quality of the shows I've seen lately downtown," she said. "I'd say they rival Miami. Maybe even out-shine it."

"You don't say..." Mick allowed, but he was instantly suspicious, not to mention secretly flattered.

"Listen, Mickey," she said, pausing to dig a seashell out of the sand. "I've been thinking."

"Uh-oh."

She ignored him. "Please don't take this the wrong way, but you don't have anyone here, Mick. I mean, besides Rose. And I know to you she's, ah … just a friend."

"Did she tell you what I did to her? Or rather, what I couldn't do?"

"Not in so many words."

Mick kicked a piece of driftwood. "I'm a flawed human being."

Grace sighed. "But I'm talking about family. You don't have any here."

"Are you trying to depress me? Because it's working. I think I need a drink now."

"Sorry, Mick. What I'm trying to say is that you have me. And Cat. And you'd keep us if you moved to Seattle."

"All it does is rain there."

"Well, yes, but it's a spitting kind of rain most of the time. Never mind what you've seen on TV. Those downpours are just for the cinematic value."

"Great. I love being spit upon."

"You'd get used to it." She spied him sideways. "I rather think it would suit your dour attitude better than this place does. You're not exactly the Margaritaville type."

What she said struck a chord in him. But there was the matter of the trouble she could conjure, being able to walk in his dreams.

As if reading his thoughts, she said, "Mickey, I'm so sorry about what I did to you back then. It was a long time ago. But I know it's affected our relationship ever since."

"Marla Gibbs was the only one who understood me as an artist."

Grace winced. She flashed on the one dream of Mick's she would never be able to forget. It had likely been an innocent pubescent fantasy. Marla Gibbs, a widower, had been kind enough to take an interest in Mick's artistic talent. He spent time at her house, and she was still youngish and pretty. He'd dreamed of kissing her, and more. Home to visit her parents, Grace had tattled on her brother, to them and several others. It was enough back then to cause a stir, and gossip spread. Gibbs moved to another town.

"I was unbearably righteous as a dreamslipper back then. I'll never forgive myself for it. What I cost you."

"Never mind me," Mick said. "I was young. I got over it. But Marla Gibbs didn't deserve that," he said. "You kind of ruined her life."

"Oh, now you're being overly dramatic, Mick." Grace sighed. "I'm sorry she had to move. But I checked into how she was doing in the Eighties, and she seemed happier there. She'd reconnected with a sister, sort of like us."

He felt swayed, emotionally, but he didn't want to let her know this, yet. He thought about how he'd miss his short jaunts to the Keys, the inspiration he'd taken there, and the place he and Donnie shared in the Everglades. He told her this.

"It's gorgeous in Seattle—the mountains, the trees, the artsy city life! There's no greater city on Earth."

"When did you become a walking commercial for your own city?"

"Since I rediscovered my own brother," Pris said, linking her arm in his.

Despite himself, he felt a lump in his throat. He held his arm in hers, and the two of them walked along for a while in silence.

Truth be told, he'd already been considering a move, and Seattle had crossed his mind. He was also turning something else over in his mind, and it involved Rose de la Crem.

"What have I got to lose?" he said to his sister. "Sure."

"Oh, Mickey! You'll love it! You must live in the Victorian with us. We've got loads of room to spare. You can paint upstairs, in the Adorable Amber Attic. And we could use your help…"

The two of them walked onward, discussing plans.

Later that afternoon, Mick dropped in on Rose de la Crem, who was in her studio, painting.

"Did you notice the railing outside?" she asked right away as she continued to stare at her easel, the tip of the paintbrush between her teeth. "It's loose again! I think it's time to get it replaced."

"Well, as my new building manager, that should be your first priority."

Mick waited a few beats for that to sink in.

Rose took the brush and set it down on her easel. "Your what?"

"My new building manager."

She put her hands on her hips. "Well, now how does that work, Mick, when you live here yourself? I can't have you breathing down my neck as the owner."

"I'm moving to Seattle. You'll be my on-site manager. You can live here rent-free, plus I'll set aside a maintenance account for repairs."

She blinked a few times and then ran over and flung her arms around him. "Oh, Mick! I'll be the best building manager in the history of building management!"

Mick laughed. "You sure? You're not still ... disappointed in me?"

"Oh, come on, Mick. You're too old for me anyway. And you can't rap worth a damn."

———

The night before the three dreamslippers were to head to Seattle together, Mick found himself falling into a dream, and at first he could not figure out for the life of him whose it was. Only Cat, Pris, and Rose were in the building, and it didn't seem to fit any of them.

He looked down at his hands, and they were a woman's, and they bore a French manicure. But man that he was, that wasn't enough to clue Mick in.

In heels, he stalked the streets of a ghetto he'd never seen before. He seemed to be looking for something, or someone. And there it was, a ramshackle house with peeling paint and a sagging front porch. That's where his host in heels wanted to go.

Inside, a man had a belt tied around his arm and was feeding a needle into it. A woman was sitting on the couch in a daze. Mick-as-whoever-he-was walked past them to a room at the back of the house, more of a porch, really, too small to be a bedroom and not adequately insulated, as he could see the sunlight through cracks in the walls. Sitting on a mattress on the floor was the redheaded girl, whose name he now knew. Angie Ramirez.

Mick realized he must be walking in Serena's dream.

Mick-as-Serena held out one hand to the girl on the mattress, and she took it. "It's a long walk," Serena said to the girl. "But you can make it. You have to." The girl looked up into Mick's eyes and nodded.

Serena took the girl out the back door and began walking with her down the street, and then the ghetto fell away, and they seemed to be in the scrub desert, and then that fell away, and they were on a beach. The dream had an endless quality to it, as if the walking took place over years and years.

Serena must have awakened at that point, as Mick was thrust out of the dream. He felt a deep longing in his chest, a longing to get there, to arrive somewhere.

He got up and walked over to the painting he had started when he blackened over the one about Cat's dream. It had started out feeling like inspiration for him at first, as he realized he could use the black paint to obscure something bright and shining beneath it that wanted to come out, not Cat's dream, but something really lovely and positive, something that everyone wanted, something that would be slipping out from under the black like it couldn't be held back.

But he'd hit a stumbling block when he didn't really know what that thing was.

Until now.

He realized it was *home*.

Acknowledgements

T hanks to all who reviewed and recommended *Cat in the Flock*. Without you, I wouldn't have had the gumption to write a sequel. These days it takes a village to publish a successful book, and you are my treasured neighbors.

And a special shout-out to my BETA readers for their honesty and insights: Ana Sprague, Anna Dobritt, Anne Harrington, Beth Poole, Chris Roman, Chris Toepker, Chrysanne Taull, Elisa Mader, Jennifer Vandenberg, Lanae Rivers-Woods, Linda Cox, Mario Russo, Marnie Roberts, Merlin G. MacReynold, Peter Wiederspan, Rebeqa Rivers, and Renee Corwin-Rey.

Most of all, thank you to the readers who've fallen in love with Cat and Granny Grace. It's my pleasure to bring you their stories.

Namaste.

About the Author

L isa Brunette is the author of the Dreamslippers mystery series. Book One, Cat in the Flock, is an indieBRAG honoree title that has been praised by *Kirkus Reviews*, Midwest Book Review, Readers Lane, and others.

Brunette is a career writer/editor whose work has appeared in major newspapers and magazines, including the *Seattle Post-Intelligencer*, *Seattle Woman*, and *Poets & Writers*. She's interviewed a Pulitzer Prize-winning author, a sex expert, homeless women, and the designer of the Batmobile, among others.

She has story design and writing credits in hundreds of bestselling video games, including the Mystery Case Files, Mystery Trackers, and Dark Tales series for Big Fish and AAA games for Nintendo and Microsoft platforms.

She holds a Master of Fine Arts in Creative Writing from University of Miami, where she was a Michener Fellow. Her short stories and poetry have appeared in *Bellingham Review*, *The Comstock Review*, *Icarus International*, and elsewhere.

She's also received many honors for her writing, including a major grant from the Tacoma Arts Commission, the William Stafford Award, and the Associated Writing Programs Intro Journals Project Award.

Brunette is a member of Mystery Writers of America and the Pacific Northwest Writers Association.

Read More at http://www.catintheflock.com.

Book Club Discussion Questions

When did you figure out the arsonist's identity? What tipped you off?

Who is your favorite dreamslipper, and why?

Which non-dreamslipping character is your favorite, and why?

Which parts of the book made you feel the most? Describe.

How do the descriptions of Miami fit with your own impressions of the place, either from experience or from media?

What did reading this book teach you?

What was most surprising about the story? Least surprising?

Quote a favorite line or passage to share with your group.

Which character's art would you most want to hang on your own walls?

What sort of jail sentence should each of the guilty characters serve? What do you think is fair?

Read on for a glimpse of the next book in the Dreamslippers Series...

Prologue

T he woman could not turn to look him in the eyes. His fist held her chin-length blonde hair in a tight nest, the tension making her scalp ache. Her pearls hung in a loose arc beneath her chin, swaying. They reminded her of the Newton's cradle on her desk at work, how she'd lift a metal ball and let it drop, hitting the next ball. The energy would travel through the three still balls in the center, forcing the one on the opposite end to rise upward. A demonstration of Newton's Law. *For every action, there is an equal and opposite reaction.*

How many times a day she did that, she did not know. It was habit. It had been for years.

The man was hard against her back. "You dirty little slut." He said it as if admiring her.

She pulled against the strength of his other hand, which held her wrists.

"Last time," she said through jagged breaths, "you really hurt me."

He laughed. She noted the slight mocking tone.

"Yes, I did. And this time," he said, pulling her hair hard enough to make her acutely aware of her roots, "I'm going to leave marks."

But his grip loosened on both her head and hand, and free now, she turned to face him.

"I was hoping you would say that." She arched an eyebrow, daring him to give her more.

Chapter 1

Finding the door to the Adorable Amber Attic not only closed, but locked, Grace permitted herself a loud knock. "Mick! You in there?"

"Who's asking?" Grace noted her brother's irritated tone.

"It's Grace."

"Grace who?"

"For heaven's sakes, Mick. Just open the door."

A pause—and the sound of a paint can toppling to the floor. "I'm indisposed."

"You're what? Come now, Mick. This is important."

The door flew open. Her brother stood there, a paint brush clenched sideways in his mouth, the brush end dripping lime green paint.

"Oh," Grace said. "I didn't realize you were working."

Mick yanked the brush from his mouth. "Well, what else would I be doing in here?"

He stalked back over to an oblong easel, where what appeared to be some sort of alien mothership painted in lime green hovered over a field of what looked like tombstones. He stabbed at the mothership with his brush.

"My word," said Grace. "What is that? An album cover?"

"I wish. That would at least pay."

Grace softened her tone. "It's the mural."

Mick turned to glare at her. "Yes. Your brainchild."

Grace smiled. Her brother had not had an easy time of it in Seattle's arts scene, what with the stigma of child pornography still surrounding him. Even though Mick himself had caught the real culprit, the initial damage to his reputation wrought by an army of online trolls and opportunists could not be undone. So she'd cooked up a plan to endear Mick to Seattleites, in the form of a large public mural, to be donated to the city as a gift from Mick.

She surveyed the mothership, which seemed to be emitting bolts of electric-orange rays onto the tombstones. "It's a little more ... representational than your usual style."

Mick put down the brush, crossing his arms over his chest. "Did you interrupt me just to give me a critique?"

"Well, I'm just not sure that an alien ship over a graveyard is what the residents of Queen Anne really need."

Mick threw up his hands. "Well, that's what they're going to get, Pris! What else am I supposed to do with this theme? 'Alien visitation.' It's bloody ridiculous if you ask me. But that's what they want. So that's what they're going to get."

"I think they meant it metaphorically."

He gave her a look that would wilt a flower.

"The notion of 'alien' is rather broad," she persisted. "And visitation. Just think of its religious connotations."

Mick picked up the brush again. "You. Are. Not. Helping."

"I'm sorry, Mick."

"Now what, dear sister of mine, did you wander all the way up here to talk to me about?"

She hesitated, her hand fluttering up to touch her throat. Her brother certainly wasn't in the mood for that topic of conversation now.

"Well?"

"Oh, never mind. You're not going to like it anyway."

"Out with it, woman."

Grace swallowed hard, figuring it was now or never. "I wanted to talk to you about a friend of mine. I think you'd really like her. She's having an art show—"

"No."

"No, what? I haven't asked you anything."

"I refuse to be set up on a date. Especially with another artist."

"But Cecily is … You'd really like her, Mick."

"No."

Grace felt frustration welling up inside her. Did he always have to be such a pain in the keister? She was only trying to help. "Mickelson Daniel Travers," she said, raising her voice. "You are impossible."

"Which is precisely why you shouldn't set me up with anyone."

"You're going to die old and alone." It was out of her mouth before she could censor it.

Mick put down his brush and sighed. "Really, Pris. Ever since I moved here, you've been up in my business. If it's not you trying to save my fledgling art career, it's you trying to set me up with Seattle's elderly eccentrics. I'm sixty-seven years old, and I've managed perfectly fine without your direction all this time. Please. Leave me alone!"

"But Mick, you could really use the help."

"Get out of my studio!" He bellowed at her, and for emphasis, he pointed at the door to the Adorable Amber Attic.

Grace turned on her Etienne Aigners and marched out. Mick slammed the door behind her.

"And stay out!"

She muttered a 'hmpf' and stepped back downstairs.

At her computer, she suggested Cecily Thompson as a contact for Mick Travers through a social networking site. Then she pulled a flyer for Cecily's art opening out of her bag and left it on the countertop in the Terra Cotta Cocina, where Mick would be sure to see it. She would not be deterred by her brother's temper.

It was time for a new class she was trying out, something called Nia, a dance class that was low-impact and supposedly choreographed with healing movements. She'd watched a few videos online.

The class was at a small studio that had just opened up at the top of Queen Anne, within walking distance of her old Victorian. A little pricey at twenty-six dollars for a drop-in, Grace pushed herself to pony up the cash anyway, thinking that it was good to support a local business. But lately she had been questioning whether or not Seattle's quickly skyrocketing prices were sustainable for her in the long run. To her delight, she discovered that her first class would be free.

The owner, Yvette Johnson, wore what Grace could only describe as "yoga clothes with flair." The hems of both her shirt and pants extended past their usual lines into scarves that fluttered as she moved about. A row of cutouts ran down the sides of the legs. She also wore a good deal of makeup, not the usual for yoga teachers in Seattle and more of a theatrical gesture. A magnolia blossom was tucked into Yvette's cornrowed hair.

After the usual questions about her experience level and physical fitness and a brief description that this would be a "barefoot dance class," Grace walked into the studio and found a place to stand. She surveyed herself in the mirror, being careful to turn off the voice in her head that liked to call attention to the less savory aspects of herself at seventy-eight, like the rings of puffy flesh around her ankles. What was it her granddaughter called them? Cankles.

Soon, a bevy of students bedecked in similar scarf-hemmed attire poured in, and Grace suddenly felt as if she were back stage at a dance show. In her simple leotard and leggings, though, she'd be playing the role of straight man. Yvette waltzed in—literally—and talked about proper form, demonstrating how to pay attention to one's center of gravity and not exaggerate the footwork.

"Small movements sometimes work better," she said. She cued the music, and they were off.

Grace wasn't the least bit intimidated or reluctant as the music swelled. Her muscle memory took her back across time to other moments in her life when she'd danced in a studio: ballet as a small-town girl, modern dance in college, African dance in the Seventies, and that undercover work she did serving as backup dancer for a drag queen. Plus, the movement incorporated a few poses from other practices she knew—yoga, martial arts, tai chi. Yvette's bare, toffee-colored shoulders shimmied and shook, and Grace's followed suit. She mimicked Yvette's quick steps and followed the instructions she belted out through a microphone headset. Grace was mindful not to give herself any trouble for her own missteps. It was her first time, after all. And what a time it was. They alternated between structured dance led by the instructor and moments of improvised "freedance" that allowed all the students to whirl throughout the room, letting their bodies move as desired. Grace enjoyed these moments best, using them to work out a kink in her low back that had sprung up during her fight with Mick.

The class ended with the dancers on the floor, in crawling, slithering movements that to Grace felt luxurious and self-indulgent. She hadn't allowed herself to move like that since the last time she'd gotten down on the floor to play with a child. By the time the class ended, with everyone taking two steps forward into their day and applause breaking out across the room, Grace wondered where this Nia had been all her life. She vowed to get Cat in that studio as soon as she came back from San Francisco.

If she came back, Grace allowed herself to worry, but just a touch. She didn't really think Cat would pick up and move to San Francisco for a man she really hardly knew. But let's just say the possibility was on Grace's radar.

The lovely Yvette, sweaty and breathless herself, beckoned them to the rear of the studio, where she retrieved towels from what looked like a microwave but turned out to be a newfangled towel warmer. They were hot and scented with eucalyptus. Grace accepted her towel gratefully, and following suit of the others, swabbed her face, neck, and arms.

"How was that?" Yvette asked Grace.

"I feel reborn."

The comment brought a thousand-watt smile to Yvette's face.

———

When she got home, Mick was in the kitchen eating a bowl of cereal. Grace held her tongue against commenting on his aberrant schedule, as it was now three in the afternoon, and he was just getting around to breakfast.

"How's the alien invasion coming along?" she asked without a hint of sarcasm. She really wanted to be positive in all her dealings with Mick. She had committed to this on her walk home.

"*Visitation*," Mick corrected.

"Oh, right," she laughed. "How could I forget the religious connotation?"

"Where did you go?" Mick asked. "Not that I minded having the house to myself. You just look, well, radiant."

At that, Grace bubbled over with enthusiasm for her new dance practice. She filled Mick's ears with a description of her first Nia class while he munched on his cereal. At least he was eating whole grains, she noted.

Once she wound down, Mick cleared his throat. "You know, you're quite a catch there, sister Grace."

Her senses tingled. Mick hardly ever called her "Grace," even though she'd made it her legal name years ago. He insisted on calling her "Pris," short for Priscilla. This was done, she realized, partly out of habit, as it was her birth name, but mostly just to get her goat. "Thank you, Mick," she said. It was her policy never to let a compliment go unacknowledged. But she waited for the other shoe to drop.

Mick waved his spoon at her. "I have a proposition for you."

"Yes?"

"You think you can take charge of my love life, fix me up on a date. Well, I'll admit I haven't done a very good job of managing that part of my existence on my own. So I'll turn it over to you—"

Grace couldn't help herself. She clapped her hands together. "Oh, Mick! You won't regret—"

"—on one condition," he continued, pointing his spoon at her for emphasis.

She waited.

"You have to let me fix *you* up on a date in return."

Grace protested. "But Mick, you don't even know anyone in Seattle."

He raised his eyebrows. "I know people … Besides, you're just making excuses. Listen, you haven't exactly been a master of your own love life, either. Too busy managing everyone else's, I suspect."

His words hit a tender place inside her. She opened her mouth to say something but then silenced.

"I'll take that as agreement," he said.

Grace smiled, placing her hand on his. "I guess we'll see if anyone will have us. A couple of well-worn dreamslippers, we are."

Made in the USA
San Bernardino, CA
01 February 2016